PENGUIN ENGLISH LIBRARY

THE SCIENCE FICTION OF
EDGAR ALLAN POE

Harold Beaver is Reader in American Literature at the University of Warwick. He has also edited for the Penguin English Library Edgar Allan Poe's *The Narrative of Arthur Gordon Pym of Nantucket*, as well as Herman Melville's *Redburn*, *Moby-Dick*, and *Billy Budd, Sailor and Other Stories*.

The Science Fiction of
Edgar Allan Poe

*Collected and edited with an
Introduction and Commentary by
Harold Beaver*

PENGUIN BOOKS

Penguin Books Ltd, Harmondsworth, Middlesex, England
Penguin Books, 625 Madison Avenue, New York, New York 10022, U.S.A.
Penguin Books Australia Ltd, Ringwood, Victoria, Australia
Penguin Books Canada Ltd, 2801 John Street, Markham, Ontario, Canada L3R 1B4
Penguin Books (N.Z.) Ltd, 182–190 Wairau Road, Auckland 10, New Zealand

This selection first published 1976
Reprinted 1977, 1978, 1979, 1982

—

Introduction and Commentary copyright © Harold Beaver, 1976
All rights reserved

Made and printed in Great Britain
by Hazell Watson & Viney Ltd,
Aylesbury, Bucks
Set in Linotype Granjon

Contents

SC
Poe

6.85

Permabound

9/84

Contents

Introduction

ELECTRO-CHEMISTRY dominated the early nineteenth century. Galvani and Watt, Volta and Ohm, Ampère, Bunsen, Morse – its pioneers embedded their very names into the language. Sir Humphry Davy's researches led to the isolation of potassium and sodium in 1807; of calcium, barium, boron, magnesium and strontium in 1808. His assistant Michael Faraday discovered electromagnetic induction and developed the first dynamo. It was the age of voltaic cells, electrodes, Leyden jars, piles, conductors, ions, insulation, electric circuits, batteries, generators, dynamos, condensers, galvanometers. The fundamental nature of all matter, it became apparent, was electrical.

Coleridge proclaimed :[1]

In short, from the time of Kepler to that of Newton, and from Newton to Hartley, not only all things in external nature, but the subtlest mysteries of life and organization, and even of the intellect and moral being, were conjured within the magic circle of mathematical formulae. And now a new light was struck by the discovery of electricity, and, in every sense of the word, both playful and serious, both for good and for evil, it may be affirmed to have electrified the whole frame of natural philosophy. Close on its heels followed the momentous discovery of the principal gases by Scheele and Priestley, the composition of water by Cavendish, and the doctrine of latent heat by Black. The scientific world was prepared for a new dynasty; accordingly, as soon as Lavoisier had reduced the infinite variety of chemical phenomena to the actions, reactions, and interchanges of a few elementary substances, or at least excited the expectation that this would speedily be effected, the hope shot up, almost instantly, into full faith, that it had been effected. Henceforward the new path, thus brilliantly opened, became the common road to all departments of knowledge: and, to this moment, it has been pursued with an eagerness and almost epidemic enthusiasm

1. Coleridge, *On the Definitions of Life Hitherto Received: Hints towards a more Comprehensive Theory* (1848).

which, scarcely less than its political revolutions, characterize the spirit of the age.

Even electrical and nervous phenomena were linked. That, too, was a tenet of the age – one of Sir John Herschel's four determinants of electromagnetism. For what of 'Animal Magnetism'? Had not Mesmer taken Paris by storm with his 'magnetic' cures? Coleridge continued: 'reproduction corresponds to magnetism, irritability to electricity, and sensibility to constructive chemical affinity'.[2] No wonder Poe was fascinated. Born midway between the practical triumphs of a Franklin and of an Edison, his aim was to be the comprehensive theorist, and seer, of the electromagnetic age. An amateur mathematician, like his contemporary Morse, 'even his most unbounded imagination' (in Dostoyevsky's phrase)[3] 'betrays the true American'. Alone he would play the conjuror, constructing a post-Newtonian hypothesis to decipher God Himself, the Father Almighty, in terms of an almighty electric code.

American newspapers of the 1830s and 1840s were agog with strange reports : of ballooning, exotic voyages, premature burials, automata, trances, plagues. In February 1838, while Poe was working in Greenwich Village, the new electric telegraph was demonstrated at the White House. On 23 April the *Sirius*, the first steamship to cross the Atlantic, chugged into New York harbour, followed that same afternoon by Isambard Kingdom Brunel's *Great Western*, a 1,300-ton ironclad, which had left England three days later. 'The Thousand-and-Second Tale of Scheherazade' was gaily to expound these marvels – with those of the electrotype, daguerreotype, and electrotelegraphic printer. But exploitation of mechanical inventions launched a parallel

2. Clarified by Coleridge as follows : When, therefore, I affirm the power of reproduction in organized bodies to be magnetism, I must be understood to mean that this power, as it exists in the magnet, and which we there (to use a strong phrase) catch in the very act, is to the same kind of power, working as reproductive, what the root is to the cube of that root. We no more confound the force in the compass needle with that of reproduction, than a man can be said to confound his liver with a lichen, because he affirms that both of them grow.

3. Dostoyevsky, *Wremia* vol. 1 (1861), p. 230.

boom in psychology. Into the vacuum left by Descartes and Newton flooded every form of transcendentalism. The doctrines of Swedenborg, Lavater and Saint-Martin now grew intellectually fashionable. Had not natural forces been harnessed? So too would supernatural. Progress, Democracy, Manifest Destiny, were the cry of the day. All things, physical and metaphysical, would be annexed – like Texas, Cuba, Mexico – to the American Dream. Father Miller and Prophet Joseph Smith, Mormons and Second Adventists, vied with each other for disciples. Mysticism, spiritualism, hypnotism, mesmeric trances, galvanic resuscitation, phrenology, flourished. In 1849, with a greedy rush, Eldorado itself was besieged.

It was an age for amateurs. De Quincey and Coleridge, Emerson and Poe, could still speak as 'philosophers', as literary gentlemen. They linger on the very edge between the old Newtonian order and the new, between Sir William Herschel and Clerk Maxwell, between Munchausen and H. G. Wells. Professionalism and the gathering complexity of research had not yet overwhelmed all but committed 'scientists'. After mid-century such confidence became less and less attainable. Between science and literature no neutral ground now remained. So no room for 'natural philosophy' remained – except in that new, eccentric and bastard form, their communal offspring, 'science fiction'.

The main line of descent is usually reckoned from Verne and H. G. Wells. But Jules Verne himself acknowledged his debt to Poe; so it was the French who first saluted the American as master: *'le créateur du roman merveilleux-scientifique'*.[4] Hubert Matthey presented 'The Facts in the Case of M. Valdemar',

4. Hubert Matthey, *Essai sur le merveilleux dans la littérature française depuis 1800* (Paris, 1915), p. 237.

H. Bruce Franklin traces the title back to 1905: ' "Science in Romance", an anonymous article in the *Saturday Review*, cited Poe (accusingly) as "probably the father" of that "pseudo-science" fiction "which still has its living practitioners in Dr Conan Doyle and Mr H. G. Wells". In 1909, Maurice Renard in "Du merveilleux scientifique et son action sur l'intelligence du progrès" (*Le Spectateur, Revue Critique*) called Poe the true founder of the marvellous-scientific romance. . .' (*Future Perfect: American Science Fiction of the Nineteenth Century*, New York: Oxford University Press, 1966, p. 93).

'A Tale of the Ragged Mountains', and 'A Descent into the Maelström' as *'les types d'un genre qui devait se développer après lui'*; the genre itself he defined as *'ce mélange de la logique et de la narration'*. And the emphasis ever since (following Poe's lead) has been on logic, on reason, on coherent forecast and calculation. As the master himself observed in praise of *Eureka*: 'these conditions themselves have been imposed upon me, as necessities, in a train of ratiocination as rigorously logical as that which establishes any demonstration in Euclid'.[5]

Facts and figures, as scholars have demonstrated, were commonly adapted – plagiarized verbatim even – from published sources. That was inevitable, no doubt. It is also irrelevant. Poe is celebrated as 'Science Fiction Pioneer' (in Clarke Olney's phrase) for being the first 'to base his stories firmly on a rational kind of extrapolation, avoiding the supernatural'.[6] Extrapolation! The very concept, borrowed from statistical projection, is his. Even in the gush of a passionate love letter, in mid-flight, he could declare:[7]

Think, too, of the rare agreement of name... think of all these coincidences, and you will no longer wonder that, to one accustomed as I am to the Calculus of Probabilities, they wore an air of positive miracle.

For the Calculus of Probabilities had been long familiar to Poe from the work of Condorcet and Laplace, Cournot and Quetelet.

'All that is necessary,' taught the Marquis de Condorcet, 'to reduce the whole of nature to laws similar to those which Newton discovered with the aid of the calculus, is to have a sufficient number of observations and a mathematics that is complex enough.'[8] From a mathematical theory of probability he turned to a social mathematics, or calculus of history, to tame the future: 'a science to foresee the progressions of the human species'. Even future moral data were to be mathematicized. In

5. *Eureka*, p. 252.

6. Clarke Olney, 'Edgar Allan Poe: Science Fiction Pioneer', *Georgia Review*, vol. 12 (1958), pp. 416–21.

7. Letter to Sarah Helen Whitman (Fordham: 1 October 1848).

8. Condorcet, *Essai sur l'application de l'analyse aux probabilités des décisions rendues à la pluralité des voix* (1785).

the *Esquisse d'un tableau historique des progrès de l'esprit humain*, he charted human development through nine epochs to the French Revolution, predicting in a tenth the ultimate perfection of man. The Marquis de Laplace,[9] in *Théorie analytique des probabilités* (1812) continued his rigorous approach to formulaic, mathematical prediction.

Poe has nothing but scorn for 'human-perfectibility' spokesmen like Condorcet. But his 'C. Auguste Dupin', master detective, is heir to the great French tradition. He is Poe's spokesman in praise of 'the theory of probabilities – that theory to which the most glorious objects of human research are indebted for the most glorious of illustration'.[10] In 'The Mystery of Marie Rogêt' he expounds, and refines on, its technique :

It is through the spirit of this principle, if not precisely through its letter, that modern science has resolved to *calculate upon the unforeseen*. But perhaps you do not comprehend me. The history of human knowledge has so uninterruptedly shown that to collateral, or incidental, or accidental events we are indebted for the most numerous and most valuable discoveries, that it has at length become necessary, in any prospective view of improvement, to make not only large, but the largest allowances for inventions that shall arise by chance, and quite out of the range of ordinary expectation. It is no longer philosophical to base, upon what has been, a vision of what is to be. *Accident* is admitted as a portion of the substructure. We make chance a matter of absolute calculation. We subject the unlooked for and unimagined, to the mathematical *formulae* of the schools.

With 'the Calculus of Probabilities' it is but a short step from

9. The Marquis de Laplace considered the philosophical and social implications of his mathematical classic in *Essai philosophique sur les probabilités* (1814).

Antoine Cournot, following Poisson, first applied mathematics to economic forecasting in *Exposition de la théorie des chances et des probabilités* (1843). Adolphe Quetelet, supervisor of Belgian statistics, first devised rules for modern census taking, by formulating the theory of the 'average man' : *Sur l'homme et le developpement de ses facultés* (1835); translated into English as *A Treatise on Man* (1842).

It was James Clerk Maxwell, in 1859, who was to apply the calculus of probabilities, not to games or public affairs, but to matter in motion.

10. 'The Murders in the Rue Morgue', 1841.

Poe's Detective to his Science Fiction. For 'this Calculus', he explains, 'is, in its essence, purely mathematical; and thus we have the anomaly of the most rigidly exact in science applied to the shadow and spirituality of the most intangible in speculation'.[11]

What was once stuff for ritual or religious myths, or tall tales for entertainment, was thus transformed by Poe to a new speculative fiction. Utopian voyages had long presented all kinds of rational laboratories; but Sir Thomas More and his successors were concerned with the permutation of mainly moral and political hypotheses. The hypotheses of science fiction were wholly material, whether psychological or technological. Their pragmatic claim was the inevitable change (for better or for worse) of both man's outer and his inner or spiritual environment. Yet, cast as fantasy, the pressure persisted towards the journal-entry, in the present tense; not to recollection, but lived intensity; not as theoretical exercises, but adventures (in the tradition of Lucian, Swift, Defoe) by sea, land or air, foraging into the unknown.

In 1785 an Oxford printer had published an anonymous shilling pamphlet, entitled *Singular Travels, Campaigns and Adventures of Baron Munchausen*. Rudolph Erich Raspe, its author, seems oddly to prefigure Poe. An amateur scientist and antiquarian, who had earlier written on volcanic geology and the Ossianic poems, he even became a fellow of the Royal Society (until a German scandal caught up with him). Equally fascinated by Lucian, the *Arabian Nights*, Captain Cook's voyages in the South Seas and the ballooning exploits of Blanchard or the Montgolfier brothers, he became an avid reader of Swift and Defoe. An anonymous and penniless hoaxer, he foisted his fantastical tall tales upon the world. Poe's 'The Unparalleled Adventure of One Hans Pfaall', however, starting from the same grotesquely exaggerated note, soars, once aloft, into a new and mathematically exacting realm. In that shift, in that unbridgeable gap between the poetic quips of Raspe and the scientific imagination of Poe lay the seeds of the new genre. Both insist on their total veracity; both delight in the elusive antics of the absurd. But while the one dallies solely with metaphoric suggestions, the other explicates, rationalizes, presses inexorably on to

11. Introduction to 'The Mystery of Marie Rogêt', 1842.

hoodwink his bourgeois, materialistic audience. The German concludes his baronial descent of Mount Etna with a plunge through the centre of the earth to the South Seas, adding:

> This was a much shorter cut than going round and one which no man has ever before accomplished, or even attempted. However, the next time I do it, I shall endeavour to make proper scientific observations.

The American – as balloonist, sailor or mesmerist – from the start played the experimental, philosophical role: making 'proper scientific observations'.

But Poe has never been without his detractors. When his originality has not been ignored, it has been undermined. H. Bruce Franklin is the most recent to launch a two-pronged attack. The first concerned his themes : [12]

> Rarely in Poe's science fiction does one find science itself as a subject and nowhere does one find any kind of true scientist as a consequential figure.

But precisely this respect for the 'true scientist' and his 'science' is what Poe himself, again and again, rejected: *'merely* scientific men' he called them, to be trusted with nothing but 'scientific *details*' : [13]

> Of all persons in the world, they are at the same time the most bigoted and the least capable of using, generalizing, or deciding upon the facts which they bring to light in the course of their experiments.

Which makes nonsense of Franklin's second objection – the matter of treatment : [14]

> But if science fiction is merely a popularizer of science rather than the literature which, growing with science, evaluates it, and relates it meaningfully to the rest of existence, it is hardly worth serious attention.

Very little science fiction, of course, could pass that exacting test. But who would claim that 'Mesmeric Revelation', *Eureka*, or 'Mellonta Tauta', for example, are 'popularizers'? Their very

12. H. Bruce Franklin, *Future Perfect*, p. 95.
13. Letter to George E. Isbell (New York : 29 February 1848).
14. H. Bruce Franklin, *Future Perfect*, p. 96.

role, successful or not, is the exact opposite: to evaluate scientific method and technological achievement, by confronting both with a vision of life ('Out of Space – out of Time') [15] in its widest spiritual dimensions.

Poe's 'Sonnet – To Science', [16] written while only twenty, begins:

> Science! true daughter of Old Time thou art!
> Who alterest all things with thy peering eyes.
> Why preyest thou thus upon the poet's heart,
> Vulture, whose wings are dull realities?

But it was not science he abhorred so much as the triumph of mechanical reason, confirmed by technical progress. In 'The Colloquy of Monos and Una' Monos denounces 'the harsh mathematical reason of the schools', [17] sweeping aside the 'rectangular obscenities' with which technology has littered our globe. Poe used speculative theory from the start to frustrate technological methods and aims. Each 'advance in practical science' meant 'a retro-gradation in the true utility'. Industrialization led only to regimentation; regimentation to that ultimate disease of the 'poetic intellect', the expropriation of the imagination. A pure mathematics – blending calculation with the ideal – of the circle, the sphere, [18] the oval, of the curving arabesques that spiral through dreams and the screwed form of a helix (as on a watch-spring or electromagnetic coil of wire), controlled his visionary quests.

One critical fight he was intent on waging: [19]

15. 'Dreamland', 1844.
16. First written in 1829, but revised with frequent variants until 1843.
17. 'The Colloquy of Monos and Una', pp. 92, 93, 90.
18. cf. Georges Poulet: 'A sort of temporal circle surrounds Poe's characters. A whirlpool envelopes them, which, like that of the Maelström, disposes its funnel by degrees from the past in which one has been caught, to the future in which one will be dead. Whether it moves in the limitless eternity of dreams or in the limited temporality of awakening, the work of Poe thus always presents a time that is *closed*.' (*Studies in Human Time*, 1949, translated by Elliott Coleman, Baltimore: The Johns Hopkins Press, 1956, pp. 330–34.)
19. 'Mr Griswold and the Poets' (*Boston Miscellany*, November 1842); *Works*, vol. 11, p. 148.

The mistake... of the old dogma, that the calculating faculties are at war with the ideal; while, in fact, it may be demonstrated that the two divisions of mental power are never to be found in perfection apart. The *highest* order of the imaginative intellect is always pre-eminently mathematical; and the converse.

His fascination with lunar investigation, sound and colour, the cosmology of Newton, von Humboldt, and Laplace, was a cult of homage to pure science. 'Poe was opening up a way,' wrote Paul Valéry, 'teaching a very strict and deeply alluring doctrine, in which a kind of mathematics and a kind of mysticism became one...' [20] The beauty of number was that point, that configuration, where mathematics and mysticism met.

Something of this ambivalence, ever since, has haunted science fiction. Itself an offshoot of gothicism, the new genre was to evoke a horror both of the future and of the science which could bring that future about. By identifying with the collapse of technology, it was already critically undermining that technology. Yet its only appeal was to science. It had nowhere to turn but to science for its salvation. The fiction, then, was that somehow science must learn to control its own disastrous career. Poe too – quite self-consciously, of course – was working in this gothic vein. Within his husk of mathematics, as often as not, lurks an old-fashioned kernel of magic. In a sense, he recreated all the traditional feats of magic in pseudo-scientific terms (of galvanism and mesmerism). Alchemy became the synthetic manufacture of 'Von Kempelen and His Discovery'; resurrection of the dead, the time travel of 'Some Words with a Mummy'; demonic possession, the hypnotic or 'magnetic relation' of 'A Tale of the Ragged Mountains'; apocalyptic vision, the cataclysmic fire of 'The Conversation of Eiros and Charmion.' Just as the pseudo-scholarship (in antiquarian statutes and genealogies) of Scott, or gothic elaboration of Hawthorne, was part of an attempt to make the imaginative spell more potent, more binding, so Poe's detailed and mathematical science intensifies his imaginative fusion with the occult.

20. Paul Valéry, 'Situation de Baudelaire', 1924, translated by James R. Lawler in *Leonardo, Poe, Mallarmé* (Princeton University Press, 1972), p. 207.

There is far more of literary burlesque, of outright parody, in all this than Sam Moskowitz, for example, or H. Bruce Franklin,[21] appeared to realize. Yet clues abound. Those zany, zestful surfaces are all deceitful. The reckless playfulness invades even the august vision of *Eureka*. For his science ultimately is admitted to be a kind of hoax; his fiction openly and ironically conceived as a lie. Like Lucian, in his *True History*, he might have declared:[22]

The motive and purpose of my journey lay in my intellectual restlessness and passion for adventure, and in my wish to find out what the end of the ocean was, and who the people were that lived on the other side.

But what he contrived was the inversion of romantic fiction from the antiquarian hoax (of a Chatterton or Macpherson) into a futuristic hoax. It proved a brilliant reversal of time-scale, made possible by the wide-spread willingness of an ever-proliferating, journal-reading, stock investing, news addicted, male and female public to be duped.

'His purpose in the hoaxes,' Constance Rourke astutely remarked, 'was to make his readers absurd, to reduce them to an involuntary imbecility. His objective was triumph...'[23] Or in Poe's own caustic words:[24]

Twenty years ago credulity was the characteristic trait of the mob, incredulity the distinctive feature of the philosophic; now the case is exactly conversed.

'Hans Pfaall' stands in a direct line of descent from the pseudoscientific 'Memoirs of Martinus Scriblerus': the literary hoax from the start was bound up with literary burlesque. Compared

21. So Franklin accepts Moskowitz's insensitive categorization of the tales (into those where 'the mood or effect is primary' and those where 'the idea was paramount') to further his own didactic argument: 'In the first, the science is merely a device; in the other, the fiction is merely a device' (*Future Perfect*, pp. 97–8).

22. Lucian, *The True History*, Book 1, lines 56–9.

23. Constance Rourke, *American Humor: A Study of the National Character* (1931), ch. 6, p. 148.

24. *Doings of Gotham* (Letter II, May 1844), p. 34.

to Queen Anne's England, however, Jacksonian America presented even more fertile ground: [25]

As the tall tale came into its great prime in the early '30s a sudden contagion was created. A series of newspaper hoaxes sprang into life in the East. The scale was western, the tone that of calm, scientific exposition of wonders such as often belonged to western comic legend.

Americans 'who like so much to be fooled', Baudelaire commented in a note to 'Hans Pfaall' [26] adding that fooling people was Poe's main 'dada', or hobbyhorse. The American hoax, or tall story, was indeed a kind of pioneer *dada* – a violent, endlessly protracted game with the absurd. What Poe, the Southerner, initiated, Mark Twain (the very name is a hoax) from the South-West was lovingly to perfect, and William Faulkner with reckless rhetoric to explore for a twentieth-century topology of the South.

But by detaching himself from the prosaic present, in imaginatively identifying with the future, Poe himself was duped. Compiling, extrapolating, closely paraphrasing, he seems to have deceived himself at last into claiming his very plagiarisms as his own. [27] Spell-bound, he became his own victim. There are moments – at the climax of 'The Colloquy of Monos and Una', *The Narrative of Arthur Gordon Pym*, or *Eureka* – when the hoax is no longer openly and ironically confessed as a 'lie', but celebrated as the 'truth' of the imagination, whose natural home is located on remote geographic horizons or pursued into the distant future. There, with intuition as guide, Truth and Beauty – science and art – will fuse in a single poetic vision. Why not fiction as a kind of science, when science itself was proving to be a kind of fiction? [28]

25. Constance Rourke, *American Humor*, ch. 2, 'The Gamecock of the Wilderness', sec. 6, pp. 56-7.

26. '*Ces Américains qui aiment tant à être dupés*', Baudelaire, note to the final instalment of 'Hans Pfaall', *Le Pays*, 20 April 1855.

27. Of which an early, and most notorious, instance is his *Conchologist's First Book* (1839).

28. As the 'intuitive *leaps*' or hypotheses of a scientist must be followed by experimental enquiry, so the intuitive expression of a poet (which is the poem) must be followed by explanatory analysis (or criticism). The

A perfect consistency, I repeat, can be nothing but an absolute truth.[29]

The plots of God are perfect. The Universe is a plot of God.[30]

All art constantly aspired towards the condition of science : all science constantly aspired towards the vision of art. The spell of science fiction for Poe derived as much from his long-drawn-out romance with science as from his scientific concept of romance.

He offered *Eureka* to his readers as [31]

this Book of Truths, not in its character of Truth-Teller, but for the Beauty that abounds in its Truth; constituting it true. To these I present the composition as an Art-Product alone: – let us say as a Romance; or, if I be not urging too lofty a claim, as a Poem.

It was to be his last stab at piercing the '*Physical, Metaphysical and Mathematical*' cloud of unknowing – 'the cloud behind which lay, forever invisible, the *object* of this attempt'.[32] In an intuitive, that is to say apocalyptic vision he proposed 'to show . . . *the plainly inevitable annihilation of at least the material Universe*'.[33] What was it but a maelström of energy, speeding away and returning, round and round, in an eternal vortex, whose '*First Cause*' was the will, 'the Volition of God'? Such is the 'plot of God' – an endless drama of expansion and contraction, of dissipation (or irradiation) and collapse (or reconstruction), of exhalation and inhalation. In the beginning was the word, the breath, the inspiration of God. Such was to be this astronomical book of *Revelation* : [34]

Then, indeed, amid unfathomable abysses, will be glaring unimaginable suns. . . The inevitable catastrophe is at hand.

The bravado of thought, the hyperbole, the sheer effrontery is breathtaking : [35]

' "Raven" was not complete until Poe had written the explanatory "Philosophy of Composition" '. (Edward H. Davidson, *Poe, A Critical Study*, 1957, p. 246.)

29. *Eureka*, p. 300.   30. *Eureka*, p. 292.   31. *Eureka*, Preface.
32. *Eureka*, p. 222.   33. *Eureka*, p. 227.   34. *Eureka*, p. 304.
35. *Eureka*, p. 236.

... a deed which shakes the Moon in her path, which causes the Sun to be no longer the Sun, and which alters forever the destiny of the multitudinous myriads of stars that roll and glow in the majestic presence of their Creator.

Poe is both the Euclidean theologian and methodological Wittgenstein of this universe, declaring 'the *modus operandi* of the Law of Gravity to be an exceedingly simple and perfectly explicable thing'.[36] For the ultimate basis of the vision rests on the imaginative primacy of the artist. If God is a poet, then only a poet can play God and reveal God. Dupin, with a hunch, could investigate the criminal mind (to reconstruct his action); but Poe intuitively enters the mind of God (to reconstruct the mystery of divine creation). He is both the creator and the solver of conundra.[37] He is both the detached observer (scientist, explorer, detective) and imaginative artist; both master and mystagogue. What is a hoax at one end can turn to a poetic vision at the other. What is mystery can as easily turn to mystification; science fiction, to use his own word, become the science of 'Mystification'.[38]

It is the poetical essence of the Universe – *of the Universe* which, in the supremeness of its symmetry, is but the most sublime of poems. Now symmetry and consistency are convertible terms: – thus Poetry and Truth are one.[39]

J. B. S. Haldane once pointed out that the human organism is exactly intermediate in size between the electron and the spiral nebula, the smallest and largest existing objects. This, he suggested, gave man a privileged position in the world of nature.[40] But to what varying effect! For Poe, what he learnt as an amateur scientist and astronomer led incontrovertibly to what he had always known (intuitively) as an artist. Just as what Teilhard

36. *Eureka*, p. 241.

37. 'And now – this Heart Divine – what is it? *It is our own.*' (*Eureka*, p. 307). cf. Denis Marion, *La Méthode intellectuelle d'Edgar Poe* (Paris, 1952).

38. First printed as 'Von Jung, the Mystic', *American Monthly Magazine* (June 1837).

39. *Eureka*, p. 300.

40. cf. 'On Being the Right Size', *Possible Worlds*, 1927.

de Chardin, a century later, learnt as geologist and palaeontologist seemed to lead incontrovertibly to what he had always known (intuitively) as a Christian.[41] Melville, in the face of science, imaginatively retreated into myth. Poe encountered science as the precise mathematical equation between Truth and Beauty; 'that is all ye know on earth, and all ye need to know'. He aspired to be nothing less than an American Keats with the mind of Newton, or rather a sublimer Newton with the soul of Keats.

All his imaginary trips – by ship, balloon, laudanum, hypnosis – were aimed at setting the soul free from the demands of the body and so from the restraints of normal perception; simultaneously releasing the mind from its own tomb, the prison of its endlessly inturned and ramifying nervous complexes (where Madeleine Usher or Fortunato were buried). For, above all, they express 'the thirst *to know* which is forever unquenchable' [42] – reaching out for knowledge, beyond waking, in sleep; beyond sleep, in death; beyond death, pushed to further and further extremes of consciousness on voyages as dreams, or dreams as voyages ('Out of Space – out of Time'), to a confrontation with the abyss, the whirlpool, the void which is eternity. There are voices of those who have plunged into the ultimate abyss, but survived (like the Norse fisherman); voices that seem to rebound from the fatal impact (like that of Arthur Gordon Pym); voices that hover suspended at the point of transition (like M. Valdemar); voices retrieved from beyond the point of no return (via bottles or Moon-men); voices that continue the quest on the far side of the grave in angelic dialogues among the stars.

Baudelaire, long ago, had mourned Poe's 'eccentric and meteoric literary destiny'.[43] Mallarmé enshrined that image in a passionate tribute, *Le Tombeau d'Edgar Poe*, recited at the unveiling over Poe's grave in 1875 of a block of basalt. Walt Whitman

41. Pierre Teilhard de Chardin, *Le Phénomène humain* (Paris, 1959), translated by Bernard Wall and others as *The Phenomenon of Man* (London, 1959).

42. 'The Power of Words', p. 171.

43. *'son excentrique et fulgurante destinée littéraire'* ('Edgar Allan Poe, sa vie et ses ouvrages', *Revue de Paris*, 1852).

attended the ceremony in Baltimore but declined to speak.[44]
Tennyson and Swinburne sent letters from England. But Mallarmé alone transfigured that tomb:

> *Calme bloc ici-bas chu d'un désastre obscur*
> *Que ce granit du moins montre à jamais sa borne*
> *Aux noirs vols du Blasphème épars dans le futur.*[45]

That meteorite, plunged down from some cosmic disaster, still survives. Far off it seems to loom – as dim, eternal witness of this interloper among 'the tribe of Stars', apocalyptic prophet and pioneer victim of science fiction.

44. 'I have felt a strong impulse to come over and be here to-day myself in memory of Poe, which I have obey'd, but not the slightest impulse to make a speech, which, my dear friends, must also be obeyed.' (*Washington Star*, 16 November 1875).

In his 'final judgement' Poe's verse probably belonged 'among the electric lights of imaginative literature, brilliant and dazzling, but with no heat'. ('Edgar Poe's Significance' *Specimen Days*, 1 January 1880).

45. The Sonnet appeared at the end of the *Memorial Volume* (Baltimore, 1876): '*désastre*', like 'disaster', literally means 'ill-starred'.

The last three lines, in Mallarmé's own word-for-word English translation, run:

[A] Stern block here fallen from a mysterious disaster,
Let this granite at least show forever their bound
To the old flights of Blasphemy [still] spread in the future.

(For Mrs Sarah Helen Whitman, 31 July 1877)

A Note on the Text

POE published and republished his stories in a wide assortment
of newspapers, books, magazines. Again and again they appeared in Richmond or Baltimore, Philadelphia or New York.
Editorial salaries apart, they were his sole source of income.
Naturally he squeezed them for all they were worth. Each new
appearance, however, offered a new chance for revision; and he
tinkered compulsively. So that even their final form – in the
edition of 1845 or the *Broadway Journal*, for example – was
often belaboured with further scribbled marginalia, emending
the text. It is essential, therefore, to determine not only the first
printing of each story, but also the last printing supervised by
him.

What provoked him, above all, was the professional slackness
of his provincial editors and hack printers. For Edgar Allan Poe
meant to rise above all such hacks. Self-consciously he was a
dandy – the first American literary dandy – and demanded perfection. But again and again as he launched his work, it returned to him flawed by his own hurried lapses or butchered by
others' carelessness. The *Broadway Journal*, at least, was under
his own eagle eye and printed under his own direction.

This edition does not aim at collating these many textual variations and corrections. The only such collation, to date, is in the
'Virginia' edition, edited by James A. Harrison (New York :
Thomas Y. Crowell & Co., 1902). Bibliographical notes at the
rear merely list the first publication, all reprints during Poe's lifetime, and the occasional autograph manuscripts available.

From which the following have been selected as standard
texts :

MS. FOUND IN A BOTTLE : *Broadway Journal* vol. 2 (11 October
    1845), pp. 203–6
THE UNPARALLELED ADVENTURE OF ONE HANS PFAALL :
    Tales of the Grotesque and Arabesque (1840) vol. 2, with

revisions, mainly of the final 'Note', first incorporated by Rufus Griswold (1849–56)

THE CONVERSATION OF EIROS AND CHARMION: *Tales of Edgar A. Poe* (New York: Wiley & Putnam, 1845) – twelve stories selected by Evert A. Duyckinck

A DESCENT INTO THE MAELSTRÖM: *Tales* (1845), incorporating Poe's manuscript corrections

THE COLLOQUY OF MONOS AND UNA: *Tales* (1845)

A TALE OF THE RAGGED MOUNTAINS: *Broadway Journal* (29 November 1845)

THE BALLOON-HOAX: *New York Sun* (13 April 1844)

MESMERIC REVELATION: *Tales* (1845)

THE THOUSAND-AND-SECOND TALE OF SCHEHERAZADE: *Broadway Journal* (25 October 1845), with revisions of the scientific data and expansion of the notes, first incorporated by Rufus Griswold

SOME WORDS WITH A MUMMY: *Broadway Journal* (1 November 1845)

THE POWER OF WORDS: *Broadway Journal* (25 October 1845)

THE SYSTEM OF DR TARR AND PROF. FETHER: *Graham's Lady's and Gentleman's Magazine* (November 1845)

THE FACTS IN THE CASE OF M. VALDEMAR: *Broadway Journal* (20 December 1845), incorporating Poe's MS. notes from his own copy

EUREKA: George P. Putnam (New York, 1848), with emendations incorporated from a copy of the first edition: 'They are in Poe's handwriting, in the faint tracing of a pencil, and are the changes the poet had in mind to make in a second edition.' (James A. Harrison, *Works* vol. 16, pp. 319–36)

MELLONTA TAUTA: *Godey's Lady's Book* (February 1849)

VON KEMPELEN AND HIS DISCOVERY: *The Flag of Our Union* (14 April 1849)

The texts themselves have been left unaltered. Bar the odd hyphen, nothing is deleted; nothing added except superior numerals to mark a reference in the commentary. All footnotes to the texts or insertions in square brackets signed 'Ed.' are authentically Poe's, denoting the 'Editor' as 'Edgar'.

Bibliography

SPECIALIZED work, devoted to individual pieces, is attached to their individual commentaries at the rear. More general work is still rare. The initial research into Poe's use of contemporary science in his fiction was consolidated in three (unpublished) doctoral theses:

CARROLL D. LAVERTY, *Science and Pseudo-Science in the Writings of Poe* (Duke University, 1951)

JOHN F. LIGON, *On Desperate Seas: A Study of Poe's Imaginary Journeys* (University of Washington, 1961)

ELVA BAER KREMENLIEV, *The Literary Uses of Astronomy in the Writings of Edgar Allan Poe* (University of California, Los Angeles, 1963)

The debate on Poe's status as the pioneer of science fiction has been conducted, among others, by:

HUBERT MATTHEY, *Essai sur le merveilleux dans la littérature française depuis 1800* (Paris: Payot, 1915)

LÉON LEMMONIER, 'Edgar Poe et le roman scientifique française', *La Grande Revue* vol. 83 (1930), pp. 214–23

H. P. LOVECRAFT, *Supernatural Horror in Literature* (New York: B. Abramson, 1945; Dover Books, 1973)

J. O. BAILEY, *Pilgrims through Space and Time: Trends and Patterns in Scientific and Utopian Fiction* (New York: Argus Books, 1947)

PETER PENZOLDT, *The Supernatural in Fiction* (London: P. Nevill, 1952; New York: Humanities Press, 1965)

CLARKE OLNEY, 'Edgar Allan Poe: Science Fiction Pioneer', *Georgia Review* vol. 12 (1958), pp. 416–21

SAM MOSKOWITZ, *Explorers of the Infinite: Shapers of Science Fiction* (Cleveland: World Publishing Co., 1963)

H. BRUCE FRANKLIN, 'Edgar Allan Poe and Science Fiction',

Future Perfect: American Science Fiction of the Nineteenth Century (New York: Oxford University Press, 1966)

BRIAN W. ALDISS, *Billion Year Spree: The True History of Science Fiction* (London: Weidenfeld and Nicolson, 1973; New York: Doubleday, 1973)

Baudelaire translated all pieces in this collection, with the exception of 'The Thousand-and-Second Tale of Scheherazade', 'Mellonta Tauta' and 'Von Kempelen and His Discovery'. Details of the first publication in France is given under each separate head.

MS. Found in a Bottle

*Qui n'a plus qu'un moment à vivre
N'a plus rien à dissimuler.*
QUINAULT – *Atys* [1]

OF my country and of my family I have little to say. Ill usage
and length of years have driven me from the one, and estranged
me from the other. Hereditary wealth afforded me an education of no common order, and a contemplative turn of mind enabled me to methodize the stores which early study very dili-
gently garnered up. – Beyond all things, the study of the German moralists gave me great delight; not from any ill-advised
admiration of their eloquent madness, but from the ease with
which my habits of rigid thought enabled me to detect their
falsities. I have often been reproached with the aridity of my
genius; a deficiency of imagination has been imputed to me as a
crime; and the Pyrrhonism of my opinions [2] has at all times rendered me notorious. Indeed, a strong relish for physical philosophy has, I fear, tinctured my mind with a very common error
of this age – I mean the habit of referring occurrences, even the
least susceptible of such reference, to the principles of that
science. Upon the whole, no person could be less liable than myself to be led away from the severe precincts of truth by the
ignes fatui of superstition. I have thought proper to premise thus
much, lest the incredible tale I have to tell should be considered
rather the raving of a crude imagination, than the positive experience of a mind to which the reveries of fancy have been
a dead letter and a nullity.

After many years spent in foreign travel, I sailed in the year
18—, from the port of Batavia, in the rich and populous island of
Java, on a voyage to the Archipelago of the Sunda islands. [3] I
went as passenger – having no other inducement than a kind of
nervous restlessness which haunted me as a fiend.

Our vessel was a beautiful ship of about four hundred tons, copper-fastened, and built at Bombay of Malabar teak. She was freighted with cotton-wool and oil, from the Lachadive islands. We had also on board coir, jaggeree, ghee,[4] cocoa-nuts, and a few cases of opium. The stowage was clumsily done, and the vessel consequently crank.[5]

We got under way with a mere breath of wind, and for many days stood along the eastern coast of Java, without any other incident to beguile the monotony of our course than the occasional meeting with some of the small grabs of the Archipelago [6] to which we were bound.

One evening, leaning over the taffrail, I observed a very singular, isolated cloud, to the N. W. It was remarkable, as well for its color, as from its being the first we had seen since our departure from Batavia. I watched it attentively until sunset, when it spread all at once to the eastward and westward, girting in the horizon with a narrow strip of vapor, and looking like a long line of low beach. My notice was soon afterwards attracted by the dusky-red appearance of the moon, and the peculiar character of the sea. The latter was undergoing a rapid change, and the water seemed more than usually transparent. Although I could distinctly see the bottom, yet, heaving the lead, I found the ship in fifteen fathoms. The air now became intolerably hot, and was loaded with spiral exhalations similar to those arising from heated iron. As night came on, every breath of wind died away, and a more entire calm it is impossible to conceive. The flame of a candle burned upon the poop without the least perceptible motion, and a long hair, held between the finger and thumb, hung without the possibility of detecting a vibration. However, as the captain said he could perceive no indication of danger, and as we were drifting in bodily to shore, he ordered the sails to be furled, and the anchor let go. No watch was set, and the crew, consisting principally of Malays, stretched themselves deliberately upon deck. I went below – not without a full presentiment of evil. Indeed, every appearance warranted me in apprehending a Simoom.[7] I told the captain my fears; but he paid no attention to what I said, and left me without deigning to give a reply. My uneasiness, however, prevented me from sleeping, and about midnight I went upon deck. – As I placed my foot upon the upper step of the companion-ladder, I was startled by a loud, humming noise, like that occasioned by the rapid revolution of a mill-wheel, and before I could ascertain its meaning, I found the ship quivering to its centre. In the next instant, a wilderness of foam hurled us upon our beam-ends, and, rushing over us fore and aft, swept the entire decks from stem to stern.

The extreme fury of the blast proved, in a great measure, the salvation of the ship. Although completely water-logged, yet, as her masts had gone by the board, she rose, after a minute, heavily from the sea, and, staggering awhile beneath the immense pressure of the tempest, finally righted.

By what miracle I escaped destruction, it is impossible to say. Stunned by the shock of the water, I found myself, upon recovery, jammed in between the stern-post and rudder. With great difficulty I gained my feet, and looking dizzily around, was, at first, struck with the idea of our being among breakers; so terrific, beyond the wildest imagination, was the whirlpool of mountainous and foaming ocean within which we were engulfed. After a while, I heard the voice of an old Swede, who had shipped with us at the moment of our leaving port. I hallooed to him with all my strength, and presently he came reeling aft. We soon discovered that we were the sole survivors of the accident. All on deck, with the exception of ourselves, had been swept overboard; – the captain and mates must have perished as they slept, for the cabins were deluged with water. Without assistance, we could expect to do little for the security of the ship, and our exertions were at first paralyzed by the momentary expectation of going down. Our cable had, of course, parted like pack-thread, at the first breath of the hurricane, or we should have been instantaneously overwhelmed. We scudded with frightful velocity before the sea,[8] and the water made clear breaches over us. The frame-work of our stern was shattered excessively, and, in almost every respect, we had received considerable injury; but to our extreme joy we found the pumps unchoked, and that we had made no great shifting of our ballast. The main fury of the blast had already blown over, and we apprehended little danger from the violence of the wind; but we looked forward to its total cessation with dismay; well believing, that, in our shattered condition, we should inevitably perish in the tremendous swell which would ensue. But this very just apprehension seemed by no means likely to be soon verified. For five entire days and nights – during which our only subsistence was a small quantity of jaggeree, procured with great difficulty from the forecastle – the hulk flew at a rate defying computation, before rapidly succeeding flaws of wind, which, without equalling the first violence of the Simoom, were still more terrific than any tempest I had before encountered. Our course for the first four days was, with trifling variations, S. E. and by S.; and we must have run down the coast of New Holland.[9] – On the fifth day the cold became extreme, although the wind had hauled round a point more to the northward. – The sun arose with a sickly yellow lustre, and clambered a very few degrees above the horizon – emitting no decisive light. – There were no clouds apparent, yet the wind was upon the increase, and blew with a fitful and unsteady fury. About noon, as nearly as we could guess, our attention was again arrested by the appearance of the sun. It gave out no light, properly so called, but a dull and sullen glow without reflection, as if all its rays were polarized. Just before sinking within the turgid sea, its central fires suddenly went out, as if hurriedly extinguished by some unaccountable power. It was a dim, silverlike rim, alone, as it rushed down the unfathomable ocean.

We waited in vain for the arrival of the sixth day – that day to me has not arrived – to the Swede, never did arrive. Thenceforward we were enshrouded in pitchy darkness, so that we could not have seen an object at twenty paces from the ship. Eternal night continued to envelop us, all unrelieved by the phosphoric sea-brilliancy to which we had been accustomed in the tropics. We observed too, that, although the tempest continued to rage with unabated violence, there was no longer to be discovered the usual appearance of surf, or foam, which had hitherto attended us. All around were horror, and thick gloom, and a black sweltering desert of ebony. – Superstitious terror crept by degrees into the spirit of the old Swede, and my own soul was wrapped up in silent wonder. We neglected all care of the ship, as worse than useless, and securing ourselves, as well as possible, to the stump of the mizen-mast, looked out bitterly into the world of ocean. We had no means of calculating time, nor could we form any guess of our situation. We were, however, well aware of having made farther to the southward than any previous navigators, and felt great amazement at not meeting with the usual impediments of ice. In the meantime every moment threatened to be our last – every mountainous billow hurried to overwhelm us. The swell surpassed anything I had imagined possible, and that we were not instantly buried is a miracle. My companion spoke of the lightness of our cargo, and reminded me of the excellent qualities of our ship; but I could not help feeling the utter hopelessness of hope itself, and prepared myself gloomily for that death which I thought nothing could defer beyond an hour, as, with every knot of way the ship made, the swelling of the black stupendous seas became more dismally appalling. At times we gasped for breath at an elevation beyond the albatross – at times became dizzy with the velocity of our descent into some watery hell, where the air grew stagnant, and no sound disturbed the slumbers of the kraken.[10]

We were at the bottom of one of these abysses, when a quick scream from my companion broke fearfully upon the night. 'See! see!' cried he, shrieking in my ears, 'Almighty God! see! see!'[11] As he spoke, I became aware of a dull, sullen glare of red light which streamed down the sides of the vast chasm where we lay, and threw a fitful brilliancy upon our deck. Casting my eyes upwards, I beheld a spectacle which froze the current of my blood. At a terrific height directly above us, and upon the very verge of the precipitous descent, hovered a gigantic ship of, perhaps, four thousand tons. Although upreared upon the summit of a wave, more than a hundred times her own altitude, her apparent size still exceeded that of any ship of the line or East Indiaman in existence. Her huge hull was of a deep dingy black, unrelieved by any of the customary carvings of a ship. A single row of brass cannon protruded from her open ports, and dashed from their polished surfaces the fires of innumerable battle-lanterns, which swung to and fro about her rigging. But what mainly inspired us with horror and astonishment, was that she bore up under a press of sail in the very teeth of that supernatural

sea, and of that ungovernable hurricane. When we first discovered her, her bows were alone to be seen, as she rose slowly
from the dim and horrible gulf beyond her. For a moment of
intense terror she paused upon the giddy pinnacle, as if in contemplation of her own sublimity, then trembled and tottered, and
– came down.

At this instant, I know not what sudden self-possession came
over my spirit. Staggering as far aft as I could, I awaited fear-
lessly the ruin that was to overwhelm. Our own vessel was at
length ceasing from her struggles, and sinking with her head to
the sea. The shock of the descending mass struck her, consequently, in that portion of her frame which was already under
water, and the inevitable result was to hurl me, with irresistible
violence, upon the rigging of the stranger.

As I fell, the ship hove in stays, and went about; and to the
confusion ensuing I attributed my escape from the notice of the
crew. With little difficulty I made my way unperceived to the
main hatchway, which was partially open, and soon found an
opportunity of secreting myself in the hold. Why I did so I can
hardly tell. An indefinite sense of awe, which at first sight of the
navigators of the ship had taken hold of my mind, was perhaps
the principle of my concealment. I was unwilling to trust myself
with a race of people who had offered, to the cursory glance I
had taken, so many points of vague novelty, doubt, and apprehension. I therefore thought proper to contrive a hiding-place
in the hold. This I did by removing a small portion of the shift-
ing-boards, in such a manner as to afford me a convenient retreat
between the huge timbers of the ship.

I had scarcely completed my work, when a footstep in the hold
forced me to make use of it. A man passed by my place of concealment with a feeble and unsteady gait. I could not see his face,
but had an opportunity of observing his general appearance.
There was about it an evidence of great age and infirmity. His
knees tottered beneath a load of years, and his entire frame
qivered under the burthen. He muttered to himself, in a low
broken tone, some words of a language which I could not understand, and groped in a corner among a pile of singular-looking
instruments, and decayed charts of navigation. His manner was

a wild mixture of the peevishness of second childhood, and the solemn dignity of a God. He at length went on deck, and I saw him no more.

*

A feeling, for which I have no name, has taken possession of my soul – a sensation which will admit of no analysis, to which the lessons of by-gone times are inadequate, and for which I fear futurity itself will offer me no key. To a mind constituted like my own, the latter consideration is an evil. I shall never – I know that I shall never – be satisfied with regard to the nature of my conceptions. Yet it is not wonderful that these conceptions are indefinite, since they have their origin in sources so utterly novel. A new sense – a new entity is added to my soul.

*

It is long since I first trod the deck of this terrible ship, and the rays of my destiny are, I think, gathering to a focus. Incomprehensible men! Wrapped up in meditations of a kind which I cannot divine, they pass me by unnoticed. Concealment is utter folly on my part, for the people *will not* see. It was but just now that I passed directly before the eyes of the mate – it was no long while ago that I ventured into the captain's own private cabin, and took thence the materials with which I write, and have written. I shall from time to time continue this journal. It is true that I may not find an opportunity of transmitting it to the world, but I will not fail to make the endeavour. At the last moment I will enclose the MS. in a bottle, and cast it within the sea.

*

An incident has occurred which has given me new room for meditation. Are such things the operation of ungoverned Chance? I had ventured upon deck and thrown myself down, without attracting any notice, among a pile of ratlin-stuff and old sails, in the bottom of the yawl. While musing upon the singularity of my fate, I unwittingly daubed with a tar-brush the edges of a neatly-folded studding-sail which lay near me on a barrel. The studding-sail is now bent upon the ship, and the thoughtless touches of the brush are spread out into the word DISCOVERY. * * *

I have made many observations lately upon the structure of the vessel. Although well armed, she is not, I think, a ship of war. Her rigging, build, and general equipment, all negate a supposition of this kind. What she *is not*, I can easily perceive – what she *is* I fear it is impossible to say. I know not how it is, but in scrutinizing her strange model and singular cast of spars, her huge size and overgrown suits of canvass, her severely simple bow and antiquated stern, there will occasionally flash across my mind a sensation of familiar things, and there is always mixed up with such indistinct shadows of recollection, an unaccountable memory of old foreign chronicles and ages long ago. * * *

I have been looking at the timbers of the ship. She is built of a material to which I am a stranger. There is a peculiar character about the wood which strikes me as rendering it unfit for the purpose to which it has been applied. I mean its extreme *porousness*, considered independently of the worm-eaten condition which is a consequence of navigation in these seas, and apart from the rottenness attendant upon age. It will appear perhaps an observation somewhat over-curious, but this wood would have every characteristic of Spanish oak, if Spanish oak were distended by any unnatural means.

In reading the above sentence a curious apothegm of an old weather-beaten Dutch navigator comes full upon my recollection. 'It is as sure,' he was wont to say, when any doubt was entertained of his veracity, 'as sure as there is a sea where the ship itself will grow in bulk like the living body of the seaman.' * * *

About an hour ago, I made bold to thrust myself among a group of the crew. They paid me no manner of attention, and, although I stood in the very midst of them all, seemed utterly unconscious of my presence. Like the one I had at first seen in the hold, they all bore about them the marks of a hoary old age.[12] Their knees trembled with infirmity; their shoulders were bent double with decrepitude; their shrivelled skins rattled in the wind; their voices were low, tremulous and broken; their eyes glistened with the rheum of years; and their gray hairs streamed terribly in the tempest. Around them on every part of the deck, lay scattered mathematical instruments of the most quaint and obsolete construction. * * *

I mentioned some time ago the bending of a studding-sail. From that period the ship, being thrown dead off the wind, has continued her terrific course due south, with every rag of canvass packed upon her, from her trucks to her lower studding-sail booms, and rolling every moment her top-gallant yard-arms into the most appalling hell of water which it can enter into the mind of man to imagine. I have just left the deck, where I find it impossible to maintain a footing, although the crew seem to experience little inconvenience. It appears to me a miracle of miracles that our enormous bulk is not swallowed up at once and forever. We are surely doomed to hover continually upon the brink of Eternity, without taking a final plunge into the abyss. From billows a thousand times more stupendous than any I have ever seen, we glide away with the facility of the arrowy sea-gull; and the colossal waters rear their heads above us like demons of the deep, but like demons confined to simple threats and forbidden to destroy. I am led to attribute these frequent escapes to the only natural cause which can account for such effect. – I must suppose the ship to be within the influence of some strong current, or impetuous under-tow. * * *

I have seen the captain face to face, and in his own cabin – but, as I expected, he paid me no attention. Although in his appearance there is, to a casual observer, nothing which might bespeak him more or less than man – still a feeling of irrepressible reverence and awe mingled with the sensation of wonder with which I regarded him. In stature he is nearly my own height; that is, about five feet eight inches.[13] He is of a well-knit and compact frame of body, neither robust nor remarkably otherwise. But it is the singularity of the expression which reigns upon the face – it is the intense, the wonderful, the thrilling evidence of old age, so utter, so extreme, which excites within my spirit a sense – a sentiment ineffable. His forehead, although little wrinkled, seems to bear upon it the stamp of a myriad of years. – His gray hairs are records of the past, and his grayer eyes are

Sybils of the future. The cabin floor was thickly strewn with strange, iron-clasped folios, and mouldering instruments of science, and obsolete long-forgotten charts. His head was bowed down upon his hands, and he pored, with a fiery unquiet eye, over a paper which I took to be a commission, and which, at all events, bore the signature of a monarch. He muttered to himself, as did the first seaman whom I saw in the hold, some low peevish syllables of a foreign tongue,[14] and although the speaker was close at my elbow, his voice seemed to reach my ears from the distance of a mile. * * *

The ship and all in it are imbued with the spirit of Eld. The crew glide to and fro like the ghosts of buried centuries; their eyes have an eager and uneasy meaning; and when their fingers fall athwart my path in the wild glare of the battle-lanterns, I feel as I have never felt before, although I have been all my life a dealer in antiquities, and have imbibed the shadows of fallen columns at Balbec, and Tadmor, and Persepolis,[15] until my very soul has become a ruin. * * *

When I look around me I feel ashamed of my former apprehensions. If I trembled at the blast which has hitherto attended us, shall I not stand aghast at a warring of wind and ocean, to convey any idea of which the words tornado and simoom are trivial and ineffective? All in the immediate vicinity of the ship is the blackness of eternal night, and a chaos of foamless water; but, about a league on either side of us, may be seen, indistinctly and at intervals, stupendous ramparts of ice, towering away into the desolate sky, and looking like the walls of the universe.[16] * * *

As I imagined, the ship proves to be in a current; if that appellation can properly be given to a tide which, howling and shrieking by the white ice, thunders on to the southward with a velocity like the headlong dashing of a cataract.[17] * * *

To conceive the horror of my sensations is, I presume, utterly impossible; yet a curiosity to penetrate the mysteries of these awful regions, predominates even over my despair, and will reconcile me to the most hideous aspect of death. It is evident that we are hurrying onwards to some exciting knowledge – some never-to-be-imparted secret, whose attainment is destruction.[18]

Perhaps this current leads us to the southern pole itself. It must be confessed that a supposition apparently so wild has every probability in its favor. * * *

The crew pace the deck with unquiet and tremulous step; but there is upon their countenances an expression more of the eagerness of hope than of the apathy of despair.

In the meantime the wind is still in our poop, and, as we carry a crowd of canvass, the ship is at times lifted bodily from out the sea – Oh, horror upon horror ! the ice opens suddenly to the right, and to the left, and we are whirling dizzily, in immense concentric circles, round and round the borders of a gigantic amphitheatre,[19] the summit of whose walls is lost in the darkness and the distance. But little time will be left me to ponder upon my destiny – the circles rapidly grow small – we are plunging madly within the grasp of the whirlpool – and amid a roaring, and bellowing, and thundering of ocean and of tempest, the ship is quivering, oh God ! and— going down.

*

NOTE. – The 'MS. Found in a Bottle', was originally published in 1831,[20] and it was not until many years afterwards that I became acquainted with the maps of Mercator, in which the ocean is represented as rushing, by four mouths, into the (northern) Polar Gulf, to be absorbed into the bowels of the earth; the Pole itself being represented by a black rock, towering to a prodigious height.

The Unparalleled Adventure of One
Hans Pfaall[1]

> With a heart of furious fancies,
>   Whereof I am commander,
> With a burning spear *and a horse of air,*
> To the wilderness I wander.
>   *Tom O'Bedlam's Song*[2]

By late accounts from Rotterdam, that city seems to be in a high
state of philosophical excitement. Indeed, phenomena have there
occurred of a nature so completely unexpected – so entirely novel
– so utterly at variance with preconceived opinions – as to leave
no doubt on my mind that long ere this all Europe is in an uproar, all physics in a ferment, all reason and astronomy together
by the ears.

It appears that on the — day of —, (I am not positive about
the date,) a vast crowd of people, for purposes not specifically
mentioned, were assembled in the great square of the Exchange
in the well-conditioned city of Rotterdam. The day was warm –
unusually so for the season – there was hardly a breath of air
stirring; and the multitude were in no bad humor at being now
and then besprinkled with friendly showers of momentary duration, that fell from large white masses of cloud profusely distributed about the blue vault of the firmament. Nevertheless, about
noon, a slight but remarkable agitation became apparent in the
assembly; the clattering of ten thousand tongues succeeded; and,
in an instant afterwards, ten thousand faces were upturned towards the heavens, ten thousand pipes descended simultaneously
from the corners of ten thousand mouths, and a shout, which
could be compared to nothing but the roaring of Niagara, re-
sounded long, loudly and furiously, through all the city and
through all the environs of Rotterdam.

The origin of this hubbub soon became sufficiently evident.
From behind the huge bulk of one of those sharply defined

masses of cloud already mentioned, was seen slowly to emerge into an open area of blue space, a queer, heterogeneous, but apparently solid substance, so oddly shaped, so whimsically put together, as not to be in any manner comprehended, and never to be sufficiently admired, by the host of sturdy burghers who stood open-mouthed below. What could it be? In the name of all the devils in Rotterdam, what could it possibly portend? No one knew; no one could imagine; no one – not even the burgomaster Mynheer Superbus Von Underduk [3] – had the slightest clew by which to unravel the mystery; so, as nothing more reasonable could be done, every one to a man replaced his pipe carefully in the corner of his mouth, and maintaining an eye steadily upon the phenomenon, puffed, paused, waddled about, and grunted significantly – then waddled back, grunted, paused, and finally – puffed again.

In the meantime, however, lower and still lower towards the goodly city, came the object of so much curiosity, and the cause of so much smoke. In a very few minutes it arrived near enough to be accurately discerned. It appeared to be – yes! it *was* undoubtedly a species of balloon; but surely no *such* balloon had ever been seen in Rotterdam before. For who, let me ask, ever heard of a balloon manufactured entirely of dirty newspapers? No man in Holland certainly; yet here, under the very noses of the people, or rather at some distance *above* their noses, was the identical thing in question, and composed, I have it on the best authority, of the precise material which no one had ever before known to be used for a similar purpose. – It was an egregious insult to the good sense of the burghers of Rotterdam. As to the shape of the phenomenon, it was even still more reprehensible. Being little or nothing better than a huge fool's-cap turned upside down. And this similitude was regarded as by no means lessened, when upon nearer inspection, the crowd saw a large tassel depending from its apex, and, around the upper rim or base of the cone, a circle of little instruments, resembling sheep-bells, which kept up a continual tinkling to the tune of Betty Martin.[4] But still worse. – Suspended by blue ribbons to the end of this fantastic machine, there hung, by way of car, an enormous drab beaver hat, with a brim superlatively broad, and a hemispherical crown with a black band and a silver buckle. It is, however, somewhat remarkable that many citizens of Rotterdam swore to having seen the same hat repeatedly before; and indeed the whole assembly seemed to regard it with eyes of familiarity; while the vrow Grettel Pfaall,[5] upon sight of it, uttered an exclamation of joyful surprise, and declared it to be the identical hat of her good man himself. Now this was a circumstance the more to be observed, as Pfaall, with three companions, had actually disappeared from Rotterdam about five years before, in a very sudden and unaccountable manner, and up to the date of this narrative all attempts at obtaining intelligence concerning them had failed. To be sure, some bones which were thought to be human, mixed up with a quantity of odd-looking rubbish, had been lately discovered in a retired situation to the east of the city; and some people went so far as to imagine that in this spot a foul murder had been committed, and that the sufferers were in all probability Hans Pfaall and his associates. – But to return.

The balloon (for such no doubt it was) had now descended to within a hundred feet of the earth, allowing the crowd below a sufficiently distinct view of the person of its occupant. This was in truth a very singular somebody. He could not have been more than two feet in height;[6] but this altitude, little as it was, would have been sufficient to destroy his *equilibrium*, and tilt him over the edge of his tiny car, but for the intervention of a circular rim reaching as high as the breast, and rigged on to the cords of the balloon. The body of the little man was more than proportionally broad, giving to his entire figure a rotundity highly absurd. His feet, of course, could not be seen at all.[7] His hands were enormously large. His hair was gray, and collected into a *queue* behind. His nose was prodigiously long, crooked and inflammatory; his eyes full, brilliant, and acute; his chin and cheeks, although wrinkled with age, were broad, puffy, and double; but of ears of any kind there was not a semblance to be discovered upon any portion of his head. This odd little gentleman was dressed in a loose surtout of sky-blue satin, with tight breeches to match, fastened with silver buckles at the knees. His vest was of some bright yellow material; a white taffety cap was set jauntily on one side of his head; and, to complete his equipment, a blood-red silk handkerchief enveloped his throat, and fell down, in a dainty manner, upon his bosom, in a fantastic bow-knot of supereminent dimensions.

Having descended, as I said before, to about one hundred feet from the surface of the earth, the little old gentleman was suddenly seized with a fit of trepidation, and appeared disinclined to make any nearer approach to *terra firma*. Throwing out, therefore, a quantity of sand from a canvas bag, which he lifted with great difficulty, he became stationary in an instant. He then proceeded in a hurried and agitated manner, to extract from a side-pocket in his surtout a large morocco pocket-book. This he poised suspiciously in his hand; then eyed it with an air of extreme surprise, and was evidently astonished at its weight. He at length opened it, and, drawing therefrom a huge letter sealed with red sealing-wax and tied carefully with red tape, let it fall precisely at the feet of the burgomaster Superbus Von Underduk. His Excellency stooped to take it up. But the aeronaut, still greatly discomposed, and having apparently no further business to detain him in Rotterdam, began at this moment to make busy preparations for departure; and, it being necessary to discharge a portion of ballast to enable him to reascend, the half dozen bags which he threw out, one after another, without taking the trouble to empty their contents, tumbled, every one of them, most unfortunately, upon the back of the burgomaster, and rolled him over and over no less than half a dozen times, in the face of every individual in Rotterdam. It is not to be supposed, however, that the great Underduk suffered this impertinence on the part of the little old man to pass off with impunity. It is said, on the contrary, that during each of his half dozen circumvolutions, he emitted no less than half a dozen distinct and furious whiffs from his pipe, to which he held fast the whole time with all his might, and to which he intends holding fast, (God willing,) until the day of his decease.

In the meantime the balloon arose like a lark, and, soaring far away above the city, at length drifted quietly behind a cloud similar to that from which it had so oddly emerged, and was thus lost forever to the wondering eyes of the good citizens of Rotterdam. All attention was now directed to the letter, the descent of which, and the consequences attending thereupon, had proved so fatally subversive of both person and personal dignity to his Excellency, Von Underduk. That functionary, however, had not failed, during his circumgyratory movements, to bestow a thought upon the important object of securing the epistle, which was seen, upon inspection, to have fallen into the most proper hands, being actually addressed to himself and Professor Rubadub, in their official capacities of President and Vice-President of the Rotterdam College of Astronomy. It was accordingly opened by those dignitaries upon the spot, and found to contain the following extraordinary, and indeed very serious, communication:

To their Excellencies Von Underduk and Rubadub, President and Vice-President of the States' College of Astronomers, in the city of Rotterdam.

Your Excellencies may perhaps be able to remember an humble artizan, by name Hans Pfaall, and by occupation a mender of bellows, who, with three others, disappeared from Rotterdam, about five years ago, in a manner which must have been considered unaccountable. If, however, it so please your Excellencies, I, the writer of this communication, am the identical Hans Pfaall himself. It is well known to most of my fellow-citizens, that for the period of forty years I continued to occupy the little square brick building, at the head of the alley called Sauerkraut, in which I resided at the time of my disappearance. My ancestors have also resided therein time out of mind – they, as well as myself, steadily following the respectable and indeed lucrative profession of mending of bellows: for, to speak the truth, until of late years, that the heads of all the people have been set agog with politics, no better business than my own could an honest citizen of Rotterdam either desire or deserve. Credit was good, employment was never wanting, and there was no lack of either money or good will. But, as I was saying, we soon began to feel the effects of liberty, and long speeches, and radicalism, and all that sort of thing. People who were formerly the very best customers in the world, had now not a moment of time to think of us at all. They had as much as they could do to read about the revolutions, and keep up with the march of intellect and the spirit of the age. If a fire wanted fanning, it could readily be fanned with a newspaper; and as the government grew weaker, I have no doubt that leather and iron acquired durability in proportion – for, in a very short time, there was not a pair of bellows in all Rotterdam that ever stood in need of a stitch or required the assistance of a hammer. This was a state of things not to be endured. I soon grew as poor as a rat, and, having a wife and children to provide for, my burdens at length became intolerable, and I spent hour after hour in reflecting upon the most convenient method of putting an end to my life. Duns, in the meantime, left me little leisure for contemplation. My house was literally besieged from morning till night. There were three fellows in particular, who worried me beyond endurance, keeping watch continually about my door, and threatening me with the law. Upon these three I vowed the bitterest revenge, if ever I should be so happy as to get them within my clutches; and I believe nothing in the world but the pleasure of this anticipation prevented me from putting my plan of suicide into immediate execution, by blowing my brains out with a blunderbuss. I thought it best, however, to dissemble my wrath, and to treat them with promises and fair words, until, by some good turn of fate, an opportunity of vengeance should be afforded me.

One day, having given them the slip, and feeling more than usually dejected, I continued for a long time to wander about the most obscure streets without object, until at length I chanced to stumble against the corner of a bookseller's stall. Seeing a chair close at hand, for the use of customers, I threw myself doggedly into it, and, hardly knowing why, opened the pages of the first volume which came within my reach. It proved to be a small pamphlet treatise on Speculative Astronomy, written either by Professor Encke of Berlin, or by a Frenchman of somewhat similar name.[8] I had some little tincture of information on matters of this nature, and soon became more and more absorbed in the contents of the book – reading it actually through twice before I awoke to a recollection of what was passing around me. By this time it began to grow dark, and I directed my steps toward home.

But the treatise (in conjunction with a discovery in pneumatics, lately communicated to me as an important secret, by a cousin from Nantz,)[9] had made an indelible impression on my mind, and, as I sauntered along the dusky streets, I revolved carefully over in my memory the wild and sometimes unintelligible reasonings of the writer. There are some particular passages which affected my imagination in an extraordinary manner. The longer I meditated upon these, the more intense grew the interest which had been excited within me. The limited nature of my education in general, and more especially my ignorance on subjects connected with natural philosophy, so far from rendering me diffident of my own ability to comprehend what I had read, or inducing me to mistrust the many vague notions which had arisen in consequence, merely served as a farther stimulus to imagination; and I was vain enough, or perhaps reasonable enough, to doubt whether those crude ideas which, arising in ill-regulated minds, have all the appearance, may not often in effect possess all the force, the reality, and other inherent properties of instinct or intuition.[10]

It was late when I reached home, and I went immediately to bed. My mind, however, was too much occupied to sleep, and I lay the whole night buried in meditation. Arising early in the morning, I repaired eagerly to the bookseller's stall, and laid out what little ready money I possessed, in the purchase of some volumes of Mechanics and Practical Astronomy. Having arrived at home safely with these, I devoted every spare moment to their perusal, and soon made such proficiency in studies of this nature as I thought sufficient for the execution of a certain design with which either the devil or my better genius had inspired me. In the intervals of this period, I made every endeavor to conciliate the three creditors who had given me so much annoyance. In this I finally succeeded – partly by selling enough of my household furniture to satisfy a moiety of their claim, and partly by a promise of paying the balance upon completion of a little project which I told them I had in view, and for assistance in which I solicited their services. By these means (for they were ignorant men) I found little difficulty in gaining them over to my purpose.

Matters being thus arranged, I contrived, by the aid of my

wife, and with the greatest secrecy and caution, to dispose of what property I had remaining, and to borrow, in small sums, under various pretences, and without giving any attention (I am ashamed to say) to my future means of repayment, no inconsiderable quantity of ready money. With the means thus accruing I proceeded to procure at intervals, cambric muslin,[11] very fine, in pieces of twelve yards each; twine; a lot of the varnish of caoutchouc; a large and deep basket of wicker-work, made to order; and several other articles necessary in the construction and equipment of a balloon of extraordinary dimensions. This I directed my wife to make up as soon as possible, and gave her all requisite information as to the particular method of proceeding. In the meantime I worked up the twine into net-work of sufficient dimensions; rigged it with a hoop and the necessary cords; and made purchase of numerous instruments and materials for experiment in the upper regions of the upper atmosphere. I then took opportunities of conveying by night, to a retired situation east of Rotterdam, five iron-bound casks, to contain about fifty gallons each, and one of a larger size; six tin tubes, three inches in diameter, properly shaped, and ten feet in length; a quantity of a *particular metallic substance, or semi-metal* which I shall not name, and a dozen demijohns of *a very common acid.*[12] The gas to be formed from these latter materials is a gas never yet generated by any other person than myself – or at least never applied to any similar purpose. I can only venture to say here, that it is *a constituent of azote,*[13] so long considered irreducible, and that its density is about 37.4 times *less than that of hydrogen.* It is tasteless, but not odorless; burns, when pure, with a greenish flame, and is instantaneously fatal to animal life. Its full secret I would make no difficulty in disclosing, but that it of right belongs (as I have before hinted) to a citizen of Nantz, in France, by whom it was conditionally communicated to myself. The same individual submitted to me, without being at all aware of my intentions, a method of constructing balloons from the membrane of a certain animal, through which substance any escape of gas was nearly an impossibility. I found it, however, altogether too expensive, and was not sure, upon the whole, whether cambric muslin with a coating of gum caoutchouc, was not equally as good. I mention this circumstance, because I think it probable that hereafter the individual in question may attempt a balloon ascension with the novel gas and material I have spoken of, and I do not wish to deprive him of the honor of a very singular invention.

On the spot which I intended each of the smaller casks to occupy respectively during the inflation of the balloon, I privately dug a small hole; the holes forming in this manner a circle twenty-five feet in diameter. In the centre of this circle, being the station designed for the large cask, I also dug a hole of greater depth. In each of the five smaller holes, I deposited a canister containing fifty pounds, and in the larger one a keg holding one hundred and fifty pounds of cannon powder. These – the keg and the canisters – I connected in a proper manner with covered trains; and having let into one of the canisters the end of about four feet of slow-match, I covered up the hole, and placed the cask over it, leaving the other end of the match protruding about an inch, and barely visible beyond the cask. I then filled up the remaining holes, and placed the barrels over them in their destined situation.

Besides the articles above enumerated, I conveyed to the *dépôt*, and there secreted, one of M. Grimm's improvements upon the apparatus for condensation of the atmospheric air.[14] I found this machine, however, to require considerable alteration before it could be adapted to the purposes to which I intended making it applicable. But, with severe labor and unremitting perseverance, I at length met with entire success in all my preparations. My balloon was soon completed. It would contain more than forty thousand cubic feet of gas; would take me up easily, I calculated, with all my implements, and, if I managed rightly, with one hundred and seventy-five pounds of ballast into the bargain. It had received three coats of varnish, and I found the cambric muslin to answer all the purposes of silk itself, being quite as strong and a good deal less expensive.

Everything being now ready, I exacted from my wife an oath of secrecy in relation to all my actions from the day of my first visit to the bookseller's stall; and promising, on my part, to return as soon as circumstances would permit, I gave her what little money I had left, and bade her farewell. Indeed I had no fear on her account. She was what people call a notable woman, and could manage matters in the world without my assistance. I believe, to tell the truth, she always looked upon me as an idle body – a mere make-weight – good for nothing but building castles in the air – and was rather glad to get rid of me. It was a dark night when I bade her good bye, and taking with me, as *aides-de-camp*, the three creditors who had given me so much trouble, we carried the balloon, with the car and accoutrements, by a roundabout way, to the station where the other articles were deposited. We there found them all unmolested, and I proceeded immediately to business.

It was the first of April. The night, as I said before, was dark; there was not a star to be seen; and a drizzling rain, falling at intervals, rendered us very uncomfortable. But my chief anxiety was concerning the balloon, which, in spite of the varnish with which it was defended, began to grow rather heavy with the moisture; the powder also was liable to damage. I therefore kept my three duns working with great diligence, pounding down ice around the central cask, and stirring the acid in the others. They did not cease, however, importuning me with questions as to what I intended to do with all this apparatus, and expressed much dissatisfaction at the terrible labor I made them undergo. They could not perceive (so they said) what good was likely to result from their getting wet to the skin, merely to take a part in such horrible incantations. I began to get uneasy, and worked away with all my might; for I verily believe the idiots supposed that I had entered into a compact with the devil, and that, in short, what I was now doing was nothing better than it should be. I was, therefore, in great fear of their leaving me altogether. I contrived, however, to pacify them by promises of payment of all scores in full, as soon as I could bring the present business to a termination. To these speeches they gave of course their own interpretation; fancying, no doubt, that at all events I should come into possession of vast quantities of ready money; and provided I paid them all I owed, and a trifle more, in consideration of their services, I dare say they cared very little what became of either my soul or my carcass.

In about four hours and a half I found the balloon sufficiently inflated. I attached the car, therefore, and put all my implements in it – a telescope; a barometer, with some important modifications; a thermometer; an electrometer; a compass; a magnetic needle; a seconds watch; a bell; a speaking trumpet, etc., etc., etc. – also a globe of glass, exhausted of air, and carefully closed with a stopper – not forgetting the condensing apparatus, some unslacked lime, a stick of sealing wax, a copious supply of water, and a large quantity of provisions, such as pemmican, in which much nutriment is contained in comparatively little bulk. I also secured in the car a pair of pigeons and a cat.

It was now nearly daybreak, and I thought it high time to take my departure. Dropping a lighted cigar on the ground, as if by accident, I took the opportunity, in stooping to pick it up, of igniting privately the piece of slow match, the end of which, as I said before, protruded a little beyond the lower rim of one of the smaller casks. This manoeuvre was totally unperceived on the part of the three duns; and, jumping into the car, I immediately cut the single cord which held me to the earth, and was pleased to find that I shot upwards with inconceivable rapidity, carrying with all ease one hundred and seventy-five pounds of leaden ballast, and able to have carried up as many more. As I left the earth, the barometer stood at thirty inches, and the centigrade thermometer at $19°$.

Scarcely, however, had I attained the height of fifty yards, when, roaring and rumbling up after me in the most tumultuous and terrible manner, came so dense a hurricane of fire, and gravel, and burning wood,[15] and blazing metal, and mangled limbs, that my very heart sunk within me, and I fell down in the bottom of the car, trembling with terror. Indeed, I now perceived that I had entirely overdone the business, and that the main consequences of the shock were yet to be experienced. Accordingly, in less than a second, I felt all the blood in my body rushing to my temples, and, immediately thereupon, a concussion, which I shall never forget, burst abruptly through the night, and seemed to rip the very firmament asunder. When I afterwards had time for reflection, I did not fail to attribute the extreme violence of the explosion, as regarded myself, to its proper cause – my situation directly above it, and in the line of its greatest power. But at the time, I thought only of preserving my life. The balloon at first collapsed, then furiously expanded, then whirled round and round with sickening velocity, and finally, reeling and staggering like a drunken man, hurled me over the rim of the car, and left me dangling, at a terrific height, with my head downward, and my face outward, by a piece of slender cord[16] about three feet in length, which hung accidentally through a crevice near the bottom of the wicker-work, and in which, as I fell, my left foot became most providentially entangled. It is impossible – utterly impossible – to form any adequate idea of the horror of my situation. I gasped convulsively for breath – a shudder resembling a fit of the ague agitated every nerve and muscle in my frame – I felt my eyes starting from their sockets – a horrible nausea overwhelmed me – and at length I lost all consciousness in a swoon.

How long I remained in this state it is impossible to say. It must, however, have been no inconsiderable time, for when I partially recovered the sense of existence, I found the day breaking, the balloon at a prodigious height over a wilderness of ocean, and not a trace of land to be discovered far and wide within the limits of the vast horizon. My sensations, however, upon thus recovering, were by no means so replete with agony as might have been anticipated. Indeed, there was much of madness in the calm survey which I began to take of my situation. I drew up to my eyes each of my hands, one after the other, and wondered what occurrence could have given rise to the swelling of the veins, and the horrible blackness of the finger nails. I afterwards carefully examined my head, shaking it repeatedly, and feeling it with minute attention, until I succeeded in satisfying myself that it was not, as I had more than half suspected, larger than my balloon. Then, in a knowing manner, I felt in both my breeches pockets, and, missing therefrom a set of tablets and a tooth-pick case, endeavored to account for their disappearance, and, not being able to do so, felt inexpressibly chagrined. It now occurred to me that I suffered great uneasiness in the joint of my left ankle, and a dim consciousness of my situation began to glimmer through my mind. But, strange to say! I was neither astonished nor horror-stricken. If I felt any emotion at all, it was a kind of chuckling satisfaction at the cleverness I was about to display in extricating myself from this dilemma; and never, for a moment, did I look upon my ultimate safety as a question susceptible of doubt. For a few minutes I remained wrapped in the profoundest meditation. I have a distinct recollection of frequently compressing my lips, putting my fore-finger to the side of my nose, and making use of other gesticulations and grimaces common to men who, at ease in their arm-chairs, meditate upon matters of intricacy or importance. Having, as I thought, sufficiently collected my ideas, I now, with great caution and deliberation, put my hands behind my back, and unfastened the large iron buckle which belonged to the waistband of my pantaloons. This buckle had three teeth, which, being somewhat rusty, turned with great difficulty on their axis. I brought them, however, after some trouble, at right angles to the body of the buckle, and was glad to find them remain firm in that position. Holding within my teeth the instrument thus obtained, I now proceeded to untie the knot of my cravat. I had to rest several times before I could accomplish this manoeuvre; but it was at length accomplished. To one end of the cravat I then made fast the buckle, and the other end I tied, for greater security, tightly around my wrist. Drawing now my body upwards, with a prodigious exertion of muscular force, I succeeded, at the very first trial, in throwing the buckle over the car, and entangling it, as I had anticipated, in the circular rim of the wicker-work.

My body was now inclined towards the side of the car, at an angle of about forty-five degrees; but it must not be understood that I was therefore only forty-five degrees below the perpendicular. So far from it, I still lay nearly level with the plane of the horizon; for the change of situation which I had acquired, had forced the bottom of the car considerably outward from my position, which was accordingly one of the most imminent peril. It should be remembered, however, that when I fell, in the first instance, from the car, if I had fallen with my face turned toward the balloon, instead of turned outwardly from it as it actually was – or if, in the second place, the cord by which I was suspended had chanced to hang over the upper edge, instead of through a crevice near the bottom of the car – I say it may readily be conceived that, in either of these supposed cases, I should have been unable to accomplish even as much as I had now accomplished, and the disclosures now made would have been utterly lost to posterity. I had therefore every reason to be grateful; although, in point of fact, I was still too stupid to be any thing at all, and hung for, perhaps, a quarter of an hour, in that extraordinary manner, without making the slightest farther exertion, and in a singularly tranquil state of idiotic enjoyment. But this feeling did not fail to die rapidly away, and thereunto succeeded horror, and dismay, and a sense of utter helplessness and ruin. In fact, the blood so long accumulating in the vessels of my head and throat, and which had hitherto buoyed up my spirits with delirium, had now begun to retire within their proper channels, and the distinctness which was thus added to my perception of the danger, merely served to deprive me of the self-possession and courage to encounter it. But this weakness was, luckily for me, of no very long duration. In good time came to my rescue the spirit of despair, and, with frantic cries and struggles, I jerked my way bodily upwards, till, at length, clutching with a vice-like grip the long-desired rim, I writhed my person over it, and fell headlong and shuddering within the car.

It was not until some time afterward that I recovered myself sufficiently to attend to the ordinary cares of the balloon. I then, however, examined it with attention, and found it, to my great relief, uninjured. My implements were all safe, and, fortunately, I had lost neither ballast nor provisions. Indeed, I had so well secured them in their places, that such an accident was entirely out of the question. Looking at my watch, I found it six o'clock. I was still rapidly ascending, and the barometer gave a present altitude of three and three-quarter miles. Immediately beneath me in the ocean, lay a small black object, slightly oblong in shape, seemingly about the size of a domino, and in every respect bearing a great resemblance to one of those toys. Bringing my telescope to bear upon it, I plainly discerned it to be a British ninety-four gun ship, close-hauled, and pitching heavily in the sea with her head to the W. S. W. Besides this ship, I saw nothing but the ocean and the sky, and the sun, which had long arisen.

It is now high time that I should explain to your Excellencies the object of my voyage. Your Excellencies will bear in mind that distressed circumstances in Rotterdam had at length driven me to the resolution of committing suicide. It was not, however, that to life itself I had any positive disgust, but that I was harassed beyond endurance by the adventitious miseries attending my situation. In this state of mind, wishing to live, yet wearied with life, the treatise at the stall of the bookseller, backed by the opportune discovery of my cousin of Nantz, opened a resource to my imagination. I then finally made up my mind. I determined to depart, yet live – to leave the world, yet continue to exist – in short, to drop enigmas, I resolved, let what would ensue, to force a passage, if I could, *to the moon*. Now, lest I should be supposed more of a madman than I actually am, I will detail, as well as I am able, the considerations which led me to believe that an achievement of this nature, although without doubt difficult, and full of danger, was not absolutely, to a bold spirit, beyond the confines of the possible.

The moon's actual distance from the earth was the first thing to be attended to. Now, the mean or average interval between the *centres* of the two planets is 59.9643 of the earth's equatorial *radii*,[17] or only about 237,000 miles. I say the mean or average interval; – but it must be borne in mind, that the form of the moon's orbit being an ellipse of eccentricity amounting to no less than 0.05484 of the major semi-axis of the ellipse itself, and the earth's centre being situated in its focus, if I could, in any manner, contrive to meet the moon in its perigee, the above-mentioned distance would be materially diminished. But to say nothing, at present, of this possibility, it was very certain that, at all events, from the 237,000 miles I would have to deduct the *radius* of the earth, say 4000, and the radius of the moon, say 1080, in all 5080, leaving an actual interval to be traversed, under average circumstances, of 231,920 miles. Now this, I reflected, was no very extraordinary distance. Travelling on the land has been repeatedly accomplished at the rate of sixty miles per hour; and indeed a much greater speed may be anticipated. But even at this velocity, it would take me no more than 161 days to reach the surface of the moon. There were, however, many particulars inducing me to believe that my average rate of travelling might possibly very much exceed that of sixty miles per hour, and, as these considerations did not fail to make a deep impression upon my mind, I will mention them more fully hereafter.

The next point to be regarded was one of far greater importance. From indications afforded by the barometer, we find that, in ascensions from the surface of the earth we have, at the height of 1,000 feet, left below us about one-thirtieth of the entire mass of atmospheric air; that at 10,600, we have ascended through nearly one-third; and that at 18,000, which is not far from the elevation of Cotopaxi,[18] we have surmounted one-half the material, or, at all events, one-half the *ponderable* body of air incumbent upon our globe. It is also calculated, that at an altitude not exceeding the hundredth part of the earth's diameter – that is, not exceeding eighty miles – the rarefaction would be so excessive that animal life could in no manner be sustained, and, moreover, that the most delicate means we possess of ascertaining the presence of the atmosphere, would be inadequate to assure us of its existence. But I did not fail to perceive that these latter calculations are founded altogether on our experimental knowledge of the properties of air, and the mechanical laws regulating its dilation and compression, in what may be called, comparatively speaking, *the immediate vicinity* of the earth itself; and, at the same time, it is taken for granted that animal life is and must be, essentially *incapable of modification* at any given unattainable distance from the surface. Now, all such reasoning and from such *data*, must of course be simply analogical. The greatest height ever reached by man was that of 25,000 feet, attained in the aeronautic expedition of Messieurs Gay–Lussac and Biot.[19] This is a moderate altitude, even when compared with the eighty miles in question; and I could not help thinking that the subject admitted room for doubt, and great latitude for speculation.

But, in point of fact, an ascension being made to any given altitude, the ponderable quantity of air surmounted in any *farther* ascension, is by no means in proportion to the additional height ascended, (as may be plainly seen from what has been stated before,) but in a *ratio* constantly decreasing. It is therefore evident that, ascend as high as we may, we cannot, literally speaking, arrive at a limit beyond which *no* atmosphere is to be found. It *must exist*, I argued; although it *may* exist in a state of infinite rarefaction.

On the other hand, I was aware that arguments have not been wanting to prove the existence of a real and definite limit to the atmosphere, beyond which there is absolutely no air whatsoever. But a circumstance which has been left out of view by those who contend for such a limit, seemed to me, although no positive refutation of their creed, still a point worthy very serious investigation. On comparing the intervals between the successive arrivals of Encke's comet at its perihelion, after giving credit, in the most exact manner, for all the disturbances due to the attractions of the planets, it appears that the periods are gradually diminishing; that is to say, the major axis of the comet's ellipse is growing shorter, in a slow but perfectly regular decrease. Now, this is precisely what ought to be the case, if we suppose a resistance experienced from the comet from an extremely *rare ethereal medium* pervading the regions of its orbit. For it is evident that such a medium must, in retarding the comet's velocity, increase its centripetal, by weakening its centrifugal force. In other words, the sun's attraction would be constantly attaining greater power, and the comet would be drawn nearer at every revolution. Indeed, there is no other way of accounting for the variation in question. But again: – The real diameter of the same comet's nebulosity, is observed to contract rapidly as it approaches the sun, and dilate with equal rapidity in its departure toward its aphelion. Was I not justifiable in supposing, with M. Valz, that this apparent condensation of volume has its origin in the compression of the same ethereal medium I have spoken of before, and which is dense in proportion to its vicinity to the sun? The lenticular-shaped phenomenon,[20] also, called the zodiacal light, was a matter worthy of attention. This radiance, so apparent in the tropics, and which cannot be mistaken for any meteoric lustre, extends from the horizon obliquely upwards, and follows generally the direction of the sun's equator. It appeared to me evidently in the nature of a rare atmosphere extending from the sun outwards, beyond the orbit of Venus at least, and I believed indefinitely farther.* Indeed, this medium I could not suppose confined to the path of the comet's ellipse, or to the immediate neighborhood of the sun. It was easy, on the contrary, to imagine it pervading the entire regions of our planetary system, condensed into what we call atmosphere at the planets themselves, and perhaps at some of them modified by considerations purely geological; that is to say, modified, or varied in its proportions (or absolute nature) by matters volatilized from the respective orbs.

Having adopted this view of the subject, I had little farther hesitation. Granting that on my passage I should meet with atmosphere *essentially* the same as at the surface of the earth, I conceived that, by means of the very ingenious apparatus of M. Grimm, I should readily be enabled to condense it in sufficient quantity for the purposes of respiration. This would remove the chief obstacle in a journey to the moon. I had indeed spent some money and great labor in adapting the apparatus to the object intended, and confidently looked forward to its successful application, if I could manage to complete the voyage within any reasonable period. – This brings me back to the *rate* at which it would be possible to travel.

It is true that balloons, in the first stage of their ascensions from the earth, are known to rise with a velocity comparatively moderate. Now, the power of elevation lies altogether in the superior gravity of the atmospheric air compared with the gas in the balloon; and, at first sight, it does not appear probable that, as the balloon acquires altitude, and consequently arrives successively in atmospheric *strata* of densities rapidly diminishing – I say, it does not appear at all reasonable that, in this its progress upward, the original velocity should be accelerated. On the other hand, I was not aware that, in any recorded ascension, a *diminution* had been proved to be apparent in the absolute rate of ascent; although such should have been the case, if on account of nothing else, on account of the escape of gas through balloons ill-constructed, and varnished with no better material than the

---

*The zodiacal light is probably what the ancients called Trabes.[21] *Emicant trabes quos docos vocant.* – Pliny lib. 2, p. 26.

ordinary varnish. It seemed, therefore, that the effect of such escape was only sufficient to counterbalance the effect of the acceleration attained in the diminishing of the balloon's distance from the gravitating centre. I now considered that, provided in my passage I found the *medium* I had imagined, and provided it should prove to be *essentially* what we denominate atmospheric air, it could make comparatively little difference at what extreme state of rarefaction I should discover it – that is to say, in regard to my power of ascending – for the gas in the balloon would not only be itself subject to similar rarefaction, (in proportion to the occurrence of which, I could suffer an escape of so much as would be requisite to prevent explosion,) but, *being what it was*, would, at all events, continue specifically lighter than any compound whatever of mere nitrogen and oxygen. Thus there was a chance – in fact, there was a strong possibility – that, *at no epoch of my ascent, I should reach a point where the united weights of my immense balloon, the inconceivably rare gas within it, the car, and its contents, should equal the weight of the mass of the surrounding atmosphere displaced*; and this will be readily understood as the sole condition upon which my upward flight would be arrested. But, if this point were even attained, I could dispense with ballast and other weight to the amount of nearly 300 pounds. In the meantime, the force of gravitation would be constantly diminishing, in proportion to the squares of the distances, and so, with a velocity prodigiously accelerating, I should at length arrive in those distant regions where the force of the earth's attraction would be superseded by that of the moon.

There was another difficulty, however, which occasioned me some little disquietude. It has been observed that, in balloon ascensions to any considerable height, besides the pain attending respiration, great uneasiness is experienced about the head and body, often accompanied with bleeding at the nose, and other symptoms of an alarming kind, and growing more and more inconvenient in proportion to the altitude attained.* This was a

---

* Since the original publication of Hans Pfaall, I find that Mr Green, of Nassau-balloon notoriety,[22] and other late æronauts, deny the assertions of Humboldt, in this respect, and speak of a *decreasing* inconvenience, – precisely in accordance with the theory here urged.

reflection of a nature somewhat startling. Was it not probable that these symptoms would increase until terminated by death itself? I finally thought not. Their origin was to be looked for in the progressive removal of the *customary* atmospheric pressure upon the surface of the body, and consequent distention of the superficial blood-vessels – not in any positive disorganization of the animal system, as in the case of difficulty in breathing, where the atmospheric density is *chemically insufficient* for the due renovation of blood in a ventricle of the heart. Unless for default of this renovation, I could see no reason, therefore, why life could not be sustained even in a *vacuum*; for the expansion and compression of chest, commonly called breathing, is action purely muscular, and the *cause*, not the *effect*, of respiration. In a word, I conceived that, as the body should become habituated to the want of atmospheric pressure, these sensations of pain would gradually diminish – and to endure them while they continued, I relied with confidence upon the iron hardihood of my constitution.

Thus, may it please your Excellencies, I have detailed some, though by no means all, the considerations which led me to form the project of a lunar voyage. I shall now proceed to lay before you the result of an attempt so apparently audacious in conception, and, at all events, so utterly unparelleled in the annals of mankind.

Having attained the altitude before mentioned – that is to say, three miles and three quarters – I threw out from the car a quantity of feathers, and found that I still ascended with sufficient rapidity; there was, therefore, no necessity for discharging any ballast. I was glad of this, for I wished to retain with me as much weight as I could carry, for the obvious reason that I could not be *positive* either about the gravitation or the atmospheric density of the moon. I as yet suffered no bodily inconvenience, breathing with great freedom, and feeling no pain whatever in the head. The cat was lying very demurely upon my coat, which I had taken off, and eyeing the pigeons with an air of *nonchalance*. These latter being tied by the leg, to prevent their escape, were busily employed in picking up some grains of rice scattered for them in the bottom of the car.

At twenty minutes past six o'clock, the barometer showed an elevation of 26,400 feet, or five miles to a fraction. The prospect seemed unbounded. Indeed, it is very easily calculated by means of spherical geometry, how great an extent of the earth's area I beheld. The convex surface of any segment of a sphere is, to the entire surface of the sphere itself, as the versed sine of the segment to the diameter of the sphere. Now, in my case, the versed sine – that is to say, the *thickness* of the segment beneath me – was about equal to my elevation, or the elevation of the point of sight above the surface. 'As five miles, then, to eight thousand', would express the proportion of the earth's area seen by me. In other words, I beheld as much as a sixteen-hundredth part of the whole surface of the globe.[23] The sea appeared unruffled as a mirror, although, by means of the telescope, I could perceive it to be in a state of violent agitation. The ship was no longer visible, having drifted away, apparently, to the eastward. I now began to experience, at intervals, severe pain in the head, especially about the ears – still, however, breathing with tolerable freedom. The cat and pigeons seemed to suffer no inconvenience whatsoever.

At twenty minutes before seven, the balloon entered a long series of dense cloud, which put me to great trouble, by damaging my condensing apparatus, and wetting me to the skin. This was, to be sure, a singular *rencontre*, for I had not believed it possible that a cloud of this nature could be sustained at so great an elevation. I thought it best, however, to throw out two five-pound pieces of ballast, reserving still a weight of one hundred and sixty-five pounds. Upon so doing, I soon rose above the difficulty, and perceived immediately, that I had obtained a great increase in my rate of ascent. In a few seconds after my leaving the cloud, a flash of vivid lightning shot from one end of it to the other, and caused it to kindle up, throughout its vast extent, like a mass of ignited charcoal. This, it must be remembered, was in the broad light of day. No fancy may picture the sublimity which might have been exhibited by a similar phenomenon taking place amid the darkness of the night. Hell itself might then have found a fitting image. Even as it was, my hair stood on end, while I gazed afar down within the yawning abysses, letting imagination descend, and stalk about in the strange vaulted halls, and ruddy gulfs, and red ghastly chasms of the hideous and unfathomable fire. I had indeed made a narrow escape. Had the balloon remained a very short while longer within the cloud – that is to say had not the inconvenience of getting wet, determined me to discharge the ballast – my destruction might, and probably would, have been the consequence. Such perils, although little considered, are perhaps the greatest which must be encountered in balloons. I had by this time, however, attained too great an elevation to be any longer uneasy on this head.

I was now rising rapidly, and by seven o'clock the barometer indicated an altitude of no less than nine miles and a half. I began to find great difficulty in drawing my breath. My head, too, was excessively painful; and, having felt for some time a moisture about my cheeks, I at length discovered it to be blood, which was oozing quite fast from the drums of my ears. My eyes, also, gave me great uneasiness. Upon passing the hand over them they seemed to have protruded from their sockets in no inconsiderable degree; and all objects in the car, and even the balloon itself, appeared distorted to my vision. These symptoms were more than I had expected, and occasioned me some alarm. At this juncture, very imprudently, and without consideration, I threw out from the car three five-pound pieces of ballast. The accelerated rate of ascent thus obtained, carried me too rapidly, and without sufficient gradation, into a highly rarefied *stratum* of the atmosphere, and the result had nearly proved fatal to my expedition and to myself. I was suddenly seized with a spasm which lasted for more than five minutes, and even when this, in a measure, ceased, I could catch my breath only at long intervals, and in a gasping manner, – bleeding all the while copiously at the nose and ears, and even slightly at the eyes. The pigeons appeared distressed in the extreme, and struggled to escape; while the cat mewed piteously, and, with her tongue hanging out of her mouth, staggered to and fro in the car as if under the influence of poison. I now too late discovered the great rashness of which I had been guilty in discharging the ballast, and my agitation was excessive. I anticipated nothing less than death, and death in a few minutes. The physical suffering I underwent contributed also to render me nearly incapable of making any exertion for the preservation of my life. I had, indeed, little power of reflection left, and the violence of the pain in my head seemed to be greatly on the increase. Thus I found that my senses would shortly give way altogether, and I had already clutched one of the valve ropes with the view of attempting a descent, when the recollection of the trick I had played the three creditors, and the possible consequences to myself, should I return, operated to deter me for the moment. I lay down in the bottom of the car, and endeavored to collect my faculties. In this I so far succeeded as to determine upon the experiment of losing blood. Having no lancet, however, I was constrained to perform the operation in the best manner I was able, and finally succeeded in opening a vein in my left arm, with the blade of my pen-knife. The blood had hardly commenced flowing when I experienced a sensible relief, and by the time I had lost about half a moderate basin-full, most of the worst symptoms had abandoned me entirely. I nevertheless did not think it expedient to attempt getting on my feet immediately; but, having tied up my arm as well as I could, I lay still for about a quarter of an hour. At the end of this time I arose, and found myself freer from absolute *pain* of any kind than I had been during the last hour and a quarter of my ascension. The difficulty of breathing, however, was diminished in a very slight degree, and I found that it would soon be positively necessary to make use of my condenser. In the meantime, looking towards the cat, who was again snugly stowed away upon my coat, I discovered, to my infinite surprise, that she had taken the opportunity of my indisposition to bring into light a litter of three little kittens. This was an addition to the number of passengers on my part altogether unexpected; but I was pleased at the occurrence. It would afford me a chance of bringing to a kind of test the truth of a surmise, which, more than any thing else, had influenced me in attempting this ascension. I had imagined that the *habitual* endurance of the atmospheric pressure at the surface of the earth was the cause, or nearly so, of the pain attending animal existence at a distance above the surface. Should the kittens be found to suffer uneasiness *in an equal degree with their mother*, I must consider my theory in fault, but a failure to do so I should look upon as a strong confirmation of my idea.

By eight o'clock I had actually attained an elevation of seventeen miles above the surface of the earth. Thus it seemed to me evident that my rate of ascent was not only on the increase, but that the progression would have been apparent in a slight degree even had I not discharged the ballast which I did. The pains in my head and ears returned, at intervals, with violence, and I still continued to bleed occasionally at the nose: but, upon the whole, I suffered much less than might have been expected. I breathed, however, at every moment, with more and more difficulty, and each inhalation was attended with a troublesome spasmodic action of the chest. I now unpacked the condensing apparatus, and got it ready for immediate use.

The view of the earth, at this period of my ascension, was beautiful indeed.[24] To the westward, the northward, and the southward, as far as I could see, lay a boundless sheet of apparently unruffled ocean, which every moment gained a deeper and deeper tint of blue. At a vast distance to the eastward, although perfectly discernible, extended the islands of Great Britain, the entire Atlantic coasts of France and Spain, with a small portion of the northern part of the continent of Africa. Of individual edifices not a trace could be discovered, and the proudest cities of mankind had utterly faded away from the face of the earth.

What mainly astonished me, in the appearance of things below, was the seeming concavity of the surface of the globe.[25] I had, thoughtlessly enough, expected to see its real *convexity* become evident as I ascended; but a very little reflection sufficed to explain the discrepancy. A line, dropped from my position perpendicularly to the earth, would have formed the perpendicular of a right-angled triangle, of which the base would have extended from the right-angle to the horizon, and the hypothenuse from the horizon to my position. But my height was little or nothing in comparison with my prospect. In other words, the base and hypothenuse of the supposed triangle would, in my case, have been so long, when compared to the perpendicular, that the two former might have been regarded as nearly parallel.

In this manner the horizon of the æronaut appears always to be *upon a level* with the car. But as the point immediately beneath him seems, and is, at a great distance below him, it seems, of course, also at a great distance below the horizon. Hence the impression of concavity; and this impression must remain, until the elevation shall bear so great a proportion to the prospect, that the apparent parallelism of the base and hypothenuse, disappears.

The pigeons about this time seeming to undergo much suffering, I determined upon giving them their liberty. I first untied one of them, a beautiful gray-mottled pigeon, and placed him upon the rim of the wicker-work. He appeared extremely uneasy, looking anxiously around him, fluttering his wings, and making a loud cooing noise, but could not be persuaded to trust himself from the car. I took him up at last, and threw him to about half-a-dozen yards from the balloon. He made, however, no attempt to descend as I had expected, but struggled with great vehemence to get back, uttering at the same time very shrill and piercing cries. He at length succeeded in regaining his former station on the rim, but had hardly done so when his head dropped upon his breast, and he fell dead within the car. The other one did not prove so unfortunate. To prevent his following the example of his companion, and accomplishing a return, I threw him downwards with all my force, and was pleased to find him continue his descent, with great velocity, making use of his wings with ease, and in a perfectly natural manner. In a very short time he was out of sight, and I have no doubt he reached home in safety. Puss, who seemed in a great measure recovered from her illness, now made a hearty meal of the dead bird, and then went to sleep with much apparent satisfaction. Her kittens were quite lively and so far evinced not the slightest sign of any uneasiness.

At a quarter-past eight, being able no longer to draw breath without the most intolerable pain, I proceeded, forthwith, to adjust around the car the apparatus belonging to the condenser. This apparatus will require some little explanation, and your Excellencies will please to bear in mind that my object, in the first place, was to surround myself and car entirely with a barricade against the highly rarefied atmosphere in which I was existing, with the intention of introducing within this barricade, by means of my condenser, a quantity of this same atmosphere sufficiently condensed for the purposes of respiration. With this object in view I had prepared a very strong, perfectly air-tight, but flexible gum-elastic bag. In this bag, which was of sufficient dimensions, the entire car was in a manner placed. That is to say, it (the bag) was drawn over the whole bottom of the car, up its sides, and so on, along the outside of the ropes, to the upper rim or hoop where the net-work is attached. Having pulled the bag up in this way, and formed a complete enclosure on all sides, and at bottom, it was now necessary to fasten up its top or mouth, by passing its material over the hoop of the net-work, – in other words, between the net-work and the hoop. But if the net-work were separated from the hoop to admit this passage, what was to sustain the car in the meantime? Now the net-work was not permanently fastened to the hoop, but attached by a series of running loops or nooses. I therefore undid only a few of these loops at one time, leaving the car suspended by the remainder. Having thus inserted a portion of the cloth forming the upper part of the bag, I refastened the loops – not to the hoop, for that would have been impossible, since the cloth now intervened, – but to a series of large buttons, affixed to the cloth itself, about three feet below the mouth of the bag; the intervals between the buttons having been made to correspond to the intervals between the loops. This done, a few more of the loops were unfastened from the rim, a farther portion of the cloth introduced, and the disengaged loops then connected with their proper buttons. In this way it was possible to insert the whole upper part of the bag between the net-work and the hoop. It is evident that the hoop would now drop down within the car, while the whole weight of the car itself, with all its contents, would be held up merely by the strength of the buttons. This, at first sight, would seem an inadequate dependence; but it was by no means so, for the buttons were not only very strong in themselves, but so close together that a very slight portion of the whole weight was supported by any one of them. Indeed, had the car and contents been three times heavier than they were, I should not have been at all uneasy. I now raised up the hoop again within the covering of gum-elastic, and propped it at nearly its former height by means of three light poles prepared for the occasion. This was done, of course, to keep the bag distended at the top, and to preserve the lower part of the net-work in its proper situation. All that now remained was to fasten up the mouth of the enclosure; and this was readily accomplished by gathering the folds of the material together, and twisting them up very tightly on the inside by means of a kind of stationary *tourniquet*.

In the sides of the covering thus adjusted round the car, had been inserted three circular panes of thick but clear glass, through which I could see without difficulty around me in every horizontal direction. In that portion of the cloth forming the bottom, was likewise a fourth window, of the same kind, and corresponding with a small aperture in the floor of the car itself. This enabled me to see perpendicularly down, but having found it impossible to place any similar contrivance overhead, on account of the peculiar manner of closing up the opening there, and the consequent wrinkles in the cloth, I could expect to see no objects situated directly in my zenith. This, of course, was a matter of little consequence; for, had I even been able to place a window at top, the balloon itself would have prevented my making any use of it.

About a foot below one of the side windows was a circular opening, three inches in diameter, and fitted with a brass rim adapted in its inner edge to the windings of a screw. In this rim was screwed the large tube of the condenser, the body of the machine being, of course, within the chamber of gum-elastic. Through this tube a quantity of the rare atmosphere circumjacent being drawn by means of a *vacuum* created in the body of the machine, was thence discharged, in a state of condensation, to mingle with the thin air already in the chamber. This operation being repeated several times, at length filled the chamber with atmosphere proper for all the purposes of respiration. But in so confined a space it would, in a short time, necessarily become foul, and unfit for use from frequent contact with the lungs. It was then ejected by a small valve at the bottom of the car; – the dense air readily sinking into the thinner atmosphere below. To avoid the inconvenience of making a total *vacuum* at any moment within the chamber, this purification was never accomplished all at once, but in a gradual manner, – the valve being opened only for a few seconds, then closed again, until one or two strokes from the pump of the condenser had supplied the place of the atmosphere ejected. For the sake of experiment I had put the cat and kittens in a small basket, and suspended it outside the car to a button at the bottom, close by the valve, through which I could feed them at any moment when necessary. I did this at some little risk, and before closing the mouth of the chamber, by reaching under the car with one of the poles before mentioned to which a hook had been attached. As soon as dense air was admitted in the chamber, the hoop and poles became unnecessary; the expansion of the enclosed atmosphere powerfully distending the gum-elastic.

By the time I had fully completed these arrangements and filled the chamber as explained, it wanted only ten minutes of nine o'clock. During the whole period of my being thus employed, I endured the most terrible distress from difficulty of respiration; and bitterly did I repent the negligence, or rather fool-hardiness, of which I had been guilty, of putting off to the last moment a matter of so much importance. But having at length accomplished it, I soon began to reap the benefit of my invention. Once again I breathed with perfect freedom and ease – and indeed why should I not? I was also agreeably surprised to find myself, in a great measure, relieved from the violent pains which had hitherto tormented me. A slight headache, accompanied with a sensation of fulness or distention about the wrists, the ankles, and the throat, was nearly all of which I had now to complain. Thus it seemed evident that a greater part of the uneasiness attending the removal of atmospheric pressure had actually *worn off*, as I had expected, and that much of the pain endured for the last two hours should have been attributed altogether to the effects of a deficient respiration.

At twenty minutes before nine o'clock – that is to say, a short time prior to my closing up the mouth of the chamber, the mercury attained its limit, or ran down, in the barometer, which, as I mentioned before, was one of an extended construction. It then indicated an altitude on my part of 132,000 feet, or five-and-twenty miles, and I consequently surveyed at that time an extent of the earth's area amounting to no less than the three-hundred-and-twentieth part of its entire superficies. At nine o'clock I had again lost sight of land to the eastward, but not before I became aware that the balloon was drifting rapidly to the N. N. W. The ocean beneath me still retained its apparent concavity, although my view was often interrupted by the masses of cloud which floated to and fro.

At half past nine I tried the experiment of throwing out a handful of feathers through the valve. They did not float as I had expected, but dropped down perpendicularly, like a bullet, *en masse*, and with the greatest velocity, – being out of sight in a very few seconds. I did not at first know what to make of this extraordinary phenomenon; not being able to believe that my rate of ascent had, of a sudden, met with so prodigious an acceleration. But it soon occurred to me that the atmosphere was now far too rare to sustain even the feathers; that they actually fell, as they appeared to do, with great rapidity; and that I had been surprised by the united velocities of their descent and my own elevation.

By ten o'clock I found that I had very little to occupy my immediate attention. Affairs went on swimmingly, and I believed the balloon to be going upwards with a speed increasing momently, although I had no longer any means of ascertaining the progression of the increase. I suffered no pain or uneasiness of any kind, and enjoyed better spirits than I had at any period since my departure from Rotterdam; busying myself now in examining the state of my various apparatus, and now in regenerating the atmosphere within the chamber. This latter point I determined to attend to at regular intervals of forty minutes, more on account of the preservation of my health, than from so frequent a renovation being absolutely necessary. In the meanwhile I could not help making anticipations. Fancy revelled in the wild and dreamy regions of the moon. Imagination, feeling herself for once unshackled, roamed at will among the ever-changing wonders of a shadowy and unstable land. Now there were hoary and time-honored forests, and craggy precipices, and waterfalls tumbling with a loud noise into abysses without a bottom. Then I came suddenly into still noonday solitudes, where no wind of heaven ever intruded, and where vast meadows of poppies, and slender, lily-looking flowers spread themselves out a weary distance, all silent and motionless for ever. Then again I journey far down away into another country where it was all one dim and vague lake, with a boundary-line of clouds.[26] But fancies such as these were not the sole possessors of my brain. Horrors of a nature most stern and most appalling would too frequently obtrude themselves upon my mind, and shake the innermost depths of my soul with the bare supposition of their possibility. Yet I would not suffer my thoughts for any length of time to dwell upon these latter speculations, rightly judging the real and palpable dangers of the voyage sufficient for my undivided attention.

At five o'clock, P.M., being engaged in regenerating the atmosphere within the chamber, I took that opportunity of observing the cat and kittens through the valve. The cat herself appeared to suffer again very much, and I had no hesitation in attributing her uneasiness chiefly to a difficulty in breathing; but my experiment with the kittens had resulted very strangely. I had expected, of course, to see them betray a sense of pain, although in a less degree than their mother; and this would have been sufficient to confirm my opinion concerning the habitual endurance of atmospheric pressure. But I was not prepared to find them, upon close examination, evidently enjoying a high degree of health, breathing with the greatest ease and perfect regularity, and evincing not the slightest sign of any uneasiness. I could only account for all this by extending my theory, and supposing that the highly rarefied atmosphere around, might perhaps not be, as I had taken for granted, chemically insufficient for the purposes of life, and that a person born in such a *medium* might, possibly, be unaware of any inconvenience attending its inhalation, while, upon removal to the denser *strata* near the earth, he might endure tortures of a similar nature to those I had so lately experienced. It has since been to me a matter of deep regret that an awkward accident, at this time, occasioned me the loss of my little family of cats,[27] and deprived me of the insight into this matter which a continued experiment might have afforded. In passing my hand through the valve, with a cup of water for the old puss, the sleeve of my shirt became entangled in the loop which sustained the basket, and thus, in a moment, loosened it from the button. Had the whole actually vanished into air, it could not have shot from my sight in a more abrupt and instantaneous manner. Positively, there could not have intervened the tenth part of a second between the disengagement of the basket and its absolute disappearance with all that it contained. My good wishes followed it to the earth, but, of course, I had no hope that either cat or kittens would ever live to tell the tale of their misfortune.

At six o'clock, I perceived a great portion of the earth's visible area to the eastward involved in thick shadow, which continued to advance with great rapidity, until, at five minutes before seven, the whole surface in view was enveloped in the darkness of night. It was not, however, until long after this time that the rays of the setting sun ceased to illumine the balloon; and this circumstance, although of course fully anticipated, did not fail to give me an infinite deal of pleasure. It was evident that, in the morning, I should behold the rising luminary many hours at least before the citizens of Rotterdam, in spite of their situation so much farther to the eastward, and thus, day after day, in proportion to the height ascended, would I enjoy the light of the sun for a longer and a longer period. I now determined to keep a journal of my passage, reckoning the days from one to twenty-four hours continuously, without taking into consideration the intervals of darkness.

At ten o'clock, feeling sleepy, I determined to lie down for the rest of the night; but here a difficulty presented itself, which, obvious as it may appear, had escaped my attention up to the very moment of which I am now speaking. If I went to sleep as I proposed, how could the atmosphere in the chamber be regenerated in the *interim*? To breathe it for more than an hour, at the farthest, would be a matter of impossibility; or, if even this term could be extended to an hour and a quarter, the most ruinous consequences might ensue. The consideration of this dilemma gave me no little disquietude; and it will hardly be believed, that, after the dangers I had undergone, I should look upon this business in so serious a light, as to give up all hope of accomplishing my ultimate design, and finally make up my mind to the necessity of a descent. But this hesitation was only momentary. I reflected that man is the veriest slave of custom, and that many points in the routine of his existence are deemed *essentially* important, which are only so *at all* by his having rendered them habitual. It was very certain that I could not do without sleep; but I might easily bring myself to feel no inconvenience from being awakened at intervals of an hour during the whole period of my repose. It would require but five minutes at most, to regenerate the atmosphere in the fullest manner – and the only real difficulty was, to contrive a method of arousing myself at the proper moment for so doing. But this was a question which, I am willing to confess, occasioned me no little trouble in its solution. To be sure, I had heard of the student who, to prevent his falling asleep over his books, held in one hand a ball of copper, the din of whose descent into a basin of the same metal on the floor beside his chair, served effectually to startle him up, if, at any moment, he should be overcome with drowsiness. My own case, however, was very different indeed, and left me no room for any similar idea; for I did not wish to keep awake, but to be aroused from slumber at regular intervals of time. I at length hit upon the following expedient, which, simple as it may seem, was hailed by me, at the moment of discovery, as an invention fully equal to that of the telescope, the steam-engine, or the art of printing itself.

It is necessary to premise, that the balloon, at the elevation now attained, continued its course upwards with an even and undeviating ascent, and the car consequently followed with a steadiness so perfect that it would have been impossible to detect in it the slightest vacillation. This circumstance favored me greatly in the project I now determined to adopt. My supply of water had been put on board in kegs containing five gallons each, and ranged very securely around the interior of the car. I unfastened one of these, and taking two ropes, tied them tightly across the rim of the wicker-work from one side to the other; placing them about a foot apart and parallel, so as to form a kind of shelf, upon which I placed the keg, and steadied it in a horizontal position. About eight inches immediately below these ropes, and four feet from the bottom of the car, I fastened another shelf – but made of thin plank, being the only similar piece of wood I had. Upon this latter shelf, and exactly beneath one of the rims of the keg, a small earthen pitcher was deposited. I now bored a hole in the end of the keg over the pitcher, and fitted in a plug of soft wood, cut in a tapering or conical shape. This plug I pushed in or pulled out, as might happen, until, after a few experiments, it arrived at that exact degree of tightness, at which the water, oozing from the hole, and falling into the pitcher below, would fill the latter to the brim in the period of sixty minutes. This, of course, was a matter briefly and easily ascertained, by noticing the proportion of the pitcher filled in any given time. Having arranged all this, the rest of the plan is obvious. My bed was so contrived upon the floor of the car, as to bring my head, in lying down, immediately below the mouth of the pitcher. It was evident, that, at the expiration of an hour, the pitcher, getting full, would be forced to run over, and to run over at the mouth, which was somewhat lower than the rim. It was also evident, that the water, thus falling from a height of more than four feet, could not do otherwise than fall upon my face, and that the sure consequence would be, to waken me up instantaneously, even from the soundest slumber in the world.

It was fully eleven by the time I had completed these arrangements, and I immediately betook myself to bed, with full confidence in the efficiency of my invention. Nor in this matter was I disappointed. Punctually every sixty minutes was I aroused by my trusty chronometer, when, having emptied the pitcher into the bung-hole of the keg, and performed the duties of the condenser, I retired again to bed. These regular interruptions to my slumber caused me even less discomfort than I had anticipated; and when I finally arose for the day, it was seven o'clock, and the sun had attained many degrees above the line of my horizon.

April 3d. I found the balloon at an immense height indeed, and the earth's convexity had now become strikingly manifest. Below me in the ocean lay a cluster of black specks, which undoubtedly were islands. Overhead, the sky was of a jetty black, and the stars were brilliantly visible; indeed they had been so constantly since the first day of ascent. Far away to the north-ward I perceived a thin, white, and exceedingly brilliant line, or streak, on the edge of the horizon, and I had no hesitation in supposing it to be the southern disc of the ices of the Polar sea. My curiosity was greatly excited, for I had hopes of passing on much farther to the north, and might possibly, at some period, find myself placed directly above the Pole itself. I now lamented that my great elevation would, in this case, prevent my taking as accurate a survey as I could wish. Much, however, might be ascertained. Nothing else of an extraordinary nature occurred during the day. My apparatus all continued in good order, and the balloon still ascended without any perceptible vacillation. The cold was intense, and obliged me to wrap up closely in an overcoat. When darkness came over the earth, I betook myself to bed, although it was for many hours afterwards broad daylight all around my immediate situation. The water-clock was punctual in its duty, and I slept until next morning soundly, with the exception of the periodical interruption.

April 4th. Arose in good health and spirits, and was astonished at the singular change which had taken place in the appearance of the sea. It had lost, in a great measure, the deep tint of blue it had hitherto worn, being now of a grayish-white, and of a lustre dazzling to the eye. The convexity of the ocean had become so evident, that the entire mass of the distant water seemed to be tumbling headlong over the abyss of the horizon, and I found myself listening on tiptoe for the echoes of the mighty cataract. The islands were no longer visible; whether they had passed down the horizon to the south-east, or whether my increasing elevation had left them out of sight, it is impossible to say. I was inclined, however, to the latter opinion. The rim of ice to the northward was growing more and more apparent. Cold by no means so intense. Nothing of importance occurred, and I passed the day in reading, having taken care to supply myself with books.

April 5th. Beheld the singular phenomenon of the sun rising while nearly the whole visible surface of the earth continued to be involved in darkness. In time, however, the light spread itself over all, and I again saw the line of ice to the northward. It was now very distinct, and appeared of a much darker hue than the waters of the ocean. I was evidently approaching it, and with great rapidity. Fancied I could again distinguish a strip of land to the eastward, and one also to the westward, but could not be certain. Weather moderate. Nothing of any consequence happened during the day. Went early to bed.

April 6th. Was surprised at finding the rim of ice at a very moderate distance, and an immense field of the same material stretching away off to the horizon in the north. It was evident that if the balloon held its present course, it would soon arrive above the Frozen Ocean, and I had now little doubt of ultimately seeing the Pole. During the whole of the day I continued to near the ice. Towards night the limits of my horizon very suddenly and materially increased, owing undoubtedly to the earth's form being that of an oblate spheroid, and my arriving above the flattened regions in the vicinity of the Arctic circle. When darkness at length overtook me, I went to bed in great anxiety, fearing to pass over the object of so much curiosity when I should have no opportunity of observing it.

April 7th. Arose early, and to my great joy, at length beheld what there could be no hesitation in supposing the northern Pole itself. It was there, beyond a doubt, and immediately beneath my feet; but, alas! I had now ascended to so vast a distance, that nothing could with accuracy be discerned. Indeed, to judge from the progression of the numbers indicating my various altitudes, respectively, at different periods, between six, A.M., on the second of April, and twenty minutes before nine, A.M., of the same day, (at which time the barometer ran down,) it might be fairly inferred that the balloon had now, at four o'clock in the morning of April the seventh, reached a height of *not less*, certainly, than 7254 miles above the surface of the sea. This elevation may appear immense, but the estimate upon which it is calculated gave a result in all probability far inferior to the truth. At all events I undoubtedly beheld the whole of the earth's major diameter;[28] the entire northern hemisphere lay beneath me like a chart orthographically projected; and the great circle of the equator itself formed the boundary line of my horizon. Your Excellencies may, however, readily imagine that the confined regions hitherto unexplored within the limits of the Arctic circle, although situated directly beneath me, and therefore seen without any appearance of being foreshortened, were still, in themselves, comparatively too diminutive, and at too great a distance from the point of sight, to admit of any very accurate examination. Nevertheless, what could be seen was of a nature singular and exciting. Northwardly from that huge rim before mentioned, and which, with slight qualification, may be called the limit of human discovery in these regions, one unbroken, or nearly unbroken sheet of ice continues to extend. In the first few degrees of this its progress, its surface is very sensibly flattened, farther on depressed into a plane, and finally, becoming *not a little concave*, it terminates, at the Pole itself, in a circular centre, sharply defined, whose apparent diameter subtended at the balloon an angle of about sixty-five seconds, and whose dusky hue, varying in intensity, was at all times darker than any other spot upon the visible hemisphere,[29] and occasionally deepened into the most absolute blackness. Farther than this, little could be ascertained. By twelve o'clock the circular centre had materially decreased in circumference, and by seven, P.M., I lost sight of it entirely; the balloon passing over the western limb of the ice, and floating away rapidly in the direction of the equator.

April 8th. Found a sensible diminution in the earth's apparent diameter, besides a material alteration in its general color and appearance. The whole visible area partook in different degrees of a tint of pale yellow, and in some portions had acquired a brilliancy even painful to the eye. My view downwards was also considerably impeded by the dense atmosphere in the vicinity of the surface being loaded with clouds, between whose masses I could only now and then obtain a glimpse of the earth itself. This difficulty of direct vision had troubled me more or less for the last forty-eight hours; but my present enormous elevation brought closer together, as it were, the floating bodies of vapor, and the inconvenience became, of course, more and more palpable in proportion to my ascent. Nevertheless, I could easily perceive that the balloon now hovered above the range of great lakes in the continent of North America, and was holding a course, due south, which would soon bring me to the tropics.

This circumstance did not fail to give me the most heartfelt satisfaction, and I hailed it as a happy omen of ultimate success. Indeed, the direction I had hitherto taken, had filled me with uneasiness; for it was evident that, had I continued it much longer, there would have been no possibility of my arriving at the moon at all, whose orbit is inclined to the ecliptic at only the small angle of 5° 8′ 48″. Strange as it may seem, it was only at this late period that I began to understand the great error I had committed, in not taking my departure from earth at some point *in the plane of the lunar ellipse*.

April 9th. To-day, the earth's diameter was greatly diminished, and the color of the surface assumed hourly a deeper tint of yellow. The balloon kept steadily on her course to the southward, and arrived, at nine, P.M., over the northern edge of the Mexican Gulf.

April 10th. I was suddenly aroused from slumber, about five o'clock this morning, by a loud, crackling, and terrific sound, for which I could in no manner account. It was of very brief duration, but, while it lasted, resembled nothing in the world of which I had any previous experience. It is needless to say that I became excessively alarmed, having, in the first instance, attributed the noise to the bursting of the balloon. I examined all my apparatus, however, with great attention, and could discover nothing out of order. Spent a great part of the day in meditating upon an occurrence so extraordinary, but could find no means whatever of accounting for it. Went to bed dissatisfied, and in a state of great anxiety and agitation.

April 11th. Found a startling diminution in the apparent diameter of the earth, and a considerable increase, now observable for the first time, in that of the moon itself, which wanted only a few days of being full. It now required long and excessive labor to condense within the chamber sufficient atmospheric air for the sustenance of life.

April 12th. A singular alteration took place in regard to the direction of the balloon, and although fully anticipated, afforded me the most unequivocal delight. Having reached, in its former course, about the twentieth parallel of southern latitude, it turned off suddenly, at an acute angle, to the eastward, and thus proceeded throughout the day, keeping nearly, if not altogether, *in the exact plane of the lunar ellipse*. What was worthy of remark, a very perceptible vacillation in the car was a consequence of this change of route, – a vacillation which prevailed, in a more or less degree, for a period of many hours.

April 13th. Was again very much alarmed by a repetition of the loud crackling noise which terrified me on the tenth. Thought long upon the subject, but was unable to form any satisfactory conclusion. Great decrease in the earth's apparent diameter, which now subtended from the balloon an angle of very little more than twenty-five degrees. The moon could not be seen at all, being nearly in my zenith. I still continued in the plane of the ellipse, but made little progress to the eastward.

April 14th. Extremely rapid decrease in the diameter of the earth. To-day I became strongly impressed with the idea, that the balloon was now actually running up the line of apsides to the point of perigee, – in other words, holding the direct course which would bring it immediately to the moon in that part of its orbit nearest to the earth. The moon itself was directly overhead, and consequently hidden from my view. Great and long continued labor necessary for the condensation of the atmosphere.

April 15th. Not even the outlines of continents and seas could now be traced upon the earth with distinctness. About twelve o'clock I became aware, for the third time, of that appalling sound which had so astonished me before. It now, however, continued for some moments, and gathered intensity as it continued. At length, while, stupefied and terror-stricken, I stood in expectation of I knew not what hideous destruction, the car vibrated with excessive violence, and a gigantic and flaming mass of some material which I could not distinguish, came with a voice of a thousand thunders, roaring and booming by the balloon. When my fears and astonishment had in some degree subsided, I had little difficulty in supposing it to be some mighty volcanic fragment ejected from that world to which I was so rapidly approaching, and, in all probability, one of that singular class of substances occasionally picked up on the earth, and termed meteoric stones for want of a better appellation.

April 16th. To-day, looking upwards as well as I could,

through each of the side windows alternately, I beheld, to my great delight, a very small portion of the moon's disc protruding, as it were, on all sides beyond the huge circumference of the balloon. My agitation was extreme; for I had now little doubt of soon reaching the end of my perilous voyage. Indeed, the labor now required by the condenser, had increased to a most oppressive degree, and allowed me scarcely any respite from exertion. Sleep was a matter nearly out of the question. I became quite ill, and my frame trembled with exhaustion. It was impossible that human nature could endure this state of intense suffering much longer. During the now brief interval of darkness a meteoric stone again passed in my vicinity, and the frequency of these phenomena began to occasion me much apprehension.

April 17th. This morning proved an epoch in my voyage. It will be remembered, that, on the thirteenth, the earth subtended an angular breadth of twenty-five degrees. On the fourteenth, this had greatly diminished; on the fifteenth, a still more rapid decrease was observable; and, in retiring for the night of the sixteenth, I had noticed an angle of no more than about seven degrees and fifteen minutes. What, therefore, must have been my amazement, on awakening from a brief and disturbed slumber, on the morning of this day, the seventeenth, at finding the surface beneath me so suddenly and wonderfully *augmented* in volume, as to subtend no less than thirty-nine degrees in apparent angular diameter! I was thunderstruck! No words can give any adequate idea of the extreme, the absolute horror and astonishment, with which I was seized, possessed, and altogether overwhelmed. My knees tottered beneath me – my teeth chattered – my hair started up on end. 'The balloon, then, had actually burst!' These were the first tumultuous ideas which hurried through my mind : 'The balloon had positively burst! – I was falling – falling with the most impetuous, the most unparalleled velocity! To judge from the immense distance already so quickly passed over, it could not be more than ten minutes, at the farthest, before I should meet the surface of the earth, and be hurled into annihilation!' But at length reflection came to my relief. I paused; I considered; and I began to doubt. The matter was impossible. I could not in any reason have so rapidly come down.

Besides, although I was evidently approaching the surface below me, it was with a speed by no means commensurate with the velocity I had at first conceived. This consideration served to calm the perturbation of my mind, and I finally succeeded in regarding the phenomenon in its proper point of view. In fact, amazement must have fairly deprived me of my senses, when I could not see the vast difference, in appearance, between the surface below me, and the surface of my mother earth. The latter was indeed over my head, and completely hidden by the balloon, while the moon – the moon itself in all its glory – lay beneath me, and at my feet.

The stupor and surprise produced in my mind by this extraordinary change in the posture of affairs, was perhaps, after all, that part of the adventure least susceptible of explanation. For the *bouleversement* in itself was not only natural and inevitable, but had been long actually anticipated, as a circumstance to be expected whenever I should arrive at that exact point of my voyage where the attraction of the planet should be superseded by the attraction of the satellite – or, more precisely, where the gravitation of the balloon towards the earth should be less powerful than its gravitation towards the moon. To be sure I arose from a sound slumber, with all my senses in confusion, to the contemplation of a very startling phenomenon, and one which, although expected, was not expected at the moment. The revolution itself must, of course, have taken place in an easy and gradual manner, and it is by no means clear that, had I even been awake at the time of the occurrence, I should have been made aware of it by any *internal* evidence of an inversion – that is to say, by any inconvenience or disarrangement, either about my person or about my apparatus.

It is almost needless to say, that, upon coming to a due sense of my situation, and emerging from the terror which had absorbed every faculty of my soul, my attention was, in the first place, wholly directed to the contemplation of the general physical appearance of the moon. It lay beneath me like a chart – and although I judged it to be still at no inconsiderable distance, the indentures of its surface were defined to my vision with a most striking and altogether unaccountable distinctness. The entire absence of ocean or sea, and indeed of any lake or river, or body of water whatsoever, struck me, at the first glance, as the most extraordinary feature in its geological condition. Yet, strange to say, I beheld vast level regions of a character decidedly alluvial, although by far the greater portion of the hemisphere in sight was covered with innumerable volcanic mountains, conical in shape,[30] and having more the appearance of artificial than of natural protuberances. The highest among them does not exceed three and three-quarter miles in perpendicular elevation; but a map of the volcanic districts of the Campi Phlegraei [31] would afford to your Excellencies a better idea of their general surface than any unworthy description I might think proper to attempt. The greater part of them were in a state of evident eruption, and gave me fearfully to understand their fury and their power, by the repeated thunders of the mis-called meteoric stones, which now rushed upwards by the balloon with a frequency more and more appalling.

April 18th. To-day I found an enormous increase in the moon's apparent bulk – and the evidently accelerated velocity of my descent, began to fill me with alarm. It will be remembered, that, in the earliest stage of my speculations upon the possibility of a passage to the moon, the existence, in its vicinity, of an atmosphere dense in proportion to the bulk of the planet, had entered largely into my calculations; this too in spite of many theories to the contrary, and, it may be added, in spite of a general disbelief in the existence of any lunar atmosphere at all. But, in addition to what I have already urged in regard to Encke's comet and the zodiacal light, I had been strengthened in my opinion by certain observations of Mr Schroeter, of Lilienthal.[32] He observed the moon, when two days and a half old, in the evening soon after sunset, before the dark part was visible, and continued to watch it until it became visible. The two cusps appeared tapering in a very sharp faint prolongation, each exhibiting its farthest extremity faintly illuminated by the solar rays, before any part of the dark hemisphere was visible. Soon afterwards, the whole dark limb became illuminated. This prolongation of the cusps beyond the semicircle, I thought, must have arisen from the refraction of the sun's rays by the moon's atmosphere. I computed, also, the height of the atmosphere (which could refract light enough into its dark hemisphere, to produce a twilight more luminous than the light reflected from the earth when the moon is about 32° from the new,) to be 1356 Paris feet; in this view, I supposed the greatest height capable of refracting the solar ray, to be 5376 feet. My ideas upon this topic had also received confirmation by a passage in the eighty-second volume of the Philosophical Transactions, in which it is stated, that, at an occultation of Jupiter's satellites, the third disappeared after having been about 1″ or 2″ of time indistinct, and the fourth became indiscernible near the limb.*

Upon the resistance, or more properly, upon the support of an atmosphere, existing in the state of density imagined, I had, of course, entirely depended for the safety of my ultimate descent. Should I then, after all, prove to have been mistaken, I had in consequence nothing better to expect, as a *finale* to my adventure, than being dashed into atoms against the rugged surface of the satellite. And, indeed, I had now every reason to be terrified. My distance from the moon was comparatively trifling, while the labor required by the condenser was diminished not at all, and I could discover no indication whatever of a decreasing rarity in the air.

April 19th. This morning, to my great joy, about nine o'clock, the surface of the moon being frightfully near, and my apprehensions excited to the utmost, the pump of my condenser at length gave evident tokens of an alteration in the atmosphere.

*Hevelius writes that he has several times found, in skies perfectly clear, when even stars of the sixth and seventh magnitude were conspicuous, that, at the same altitude of the moon, at the same elongation from the earth, and with one and the same excellent telescope, the moon and its maculæ did not appear equally lucid at all times. From the circumstances of the observation, it is evident that the cause of this phenomenon is not either in our air, in the tube, in the moon, or in the eye of the spectator, but must be looked for in something (an atmosphere?) existing about the moon.

Cassini frequently observed Saturn, Jupiter, and the fixed stars, when approaching the moon to occultation, to have their circular figure changed into an oval one; and, in other occultations, he found no alteration of figure at all. Hence it might be supposed, that *at some times*, and not at others, there is a dense matter encompassing the moon wherein the rays of the stars are refracted.

By ten, I had reason to believe its density considerably increased. By eleven, very little labor was necessary at the apparatus; and at twelve o'clock, with some hesitation, I ventured to unscrew the *tourniquet*, when, finding no inconvenience from having done so, I finally threw open the gum-elastic chamber, and unrigged it from around the car. As might have been expected, spasms and violent headache were the immediate consequences of an experiment so precipitate and full of danger. But these and other difficulties attending respiration, as they were by no means so great as to put me in peril of my life, I determined to endure as I best could, in consideration of my leaving them behind me momently in my approach to the denser *strata* near the moon. This approach, however, was still impetuous in the extreme; and it soon became alarmingly certain that, although I had probably not been deceived in the expectation of an atmosphere dense in proportion to the mass of the satellite, still I had been wrong in supposing this density, even at the surface, at all adequate to the support of the great weight contained in the car of my balloon. Yet this *should* have been the case, and in an equal degree as at the surface of the earth, the actual gravity of bodies at either planet supposed in the ratio of the atmospheric condensation. That it *was not* the case, however, my precipitous downfall gave testimony enough; *why* it was not so, can only be explained by a reference to those possible geological disturbances to which I have formerly alluded. At all events I was now close upon the planet, and coming down with the most terrible impetuosity. I lost not a moment, accordingly, in throwing overboard first my ballast, then my water-kegs, then my condensing apparatus and gum-elastic chamber, and finally every article within the car. But it was all to no purpose. I still fell with horrible rapidity, and was now not more than half a mile from the surface. As a last resource, therefore, having got rid of my coat, hat, and boots, I cut loose from the balloon *the car itself*, which was of no inconsiderable weight, and thus, clinging with both hands to the net-work, I had barely time to observe that the whole country, as far as the eye could reach, was thickly interspersed with diminutive habitations, ere I tumbled headlong into the very heart of a fantastical-looking city, and into the middle of a vast crowd of ugly little people,[33] who none of them uttered a single syllable, or gave themselves the least trouble to render me assistance, but stood, like a parcel of idiots, grinning in a ludicrous manner, and eyeing me and my balloon askant, with their arms set a-kimbo. I turned from them in contempt, and, gazing upwards at the earth so lately left, and left perhaps for ever, beheld it like a huge, dull, copper shield, about two degrees in diameter, fixed immovably in the heavens [34] overhead, and tipped on one of its edges with a crescent border of the most brilliant gold. No traces of land or water could be discovered, and the whole was clouded with variable spots, and belted with tropical and equatorial zones.

Thus, may it please your Excellencies, after a series of great anxieties, unheard-of dangers, and unparalleled escapes, I had, at length, on the nineteenth day of my departure from Rotterdam, arrived in safety at the conclusion of a voyage undoubtedly the most extraordinary, and the most momentous, ever accomplished, undertaken, or conceived by any denizen of earth. But my adventures yet remained to be related. And indeed your Excellencies may well imagine that, after a residence of five years upon a planet not only deeply interesting in its own peculiar character, but rendered doubly so by its intimate connection, in capacity of satellite, with the world inhabited by man, I may have intelligence for the private ear of the States' College of Astronomers of far more importance than the details, however wonderful, of the mere *voyage* which so happily concluded. This is, in fact, the case. I have much – very much which it would give me the greatest pleasure to communicate. I have much to say of the climate of the planet;[35] of its wonderful alternations of heat and cold; of unmitigated and burning sunshine for one fortnight, and more than polar frigidity for the next; of a constant transfer of moisture, by distillation like that *in vacuo*, from the point beneath the sun to the point the farthest from it; of a variable zone of running water; of the people themselves; of their manners, customs, and political institutions; of their peculiar physical construction; of their ugliness; of their want of ears, those useless appendages in an atmosphere so peculiarly modified; of their consequent ignorance of the use and properties of speech; of their substitute for speech in a singular method of inter-communication; of the incomprehensible connection between each particular individual [36] in the moon, with some particular individual on the earth – a connection analogous with, and depending upon that of the orbs of the planet and the satellite, and by means of which the lives and destinies of the inhabitants of the one are interwoven with the lives and destinies of the inhabitants of the other; and above all, if it so please your Excellencies – above all of those dark and hideous mysteries which lie in the outer regions of the moon, – regions which, owing to the almost miraculous accordance of the satellite's rotation on its own axis with its sidereal revolution about the earth, have never yet been turned, and, by God's mercy, never shall be turned, to the scrutiny of the telescopes of man. All this, and more – much more – would I most willingly detail. But, to be brief, I must have my reward. I am pining for a return to my family and to my home : and as the price of any farther communications on my part – in consideration of the light which I have it in my power to throw upon many very important branches of physical and metaphysical science – I must solicit, through the influence of your honorable body, a pardon for the crime of which I have been guilty in the death of the creditors upon my departure from Rotterdam. This, then, is the object of the present paper. Its bearer, an inhabitant of the moon, whom I have prevailed upon, and properly instructed, to be my messenger to the earth, will await your Excellencies' pleasure, and return to me with the pardon in question, if it can, in any manner, be obtained.

I have the honor to be, &c., your Excellencies' very humble servant,

HANS PFAALL

Upon finishing the perusal of this very extraordinary document, Professor Rubadub, it is said, dropped his pipe upon the ground in the extremity of his surprise, and Mynheer Superbus Von Underduk having taken off his spectacles, wiped them, and deposited them in his pocket, so far forgot both himself and his dignity, as to turn round three times upon his heel in the quintessence of astonishment and admiration. There was no doubt about the matter – the pardon should be obtained. So at least swore, with a round oath, Professor Rubadub, and so finally thought the illustrious Von Underduk, as he took the arm of his brother in science, and without saying a word, began to make the best of his way home to deliberate upon the measures to be adopted. Having reached the door, however, of the burgomaster's dwelling, the professor ventured to suggest that as the messenger had thought proper to disappear – no doubt frightened to death by the savage appearance of the burghers of Rotterdam – the pardon would be of little use, as no one but a man of the moon would undertake a voyage to so vast a distance. To the truth of this observation the burgomaster assented, and the matter was therefore at an end. Not so, however, rumors and speculations. The letter, having been published, gave rise to a variety of gossip and opinion. Some of the over-wise even made themselves ridiculous by decrying the whole business as nothing better than a hoax. But hoax, with these sort of people, is, I believe, a general term for all matters above their comprehension. For my part, I cannot conceive upon what data they have founded such an accusation. Let us see what they say:

Imprimis. That certain wags in Rotterdam have certain especial antipathies to certain burgomasters and astronomers.

Secondly. That an odd little dwarf and bottle conjurer, both of whose ears, for some misdemeanor, have been cut off close to his head, has been missing for several days from the neighboring city of Bruges.

Thirdly. That the newspapers which were stuck all over the little balloon, were newspapers of Holland, and therefore could not have been made in the moon. They were dirty papers – very dirty – and Gluck, the printer, would take his bible oath to their having been printed in Rotterdam.

Fourthly. That Hans Pfaall himself, the drunken villain, and the three very idle gentlemen styled his creditors, were all seen, no longer than two or three days ago, in a tippling house in the suburbs, having just returned, with money in their pockets, from a trip beyond the sea.

Lastly. That it is an opinion very generally received, or which ought to be generally received, that the College of Astronomers in the city of Rotterdam, as well as all other colleges in all other parts of the world, – not to mention colleges and astronomers in general, – are, to say the least of the matter, not a whit better, nor greater, nor wiser than they ought to be.

*

NOTE.[37] – Strictly speaking, there is but little similarity between the above sketchy trifle, and the celebrated 'Moon-Story' of Mr Locke;[38] but as both have the character of *hoaxes*, (although the one is in a tone of banter, the other of downright earnest,) and as both hoaxes are on the same subject, the moon – moreover, as both attempt to give plausibility by scientific detail – the author of 'Hans Pfaall' thinks it necessary to say, *in self-defence*, that his own *jeu d'esprit* was published, in the 'Southern Literary Messenger', about three weeks before the commencement of Mr L.'s in the 'New York Sun'. Fancying a likeness which, perhaps, does not exist, some of the New York papers copied 'Hans Pfaall', and collated it with the 'Moon-Hoax', by way of detecting the writer of the one in the writer of the other.

As many more persons were actually gulled by the 'Moon-Hoax' than would be willing to acknowledge the fact, it may here afford some little amusement to show why no one should have been deceived – to point out those particulars of the story which should have been sufficient to establish its real character. Indeed, however rich the imagination displayed in this ingenious fiction, it wanted much of the force which might have been given it by a more scrupulous attention to facts and to general analogy. That the public were misled, even for an instant, merely proves the gross ignorance which is so generally prevalent upon subjects of an astronomical nature.

The moon's distance from the earth is, in round numbers, 240,000 miles. If we desire to ascertain how near, apparently, a lens would bring the satellite, (or any distant object,) we, of course, have but to divide the distance by the magnifying, or more strictly, by the space-penetrating power of the glass. Mr L. makes his lens have a power of 42,000 times. By this divide 240,000 (the moon's real distance,) and we have five miles and five-sevenths, as the apparent distance. No animal at all could be seen so far; much less the minute points particularized in the story. Mr L. speaks about Sir John Herschel's perceiving flowers (the Papaver rhœas, &c.,) and even detecting the color and the shape of the eyes of small birds. Shortly before, too, he has himself observed that the lens would not render perceptible objects of less than eighteen inches in diameter; but even this, as I have said, is giving the glass by far too great power. It may be observed, in passing, that this prodigious glass is said to have been moulded at the glass-house of Messrs Hartley and Grant, in Dumbarton; but Messrs H. and G.'s establishment had ceased operations for many years previous to the publication of the hoax.

On page 13, pamphlet edition, speaking of 'a hairy veil' over the eyes of a species of bison, the author says – 'It immediately occurred to the acute mind of Dr Herschel that this was a providential contrivance to protect the eyes of the animal from the great extremes of light and darkness to which all the inhabitants of our side of the moon are periodically subjected.' But this cannot be thought a very 'acute' observation of the Doctor's. The inhabitants of our side of the moon have, evidently, no darkness at all; so there can be nothing of the 'extremes' mentioned. In the absence of the sun they have a light from the earth equal to that of thirteen full unclouded moons.

The topography, throughout, even when professing to accord with Blunt's Lunar Chart, is entirely at variance with that or any other lunar chart, and even grossly at variance with itself. The points of the compass, too, are in inextricable confusion; the writer appearing to be ignorant that, on a lunar map, these are not in accordance with terrestrial points; the east being to the left, &c.

Deceived, perhaps, by the vague titles, *Mare Nubium, Mare Tranquillitatis, Mare Fœcunditatis*, &c., given to the dark spots by former astronomers, Mr L. has entered into details regarding oceans and other large bodies of water in the moon; whereas there is no astronomical point more positively ascertained than that no such bodies exist there. In examining the boundary between light and darkness (in the crescent or gibbous moon) where this boundary crosses any of the dark places, the line of division is found to be rough and jagged; but, were these dark places liquid, it would evidently be even.

The description of the wings of the man-bat, on page 21, is but a literal copy of Peter Wilkins' account of the wings of his flying islanders.[39] This simple fact should have induced suspicion, at least, it might be thought.

On page 23, we have the following : 'What a prodigious influence must our thirteen times larger globe have exercised upon this satellite when an embryo in the womb of time, the passive subject of chemical affinity!' This is very fine; but it should be observed that no astronomer would have made such remark, especially to any Journal of Science; for the earth, in the sense intended, is not only thirteen, but forty-nine times *larger* than the moon. A similar objection applies to the whole of the concluding pages, where, by way of introduction to some discoveries in Saturn, the philosophical correspondent enters into a minute schoolboy account of that planet: – this to the Edinburgh Journal of Science!

But there is one point, in particular, which should have betrayed the fiction. Let us imagine the power actually possessed of seeing animals upon the moon's surface; – what would *first* arrest the attention of an observer from the earth? Certainly neither their shape, size, nor any other such peculiarity, so soon as their remarkable *situation*. They would appear to be walking, with heels up and head down, in the manner of flies on a ceiling. The *real* observer would have uttered an instant ejaculation of surprise (however prepared by previous knowledge) at the singularity of their position; the *fictitious* observer has not even mentioned the subject, but speaks of seeing the entire bodies of such creatures, when it is demonstrable that he could have seen only the diameter of their heads!

It might as well be remarked, in conclusion, that the size, and particularly the powers of the man-bats (for example, their ability to fly in so rare an atmosphere – if, indeed, the moon have any) – with most of the other fancies in regard to animal and vegetable existence, are at variance, generally, with all analogical reasoning on these themes; and that analogy here will often amount to conclusive demonstration. It is, perhaps, scarcely necessary to add, that all the suggestions attributed to Brewster and Herschel, in the beginning of the article, about 'a transfusion of artificial light through the focal object of vision', &c., &c., belong to that species of figurative writing which comes, most properly, under the denomination of rigmarole.

There is a real and very definite limit to optical discovery among the stars – a limit whose nature need only be stated to be understood. If, indeed, the casting of large lenses were all that is required, man's ingenuity would ultimately prove equal to the task, and we might have them of any size demanded. But, unhappily, in proportion to the increase of size in the lens, and, consequently, of space-penetrating power, is the diminution of light from the object, by diffusion of its rays. And for this evil there is no remedy within human ability; for an object is seen by means of that light alone which proceeds from itself, whether direct or reflected. Thus the only *'artificial'* light which could avail Mr Locke, would be some artificial light which he should be able to throw – not upon the 'focal object of vision', but upon the real object to be viewed – to wit : *upon the moon*. It has been easily calculated that, when the light proceeding from a star becomes so diffused as to be as weak as the natural light proceeding from the whole of the stars, in a clear and moonless night, then the star is no longer visible for any practical purpose.

The Earl of Ross telescope, lately constructed in England,[40] has a *speculum* with a reflecting surface of 4071 square inches; the Herschel telescope having one of only 1811. The metal of the Earl of Ross' is 6 feet diameter; it is $5\frac{1}{2}$ inches thick at the edges, and 5 at the centre. The weight is 3 tons. The focal length is 50 feet.

I have lately read a singular and somewhat ingenious little book, whose title page runs thus : – 'L'Homme dans la lvne, ou le Voyage Chimerique fait au Monde de la Lvne, nouuellement decouuert par Dominique Gonzales, Aduanturier Espagnol, autremèt dit le Courier volant. Mis en notre langve par J. B. D. A. Paris, chez Francois Piot, pres la Fontaine de Saint Benoist. Et chez J. Goignard, au premier pilier de la grand' salle du Palais, proche les Consultations, MDCXLVIII.' pp. 176.

The writer professes to have translated his work from the English of one Mr D'Avisson [41] (Davidson?) although there is a terrible ambiguity in the statement. 'I'en ai eu,' says he, 'l'original de Monsieur D'Avisson, medecin des mieux versez qui soient aujourd'huy dans la cònoissance des Belles Lettres, et sur tout de la Philosophie Naturelle. Je lui ai cette obligation entre les autres, de m'auoir non seulement mis en main ce Livre en anglois, mais encore le Manuscrit du Sieur Thomas D'Anan, gentilhomme Eccossois, recommendable pour sa vertu, sur la version duquel j'advoue que j'ay tiré le plan de la mienne.'

After some irrelevant adventures, much in the manner of Gil Blas, and which occupy the first thirty pages, the author relates that, being ill during a sea voyage, the crew abandoned him, together with a negro servant, on the island of St Helena. To increase the chances of obtaining food, the two separate, and live as far apart as possible. This brings about a training of birds, to serve the purpose of carrier-pigeons between them. By and by these are taught to carry parcels of some weight – and this weight is gradually increased. At length the idea is entertained of uniting the force of a great number of birds, with a view to raising the author himself. A machine is contrived for the purpose, and we have a minute description of it, which is materially helped out by a steel engraving. Here we perceive the Signor Gonzales, with point ruffles and a huge periwig, seated astride something which resembles very closely a broomstick, and borne aloft by a multitude of wild swans (*ganzas*) who had strings reaching from their tails to the machine.

The main event detailed in the Signor's narrative depends upon a very important fact, of which the reader is kept in ignorance until near the end of the book. The *ganzas*, with whom he had become so familiar, were not really denizens of St Helena, but of the moon. Thence it had been their custom, time out of mind, to migrate annually to some portion of the earth. In proper season, of course they would return home; and the author, happening, one day, to require their services for a short voyage, is unexpectedly carried straight up, and in a very brief period arrives at the satellite. Here he finds, among other odd things, that the people enjoy extreme happiness; that they have no *law*; that they die without pain; that they are from ten to thirty feet in height; that they live five thousand years; that they have an emperor called Irdonozur; and that they can jump sixty feet high, when, being out of the gravitating influence, they fly about with fans.

I cannot forbear giving a specimen of the general *philosophy* of the volume.

'I must now declare to you,' says the Signor Gonzales, 'the nature of the place in which I found myself. All the clouds were beneath my feet, or, if you please, spread between me and the earth. As to the stars, *since there was no night where I was, they always had the same appearance; not brilliant, as usual, but pale, and very nearly like the moon of a morning.* But few of them were visible, and these ten times larger (as well as I could judge,) than they seem to the inhabitants of the earth. The moon which wanted two days of being full, was of a terrible bigness.

'I must not forget here, that the stars appeared only on that side of the globe turned towards the moon, and that the closer they were to it the larger they seemed. I have also to inform you that, whether it was calm weather or stormy, I found myself *always immediately between the moon and the earth.* I was convinced of this for two reasons – because my birds always flew in a straight line; and because whenever we attempted to rest, *we were carried insensibly around the globe of the earth.* For I admit the opinion of Copernicus, who maintains that it never ceases to revolve *from the east to the west*, not upon the poles of the Equinoctial, commonly called the poles of the world, but upon those of the Zodiac, a question of which I propose to speak more at length hereafter, when I shall have leisure to refresh my memory in regard to the astrology which I learned at Salamanca when young, and have since forgotten.'

Notwithstanding the blunders italicised, the book is not without some claim to attention, as affording a naïve specimen of the current astronomical notions of the time. One of these assumed, that the 'gravitating power' extended but a short distance from the earth's surface, and, accordingly, we find our voyager 'carried insensibly around the globe', &c.

There have been other 'voyages to the moon', but none of higher merit than the one just mentioned. That of Bergerac is utterly meaningless.[42] In the third volume of the 'American Quarterly Review' will be found an elaborate criticism upon a certain 'Journey' of the kind in question; – a criticism in which it is difficult to say whether the critic most exposes the stupidity of the book, or his own absurd ignorance of astronomy. I forget the title of the work;[43] but the *means* of the voyage are more deplorably ill conceived than are even the *ganzas* of our friend the Signor Gonzales. The adventurer, in digging the earth, happens to discover a peculiar metal for which the moon has a strong attraction, and straightway constructs of it a box, which, when cast loose from its terrestrial fastenings, flies with him, forthwith, to the satellite. The 'Flight of Thomas O'Rouke',[44] is a *jeu d'esprit* not altogether contemptible, and has been translated into German. Thomas, the hero, was, in fact, the gamekeeper of an Irish peer, whose eccentricities gave rise to the tale. The 'flight' is made on an eagle's back, from Hungry Hill, a lofty mountain at the end of Bantry Bay.

In these various *brochures* the aim is always satirical; the theme being a description of Lunarian customs as compared with ours. In none, is there any effort at *plausibility* in the details of the voyage itself. The writers seem, in each instance, to be utterly uninformed in respect to astronomy. In 'Hans Pfaall' the design is original, inasmuch as regards an attempt at *verisimilitude*, in the application of scientific principles (so far as the whimsical nature of the subject would permit,) to the actual passage between the earth and the moon.

The Conversation of Eiros and Charmion[1]

Πῦρ σοι προσοίσω.

EURIPIDES, *Androm.*[2]

I will bring fire to thee.

EIROS

Why do you call me Eiros?[3]

CHARMION

So henceforward will you always be called. You must forget, too, *my* earthly name, and speak to me as Charmion.

EIROS

This is indeed no dream!

CHARMION

Dreams are with us no more; – but of these mysteries anon. I rejoice to see you looking life-like and rational. The film of the shadow has already passed from off your eyes. Be of heart, and fear nothing. Your allotted days of stupor have expired; and, to-morrow, I will myself induct you into the full joys and wonders of your novel existence.

EIROS

True – I feel no stupor – none at all. The wild sickness and the terrible darkness have left me, and I hear no longer that mad, rushing, horrible sound, like the 'voice of many waters'.[4] Yet my senses are bewildered, Charmion, with the keenness of their perception of *the new*.

CHARMION

A few days will remove all this; – but I fully understand you, and feel for you. It is now ten earthly years since I underwent what you undergo – yet the remembrance of it hangs by me still. You have now suffered all of pain, however, which you will suffer in Aidenn.[5]

EIROS

In Aidenn?

CHARMION

In Aidenn.

EIROS

Oh God! – pity me, Charmion! – I am overburthened with the majesty of all things – of the unknown now known – of the speculative Future merged in the august and certain Present.

CHARMION

Grapple not now with such thoughts. To-morrow we will speak of this. Your mind wavers, and its agitation will find relief in the exercise of simple memories. Look not around, nor forward – but back. I am burning with anxiety to hear the details of that stupendous event which threw you among us. Tell me of it. Let us converse of familiar things, in the old familiar language of the world which has so fearfully perished.

EIROS

Most fearfully, fearfully! – this is indeed no dream.

CHARMION

Dreams are no more. Was I much mourned, my Eiros?

EIROS

Mourned, Charmion? – oh deeply. To that last hour of all, there hung a cloud of intense gloom and devout sorrow over your household.

CHARMION

And that last hour – speak of it. Remember that, beyond the naked fact from the catastrophe itself, I know nothing. When, coming out from among mankind, I passed into Night through the Grave – at that period, if I remember aright, the calamity which overwhelmed you was utterly unanticipated. But, indeed, I knew little of the speculative philosophy of the day.

EIROS

The individual calamity was, as you say, entirely unanticipated; but analogous misfortunes had been long a subject of discussion with astronomers. I need scarce tell you, my friend, that, even when you left us, men had agreed to understand those passages in the most holy writings which speak of the final destruction of all things by fire, as having reference to the orb of the earth alone. But in regard to the immediate agency of the ruin, speculation had been at fault from that epoch in astronomical knowledge in which the comets were divested of the terrors of flame. The very moderate density of these bodies had been well established. They had been observed to pass among the satellites of Jupiter, without bringing about any sensible alteration either in the masses or in the orbits of these secondary planets. We had long regarded the wanderers as vapory creations of inconceivable tenuity, and as altogether incapable of doing injury to our substantial globe, even in the event of contact. But contact was not in any degree dreaded; for the elements of all the comets were accurately known. That among *them* we should look for the agency of the threatened fiery destruction had been for many years considered an inadmissible idea. But wonders and wild fancies had been, of late days, strangely rife among mankind;[6] and, although it was only with a few of the ignorant that actual apprehension prevailed, upon the announcement by astronomers of a *new* comet,[7] yet this announcement was generally received with I know not what of agitation and mistrust.

The elements of the strange orb were immediately calculated, and it was at once conceded by all observers, that its path, at perihelion, would bring it into very close proximity with the earth. There were two or three astronomers, of secondary note, who resolutely maintained that a contact was inevitable. I cannot very well express to you the effect of this intelligence upon the people. For a few short days they would not believe an assertion which their intellect, so long employed among worldly considerations, could not in any manner grasp. But the truth of a vitally important fact soon makes its way into the understanding of even the most stolid. Finally, all men saw that astronomical knowledge lied not, and they awaited the comet. Its approach was not, at first, seemingly rapid; nor was its appearance of very unusual character. It was of a dull red, and had little perceptible train. For seven or eight days we saw no material increase in its apparent diameter, and but a partial alteration in its color. Meantime, the ordinary affairs of men were discarded, and all interests absorbed in a growing discussion, instituted by the philosophic, in respect to the cometary nature. Even the grossly ignorant aroused their sluggish capacities to such considerations. The learned *now* gave their intellect – their soul – to no such points as the allaying of fear, or to the sustenance of loved theory. They sought – they panted for right views. They groaned for perfected knowledge. *Truth* arose in the purity of her strength and exceeding majesty, and the wise bowed down and adored.

That material injury to our globe or to its inhabitants would result from the apprehended contact, was an opinion which hourly lost ground among the wise; and the wise were now freely permitted to rule the reason and the fancy of the crowd. It was demonstrated, that the density of the comet's *nucleus* was far less than that of our rarest gas; and the harmless passage of a similar visitor among the satellites of Jupiter was a point strongly insisted upon, and which served greatly to allay terror. Theologists, with an earnestness, fear-enkindled, dwelt upon the biblical prophecies, and expounded them to the people with a directness and simplicity of which no previous instance had been known. That the final destruction of the earth must be brought about by the agency of fire, was urged with a spirit that enforced everywhere conviction; and that the comets were of no fiery nature (as all men now knew) was a truth which relieved all, in a great measure, from the apprehension of the great calamity foretold. It is noticeable that the popular prejudices and vulgar errors in regard to pestilence and wars – errors which were wont to prevail upon every appearance of a comet – were now altogether unknown. As if by some sudden convulsive exertion, reason had at once hurled superstition from her throne. The feeblest intellect had derived vigor from excessive interest.

What minor evils might arise from the contact were points of elaborate question. The learned spoke of slight geological disturbances, of probable alterations in climate, and consequently in vegetation; of possible magnetic and electric influences. Many held that no visible or perceptible effect would in any manner be produced. While such discussions were going on, their subject gradually approached, growing larger in apparent diameter, and of a more brilliant lustre. Mankind grew paler as it came. All human operations were suspended.

There was an epoch in the course of the general sentiment when the comet had attained, at length, a size surpassing that of any previously recorded visitation. The people now, dismissing any lingering hope that the astronomers were wrong, experienced all the certainty of evil. The chimerical aspect of their terror was gone. The hearts of the stoutest of our race beat violently within their bosoms. A very few days sufficed, however, to merge even such feelings in sentiments more unendurable. We could no longer apply to the strange orb any *accustomed* thoughts. Its *historical* attributes had disappeared. It oppressed us with a hideous *novelty* of emotion. We saw it not as an astronomical phenomenon in the heavens, but as an incubus upon our hearts, and a shadow upon our brains. It had taken, with inconceivable rapidity, the character of a gigantic mantle of rare flame,[8] extending from horizon to horizon.

Yet a day, and men breathed with greater freedom. It was clear that we were already within the influence of the comet; yet we lived. We even felt an unusual elasticity of frame and vivacity of mind. The exceeding tenuity of the object of our dread was apparent; for all heavenly objects were plainly visible through it. Meantime, our vegetation had perceptibly altered; and we gained faith, from this predicted circumstance, in the foresight of the wise. A wild luxuriance of foliage, utterly unknown before, burst out upon every vegetable thing.

Yet another day – and the evil was not altogether upon us. It was now evident that its nucleus would first reach us. A wild change had come over all men; and the first sense of *pain* was the wild signal for general lamentation and horror. This first sense of pain lay in a rigorous constriction of the breast and lungs, and an insufferable dryness of the skin. It could not be denied that our atmosphere was radically affected; the conformation of this atmosphere and the possible modifications to which it might be subjected, were now the topics of discussion. The result of investigation sent an electric thrill of the intensest terror through the universal heart of man.

It had been long known that the air which encircled us was a compound of oxygen and nitrogen gases, in the proportion of twenty-one measures of oxygen, and seventy-nine of nitrogen,[9] in every one hundred of the atmosphere. Oxygen, which was the principle of combustion, and the vehicle of heat, was absolutely necessary to the support of animal life, and was the most powerful and energetic agent in nature. Nitrogen, on the contrary, was incapable of supporting either animal life or flame. An unnatural excess of oxygen would result, it had been ascertained, in just such an elevation of the animal spirits as we had latterly experienced. It was the pursuit, the extension of the idea, which had engendered awe. What would be the result of a total extraction of the nitrogen? A combustion irresistible, all-devouring, omni-prevalent, immediate; – the entire fulfilment, in all their minute and terrible details, of the fiery and horror-inspiring denunciations of the prophecies of the Holy Book.[10]

Why need I paint, Charmion, the now disenchained frenzy of mankind? That tenuity in the comet which had previously inspired us with hope, was now the source of the bitterness of despair. In its impalpable gaseous character we clearly perceived the consummation of Fate. Meantime a day again passed – bearing away with it the last shadow of Hope. We gasped in the rapid modification of the air. The red blood bounded tumultuously through its strict channels. A furious delirium possessed all men; and, with arms rigidly outstretched towards the threatening heavens, they trembled and shrieked aloud. But the nucleus of the destroyer was now upon us; – even here in Aidenn, I shudder while I speak. Let me be brief – brief as the ruin that overwhelmed. For a moment there was a wild lurid light alone, visiting and penetrating all things. Then let us bow down, Charmion, before the excessive majesty of the great God ! – then, there came a shouting and pervading sound, as if from the mouth itself of HIM; while the whole incumbent mass of ether in which we existed, burst at once into a species of intense flame, for whose surpassing brilliancy and all-fervid heat even the angels in the high Heaven of pure knowledge have no name. Thus ended all.

A Descent into the Maelström

The ways of God in Nature, as in Providence, are not as *our* ways; nor are the models that we frame any way commensurate to the vastness, profundity, and unsearchableness of His works, *which have a depth in them greater than the well of Democritus.*[1]

JOSEPH GLANVILLE

WE had now reached the summit of the loftiest crag. For some minutes the old man seemed too much exhausted to speak.

'Not long ago,' said he at length, 'and I could have guided you on this route as well as the youngest of my sons; but, about three years past, there happened to me an event such as never happened before to mortal man – or at least such as no man ever survived to tell of – and the six hours of deadly terror which I then endured have broken me up body and soul. You suppose me a *very* old man – but I am not. It took less than a single day to change these hairs from a jetty black to white, to weaken my limbs, and to unstring my nerves, so that I tremble at the least exertion, and am frightened at a shadow. Do you know I can scarcely look over this little cliff without getting giddy?'

The 'little cliff', upon whose edge he had so carelessly thrown himself down to rest that the weightier portion of his body hung over it, while he was only kept from falling by the tenure of his elbow on its extreme and slippery edge – this 'little cliff' arose, a sheer unobstructed precipice of black shining rock, some fifteen or sixteen hundred feet from the world of crags beneath us. Nothing would have tempted me to within half a dozen yards of its brink. In truth so deeply was I excited by the perilous position of my companion, that I fell at full length upon the ground, clung to the shrubs around me, and dared not even glance upward at the sky – while I struggled in vain to divest myself of the idea that the very foundations of the mountain were in danger from the fury of the winds. It was long before I could reason myself into sufficient courage to sit up and look out into the distance.

'You must get over these fancies,' said the guide, 'for I have brought you here that you might have the best possible view of the scene of that event I mentioned – and to tell you the whole story with the spot just under your eye.'

'We are now,' he continued, in that particularizing manner which distinguished him – 'we are now close upon the Norwegian coast – in the sixty-eighth degree of latitude – in the great province of Nordland – and in the dreary district of Lofoden. The mountain upon whose top we sit is Helseggen, the Cloudy.[2] Now raise yourself up a little higher – hold on to the grass if you feel giddy – so – and look out beyond the belt of vapor beneath us, into the sea.'

I looked dizzily, and beheld a wide expanse of ocean, whose waters wore so inky a hue as to bring at once to my mind the Nubian geographer's account of the *Mare Tenebrarum*.[3] A panorama more deplorably desolate no human imagination can conceive. To the right and left, as far as the eye could reach, there lay outstretched, like ramparts of the world, lines of horridly black and beetling cliff, whose character of gloom was but the more forcibly illustrated by the surf which reared high up against it its white and ghastly crest, howling and shrieking for ever. Just opposite the promontory upon whose apex we were placed, and at a distance of some five or six miles out at sea, there was visible a small, bleak-looking island; or, more properly, its position was discernible through the wilderness of surge in which it was enveloped. About two miles nearer the land, arose another of smaller size, hideously craggy and barren, and encompassed at various intervals by a cluster of dark rocks.

The appearance of the ocean, in the space between the more distant island and the shore, had something very unusual about it. Although, at the time, so strong a gale was blowing landward that a brig in the remote offing lay to under a double-reefed trysail, and constantly plunged her whole hull out of sight, still there was here nothing like a regular swell, but only a short, quick, angry cross dashing of water in every direction – as well in the teeth of the wind as otherwise. Of foam there was little except in the immediate vicinity of the rocks.

'The island in the distance,' resumed the old man, 'is called by the Norwegians Vurrgh. The one midway is Moskoe. That a mile to the northward is Ambaaren. Yonder are Iflesen, Hoeyholm, Kieldholm, Suarven, and Buckholm. Farther off – between Moskoe and Vurrgh – are Otterholm, Flimen, Sandflesen, and Skarholm. These are the true names of the places – but why it has been thought necessary to name them at all, is more than either you or I can understand. Do you hear any thing? Do you see any change in the water?'

We had now been about ten minutes upon the top of Helseggen, to which we had ascended from the interior of Lofoden, so that we had caught no glimpse of the sea until it had burst upon us from the summit. As the old man spoke, I became aware of a loud and gradually increasing sound,[4] like the moaning of a vast herd of buffaloes upon an American prairie; and at the same moment I perceived that what seamen term the *chopping* character of the ocean beneath us, was rapidly changing into a current which set to the eastward. Even while I gazed, this current acquired a monstrous velocity. Each moment added to its speed – to its headlong impetuosity. In five minutes the whole sea, as far as Vurrgh, was lashed into ungovernable fury; but it was between Moskoe and the coast that the main uproar held its sway. Here the vast bed of the waters, seamed and scarred into a thousand conflicting channels, burst suddenly into phrensied convulsion – heaving, boiling, hissing – gyrating in gigantic and innumerable vortices, and all whirling and plunging on to the eastward with a rapidity which water never elsewhere assumes except in precipitous descents.

In a few minutes more, there came over the scene another radical alteration. The general surface grew somewhat more smooth, and the whirlpools, one by one, disappeared, while prodigious streaks of foam became apparent where none had been seen before. These streaks, at length, spreading out to a great distance, and entering into combination, took unto themselves the gyratory motion of the subsided vortices, and seemed to form the germ of another more vast. Suddenly – very suddenly – this assumed a distinct and definite existence, in a circle of more than half a mile in diameter. The edge of the whirl was represented by a broad belt of gleaming spray; but no particle of this slipped into the mouth of the terrific funnel, whose interior, as far as the eye could fathom it, was a smooth, shining, and jet-black wall of water, inclined to the horizon at an angle of some forty-five degrees, speeding dizzily round and round with a swaying and sweltering motion, and sending forth to the winds an appalling voice, half shriek, half roar, such as not even the mighty cataract of Niagara ever lifts up in its agony to Heaven.

The mountain trembled to its very base, and the rock rocked. I threw myself upon my face, and clung to the scant herbage in an excess of nervous agitation.

'This,' said I at length, to the old man – 'this *can* be nothing else than the great whirlpool of the Maelström.'

'So it is sometimes termed,' said he. 'We Norwegians call it the Moskoe-ström, from the island of Moskoe in the midway.'

The ordinary accounts of this vortex had by no means prepared me for what I saw. That of Jonas Ramus, which is perhaps the most circumstantial of any,[5] cannot impart the faintest conception either of the magnificence, or of the horror of the scene – or of the wild bewildering sense of *the novel* which confounds the beholder. I am not sure from what point of view the writer in question surveyed it, nor at what time; but it could neither have been from the summit of Helseggen, nor during a storm. There are some passages of his description, nevertheless, which may be quoted for their details, although their effect is exceedingly feeble in conveying an impression of the spectacle.

'Between Lofoden and Moskoe,' he says, 'the depth of the water is between thirty-six and forty fathoms; but on the other side, toward Ver (Vurrgh) this depth decreases so as not to afford a convenient passage for a vessel, without the risk of splitting on the rocks, which happens even in the calmest weather. When it is flood, the stream runs up the country between Lofoden and Moskoe with a boisterous rapidity; but the roar of its impetuous ebb to the sea is scarce equalled by the loudest and most dreadful cataracts; the noise being heard several leagues off, and the vortices or pits are of such an extent and depth, that if a ship comes within its attraction, it is inevitably absorbed and carried down to the bottom, and there beat to pieces against the rocks; and when the water relaxes, the fragments thereof are thrown up again. But these intervals of tranquillity are only at the turn of the ebb and flood, and in calm weather, and last but a quarter of an hour, its violence gradually returning. When the stream is most boisterous, and its fury heightened by a storm, it is dangerous to come within a Norway mile of it. Boats, yachts, and ships have been carried away by not guarding against it before they were within its reach. It likewise happens frequently, that whales come too near the stream, and are overpowered by its violence; and then it is impossible to describe their howlings and bellowings in their fruitless struggles to disengage themselves. A bear once, attempting to swim from Lofoden to Moskoe, was caught by the stream and borne down, while he roared terribly, so as to be heard on shore. Large stocks of firs and pine trees, after being absorbed by the current, rise again broken and torn to such a degree as if bristles grew upon them. This plainly shows the bottom to consist of craggy rocks, among which they are whirled to and fro. This stream is regulated by the flux and reflux of the sea – it being constantly high and low water every six hours. In the year 1645, early in the morning of Sexagesima Sunday, it raged with such noise and impetuosity that the very stones of the houses on the coast fell to the ground.'

In regard to the depth of the water, I could not see how this could have been ascertained at all in the immediate vicinity of the vortex. The 'forty fathoms' must have reference only to portions of the channel close upon the shore either of Moskoe or Lofoden. The depth in the centre of the Moskoe-ström must be immeasurably greater; and no better proof of this fact is necessary than can be obtained from even the side-long glance into the abyss of the whirl which may be had from the highest crag of Helseggen. Looking down from this pinnacle upon the howling Phlegethon below, I could not help smiling at the simplicity with which the honest Jonas Ramus records, as a matter difficult of belief, the anecdotes of the whales and the bears; for it appeared to me, in fact, a self-evident thing, that the largest ships of the line in existence, coming within the influence of that deadly attraction, could resist it as little as a feather the hurricane, and must disappear bodily and at once.

The attempts to account for the phenomenon – some of which, I remember, seemed to me sufficiently plausible in perusal – now wore a very different and unsatisfactory aspect. The idea generally received is that this, as well as three smaller vortices among the Feroe islands, 'have no other cause than the collision of waves rising and falling, at flux and reflux, against a ridge of rocks and shelves, which confines the water so that it precipitates itself like a cataract; and thus the higher the flood rises, the deeper must the fall be, and the natural result of all is a whirlpool or vortex, the prodigious suction of which is sufficiently known by lesser experiments'. – These are the words of the Encyclopædia Britannica. Kircher and others imagine that in the centre of the channel of the Maelström is an abyss penetrating the globe, and issuing in some very remote part – the Gulf of Bothnia being somewhat decidedly named in one instance. This opinion, idle in itself, was the one to which, as I gazed, my imagination most readily assented; and, mentioning it to the guide, I was rather surprised to hear him say that, although it was the view almost universally entertained of the subject by the Norwegians, it nevertheless was not his own. As to the former notion he confessed his inability to comprehend it; and here I agreed with him – for, however conclusive on paper, it becomes altogether unintelligible, and even absurd, amid the thunder of the abyss.

'You have had a good look at the whirl now,' said the old man, 'and if you will creep round this crag, so as to get in its lee, and deaden the roar of the water, I will tell you a story that will convince you I ought to know something of the Moskoe-ström.'

I placed myself as desired, and he proceeded.

'Myself and my two brothers once owned a schooner-rigged smack of about seventy tons burthen, with which we were in the habit of fishing among the islands beyond Moskoe, nearly to Vurrgh. In all violent eddies at sea there is good fishing, at proper opportunities, if one has only the courage to attempt it; but among the whole of the Lofoden coastmen, we three were the only ones who made a regular business of going out to the islands, as I tell you. The usual grounds are a great way lower down to the southward. There fish can be got at all hours, without much risk, and therefore these places are preferred. The choice spots over here among the rocks, however, not only yield the finest variety, but in far greater abundance; so that we often got in a single day, what the more timid of the craft could not scrape together in a week. In fact, we made it a matter of desperate speculation – the risk of life standing instead of labor, and courage answering for capital.

'We kept the smack in a cove about five miles higher up the coast than this; and it was our practice, in fine weather, to take advantage of the fifteen minutes' slack to push across the main channel of the Moskoe-ström, far above the pool, and then drop down upon anchorage somewhere near Otterholm, or Sand-flesen, when the eddies are not so violent as elsewhere. Here we used to remain until nearly time for slack-water again, when we weighed and made for home. We never set out upon this expedition without a steady side wind for going and coming – one that we felt sure would not fail us before our return – and we seldom made a mis-calculation upon this point. Twice, during six years, we were forced to stay all night at anchor on account of a dead calm, which is a rare thing indeed just about here; and once we had to remain on the grounds nearly a week, starving to death, owing to a gale which blew up shortly after our arrival, and made the channel too boisterous to be thought of. Upon this occasion we should have been driven out to sea in spite of everything, (for the whirlpools threw us round and round so violently, that, at length, we fouled our anchor and dragged it) if it had not been that we drifted into one of the innumerable cross currents – here today and gone tomorrow – which drove us under the lee of Flimen, where, by good luck, we brought up.

'I could not tell you the twentieth part of the difficulties we encountered "on the ground" – it is a bad spot to be in, even in good weather – but we made shift always to run the gauntlet of the Moskoe-ström itself without accident; although at times my heart has been in my mouth when we happened to be a minute or so behind or before the slack. The wind sometimes was not as strong as we thought it at starting, and then we made rather less way than we could wish, while the current rendered the smack unmanageable. My eldest brother had a son eighteen years old, and I had two stout boys of my own. These would have been of great assistance at such times, in using the sweeps, as well as afterward in fishing – but, somehow, although we ran the risk ourselves, we had not the heart to let the young ones get into the danger – for, after all said and done, it *was* a horrible danger, and that is the truth.

'It is now within a few days of three years since what I am going to tell you occurred. It was on the tenth of July, 18—, a day which the people of this part of the world will never forget – for it was one in which blew the most terrible hurricane that ever came out of the heavens. And yet all the morning, and indeed until late in the afternoon, there was a gentle and steady breeze from the south-west, while the sun shone brightly, so that the oldest seaman among us could not have foreseen what was to follow.

'The three of us – my two brothers and myself – had crossed over to the islands about two o'clock P. M., and soon nearly loaded the smack with fine fish, which, we all remarked, were more plenty that day than we had ever known them. It was just seven, *by my watch*, when we weighed and started for home, so as to make the worst of the Ström at slack water, which we knew would be at eight.

'We set out with a fresh wind on our starboard quarter, and for some time spanked along at a great rate, never dreaming of danger, for indeed we saw not the slightest reason to apprehend it. All at once we were taken aback by a breeze from over Helseggen. This was most unusual – something that had never happened to us before – and I began to feel a little uneasy, without exactly knowing why. We put the boat on the wind, but could make no headway at all for the eddies, and I was upon the point of proposing to return to the anchorage, when, looking astern, we saw the whole horizon covered with a singular copper-colored cloud that rose with the most amazing velocity.

'In the meantime the breeze that had headed us off fell away, and we were dead becalmed, drifting about in every direction. This state of things, however, did not last long enough to give us time to think about it. In less than a minute the storm was upon us – in less than two the sky was entirely overcast – and what with this and the driving spray, it became suddenly so dark that we could not see each other in the smack.

'Such a hurricane as then blew it is folly to attempt describing. The oldest seaman in Norway never experienced any thing like it. We had let our sails go by the run before it cleverly took us; but, at the first puff, both our masts went by the board as if they had been sawed off – the mainmast taking with it my youngest brother, who had lashed himself to it for safety.

'Our boat was the lightest feather of a thing that ever sat upon water. It had a complete flush deck, with only a small hatch near the bow, and this hatch it had always been our custom to batten down when about to cross the Ström, by way of precaution against the chopping seas. But for this circumstance we should have foundered at once – for we lay entirely buried for some moments. How my elder brother escaped destruction I cannot say, for I never had an opportunity of ascertaining. For my part, as soon as I had let the foresail run, I threw myself flat on deck, with my feet against the narrow gunwale of the bow, and with my hands grasping a ring-bolt near the foot of the fore-mast. It was mere instinct that prompted me to do this – which was undoubtedly the very best thing I could have done – for I was too much flurried to think.

'For some moments we were completely deluged, as I say, and all this time I held my breath, and clung to the bolt. When I could stand it no longer I raised myself upon my knees, still keeping hold with my hands, and thus got my head clear. Presently our little boat gave herself a shake, just as a dog does in coming out of the water, and thus rid herself, in some measure, of the seas. I was now trying to get the better of the stupor that had come over me, and to collect my senses so as to see what was to be done, when I felt somebody grasp my arm. It was my elder brother, and my heart leaped for joy, for I had made sure that he was overboard – but the next moment all this joy was turned into horror – for he put his mouth close to my ear, and screamed out the word *"Moskoe-ström!"*

'No one ever will know what my feelings were at that

moment. I shook from head to foot as if I had had the most violent fit of the ague. I knew what he meant by that one word well enough – I knew what he wished to make me understand. With the wind that now drove us on, we were bound for the whirl of the Ström, and nothing could save us!

'You perceive that in crossing the Ström *channel*, we always went a long way up above the whirl, even in the calmest weather, and then had to wait and watch carefully for the slack – but now we were driving right upon the pool itself, and in such a hurricane as this! "To be sure," I thought, "we shall get there just about the slack – there is some little hope in that" – but in the next moment I cursed myself for being so great a fool as to dream of hope at all. I knew very well that we were doomed, had we been ten times a ninety-gun ship.

'By this time the first fury of the tempest had spent itself, or perhaps we did not feel it so much, as we scudded before it, but at all events the seas, which at first had been kept down by the wind, and lay flat and frothing, now got up into absolute mountains. A singular change, too, had come over the heavens. Around in every direction it was still as black as pitch, but nearly overhead there burst out, all at once, a circular rift of clear sky – as clear as I ever saw – and of a deep bright blue – and through it there blazed forth the full moon with a lustre that I never before knew her to wear. She lit up every thing about us with the greatest distinctness – but, oh God, what a scene it was to light up!

'I now made one or two attempts to speak to my brother – but in some manner which I could not understand, the din had so increased that I could not make him hear a single word, although I screamed at the top of my voice in his ear. Presently he shook his head, looking as pale as death, and held up one of his fingers, as if to say *"listen!"*

'At first I could not make out what he meant – but soon a hideous thought flashed upon me. I dragged my watch from its fob. It was not going. I glanced at its face by the moonlight, and then burst into tears as I flung it far away into the ocean. *It had run down at seven o'clock! We were behind the time of the slack, and the whirl of the Ström was in full fury!*

'When a boat is well built, properly trimmed, and not deep laden, the waves in a strong gale, when she is going large, seem always to slip from beneath her – which appears very strange to a landsman – and this is what is called *riding*, in sea phrase.

'Well, so far we had ridden the swells very cleverly; but presently a gigantic sea happened to take us right under the counter, and bore us with it as it rose – up – up – as if into the sky. I would not have believed that any wave could rise so high. And then down we came with a sweep, a slide, and a plunge, that made me feel sick and dizzy, as if I was falling from some lofty mountain-top in a dream. But while we were up I had thrown a quick glance around – and that one glance was all sufficient. I saw our exact position in an instant. The Moskoe-ström whirlpool was about a quarter of a mile dead ahead – but no more like the every-day Moskoe-ström, than the whirl as you now see it, is like a mill-race. If I had not known where we were, and what we had to expect, I should not have recognized the place at all. As it was, I involuntarily closed my eyes in horror. The lids clenched themselves together as if in a spasm.

'It could not have been more than two minutes afterwards until we suddenly felt the waves subside, and were enveloped in foam. The boat made a sharp half turn to larboard, and then shot off in its new direction like a thunderbolt. At the same moment the roaring noise of the water was completely drowned in a kind of shrill shriek – such a sound as you might imagine given out by the water-pipes of many thousand steam-vessels, letting off their steam all together. We were now in the belt of surf that always surrounds the whirl; and I thought, of course, that another moment would plunge us into the abyss – down which we could only see indistinctly on account of the amazing velocity with which we were borne along. The boat did not seem to sink into the water at all, but to skim like an air-bubble upon the surface of the surge. Her starboard side was next the whirl, and on the larboard arose the world of ocean we had left. It stood like a huge writhing wall between us and the horizon.

'It may appear strange, but now, when we were in the very jaws of the gulf, I felt more composed than when we were only approaching it. Having made up my mind to hope no more, I

got rid of a great deal of that terror which unmanned me at first.
I suppose it was despair that strung my nerves.

'It may look like boasting – but what I tell you is truth – I
began to reflect how magnificent a thing it was to die in such a
manner, and how foolish it was in me to think of so paltry a
consideration as my own individual life, in view of so wonderful
a manifestation of God's power. I do believe that I blushed with
shame when this idea crossed my mind. After a little while I became possessed with the keenest curiosity about the whirl itself.
I positively felt a *wish* to explore its depths, even at the sacrifice I
was going to make; and my principal grief was that I should
never be able to tell my old companions on shore about the
mysteries I should see. These, no doubt, were singular fancies
to occupy a man's mind in such extremity – and I have often
thought since, that the revolutions of the boat around the pool
might have rendered me a little light-headed.

'There was another circumstance which tended to restore my
self-possession; and this was the cessation of the wind, which
could not reach us in our present situation – for, as you saw yourself, the belt of surf is considerably lower than the general bed of
the ocean, and this latter now towered above us, a high, black,
mountainous ridge. If you have never been at sea in a heavy gale,
you can form no idea of the confusion of mind occasioned by
the wind and spray together. They blind, deafen and strangle
you, and take away all power of action or reflection. But we were
now, in a great measure, rid of these annoyances – just as death-
condemned felons in prison are allowed petty indulgences, forbidden them while their doom is yet uncertain.

'How often we made the circuit of the belt it is impossible to
say. We careered round and round for perhaps an hour, flying
rather than floating, getting gradually more and more into the
middle of the surge, and then nearer and nearer to its horrible
inner edge. All this time I had never let go of the ring-bolt. My
brother was at the stern, holding on to a large empty water-cask
which had been securely lashed under the coop of the counter,
and was the only thing on deck that had not been swept overboard when the gale first took us. As we approached the brink of
the pit he let go his hold upon this, and made for the ring, from

which, in the agony of his terror, he endeavored to force my hands, as it was not large enough to afford us both a secure grasp. I never felt deeper grief than when I saw him attempt this act – although I knew he was a madman when he did it – a raving maniac through sheer fright. I did not care, however, to contest the point with him. I thought it could make no difference whether either of us held on at all; so I let him have the bolt, and went astern to the cask. This there was no great difficulty in doing; for the smack flew round steadily enough, and upon an even keel – only swaying to and fro, with the immense sweeps and swelters of the whirl. Scarcely had I secured myself in my new position, when we gave a wild lurch to starboard, and rushed headlong into the abyss. I muttered a hurried prayer to God, and thought all was over.

'As I felt the sickening sweep of the descent, I had instinctively tightened my hold upon the barrel, and closed my eyes. For some seconds I dared not open them – while I expected instant destruction, and wondered that I was not already in my death-struggles with the water. But moment after moment elapsed. I still lived. The sense of falling had ceased; and the motion of the vessel seemed much as it had been before while in the belt of foam, with the exception that she now lay more along. I took courage and looked once again upon the scene.

'Never shall I forget the sensations of awe, horror, and admiration with which I gazed about me. The boat appeared to be hanging, as if by magic, midway down, upon the interior surface of a funnel vast in circumference, prodigious in depth, and whose perfectly smooth sides might have been mistaken for ebony, but for the bewildering rapidity with which they spun around, and for the gleaming and ghastly radiance they shot forth, as the rays of the full moon, from that circular rift amid the clouds which I have already described, streamed in a flood of golden glory along the black walls, and far away down into the inmost recesses of the abyss.

'At first I was too much confused to observe anything accurately. The general burst of terrific grandeur was all that I beheld. When I recovered myself a little, however, my gaze fell instinctively downward. In this direction I was able to obtain an unobstructed view, from the manner in which the smack hung on the inclined surface of the pool. She was quite upon an even keel – that is to say, her deck lay in a plane parallel with that of the water – but this latter sloped at an angle of more than forty-five degrees, so that we seemed to be lying upon our beam-ends. I could not help observing, nevertheless, that I had scarcely more difficulty in maintaining my hold and footing in this situation, than if we had been upon a deal level; and this, I suppose, was owing to the speed at which we revolved.

'The rays of the moon seemed to search the very bottom of the profound gulf; but still I could make out nothing distinctly, on account of a thick mist in which everything there was enveloped, and over which there hung a magnificent rainbow, like that narrow and tottering bridge which Mussulmen say is the only pathway between Time and Eternity. This mist, or spray, was no doubt occasioned by the clashing of the great walls of the funnel, as they all met together at the bottom – but the yell that went up to the Heavens from out of that mist, I dare not attempt to describe.

'Our first slide into the abyss itself, from the belt of foam above, had carried us to a great distance down the slope; but our farther descent was by no means proportionate. Round and round we swept – not with any uniform movement – but in dizzying swings and jerks, that sent us sometimes only a few hundred feet – sometimes nearly the complete circuit of the whirl. Our progress downward, at each revolution, was slow, but very perceptible.

'Looking about me upon the wide waste of liquid ebony on which we were thus borne, I perceived that our boat was not the only object in the embrace of the whirl. Both above and below us were visible fragments of vessels, large masses of building timber and trunks of trees, with many smaller articles, such as pieces of house furniture, broken boxes, barrels and staves. I have already described the unnatural curiosity which had taken the place of my original terrors. It appeared to grow upon me as I drew nearer and nearer to my dreadful doom. I now began to watch, with a strange interest, the numerous things that floated in our company. I *must* have been delirious –

for I even sought *amusement* in speculating upon the relative velocities of their several descents toward the foam below. "This fir tree," I found myself at one time saying, "will certainly be the next thing that takes the awful plunge and disappears," – and then I was disappointed to find that the wreck of a Dutch merchant ship overtook it and went down before. At length, after making several guesses of this nature, and being deceived in all – this fact – the fact of my invariable miscalculation, set me upon a train of reflection that made my limbs again tremble, and my heart beat heavily once more.

'It was not a new terror that thus affected me, but the dawn of a more exciting *hope*. This hope arose partly from memory, and partly from present observation. I called to mind the great variety of buoyant matter that strewed the coast of Lofoden, having been absorbed and then thrown forth by the Moskoe-ström. By far the greater number of the articles were shattered in the most extraordinary way – so chafed and roughened as to have the appearance of being stuck full of splinters – but then I distinctly recollected that there were *some* of them which were not disfigured at all. Now I could not account for this difference except by supposing that the roughened fragments were the only ones which had been *completely absorbed* – that the others had entered the whirl at so late a period of the tide, or, from some reason, had descended so slowly after entering, that they did not reach the bottom before the turn of the flood came, or of the ebb, as the case might be. I conceived it possible, in either instance, that they might thus be whirled up again to the level of the ocean, without undergoing the fate of those which had been drawn in more early or absorbed more rapidly. I made, also, three important observations. The first was, that as a general rule, the larger the bodies were, the more rapid their descent; – the second, that, between two masses of equal extent, the one spherical, and the other *of any other shape*, the superiority in speed of descent was with the sphere; – the third, that, between two masses of equal size, the one cylindrical, and the other of any other shape, the cylinder was absorbed the more slowly.

'Since my escape, I have had several conversations on this subject with an old school-master of the district; and it was from him that I learned the use of the words "cylinder" and "sphere". He explained to me – although I have forgotten the explanation – how what I observed was, in fact, the natural consequence of the forms of the floating fragments – and showed me how it happened that a cylinder, swimming in a vortex, offered more resistance to its suction, and was drawn in with greater difficulty than an equally bulky body, of any form whatever.*

'There was one startling circumstance which went a great way in enforcing these observations, and rendering me anxious to turn them to account, and this was that, at every revolution, we passed something like a barrel, or else the broken yard or the mast of a vessel, while many of these things, which had been on our level when I first opened my eyes upon the wonders of the whirlpool, were now high up above us, and seemed to have moved but little from their original station.

'I no longer hesitated what to do. I resolved to lash myself securely to the water cask upon which I now held, to cut it loose from the counter, and to throw myself with it into the water. I attracted my brother's attention by signs, pointed to the floating barrels that came near us, and did everything in my power to make him understand what I was about to do. I thought at length that he comprehended my design – but, whether this was the case or not, he shook his head despairingly, and refused to move from his station by the ring-bolt. It was impossible to force him; the emergency admitted no delay; and so, with a bitter struggle, I resigned him to his fate, fastened myself to the cask by means of the lashings which secured it to the counter, and precipitated myself with it into the sea, without another moment's hesitation.

'The result was precisely what I had hoped it might be. As it is myself who now tell you this tale – as you see that I *did* escape – and as you are already in possession of the mode in which this escape was effected, and must therefore anticipate all that I have farther to say – I will bring my story quickly to conclusion. It might have been an hour, or thereabout, after my quitting the smack, when, having descended to a vast distance beneath me, it made three or four wild gyrations in rapid succession, and,

* See Archimedes, *'De Incidentibus in Fluido'*. – lib. 2.[6]

bearing my loved brother with it, plunged headlong, at once and forever, into the chaos of foam below. The barrel to which I was attached sunk very little farther than half the distance between the bottom of the gulf and the spot at which I leaped overboard, before a great change took place in the character of the whirlpool. The slope of the sides of the vast funnel became momently less and less steep. The gyrations of the whirl grew, gradually, less and less violent. By degrees, the froth and the rainbow disappeared, and the bottom of the gulf seemed slowly to uprise. The sky was clear, the winds had gone down, and the full moon was setting radiantly in the west, when I found myself on the surface of the ocean, in full view of the shores of Lofoden, and above the spot where the pool of the Moskoe-ström *had been*. It was the hour of the slack – but the sea still heaved in mountainous waves from the effects of the hurricane. I was borne violently into the channel of the Ström, and in a few minutes, was hurried down the coast into the "grounds" of the fishermen. A boat picked me up – exhausted from fatigue – and (now that the danger was removed) speechless from the memory of its horror. Those who drew me on board were my old mates and daily companions – but they knew me no more than they would have known a traveller from the spirit-land. My hair, which had been raven-black the day before, was as white as you see it now. They say too that the whole expression of my countenance had changed. I told them my story – they did not believe it. I now tell it to *you* – and I can scarcely expect you to put more faith in it than did the merry fishermen of Lofoden.'

The Colloquy of Monos and Una[1]

Μέλλοντα ταῦτα
SOPHOCLES, *Antig.*
These things are in the future.[2]

Una. 'Born again?'

Monos. Yes, fairest and best-beloved Una, 'born again'. These were the words upon whose mystical meaning I had so long pondered, rejecting the explanations of the priesthood, until Death himself resolved for me the secret.

Una. Death!

Monos. How strangely, sweet Una, you echo my words! I observe, too, a vacillation in your step – a joyous inquietude in your eyes. You are confused and oppressed by the majestic novelty of the Life Eternal.[3] Yes, it was of Death I spoke. And here how singularly sounds that word which of old was wont to bring terror to all hearts – throwing a mildew upon all pleasures!

Una. Ah, Death, the spectre which sate at all feasts! How often, Monos, did we lose ourselves in speculations upon its nature! How mysteriously did it act as a check to human bliss – saying unto it 'thus far, and no farther!' That earnest mutual love, my own Monos, which burned within our bosoms – how vainly did we flatter ourselves, feeling happy in its first up-springing, that our happiness would strengthen with its strength! Alas! as it grew, so grew in our hearts the dread of that evil hour which was hurrying to separate us forever! Thus, in time, it became painful to love. Hate would have been mercy then.

Monos. Speak not here of these griefs, dear Una mine, mine forever now!

Una. But the memory of past sorrow – is it not present joy? I have much to say yet of the things which have been. Above all, I burn to know the incidents of your own passage through the dark Valley and Shadow.

89

Monos. And when did the radiant Una ask anything of her Monos in vain? I will be minute in relating all – but at what point shall the weird narrative begin?

Una. At what point?

Monos. You have said.

Una. Monos, I comprehend you. In Death we have both learned the propensity of man to define the indefinable. I will not say, then, commence with the moment of life's cessation – but commence with that sad, sad instant when, the fever having abandoned you, you sank into a breathless and motionless torpor, and I pressed down your pallid eyelids with the passionate fingers of love.

Monos. One word first, my Una, in regard to man's general condition at this epoch. You will remember that one or two of the wise among our forefathers – wise in fact, although not in the world's esteem – had ventured to doubt the propriety of the term 'improvement', as applied to the progress of our civilization. There were periods in each of the five or six centuries immediately preceding our dissolution, when arose some vigorous intellect, boldly contending for those principles whose truth appears now, to our disenfranchised reason, so utterly obvious – principles which should have taught our race to submit to the guidance of the natural laws, rather than attempt their control. At long intervals some master-minds appeared, looking upon each advance in practical science as a retro-gradation in the true utility.[4] Occasionally the poetic intellect – that intellect which we now feel to have been the most exalted of all – since those truths which to us were of the most enduring importance could only be reached by that *analogy* which speaks in proof-tones to the imagination alone, and to the unaided reason bears no weight – occasionally did this poetic intellect proceed a step farther in the evolving of the vague idea of the philosophic, and find in the mystic parable that tells of the tree of knowledge, and of its forbidden fruit, death-producing, a distinct intimation that knowledge was not meet for man in the infant condition of his soul. And these men – the poets – living and perishing amid the scorn of the 'utilitarians' – of rough pedants, who arrogated to themselves a title which could have been properly applied only to the scorned – these men, the poets, pondered piningly, yet not unwisely, upon the ancient days when our wants were not more simple than our enjoyments were keen – days when *mirth* was a word unknown, so solemnly deep-toned was happiness – holy, august and blissful days, when blue rivers ran undammed, between hills unhewn, into far forest solitudes, primæval, odorous, and unexplored.

Yet these noble exceptions from the general misrule served but to strengthen it by opposition. Alas! we had fallen upon the most evil of all our evil days. The great 'movement' – that was the cant term – went on: a diseased commotion, moral and physical. Art – the Arts – arose supreme, and, once enthroned, cast chains upon the intellect which had elevated them to power. Man, because he could not but acknowledge the majesty of Nature, fell into childish exultation at his acquired and still-increasing dominion over her elements. Even while he stalked a God in his own fancy, an infantine imbecility came over him. As might be supposed from the origin of his disorder, he grew infected with system, and with abstraction. He enwrapped himself in generalities. Among other odd ideas, that of universal equality gained ground; and in the face of analogy and of God – in despite of the loud warning voice of the laws of *gradation* so visibly pervading all things in Earth and Heaven – wild attempts at an omni-prevalent Democracy were made. Yet this evil sprang necessarily from the leading evil, Knowledge. Man could not both know and succumb. Meantime huge smoking cities arose, innumerable. Green leaves shrank before the hot breath of furnaces. The fair face of Nature was deformed as with the ravages of some loathsome disease. And methinks, sweet Una, even our slumbering sense of the forced and of the far-fetched might have arrested us here. But now it appears that we had worked out our own destruction in the perversion of our *taste*, or rather in the blind neglect of its culture in the schools. For, in truth, it was at this crisis that taste alone – that faculty which, holding a middle position between the pure intellect and the moral sense, could never safely have been disregarded – it was now that taste alone could have led us gently back to Beauty, to Nature, and to Life. But alas for the pure contemplative spirit and majestic intuition of

Plato! Alas for the μουσική which he justly regarded as an all-sufficient education for the soul! Alas for him and for it! – since both were so desperately needed when both were most entirely forgotten or despised.*

Pascal, a philosopher whom we both love, has said, how truly! – 'que tout notre raisonnement se réduit à céder au sentiment';[5] and it is not impossible that the sentiment of the natural, had time permitted it, would have regained its old ascendancy over the harsh mathematical reason of the schools. But this thing was not to be. Prematurely induced by intemperance of knowledge, the old age of the world drew on. This the mass of mankind saw not, or, living lustily although unhappily, affected not to see. But, for myself, the Earth's records had taught me to look for widest ruin as the price of highest civilization. I had imbibed a prescience of our Fate from comparison of China the simple and enduring, with Assyria the architect, with Egypt the astrologer, with Nubia, more crafty than either, the turbulent mother of all Arts. In history† of these regions I met with a ray from the Future. The individual artificialities of the three latter were local diseases of the Earth, and in their individual overthrows we had seen local remedies applied; but for the infected world at large I could anticipate no regeneration save in death.[6] That man, as a race, should not become extinct, I saw that he must be 'born again'.

---

*'It will be hard to discover a better [method of education] than that which the experience of so many ages has already discovered; and this may be summed up as consisting in gymnastics for the body, and music for the soul.' – Repub. lib. 2. 'For this reason is a musical education most essential; since it causes Rhythm and Harmony to penetrate most intimately into the soul, taking the strongest hold upon it, filling it with beauty and making the man beautiful-minded. . . . He will praise and admire the beautiful; will receive it with joy into his soul, will feed upon it, and assimilate his own condition with it.' – Ibid. lib. 3. Music (μουσική) had, however, among the Athenians, a far more comprehensive signification than with us. It included not only the harmonies of time and of tune, but the poetic diction, sentiment, and creation, each in its widest sense. The study of music was with them, in fact, the general cultivation of the taste – of that which recognises the beautiful – in contra-distinction from reason, which deals only with the true.

†'History', from ἱστορεῖν, to contemplate.

And now it was, fairest and dearest, that we wrapped our spirits, daily, in dreams. Now it was that, in twilight, we discoursed of the days to come, when the Art-scarred surface of the Earth, having undergone that purification* which alone could efface its rectangular obscenities, should clothe itself anew in the verdure and the mountain-slopes and the smiling waters of Paradise, and be rendered at length a fit dwelling-place for man : – for man the Death-purged – for man to whose now exalted intellect there should be poison in knowledge no more – for the redeemed, regenerated, blissful, and now immortal, but still for the *material*, man.

Una. Well do I remember these conversations, dear Monos; but the epoch of the fiery overthrow was not so near at hand as we believed, and as the corruption you indicate did surely warrant us in believing. Men lived; and died individually. You yourself sickened, and passed into the grave; and thither your constant Una speedily followed you. And though the century which has since elapsed, and whose conclusion brings us thus together once more, tortured our slumbering senses with no impatience of duration, yet, my Monos, it was a century still.

Monos. Say, rather, a point in the vague infinity. Unquestionably, it was in the Earth's dotage that I died. Wearied at heart with anxieties which had their origin in the general turmoil and decay, I succumbed to the fierce fever. After some few days of pain, and many of dreamy delirium replete with ecstasy, the manifestations of which you mistook for pain, while I longed but was impotent to undeceive you – after some days there came upon me, as you have said, a breathless and motionless torpor; and this was termed *Death* by those who stood around me.

Words are vague things. My condition did not deprive me of sentience. It appeared to me not greatly dissimilar to the extreme quiescence of him, who, having slumbered long and profoundly, lying motionless and fully prostrate in a midsummer noon, begins to steal slowly back into consciousness, through the mere sufficiency of his sleep, and without being awakened by external disturbances.

---

* The word '*purification*' seems here to be used with reference to its root in the Greek $\pi \tilde{\upsilon} \rho$, fire.

I breathed no longer. The pulses were still. The heart had ceased to beat. Volition had not departed, but was powerless. The senses were unusually active, although eccentrically so – assuming often each other's functions at random. The taste and the smell were inextricably confounded,[7] and became one sentiment, abnormal and intense. The rose-water with which your tenderness had moistened my lips to the last, affected me with sweet fancies of flowers – fantastic flowers, far more lovely than any of the old Earth, but whose prototypes we have here blooming around us. The eyelids, transparent and bloodless, offered no complete impediment to vision. As volition was in abeyance, the balls could not roll in their sockets – but all objects within the range of the visual hemisphere were seen with more or less distinctness; the rays which fell upon the external retina, or into the corner of the eye, producing a more vivid effect than those which struck the front or interior surface. Yet, in the former instance, this effect was so far anomalous that I appreciated it only as *sound*[8] – sound sweet or discordant as the matters presenting themselves at my side were light or dark in shade – curved or angular in outline. The hearing, at the same time, although excited in degree, was not irregular in action – estimating real sounds with an extravagance of precision, not less than of sensibility. Touch had undergone a modification more peculiar. Its impressions were tardily received, but pertinaciously retained, and resulted always in the highest physical pleasure. Thus the pressure of your sweet fingers upon my eyelids, at first only recognised through vision, at length, long after their removal, filled my whole being with a sensual delight immeasurable. I say with a sensual delight. *All* my perceptions were purely sensual. The materials furnished the passive brain by the senses were not in the least degree wrought into shape by the deceased understanding. Of pain there was some little; of pleasure there was much; but of moral pain or pleasure none at all. Thus your wild sobs floated into my ear with all their mournful cadences, and were appreciated in their every variation of sad tone; but they were soft musical sounds and no more; they conveyed to the extinct reason no intimation of the sorrows which gave them birth; while the large and constant tears which fell upon my face, telling the bystanders of a heart which broke, thrilled every fibre of my frame with ecstasy alone. And this was in truth the *Death* of which these bystanders spoke reverently, in low whispers – you, sweet Una, gaspingly, with loud cries.

They attired me for the coffin – three or four dark figures which flitted busily to and fro. As these crossed the direct line of my vision, they affected me as *forms*; but upon passing to my side their images impressed me with the idea of shrieks, groans, and other dismal expressions of terror, or horror, or of woe. You alone, habited in a white robe, passed in all directions musically about me.

The day waned; and, as its light faded away, I became possessed by a vague uneasiness – an anxiety such as the sleeper feels when sad real sounds fall continuously within his ear – low distant bell-tones, solemn, at long but equal intervals, and commingling with melancholy dreams. Night arrived; and with its shadows a heavy discomfort. It oppressed my limbs with the oppression of some dull weight, and was palpable. There was also a moaning sound, not unlike the distant reverberation of surf, but more continuous, which, beginning with the first twilight, had grown in strength with the darkness. Suddenly lights were brought into the room, and this reverberation became forthwith interrupted into frequent unequal bursts of the same sound, but less dreary and less distinct. The ponderous oppression was in a great measure relieved; and, issuing from the flame of each lamp, (for there were many,) there flowed unbrokenly into my ears a strain of melodious monotone. And when now, dear Una, approaching the bed upon which I lay outstretched, you sat gently by my side, breathing odor from your sweet lips, and pressing them upon my brow, there arose tremulously within my bosom, and mingling with the merely physical sensations which circumstances had called forth, a something akin to sentiment itself – a feeling that, half appreciating, half responded to your earnest love and sorrow; but this feeling took no root in the pulseless heart, and seemed indeed rather a shadow than a reality, and faded quickly away, first into extreme quiescence, and then into a purely sensual pleasure as before.

And now, from the wreck and the chaos of the usual senses,

there appeared to have arisen within me a sixth, all perfect. In its exercise I found a wild delight – yet a delight still physical, inasmuch as the understanding had in it no part. Motion in the animal frame had fully ceased. No muscle quivered; no nerve thrilled; no artery throbbed. But there seemed to have sprung up in the brain, *that* of which no words could convey to the merely human intelligence even an indistinct conception. Let me term it a mental pendulous pulsation. It was the moral embodiment of man's abstract idea of *Time*. By the absolute equalization of this movement – or of such as this – had the cycles of the firmamental orbs themselves, been adjusted. By its aid I measured the irregularities of the clock upon the mantel,[9] and of the watches of the attendants. Their tickings came sonorously to my ears. The slightest deviations from the true proportion – and these deviations were omni-prævalent – affected me just as violations of abstract truth were wont, on earth, to affect the moral sense. Although no two of the time-pieces in the chamber struck the individual seconds accurately together, yet I had no difficulty in holding steadily in mind the tones and the respective momentary errors of each. And this – this keen, perfect, self-existing sentiment of *duration* – this sentiment existing (as man could not possibly have conceived it to exist) independently of any succession of events – this idea – this sixth sense, upspringing from the ashes of the rest, was the first obvious and certain step of the intemporal soul upon the threshold of the temporal Eternity.

It was midnight; and you still sat by my side. All others had departed from the chamber of Death. They had deposited me in the coffin. The lamps burned flickeringly; for this I knew by the tremulousness of the monotonous strains. But, suddenly these strains diminished in distinctness and in volume. Finally they ceased. The perfume in my nostrils died away. Forms affected my vision no longer. The oppression of the Darkness uplifted itself from my bosom. A dull shock like that of electricity pervaded my frame, and was followed by total loss of the idea of contact. All of what man has termed sense was merged in the sole consciousness of entity, and in the one abiding sentiment of duration. The mortal body had been at length stricken with the hand of the deadly *Decay*.

Yet had not all sentience departed; for the consciousness and the sentiment remaining supplied some of its functions by a lethargic intuition. I appreciated the direful change now in operation upon the flesh, and, as the dreamer is sometimes aware of the bodily presence of one who leans over him, so, sweet Una, I still dully felt that you sat by my side. So, too, when the noon of the second day came, I was not unconscious of those movements which displaced you from my side, which confined me within the coffin, which deposited me within the hearse, which bore me to the grave, which lowered me within it, which heaped heavily the mould upon me, and which thus left me, in blackness and corruption, to my sad and solemn slumbers with the worm.

And here, in the prison-house which has few secrets to disclose, there rolled away days and weeks and months; and the soul watched narrowly each second as it flew, and, without effort, took record of its flight – without effort and without object.

A year passed. The consciousness of *being* had grown hourly more indistinct, and that of mere *locality* had, in great measure, usurped its position. The idea of entity was becoming merged in that of *place*. The narrow space immediately surrounding what had been the body, was now growing to be the body itself. At length, as often happens to the sleeper (by sleep and its world alone is *Death* imaged) – at length, as sometimes happened on Earth to the deep slumberer, when some flitting light half startled him into awaking, yet left him half enveloped in dreams – so to me, in the strict embrace of the *Shadow*, came *that* light which alone might have had power to startle – the light of enduring *Love*. Men toiled at the grave in which I lay darkling. They upthrew the damp earth. Upon my mouldering bones there descended the coffin of Una.

And now again all was void. That nebulous light had been extinguished. That feeble thrill had vibrated itself into quiescence. Many *lustra* had supervened. Dust had returned to dust. The worm had food no more. The sense of being had at length utterly departed, and there reigned in its stead – instead of all things – dominant and perpetual – the autocrats *Place* and *Time*. For *that* which *was not* – for that which had no form – for that which had no thought – for that which had no sentience – for

that which was soulless, yet of which matter formed no portion –
for all this nothingness, yet for all this immortality, the grave
was still a home, and the corrosive hours, co-mates.

A Tale of the Ragged Mountains

DURING the fall of the year 1827, while residing near Charlottes-ville, Virginia, I casually made the acquaintance of Mr Augustus Bedloe. This young gentleman was remarkable in every respect, and excited in me a profound interest and curiosity. I found it impossible to comprehend him either in his moral or his physical relations. Of his family I could obtain no satisfactory account. Whence he came, I never ascertained. Even about his age – al-though I call him a young gentleman – there was something which perplexed me in no little degree. He certainly *seemed* young – and he made a point of speaking about his youth – yet there were moments when I should have had little trouble in imagining him a hundred years of age. But in no regard was he more peculiar than in his personal appearance. He was singularly tall and thin. He stooped much. His limbs were exceedingly long and emaciated. His forehead was broad and low. His complexion was absolutely bloodless. His mouth was large and flexible, and his teeth were more wildly uneven, although sound, than I had ever before seen teeth in a human head. The expression of his smile, however, was by no means unpleasing, as might be sup-posed; but it had no variation whatever. It was one of profound melancholy – of a phaseless and unceasing gloom. His eyes were abnormally large, and round like those of a cat. The pupils, too, upon any accession or diminution of light, underwent contrac-tion or dilation, just such as is observed in the feline tribe. In moments of excitement the orbs grew bright to a degree almost inconceivable; seeming to emit luminous rays,[1] not of a reflected, but of an intrinsic lustre, as does a candle or the sun; yet their ordinary condition was so totally vapid, filmy and dull, as to con-vey the idea of the eyes of a long-interred corpse.

These peculiarities of person appeared to cause him much an-noyance, and he was continually alluding to them in a sort of half explanatory, half apologetic strain, which, when I first heard it, impressed me very painfully. I soon, however, grew accustomed to it, and my uneasiness wore off. It seemed to be his design rather to insinuate than directly to assert that, physically, he had not always been what he was – that a long series of neuralgic attacks had reduced him from a condition of more than usual personal beauty, to that which I saw. For many years past he had been attended by a physician, named Templeton – an old gentleman, perhaps seventy years of age – whom he had first encountered at Saratoga,[2] and from whose attention, while there, he either received, or fancied that he received, great benefit. The result was that Bedloe, who was wealthy, had made an arrangement with Doctor Templeton, by which the latter, in consideration of a liberal annual allowance, had consented to devote his time and medical experience exclusively to the care of the invalid.

Doctor Templeton had been a traveller in his younger days, and, at Paris, had become a convert, in great measure, to the doctrines of Mesmer.[3] It was altogether by means of magnetic remedies that he had succeeded in alleviating the acute pains of his patient; and this success had very naturally inspired the latter with a certain degree of confidence in the opinions from which the remedies had been educed. The Doctor, however, like all enthusiasts, had struggled hard to make a thorough convert of his pupil, and finally so far gained his point as to induce the sufferer to submit to numerous experiments. – By a frequent repetition of these, a result had arisen, which of late days has become so common as to attract little or no attention, but which, at the period of which I write, had very rarely been known in America. I mean to say, that between Doctor Templeton and Bedloe there had grown up, little by little, a very distinct and strongly marked *rapport*, or magnetic relation. I am not prepared to assert, however, that this *rapport* extended beyond the limits of the simple sleep-producing power; but this power itself had attained great intensity. At the first attempt to induce the magnetic somnolency, the mesmerist entirely failed. In the fifth or sixth he succeeded very partially, and after long continued effort. Only at the twelfth was the triumph complete. After this the will of the patient succumbed rapidly to that of the physician, so that, when I first became acquainted with the two, sleep was brought about almost instantaneously, by the mere volition of the operator, even when the invalid was unaware of his presence. It is only now, in the year 1845, when similar miracles are witnessed daily by thousands, that I dare venture to record this apparent impossibility as a matter of serious fact.

The temperament of Bedloe was, in the highest degree, sensitive, excitable, enthusiastic. His imagination was singularly vigorous and creative; and no doubt it derived additional force from the habitual use of morphine, which he swallowed in great quantity,[4] and without which he would have found it impossible to exist. It was his practice to take a very large dose of it immediately after breakfast, each morning – or rather immediately after a cup of strong coffee, for he ate nothing in the forenoon – and then set forth alone, or attended only by a dog, upon a long ramble among the chain of wild and dreary hills that lie westward and southward of Charlottesville, and are there dignified by the title of the Ragged Mountains.

Upon a dim, warm, misty day, towards the close of November, and during the strange *interregnum* of the seasons which in America is termed the Indian Summer, Mr Bedloe departed, as usual, for the hills. The day passed, and still he did not return.

About eight o'clock at night, having become seriously alarmed at his protracted absence, we were about setting out in search of him, when he unexpectedly made his appearance, in health no worse than usual, and in rather more than ordinary spirits. The account which he gave of his expedition, and of the events which had detained him, was a singular one indeed.

'You will remember,' said he, 'that it was about nine in the morning when I left Charlottesville. I bent my steps immediately to the mountains, and, about ten, entered a gorge which was entirely new to me. I followed the windings of this pass with much interest. – The scenery which presented itself on all sides, although scarcely entitled to be called grand, had about it an indescribable, and to me, a delicious aspect of dreary desolation. The solitude seemed absolutely virgin. I could not help believing that the green sods and the gray rocks upon which I trod, had been trodden never before by the foot of a human being. So entirely secluded, and in fact inaccessible, except through a series of accidents, is the entrance of the ravine, that it is by no means impossible that I was indeed the first adventurer – the very first and sole adventurer who had ever penetrated its recesses.

'The thick and peculiar mist, or smoke, which distinguishes the Indian Summer, and which now hung heavily over all objects, served, no doubt, to deepen the vague impressions which these objects created. So dense was this pleasant fog, that I could at no time see more than a dozen yards of the path before me. This path was excessively sinuous, and as the sun could not be seen, I soon lost all idea of the direction in which I journeyed. In the meantime the morphine had its customary effect – that of enduing all the external world with an intensity of interest. In the quivering of a leaf – in the hue of a blade of grass – in the shape of a trefoil – in the humming of a bee – in the gleaming of a dew-drop – in the breathing of the wind – in the faint odors that came from the forest – there came a whole universe of suggestion – a gay and motly train of rhapsodical and immethodical thought.

'Busied in this, I walked on for several hours, during which the mist deepened around me to so great an extent, that at length I was reduced to an absolute groping of the way. And now an indescribable uneasiness possessed me – a species of nervous hesitation and tremor. – I feared to tread, lest I should be precipitated into some abyss. I remembered, too, strange stories told about these Ragged Hills, and of the uncouth and fierce races of men who tenanted their groves and caverns. A thousand vague fancies oppressed and disconcerted me – fancies the more distressing because vague. Very suddenly my attention was arrested by the loud beating of a drum.

'My amazement was, of course, extreme. A drum in these hills was a thing unknown. I could not have been more surprised at the sound of the trump of the Archangel. But a new and still more astounding source of interest and perplexity arose. There came a wild rattling or jingling sound, as if of a bunch of large keys – and upon the instant a dusky-visaged and half-naked man rushed past me with a shriek. He came so close to my person that I felt his hot breath upon my face. He bore in one hand an instrument composed of an assemblage of steel rings, and shook them vigorously as he ran. Scarcely had he disappeared in the mist, before, panting after him, with open mouth and glaring eyes, there darted a huge beast. I could not be mistaken in its character. It was a hyena.

'The sight of this monster rather relieved than heightened my terrors – for I now made sure that I dreamed, and endeavored to arouse myself to waking consciousness. I stepped boldly and briskly forward. I rubbed my eyes. I called aloud. I pinched my limbs. A small spring of water presented itself to my view, and here, stooping, I bathed my hands and my head and neck. This seemed to dissipate the equivocal sensations which had hitherto annoyed me. I arose, as I thought, a new man, and proceeded steadily and complacently on my unknown way.

'At length, quite overcome by exertion, and by a certain oppressive closeness of the atmosphere, I seated myself beneath a tree. Presently there came a feeble gleam of sunshine, and the shadow of the leaves of the tree fell faintly but definitely upon the grass. At this shadow I gazed wonderingly for many minutes. Its character stupified me with astonishment. I looked upward. The tree was a palm.

'I now arose hurriedly, and in a state of fearful agitation – for the fancy that I dreamed would serve me no longer. I saw – I felt that I had perfect command of my senses – and these senses now brought to my soul a world of novel and singular sensation. The heat became all at once intolerable. A strange odor loaded the breeze. – A low continuous murmur, like that arising from a full, but gently-flowing river, came to my ears, intermingled with the peculiar hum of multitudinous human voices.

'While I listened in an extremity of astonishment which I need not attempt to describe, a strong and brief gust of wind bore off the incumbent fog as if by the wand of an enchanter.

'I found myself at the foot of a high mountain, and looking down into a vast plain, through which wound a majestic river. On the margin of this river stood an Eastern-looking city, such as we read of in the Arabian Tales, but of a character even more singular than any there described. From my position, which was far above the level of the town, I could perceive its every nook and corner, as if delineated on a map. The streets seemed innumerable, and crossed each other irregularly in all directions, but were rather long winding alleys than streets, and absolutely swarmed with inhabitants. The houses were wildly picturesque. On every hand was a wilderness of balconies, of verandahs, of minarets, of shrines, and fantastically carved oriels. Bazaars abounded; and in these were displayed rich wares in infinite variety and profusion – silks, muslins, the most dazzling cutlery, the most magnificent jewels and gems. Besides these things, were seen, on all sides, banners and palanquins, litters with stately dames close veiled, elephants gorgeously caparisoned, idols grotesquely hewn, drums, banners and gongs, spears, silver and gilded maces. And amid the crowd, and the clamor, and the general intricacy and confusion – amid the million of black and yellow men, turbaned and robed, and of flowing beard, there roamed a countless multitude of holy filleted bulls, while vast legions of the filthy but sacred ape clambered, chattering and shrieking, about the cornices of the mosques, or clung to the minarets and oriels. From the swarming streets to the banks of the river, there descended innumerable flights of steps leading to bathing places, while the river itself seemed to force a passage with difficulty through the vast fleets of deeply-burthened ships that far and wide encumbered its surface. Beyond the limits of the city arose, in frequent majestic groups, the palm and the cocoa, with other gigantic and weird trees of vast age; and here and there might be seen a field of rice, the thatched hut of a peasant, a tank, a stray temple, a gypsy camp, or a solitary graceful maiden taking her way, with a pitcher upon her head, to the banks of the magnificent river.

'You will say now, of course, that I dreamed; but not so. What I saw – what I heard – what I felt – what I thought – had about it nothing of the unmistakeable idiosyncrasy of the dream. All was rigorously self-consistent. At first, doubting that I was really awake, I entered into a series of tests, which soon convinced me that I really was. Now, when one dreams, and, in the dream, suspects that he dreams, the suspicion *never fails to confirm itself*, and the sleeper is almost immediately aroused. – Thus Novalis errs not in saying that "we are near waking when we dream that we dream".[5] Had the vision occurred to me as I describe it, without my suspecting it as a dream, then a dream it might absolutely have been, but, occurring as it did, and suspected and tested as it was, I am forced to class it among other phenomena.'

'In this I am not sure that you are wrong,' observed Dr Templeton, 'but proceed. You arose and descended into the city.'

'I arose,' continued Bedloe, regarding the Doctor with an air of profound astonishment, 'I arose, as you say, and descended into the city. On my way, I fell in with an immense populace, crowding, through every avenue, all in the same direction, and exhibiting in every action the wildest excitement. Very suddenly, and by some inconceivable impulse, I became intensely imbued with personal interest in what was going on. I seemed to feel that I had an important part to play, without exactly understanding what it was. Against the crowd which environed me, however, I experienced a deep sentiment of animosity. I shrank from amid them, and, swiftly, by a circuitous path, reached and entered the city. Here all was the wildest tumult and contention. A small party of men, clad in garments half-Indian, half-European, and officered by gentlemen in a uniform partly British, were engaged, at great odds, with the swarming rabble of the alleys. I joined the weaker party, arming myself with the weapons of a fallen officer, and fighting I knew not whom with the nervous ferocity of despair. We were soon overpowered by numbers, and driven to seek refuge in a species of kiosk. Here we barricaded ourselves, and, for the present, were secure. From a loop-hole near the summit of the kiosk, I perceived a vast crowd, in furious agitation, surrounding and assaulting a gay palace that overhung the river. Presently, from an upper window of this palace, there descended an effeminate-looking person, by means of a string made of the turbans of his attendants. A boat was at hand, in which he escaped to the opposite bank of the river.

'And now a new object took possession of my soul. I spoke a few hurried but energetic words to my companions, and, having succeeded in gaining over a few of them to my purpose, made a frantic sally from the kiosk. We rushed amid the crowd that surrounded it. They retreated, at first, before us. They rallied, fought madly, and retreated again. In the mean time we were borne far from the kiosk, and became bewildered and entangled among the narrow streets of tall overhanging houses, into the recesses of which the sun had never been able to shine. The rabble pressed impetuously upon us, harassing us with their spears, and overwhelming us with flights of arrows. These latter were very remarkable, and resembled in some respects the writhing creese of the Malay.[6] They were made to imitate the body of a creeping serpent, and were long and black, with a poisoned barb. One of them struck me upon the right temple.[7] I reeled and fell. An instantaneous and dreadful sickness seized me. I struggled – I gasped – I died.'

'You will hardly persist *now*,' said I, smiling, 'that the whole of your adventure was not a dream. You are not prepared to maintain that you are dead?'

When I said these words, I of course expected some lively sally from Bedloe in reply; but, to my astonishment, he hesitated, trembled, became fearfully pallid, and remained silent. I looked towards Templeton. He sat erect and rigid in his chair – his teeth chattered, and his eyes were starting from their sockets. 'Proceed !' he at length said hoarsely to Bedloe.

'For many minutes,' continued the latter, 'my sole sentiment – my sole feeling – was that of darkness and nonentity, with the consciousness of death. At length, there seemed to pass a violent and sudden shock through my soul, as if of electricity.[8] With it came the sense of elasticity and of light. This latter I felt – not saw. In an instant I seemed to rise from the ground. But I had no bodily, no visible, audible, or palpable presence. The crowd had departed. The tumult had ceased. The city was in comparative repose. Beneath me lay my corpse, with the arrow in my temple, the whole head greatly swollen and disfigured. But all these things I felt – not saw. I took interest in nothing. Even the corpse seemed a matter in which I had no concern. Volition I had none, but appeared to be impelled into motion, and flitted buoyantly out of the city, retracing the circuitous path by which I had entered it. When I had attained that point of the ravine in the mountains, at which I had encountered the hyena, I again experienced a shock as of a galvanic battery; the sense of weight, of volition, of substance, returned. I became my original self, and bent my steps eagerly homewards – but the past had not lost the vividness of the real – and not now, even for an instant, can I compel my understanding to regard it as a dream.'

'Nor was it,' said Templeton, with an air of deep solemnity, 'yet it would be difficult to say how otherwise it should be termed. Let us suppose only, that the soul of the man of to-day is upon the verge of some stupendous psychal discoveries. Let us content ourselves with this supposition. For the rest I have some explanation to make. Here is a water-colour drawing, which I should have shown you before, but which an unaccountable sentiment of horror has hitherto prevented me from showing.'

We looked at the picture which he presented. I saw nothing in it of an extraordinary character; but its effect upon Bedloe was prodigious. He nearly fainted as he gazed. And yet it was but a miniature portrait – a miraculously accurate one, to be sure – of his own very remarkable features. At least this was my thought as I regarded it.

'You will perceive,' said Templeton, 'the date of this picture – it is here, scarcely visible, in this corner – 1780. In this year was the portrait taken. It is the likeness of a dead friend – a Mr Oldeb [9] – to whom I became much attached at Calcutta, during the administration of Warren Hastings. I was then only twenty years old. – When I first saw you, Mr Bedloe, at Saratoga, it was the miraculous similarity which existed between yourself and the painting, which induced me to accost you, to seek your friendship, and to bring about those arrangements which resulted in my becoming your constant companion. In accomplishing this point, I was urged partly, and perhaps principally, by a regretful memory of the deceased, but also, in part, by an uneasy, and not altogether horrorless curiosity respecting yourself.

'In your detail of the vision which presented itself to you amid the hills, you have described, with the minutest accuracy, the Indian city of Benares, upon the Holy River. The riots, the combats, the massacre, were the actual events of the insurrection of Cheyte Sing, which took place in 1780,[10] when Hastings was put in imminent peril of his life. The man escaping by the string of turbans, was Cheyte Sing himself. The party in the kiosk were sepoys and British officers, headed by Hastings. Of this party I was one, and did all I could to prevent the rash and fatal sally of the officer who fell, in the crowded alleys, by the poisoned arrow of a Bengalee. That officer was my dearest friend. It was Oldeb. You will perceive by these manuscripts,' (here the speaker produced a note-book in which several pages appeared to have been freshly written) 'that at the very period in which you fancied these things amid the hills, I was engaged in detailing them upon paper [11] here at home.'

In about a week after this conversation, the following paragraphs appeared in a Charlottesville paper.

'We have the painful duty of announcing the death of Mr AUGUSTUS BEDLO, a gentleman whose amiable manners and many virtues have long endeared him to the citizens of Charlottesville.

'Mr B., for some years past, has been subject to neuralgia, which has often threatened to terminate fatally; but this can be regarded only as the mediate cause of his decease. The proximate cause was one of especial singularity. In an excursion to the Ragged Mountains, a few days since, a slight cold and fever were contracted, attended with great determination of blood to the head. To relieve this, Dr Templeton resorted to topical bleeding. Leeches were applied to the temples. In a fearfully brief period the patient died, when it appeared that, in the jar containing the leeches, had been introduced, by accident, one of the venomous vermicular sangsues [12] which are now and then found in the neighboring ponds. This creature fastened itself upon a small artery in the right temple. Its close resemblance to the medicinal leech caused the mistake to be overlooked until too late.

'N.B. The poisonous sangsue of Charlottesville may always be distinguished from the medicinal leech by its blackness, and especially by its writhing or vermicular motions, which very nearly resemble those of a snake.'

I was speaking with the editor of the paper in question, upon the topic of this remarkable accident, when it occurred to me to ask how it happened that the name of the deceased had been given as Bedlo. [13]

'I presume,' said I, 'you have authority for this spelling, but I have always supposed the name to be written with an *e* at the end.'

'Authority? – no,' he replied. 'It is a mere typographical error. The name is Bedlo with an *e*, all the world over, and I never knew it to be spelt otherwise in my life.'

'Then,' said I mutteringly, as I turned upon my heel, 'then indeed has it come to pass that one truth is stranger than any fiction – for Bedlo, without the *e*, what is it but Oldeb conversed? And this man tells me it is a typographical error.'

The Balloon-Hoax

ASTOUNDING
NEWS!
BY EXPRESS VIA NORFOLK!
THE
ATLANTIC CROSSED
in
THREE DAYS!

Signal Triumph
of
Mr Monck Mason's
FLYING
MACHINE!!!![1]

Arrival at Sullivan's Island[2]
near Charleston, S. C.
of Mr Mason, Mr Robert
Holland, Mr Henson, Mr
Harrison Ainsworth, and
four others, in the Steer-
ing Balloon 'Victoria' –
After a passage of
Seventy-Five Hours
From Land to Land!
Full Particulars of the Voyage!*

THE great problem is at length solved! The air, as well as the earth and the ocean, has been subdued by science, and will become a common and convenient highway for mankind. *The*

---

*The subjoined *jeu d'esprit* with the preceding heading in magnificent capitals, well interspersed with notes of admiration, was originally published, as matter of fact, in the 'New York Sun', a daily newspaper, and therein fully subserved the purpose of creating indigestible aliment for the

Atlantic has been actually crossed in a Balloon! and this too without difficulty – without any great apparent danger – with
thorough control of the machine – and in the inconceivably brief
period of seventy-five hours from shore to shore ! By the energy of
an agent at Charleston, S.C.,[3] we are enabled to be the first to
furnish the public with a detailed account of this most extraordinary voyage, which was performed between Saturday, the
6th instant, at 11, A.M., and 2, P.M., on Tuesday, the 9th instant,
by Sir Everard Bringhurst; Mr Osborne, a nephew of Lord
Bentinck's; Mr Monck Mason and Mr Robert Holland, the well-
known æronauts; Mr Harrison Ainsworth, author of 'Jack Sheppard', &c.;[4] and Mr Henson, the projector of the late unsuccessful
flying machine [5] – with two seamen from Woolwich – in all,
eight persons. The particulars furnished below may be relied on
as authentic and accurate in every respect, as, with a slight exception, they are copied *verbatim* from the joint diaries of Mr Monck
Mason and Mr Harrison Ainsworth, to whose politeness our
agent is also indebted for much verbal information respecting the
balloon itself, its construction, and other matters of interest. The
only alteration in the MS. received, has been made for the purpose of throwing the hurried account of our agent, Mr Forsyth,
in a connected and intelligible form.

THE BALLOON

Two very decided failures, of late – those of Mr Henson and Sir
George Cayley – had much weakened the public interest in the
subject of aerial navigation. Mr Henson's scheme (which at first
was considered very feasible even by men of science,) was
founded upon the principle of an inclined plane, started from an
eminence by an extrinsic force, applied and continued by the
revolution of impinging vanes, in form and number resembling
the vanes of a windmill. But, in all the experiments made with

quidnuncs during the few hours intervening between a couple of the Charleston mails. The rush for the 'sole paper which had the news', was something beyond even the prodigious; and, in fact, if (as some assert) the 'Victoria' *did* not absolutely accomplish the voyage recorded, it will be difficult
to assign a reason why she *should* not have accomplished it.

models at the Adelaide Gallery, it was found that the operation of these fans not only did not propel the machine, but actually impeded its flight. The only propelling force it ever exhibited, was the mere *impetus* acquired from the descent of the inclined plane; and this *impetus* carried the machine farther when the vanes were at rest, than when they were in motion – a fact which sufficiently demonstrates their inutility; and in the absence of the propelling, which was also the *sustaining* power, the whole fabric would necessarily descend. This consideration led Sir George Cayley to think only of adapting a propeller to some machine having of itself an independent power of support – in a word, to a balloon; the idea, however, being novel, or original, with Sir George, only so far as regards the mode of its application to practice. He exhibited a model of his invention at the Polytechnic Institution. The propelling principle, or power, was here, also, applied to interrupted surfaces, or vanes, put in revolution. These vanes were four in number, but were found entirely ineffectual in moving the balloon, or in aiding its ascending power. The whole project was thus a complete failure.

It was at this juncture that Mr Monck Mason (whose voyage from Dover to Weilburg in the balloon, 'Nassau',[6] occasioned so much excitement in 1837,) conceived the idea of employing the principle of the Archimedean screw for the purpose of propulsion through the air – rightly attributing the failure of Mr Henson's scheme, and of Sir George Cayley's,[7] to the interruption of surface in the independent vanes. He made the first public experiment at Willis's Rooms, but afterwards removed his model to the Adelaide Gallery.

Like Sir George Cayley's balloon, his own was an ellipsoid.[8] Its length was thirteen feet six inches – height, six feet eight inches. It contained about three hundred and twenty cubic feet of gas, which, if pure hydrogen, would support twenty-one pounds upon its first inflation, before the gas has time to deteriorate or escape. The weight of the whole machine and apparatus was seventeen pounds – leaving about four pounds to spare. Beneath the centre of the balloon, was a frame of light wood, about nine feet long, and rigged on to the balloon itself with a network in the customary manner. From this framework was suspended a wicker basket or car.

The screw consists of an axis of hollow brass tube, eighteen inches in length, through which, upon a semi-spiral inclined at fifteen degrees, pass a series of steel wire radii, two feet long, and thus projecting a foot on either side. These radii are connected at the outer extremities by two bands of flattened wire – the whole in this manner forming the framework of the screw, which is completed by a covering of oiled silk cut into gores,[9] and tightened so as to present a tolerably uniform surface. At each end of its axis this screw is supported by pillars of hollow brass tube descending from the hoop. In the lower ends of these tubes are holes in which the pivots of the axis revolve. From the end of the axis which is next the car, proceeds a shaft of steel, connecting the screw with the pinion of a piece of spring machinery fixed in the car. By the operation of this spring, the screw is made to revolve with great rapidity, communicating a progressive motion to the whole. By means of the rudder, the machine was readily turned in any direction. The spring was of great power, compared with its dimensions, being capable of raising forty-five pounds upon a barrel of four inches diameter, after the first turn, and gradually increasing as it was wound up. It weighed, altogether, eight pounds six ounces. The rudder was a light frame of cane covered with silk, shaped somewhat like a battledoor,[10] and was about three feet long, and at the widest, one foot. Its weight was about two ounces. It could be turned *flat*, and directed upwards or downwards, as well as to the right or left; and thus enabled the æronaut to transfer the resistance of the air which in an inclined position it must generate in its passage, to any side upon which he might desire to act; thus determining the balloon in the opposite direction.

This model (which, through want of time, we have necessarily described in an imperfect manner,) was put in action at the Adelaide Gallery, where it accomplished a velocity of five miles per hour; although, strange to say, it excited very little interest in comparison with the previous complex machine of Mr Henson – so resolute is the world to despise anything which carries with it an air of simplicity. To accomplish the great desideratum of ærial navigation, it was very generally supposed that some exceedingly complicated application must be made of some unusually profound principle in dynamics.

So well satisfied, however, was Mr Mason of the ultimate success of his invention, that he determined to construct immediately, if possible, a balloon of sufficient capacity to test the question by a voyage of some extent – the original design being to cross the British Channel, as before, in the Nassau balloon. To carry out his views, he solicited and obtained the patronage of Sir Everard Bringhurst and Mr Osborne, two gentlemen well known for scientific acquirement, and especially for the interest they have exhibited in the progress of ærostation. The project, at the desire of Mr Osborne, was kept a profound secret from the public – the only persons entrusted with the design being those actually engaged in the construction of the machine, which was built (under the superintendence of Mr Mason, Mr Holland, Sir Everard Bringhurst, and Mr Osborne,) at the seat of the latter gentleman near Penstruthal, in Wales. Mr Henson, accompanied by his friend Mr Ainsworth, was admitted to a private view of the balloon, on Saturday last – when the two gentlemen made final arrangements to be included in the adventure. We are not informed for what reason the two seamen were also included in the party – but, in the course of a day or two, we shall put our readers in possession of the minutest particulars respecting this extraordinary voyage.

The balloon is composed of silk, varnished with the liquid gum caoutchouc. It is of vast dimensions, containing more than 40000 cubic feet of gas; but as coal gas was employed in place of the more expensive and inconvenient hydrogen, the supporting power of the machine, when fully inflated, and immediately after inflation, is not more than about 2500 pounds. The coal gas is not only much less costly, but is easily procured and managed.

For its introduction into common use for purposes of ærostation, we are indebted to Mr Charles Green.[11] Up to his discovery, the process of inflation was not only exceedingly expensive, but uncertain. Two, and even three days, have frequently been wasted in futile attempts to procure a sufficiency of hydrogen to fill a balloon, from which it had great tendency to escape owing to its extreme subtlety, and its affinity for the surrounding atmosphere. In a balloon sufficiently perfect to retain its contents of coal-gas unaltered, in quality or amount, for six months, an equal quantity of hydrogen could not be maintained in equal purity for six weeks.

The supporting power being estimated at 2500 pounds, and the united weights of the party amounting only to about 1200, there was left a surplus of 1300, of which again 1200 was exhausted by ballast, arranged in bags of different sizes, with their respective weights marked upon them – by cordage, barometers, telescopes, barrels containing provision for a fortnight, water-casks, cloaks, carpet-bags, and various other indispensable matters, including a coffee-warmer, contrived for warming coffee by means of slacklime,[12] so as to dispense altogether with fire, if it should be judged prudent to do so. All these articles, with the exception of the ballast, and a few trifles, were suspended from the hoop over head. The car is much smaller and lighter, in proportion, than the one appended to the model. It is formed of a light wicker, and is wonderfully strong, for so frail looking a machine. Its rim is about four feet deep. The rudder is also very much larger, in proportion, than that of the model; and the screw is considerably smaller. The balloon is furnished besides, with a grapnel, and a guide-rope; which latter is of the most indispensable importance. A few words, in explanation, will here be necessary for such of our readers as are not conversant with the details of aerostation.

As soon as the balloon quits the earth, it is subjected to the influence of many circumstances tending to create a difference in its weight; augmenting or diminishing its ascending power. For example, there may be a deposition of dew upon the silk, to the extent, even, of several hundred pounds; ballast has then to be thrown out, or the machine may descend. This ballast being discarded, and a clear sunshine evaporating the dew, and at the same time expanding the gas in the silk, the whole will again rapidly ascend. To check this ascent, the only resource is, (or rather *was*, until Mr Green's invention of the guide-rope,)[13] the permission of the escape of gas from the valve; but, in the loss of gas, is a proportionate general loss of ascending power; so that, in a comparatively brief period, the best constructed balloon must necessarily exhaust all its resources, and come to the earth. This was the great obstacle to voyages of length.

The guide-rope remedies the difficulty in the simplest manner conceivable. It is merely a very long rope which is suffered to trail from the car, and the effect of which is to prevent the balloon from changing its level in any material degree. If, for example, there should be a deposition of moisture upon the silk, and the machine begins to descend in consequence, there will be no necessity for discharging ballast to remedy the increase of weight, for it is remedied, or counteracted, in an exactly just proportion, by the deposit on the ground of just so much of the end of the rope as is necessary. If, on the other hand, any circumstances should cause undue levity, and consequent ascent, this levity is immediately counteracted by the additional weight of rope upraised from the earth. Thus, the balloon can neither ascend or descend, except within very narrow limits, and its resources, either in gas or ballast, remain comparatively unimpaired. When passing over an expanse of water, it becomes necessary to employ small kegs of copper or wood, filled with liquid ballast of a lighter nature than water. These float, and serve all the purposes of a mere rope on land. Another most important office of the guide-rope, is to point out the *direction* of the balloon. The rope *drags*, either on land or sea, while the balloon is free; the latter, consequently, is always in advance, when any progress whatever is made: a comparison, therefore, by means of the compass, of the relative positions of the two objects, will always indicate the *course*. In the same way, the angle formed by the rope with the vertical axis of the machine, indicates the *velocity*. When there is *no* angle – in other words, when the rope hangs perpendicularly, the whole apparatus is stationary; but the larger the angle, that is to say, the farther the balloon precedes the end of the rope, the greater the velocity; and the converse.

As the original design was to cross the British Channel, and alight as near Paris as possible, the voyagers had taken the precaution to prepare themselves with passports directed to all parts of the Continent, specifying the nature of the expedition, as in the case of the Nassau voyage, and entitling the adventurers to exemption from the usual formalities of office : unexpected events, however, rendered these passports superfluous.

The inflation was commenced very quietly at daybreak, on Saturday morning, the 6th instant, in the Court-Yard of Wheal-Vor House, Mr Osborne's seat, about a mile from Penstruthal,[14] in North Wales; and at 7 minutes past 11, every thing being ready for departure, the balloon was set free, rising gently but steadily, in a direction nearly South; no use being made, for the first half hour, of either the screw or the rudder. We proceed now with the journal, as transcribed by Mr Forsyth from the joint MSS. of Mr Monck Mason, and Mr Ainsworth. The body of the journal, as given, is in the hand-writing of Mr Mason, and a P. S. is appended, each day, by Mr Ainsworth, who has in preparation, and will shortly give the public a more minute, and no doubt, a thrillingly interesting account of the voyage.

THE JOURNAL

Saturday, April the 6th. – Every preparation likely to embarrass us, having been made over night, we commenced the inflation this morning at daybreak; but owing to a thick fog, which encumbered the folds of the silk and rendered it unmanageable, we did not get through before nearly eleven o'clock. Cut loose, then, in high spirits, and rose gently but steadily, with a light breeze at North, which bore us in the direction of the British Channel. Found the ascending force greater than we had expected; and as we arose higher and so got clear of the cliffs, and more in the sun's rays, our ascent became very rapid. I did not wish, however, to lose gas at so early a period of the adventure, and so concluded to ascend for the present. We soon ran out our guide-rope; but even when we had raised it clear of the earth, we still went up very rapidly. The balloon was unusually steady, and looked beautifully. In about ten minutes after starting, the barometer indicated an altitude of 15,000 feet. The weather was remarkably fine, and the view of the subjacent country – a most romantic one when seen from any point, – was now especially sublime. The numerous deep gorges presented the appearance of lakes, on account of the dense vapors with which they were filled, and the pinnacles and crags to the South East, piled in inextricable confusion, resembled nothing so much as the giant cities of eastern fable. We were rapidly approaching the mountains in the South; but our elevation was more than sufficient to enable us to pass them in safety. In a few minutes we soared over them in fine style; and Mr Ainsworth, with the seamen, were surprised at their apparent want of altitude when viewed from the car, the tendency of great elevation in a balloon being to reduce inequalities of the surface below, to nearly a dead level. At half-past eleven still proceeding nearly South, we obtained our first view of the Bristol Channel; and, in fifteen minutes afterwards, the line of breakers on the coast appeared immediately beneath us, and we were fairly out at sea. We now resolved to let off enough gas [15] to bring our guide-rope, with the buoys affixed, into the water. This was immediately done, and we commenced a gradual descent. In about twenty minutes our first buoy dipped, and at the touch of the second soon afterwards, we remained stationary as to elevation. We were all now anxious to test the efficiency of the rudder and screw, and we put them both into requisition forthwith, for the purpose of altering our direction more to the eastward, and in a line for Paris. By means of the rudder we instantly effected the necessary change of direction, and our course was brought nearly at right angles to that of the wind; when we set in motion the spring of the screw, and were rejoiced to find it propel us readily as desired. Upon this we gave nine hearty cheers, and dropped in the sea a bottle, enclosing a slip of parchment with a brief account of the principle of the invention. Hardly, however, had we done with our rejoicings, when an unforeseen accident occurred which discouraged us in no little degree. The steel rod connecting the spring with the propeller was suddenly jerked out of place, at the car end, (by a swaying of the car through some movement of one of the two seamen we had taken up,) and in an instant hung dangling out of reach, from the pivot of the axis of the screw. While we were endeavoring to regain it, our attention being completely absorbed, we became involved in a strong current of wind from the East,[16] which bore us, with rapidly increasing force, towards the

Atlantic. We soon found ourselves driving out to sea at the rate of not less, certainly, than fifty or sixty miles an hour, so that we came up with Cape Clear, at some forty miles to our North, before we had secured the rod, and had time to think what we were about. It was now that Mr Ainsworth made an extraordinary, but to my fancy, a by no means unreasonable or chimerical proposition, in which he was instantly seconded by Mr Holland – viz. : that we should take advantage of the strong gale which bore us on, and in place of beating back to Paris, make an attempt to reach the coast of North America. After slight reflection I gave a willing assent to this bold proposition, which (strange to say) met with objection from the two seamen only. As the stronger party, however, we overruled their fears, and kept resolutely upon our course. We steered due West; but as the trailing of the buoys materially impeded our progress, and we had the balloon abundantly at command, either for ascent or descent, we first threw out fifty pounds of ballast, and then wound up (by means of a windlass) so much of a rope as brought it quite clear of the sea. We perceived the effect of this manœuvre immediately, in a vastly increased rate of progress; and, as the gale freshened, we flew with a velocity nearly inconceivable; the guide-rope flying out behind the car, like a streamer from a vessel. It is needless to say that a very short time sufficed us to lose sight of the coast. We passed over innumerable vessels of all kinds, a few of which were endeavoring to beat up, but the most of them lying to. We occasioned the greatest excitement on board all – an excitement greatly relished by ourselves, and especially by our two men, who, now under the influence of a dram of Geneva, seemed resolved to give all scruple, or fear, to the wind. Many of the vessels fired signal guns; and in all we were saluted with loud cheers (which we heard with surprising distinctness) and the waving of caps and handkerchiefs. We kept on in this manner throughout the day, with no material incident, and, as the shades of night closed around us, we made a rough estimate of the distance traversed. It could not have been less than five hundred miles, and was probably much more. The propeller was kept in constant operation, and, no doubt, aided our progress materially. As the sun went down, the gale freshened into an absolute hurricane, and the ocean beneath was clearly visible on account of its phosphorescence. The wind was from the East all night, and gave us the brightest omen of success. We suffered no little from cold, and the dampness of the atmosphere was most unpleasant; but the ample space in the car enabled us to lie down, and by means of cloaks and a few blankets, we did sufficiently well.

P.S. (by Mr Ainsworth). The last nine hours have been unquestionably the most exciting of my life. I can conceive nothing more sublimating than the strange peril and novelty of an adventure such as this. May God grant that we succeed! I ask not success for mere safety to my insignificant person, but for the sake of human knowledge and – for the vastness of the triumph. And yet the feat is only so evidently feasible that the sole wonder is why men have scrupled to attempt it before. One single gale such as now befriends us – let such a tempest whirl forward a balloon for four or five days (these gales often last longer) and the voyager will be easily borne, in that period, from coast to coast. In view of such a gale the broad Atlantic becomes a mere lake. I am more struck, just now, with the supreme silence which reigns in the sea beneath us, notwithstanding its agitation, than with any other phenomenon presenting itself. The waters give up no voice to the heavens. The immense flaming ocean writhes and is tortured uncomplainingly. The mountainous surges suggest the idea of innumerable dumb gigantic fiends struggling in impotent agony. In a night such as is this to me, a man *lives* – lives a whole century of ordinary life – nor would I forego this rapturous delight for that of a whole century of ordinary existence.

Sunday, the seventh. [Mr Mason's MS.] This morning the gale, by 10, had subsided to an eight or nine knot breeze, (for a vessel at sea,) and bears us, perhaps, thirty miles per hour, or more. It has veered however, very considerably to the north; and now, at sundown, we are holding our course due west, principally by the screw and rudder, which answer their purposes to admiration. I regard the project as thoroughly successful, and the easy navigation of the air in any direction (not exactly in the teeth of a gale) as no longer problematical. We could not have made head against the strong wind of yesterday; but, by ascending, we might have got out of its influence, if requisite. Against a pretty stiff breeze, I feel convinced, we can make our way with the propeller. At noon, today, ascended to an elevation of nearly 25,000 feet, by discharging ballast. Did this to search for a more direct current, but found none so favorable as the one we are now in. We have an abundance of gas to take us across this small pond, even should the voyage last three weeks. I have not the slightest fear for the result. The difficulty has been strangely exaggerated and misapprehended. I can choose my current, and should I find *all* currents against me, I can make very tolerable headway with the propeller. We have had no incidents worth recording. The night promises fair.

P.S. [By Mr Ainsworth.] I have little to record, except the fact (to me quite a surprising one) that, at an elevation equal to that of Cotopaxi,[17] I experienced neither very intense cold, nor headache, nor difficulty of breathing; neither, I find, did Mr Mason, nor Mr Holland, nor Sir Everard. Mr Osborne complained of constriction of the chest – but this soon wore off. We have flown at a great rate during the day, and we must be more than half way across the Atlantic. We have passed over some twenty or thirty vessels of various kinds, and all seem to be delightfully astonished. Crossing the ocean in a balloon is not so difficult a feat after all. *Omne ignotum pro magnifico. Mem:* at 25,000 feet elevation the sky appears nearly black, and the stars are distinctly visible; while the sea does not seem convex (as one might suppose) but absolutely and most unequivocally *concave.**[18]

*Note. – Mr Ainsworth has not attempted to account for this phenomena, which, however, is quite susceptible of explanation. A line dropped from an elevation of 25,000 feet, perpendicularly to the surface of the earth (or sea), would form the perpendicular of a right-angled triangle, of which the base would extend from the right angle to the horizon, and the hypothenuse from the horizon to the balloon. But the 25,000 feet of altitude is little or nothing, in comparison with the extent of the prospect. In other words, the base and hypothenuse of the supposed triangle would be so long when compared with the perpendicular that the two former may be regarded as nearly parallel. In this manner the horizon of the æronaut would appear to be *on a level* with the car. But, as the point immediately beneath him seems, and is, at a great distance below him, it seems, of course, also, at a great distance below the horizon. Hence the impression of *concavity*;

Monday, the 8th. [Mr Mason's MS.] This morning we had again some little trouble with the rod of the propeller, which must be entirely remodelled, for fear of serious accident – I mean the steel rod not the vanes. The latter could not be improved. The wind has been blowing steadily and strongly from the north-east all day; and so far fortune seems bent upon favoring us. Just before day, we were all somewhat alarmed at some odd noises and concussions in the balloon, accompanied with the apparent rapid subsidence of the whole machine. These phenomena were occasioned by the expansion of the gas, through increase of heat in the atmosphere, and the consequent disruption of the minute particles of ice with which the network had become encrusted during the night. Threw down several bottles to the vessels below. Saw one of them picked up by a large ship – seemingly one of the New York line packets. Endeavored to make out her name, but could not be sure of it. Mr Osborne's telescope made it out something like 'Atalanta'. It is now 12, at night, and we are still going nearly west, at a rapid pace. The sea is peculiarly phosphorescent.

P.S. [By Mr Ainsworth.] It is now 2, A. M., and nearly calm, as well as I can judge – but it is very difficult to determine this point, since we move *with* the air so completely. I have not slept since quitting Wheal-Vor, but can stand it no longer, and must take a nap. We cannot be far from the American coast.

Tuesday, the 9th. [Mr Ainsworth's MS.] *One, P. M. We are in full view of the low coast of South Carolina.* The great problem is accomplished. We have crossed the Atlantic – fairly and *easily* crossed it in a balloon! God be praised! Who shall say that anything is impossible hereafter?

*

The Journal here ceases. Some particulars of the descent were communicated, however, by Mr Ainsworth to Mr Forsyth. It was nearly dead calm when the voyagers first came in view of the

and this impression must remain, until the elevation shall bear so great a proportion to the extent of prospect, that the apparent parallelism of the base and hypothenuse disappears – when the earth's real convexity must become apparent.

coast, which was immediately recognized by both the seamen, and by Mr Osborne. The latter gentleman having acquaintances at Fort Moultrie, it was immediately resolved to descend in its vicinity. The balloon was brought over the beach (the tide being out and the sand hard, smooth, and admirably adapted for a descent,) and the grapnel let go, which took firm hold at once. The inhabitants of the island, and of the fort, thronged out, of course, to see the balloon; but it was with the greatest difficulty that any one could be made to credit the actual voyage – *the crossing of the Atlantic*. The grapnel caught at 2, P. M., precisely,[19] and thus the whole voyage was completed in seventy-five hours; or rather less, counting from shore to shore. No serious accident occurred. No real danger was at any time apprehended. The balloon was exhausted and secured without trouble; and when the MS. from which this narrative is compiled was despatched from Charleston, the party were still at Fort Moultrie. Their farther intentions were not ascertained; but we can safely promise our readers some additional information either on Monday or in the course of the next day, at farthest.

This is unquestionably the most stupendous, the most interesting, and the most important undertaking, ever accomplished or even attempted by man. What magnificent events may ensue, it would be useless now to think of determining.

Mesmeric Revelation

WHATEVER doubt may still envelop the *rationale* of mesmerism, its startling *facts* [1] are now almost universally admitted. Of these latter, those who doubt, are your mere doubters by profession – an unprofitable and disreputable tribe. There can be no more absolute waste of time than the attempt to *prove*, at the present day, that man, by mere exercise of will, can so impress his fellow, as to cast him into an abnormal condition, of which the phenomena resemble very closely those of *death*, or at least resemble them more nearly than they do the phenomena of any other normal condition within our cognizance; that, while in this state, the person so impressed employs only with effort, and then feebly, the external organs of sense, yet perceives, with keenly refined perception, and through channels supposed unknown, matters beyond the scope of the physical organs; that, moreover, his intellectual faculties are wonderfully exalted and invigorated; that his sympathies with the person so impressing him are profound; and, finally, that his susceptibility to the impression increases with its frequency, while, in the same proportion, the peculiar phenomena elicited are more extended and more *pronounced*.

I say that these – which are the laws of mesmerism in its general features – it would be supererogation to demonstrate; nor shall I inflict upon my readers so needless a demonstration today. My purpose at present is a very different one indeed. I am impelled, even in the teeth of a world of prejudice, to detail without comment the very remarkable substance of a colloquy, occurring between a sleep-waker and myself. [2]

I had been long in the habit of mesmerizing the person in question, (Mr Vankirk,) and the usual acute susceptibility and exaltation of the mesmeric perception had supervened. For many months he had been laboring under confirmed phthisis, the more distressing effects of which had been relieved by my manipulations; and on the night of Wednesday, the fifteenth instant, I was summoned to his bedside.

The invalid was suffering with acute pain in the region of the heart, and breathed with great difficulty, having all the ordinary symptoms of asthma. In spasms such as these he had usually found relief from the application of mustard to the nervous centres, but to-night this had been attempted in vain.

As I entered his room he greeted me with a cheerful smile, and although evidently in much bodily pain, appeared to be, mentally, quite at ease.

'I sent for you tonight,' he said, 'not so much to administer to my bodily ailment, as to satisfy me concerning certain psychal impressions which, of late, have occasioned me much anxiety and surprise. I need not tell you how sceptical I have hitherto been on the topic of the soul's immortality. I cannot deny that there has always existed, as if in that very soul which I have been denying, a vague half-sentiment of its own existence. But this half-sentiment at no time amounted to conviction. With it my reason had nothing to do. All attempts at logical inquiry resulted, indeed, in leaving me more sceptical than before. I had been advised to study Cousin.[3] I studied him in his own works as well as in those of his European and American echoes. The "Charles Elwood" of Mr Brownson,[4] for example, was placed in my hands. I read it with profound attention. Throughout I found it logical, but the portions which were not *merely* logical were unhappily the initial arguments of the disbelieving hero of the book. In his summing up it seemed evident to me that the reasoner had not even succeeded in convincing himself. His end had plainly forgotten his beginning, like the government of Trinculo.[5] In short, I was not long in perceiving that if man is to be intellectually convinced of his own immortality, he will never be so convinced by the mere abstractions which have been so long the fashion of the moralists of England, of France, and of Germany. Abstractions may amuse and exercise, but take no hold on the mind. Here upon earth, at least, philosophy, I am persuaded, will always in vain call upon us to look upon qualities as things. The will may assent – the soul – the intellect, never.

'I repeat, then, that I only half felt, and never intellectually believed. But latterly there has been a certain deepening of the feeling, until it has come so nearly to resemble the acquiescence of reason, that I find it difficult to distinguish between the two. I am enabled, too, plainly to trace this effect to the mesmeric influence. I cannot better explain my meaning than by the hypothesis that the mesmeric exaltation enables me to perceive a train of ratiocination which, in my abnormal existence, convinces, but which, in full accordance with the mesmeric phenomena, does not extend, except through its *effect*, into my normal condition. In sleep-waking, the reasoning and its conclusion – the cause and its effect – are present together. In my natural state, the cause vanishing, the effect only, and perhaps only partially, remains.

'These considerations have led me to think that some good results might ensue from a series of well-directed questions propounded to me while mesmerized. You have often observed the profound self-cognizance evinced by the sleep-waker – the extensive knowledge he displays upon all points relating to the mesmeric condition itself; and from this self-cognizance may be deduced hints for the proper conduct of a catechism.'

I consented of course to make this experiment. A few passes threw Mr Vankirk into the mesmeric sleep. His breathing became immediately more easy, and he seemed to suffer no physical uneasiness. The following conversation then ensued : – V. in the dialogue representing the patient, and P. myself.

P. Are you asleep?

V. Yes – no; I would rather sleep more soundly.

P. [*After a few more passes.*] Do you sleep now?

V. Yes.

P. How do you think your present illness will result?

V. [*After a long hesitation and speaking as if with effort.*] I must die.

P. Does the idea of death afflict you?

V. [*Very quickly.*] No – no !

P. Are you pleased with the prospect?

V. If I were awake I should like to die, but now it is no matter. The mesmeric condition is so near death as to content me.

P. I wish you would explain yourself, Mr Vankirk.

V. I am willing to do so, but it requires more effort than I feel able to make. You do not question me properly.

P. What then shall I ask?

V. You must begin at the beginning.

P. The beginning! but where is the beginning?

V. You know that the beginning is GOD. [*This was said in a low, fluctuating tone, and with every sign of the most profound veneration.*]

P. What then is God?

V. [*Hesitating for many minutes.*] I cannot tell.

P. Is not God spirit?

V. While I was awake I knew what you meant by 'spirit', but now it seems only a word – such for instance as truth, beauty – a quality, I mean.

P. Is not God immaterial?

V. There is no immateriality – it is a mere word. That which is not matter, is not at all – unless qualities are things.

P. Is God, then, material?

V. No. [*This reply startled me very much.*]

P. What then is he?

V. [*After a long pause, and mutteringly.*] I see – but it is a thing difficult to tell. [*Another long pause.*] He is not spirit, for he exists. Nor is he matter, *as you understand it*. But there are *gradations* of matter of which man knows nothing; the grosser impelling the finer, the finer pervading the grosser. The atmosphere, for example, impels the electric principle, while the electric principle permeates the atmosphere. These gradations of matter increase in rarity or fineness, until we arrive at a matter *unparticled* – without particles – indivisible – *one*; and here the law of impulsion and permeation is modified. The ultimate, or unparticled matter, not only permeates all things but impels all things – and thus *is* all things within itself. This matter is God. What men attempt to embody in the word 'thought', is this matter in motion.

P. The metaphysicians maintain that all action is reducible to motion and thinking, and that the latter is the origin of the former.

V. Yes; and I now see the confusion of idea. Motion is the action of *mind* – not of *thinking*. The unparticled matter, or God, in quiescence, is (as nearly as we can conceive it) what men call mind. And the power of self-movement (equivalent in effect to human volition) is, in the unparticled matter, the result of its unity and omniprevalence; *how* I know not, and now clearly see that I shall never know. But the unparticled matter, set in motion by a law, or quality, existing within itself, is thinking.

P. Can you give me no more precise idea of what you term the unparticled matter?

V. The matters of which man is cognizant, escape the senses in gradation. We have, for example, a metal, a piece of wood, a drop of water, the atmosphere, a gas, caloric, electricity, the luminiferous ether. Now we call all these things matter, and embrace all matter in one general definition; but in spite of this, there can be no two ideas more essentially distinct than that which we attach to a metal, and that which we attach to the luminiferous ether. When we reach the latter, we feel an almost irresistible inclination to class it with spirit, or with nihility. The only consideration which restrains us is our conception of its atomic constitution; and here, even, we have to seek aid from our notion of an atom, as something possessing in infinite minuteness, solidity, palpability, weight. Destroy the idea of the atomic constitution and we should no longer be able to regard the ether as an entity, or at least as matter. For want of a better word we might term it spirit. Take, now, a step beyond the luminiferous ether – conceive a matter as much more rare than the ether, as this ether is more rare than the metal, and we arrive at once (in spite of all the school dogmas) at a unique mass – an unparticled matter. For although we may admit infinite littleness in the atoms themselves, the infinitude of littleness in the spaces between them is an absurdity. There will be a point – there will be a degree of rarity, at which, if the atoms are sufficiently numerous, the interspaces must vanish, and the mass absolutely coalesce. But the consideration of the atomic constitution being now taken away, the nature of the mass inevitably glides into what we conceive of spirit. It is clear, however, that it is as fully matter as before. The truth is, it is impossible to conceive spirit,[6] since it is impossible to imagine what is not. When we flatter ourselves that we have formed its conception, we have merely deceived our understanding by the consideration of infinitely rarified matter.

P. There seems to me an insurmountable objection[7] to the idea of absolute coalescence; – and that is the very slight resistance experienced by the heavenly bodies in their revolutions through space – a resistance now ascertained, it is true, to exist in *some* degree, but which is, nevertheless, so slight as to have been quite overlooked by the sagacity even of Newton. We know that the resistance of bodies is, chiefly, in proportion to their density. Absolute coalescence is absolute density. Where there are no interspaces, there can be no yielding. An ether, absolutely dense, would put an infinitely more effectual stop to the progress of a star than would an ether of adamant or of iron.

V. Your objection is answered with an ease which is nearly in the ratio of its apparent unanswerability. – As regards the progress of the star, it can make no difference whether the star passes through the ether *or the ether through it*. There is no astronomical error more unaccountable than that which reconciles the known retardation of the comets with the idea of their passage through an ether: for, however rare this ether be supposed, it would put a stop to all sidereal revolution in a very far briefer period than has been admitted by those astronomers who have endeavored to slur over a point which they found it impossible to comprehend. The retardation actually experienced is, on the other hand, about that which might be expected from the *friction* of the ether in the instantaneous passage through the orb. In the one case, the retarding force is momentary and complete within itself – in the other it is endlessly accumulative.

P. But in all this – in this identification of mere matter with God – is there nothing of irreverence? [*I was forced to repeat this question before the sleep-waker fully comprehended my meaning.*]

V. Can you say *why* matter should be less reverenced than mind? But you forget that the matter of which I speak is, in all respects, the very 'mind' or 'spirit' of the schools, so far as regards its high capacities, and is, moreover, the 'matter' of these schools at the same time. God, with all the powers attributed to spirit, is but the perfection of matter.

P. You assert, then, that the unparticled matter, in motion, is thought?

V. In general, this motion is the universal thought of the universal mind. This thought creates. All created things are but the thoughts of God.

P. You say, 'in general'.

V. Yes. The universal mind is God. For new individualities, *matter* is necessary.

P. But you now speak of 'mind' and 'matter' as do the metaphysicians.

V. Yes – to avoid confusion. When I say 'mind', I mean the unparticled or ultimate matter; by 'matter,' I intend all else.

P. You were saying that 'for new individualities matter is necessary'.

V. Yes; for mind, existing unincorporate, is merely God. To create individual, thinking beings, it was necessary to incarnate portions of the divine mind. Thus man is individualized. Divested of corporate investiture, he were God. Now, the particular motion of the incarnated portions of the unparticled matter is the thought of man; as the motion of the whole is that of God.

P. You say that divested of the body man will be God?

V. [*After much hesitation.*] I could not have said this; it is an absurdity.

P. [*Referring to my notes.*] You *did* say that 'divested of corporate investiture man were God'.

V. And this is true. Man thus divested *would be* God – would be unindividualized. But he can never be thus divested – at least never *will be* – else we must imagine an action of God returning upon itself – a purposeless and futile action. Man is a creature. Creatures are thoughts of God. It is the nature of thought to be irrevocable.

P. I do not comprehend. You say that man will never put off the body?

V. I say that he will never be bodiless.

P. Explain.

V. There are two bodies – the rudimental and the complete; corresponding with the two conditions of the worm and the butterfly. What we call 'death', is but the painful metamorphosis.

Our present incarnation is progressive, preparatory, temporary. Our future is perfected, ultimate, immortal. The ultimate life is the full design.

P. But of the worm's metamorphosis we are palpably cognizant.

V. *We*, certainly – but not the worm. The matter of which our rudimental body is composed, is within the ken of the organs of that body; or, more distinctly, our rudimental organs are adapted to the matter of which is formed the rudimental body; but not to that of which the ultimate is composed. The ultimate body thus escapes our rudimental senses, and we perceive only the shell which falls, in decaying, from the inner form; not that inner form itself; but this inner form, as well as the shell, is appreciable by those who have already acquired the ultimate life.

P. You have often said that the mesmeric state very nearly resembles death. How is this?

V. When I say that it resembles death, I mean that it resembles the ultimate life; for when I am entranced the senses of my rudimental life are in abeyance, and I perceive external things directly, without organs, through a medium which I shall employ in the ultimate, unorganized life.

P. Unorganized?

V. Yes; organs are contrivances by which the individual is brought into sensible relation with particular classes and forms of matter, to the exclusion of other classes and forms. The organs of man are adapted to his rudimental condition, and to that only; his ultimate condition, being unorganized, is of unlimited comprehension in all points but one – the nature of the volition of God – that is to say, the motion of the unparticled matter. You will have a distinct idea of the ultimate body by conceiving it to be entire brain. This it is *not*; but a conception of this nature will bring you near a comprehension of what it *is*. A luminous body imparts vibration to the luminiferous ether. The vibrations generate similar ones within the retina; these again communicate similar ones to the optic nerve. The nerve conveys similar ones to the brain; the brain, also, similar ones to the unparticled matter which permeates it. The motion of this latter is thought, of which perception is the first undulation. This is the mode by which the mind of the rudimental life communicates with the external world; and this external world is, to the rudimental life, limited, through the idiosyncrasy of its organs. But in the ultimate, unorganized life, the external world reaches the whole body, (which is of a substance having affinity to brain, as I have said,) with no other intervention than that of an infinitely rarer ether than even the luminiferous; and to this ether – in unison with it – the whole body vibrates, setting in motion the unparticled matter which permeates it. It is to the absence of idiosyncratic organs, therefore, that we must attribute the nearly unlimited perception of the ultimate life. To rudimental beings, organs are the cages necessary to confine them until fledged.

P. You speak of rudimental 'beings'. Are there other rudimental thinking beings than man?

V. The multitudinous conglomeration of rare matter into nebulae, planets, suns, and other bodies which are neither nebulae, suns, nor planets, is for the sole purpose of supplying *pabulum* for the idiosyncrasy of the organs of an infinity of rudimental beings. But for the necessity of the rudimental, prior to the ultimate life, there would have been no bodies such as these. Each of these is tenanted by a distinct variety of organic, rudimental, thinking creatures. In all, the organs vary with the features of the place tenanted. At death, or metamorphosis, these creatures, enjoying the ultimate life – immortality – and cognizant of all secrets but *the one,* act all things and pass everywhere by mere volition : – indwelling, not the stars, which to us seem the sole palpabilities, and for the accommodation of which we blindly deem space created – but that SPACE itself – that infinity of which the truly substantive vastness swallows up the star-shadows – blotting them out as non-entities from the perception of the angels.[8]

P. You say that ' but for the *necessity* of the rudimental life' there would have been no stars. But why this necessity?

V. In the inorganic life, as well as in the inorganic matter generally, there is nothing to impede the action of one simple *unique* law – the Divine Volition. With the view of producing impediment, the organic life and matter, (complex, substantial, and law-encumbered,) were contrived.

P. But again – why need this impediment have been produced?

V. The result of law inviolate is perfection – right – negative happiness. The result of law violate is imperfection, wrong, positive pain. Through the impediments afforded by the number, complexity, and substantiality of the laws of organic life and matter, the violation of law is rendered, to a certain extent, practicable. Thus pain, which in the inorganic life is impossible, is possible in the organic.

P. But to what good end is pain thus rendered possible?

V. All things are either good or bad by comparison. A sufficient analysis will show that pleasure, in all cases, is but the contrast of pain. *Positive* pleasure is a mere idea. To be happy at any one point we must have suffered at the same. Never to suffer would have been never to have been blessed. But it has been shown that, in the inorganic life, pain cannot be; thus the necessity for the organic. The pain of the primitive life of Earth, is the sole basis of the bliss of the ultimate life in Heaven.

P. Still, there is one of your expressions which I find it impossible to comprehend – 'the truly *substantive* vastness of infinity'.

V. This, probably, is because you have no sufficiently generic conception of the term *'substance'* itself. We must not regard it as a quality, but as a sentiment : – it is the perception, in thinking beings, of the adaptation of matter to their organization. There are many things on the Earth, which would be nihility to the inhabitants of Venus – many things visible and tangible in Venus, which we could not be brought to appreciate as existing at all. But to the inorganic beings – to the angels – the whole of the unparticled matter is substance; that is to say, the whole of what we term 'space' is to them the truest substantiality; – the stars, meantime, through what we consider their materiality, escaping the angelic sense, just in proportion as the unparticled matter, through what we consider its immateriality, eludes the organic.

As the sleep-waker pronounced these latter words, in a feeble tone, I observed on his countenance a singular expression, which somewhat alarmed me, and induced me to awake him at once.

No sooner had I done this, than, with a bright smile irradiating all his features, he fell back upon his pillow and expired. I noticed that in less than a minute afterward his corpse had all the stern rigidity of stone. His brow was of the coldness of ice. Thus, ordinarily, should it have appeared, only after long pressure from Azrael's hand.[9] Had the sleep-waker, indeed, during the latter portion of his discourse, been addressing me from out the region of the shadows?

The Thousand–and–Second Tale of Scheherazade

Truth is stranger than fiction
Old Saying

HAVING had occasion, lately, in the course of some oriental investigations, to consult the *Tellmenow Isitsoörnot*, a work which (like the Zohar of Simeon Jochaides)[1] is scarcely known at all, even in Europe, and which has never been quoted to my knowledge, by any American – if we except, perhaps, the author of the 'Curiosities of American Literature'; – having had occasion, I say, to turn over some pages of the first-mentioned very remarkable work, I was not a little astonished to discover that the literary world has hitherto been strangely in error respecting the fate of the vizier's daughter, Scheherazade, as that fate is depicted in the 'Arabian Nights', and that the *dénouement* there given, if not altogether inaccurate, as far as it goes, is at least to blame in not having gone very much farther.

For full information on this interesting topic, I must refer the inquisitive reader to the 'Isitsoörnot' itself: but, in the mean time, I shall be pardoned for giving a summary of what I there discovered.

It will be remembered that, in the usual version[2] of the tales, a certain monarch, having good cause to be jealous of his queen, not only puts her to death, but makes a vow, by his beard and the prophet, to espouse each night the most beautiful maiden in his dominions, and the next morning to deliver her up to the executioner.

Having fulfilled this vow for many years to the letter, and with a religious punctuality and method that conferred great credit upon him as a man of devout feelings and excellent sense, he was interrupted one afternoon (no doubt at his prayers) by a visit from his grand vizier, to whose daughter, it appears, there had occurred an idea.

Her name was Scheherazade, and her idea was, that she would either redeem the land from the depopulating tax upon its beauty, or perish, after the approved fashion of all heroines, in the attempt.

Accordingly, and although we do not find it to be leap-year, (which makes the sacrifice more meritorious,) she deputes her father, the grand vizier, to make an offer to the king of her hand. This hand the king eagerly accepts – (he had intended to take it at all events, and had put off the matter from day to day, only through fear of the vizier) – but, in accepting it now, he gives all parties very distinctly to understand that, grand vizier or no grand vizier, he has not the slightest design of giving up one iota of his vow or of his privileges. When, therefore, the fair Scheherazade insisted upon marrying the king, and did actually marry him despite her father's excellent advice not to do anything of the kind – when she would and did marry him, I say, will I nill I, it was with her beautiful black eyes as thoroughly open as the nature of the case would allow.

It seems, however, that this politic damsel (who had been reading Machiavelli, beyond doubt,) had a very ingenious little plot in her mind. On the night of the wedding she contrived, upon I forget what specious pretence, to have her sister occupy a couch sufficiently near that of the royal pair to admit of easy conversation from bed to bed; and, a little before cock-crowing, she took care to awaken the good monarch, her husband, (who bore her none the worse will because he intended to wring her neck on the morrow,) – she managed to awaken him, I say, (although, on account of a capital conscience and an easy digestion, he slept well,) by the profound interest of a story (about a rat and a black cat, I think,) which she was narrating (all in an under-tone, of course,) to her sister. When the day broke, it so happened that this history was not altogether finished, and that Scheherazade, in the nature of things, could not finish it just then, since it was high time for her to get up and be bowstrung – a thing very little more pleasant than hanging, only a trifle more genteel.

The king's curiosity, however, prevailing, I am sorry to say, even over his sound religious principles, induced him for this once to postpone the fulfilment of his vow until next morning, for the purpose and with the hope of hearing that night how it fared in the end with the black cat (a black cat I think it was) and the rat.

The night having arrived, however, the lady Scheherazade not only put the finishing stroke to the black cat and the rat, (the rat was blue,) but before she well knew what she was about, found herself deep in the intricacies of a narration, having reference (if I am not altogether mistaken) to a pink horse (with green wings) that went, in a violent manner, by clockwork, and was wound up with an indigo key. With this history the king was even more profoundly interested than with the other, and as the day broke before its conclusion, (notwithstanding all the queen's endeavours to get through with it in time for the bowstringing,) there was again no resource but to postpone that ceremony as before, for twenty-four hours. The next night there happened a similar accident with a similar result; and then the next – and then again the next; so that, in the end, the good monarch, having been unavoidably deprived of all opportunity to keep his vow during a period of no less than one thousand and one nights, either forgets it altogether by the expiration of this time or gets himself absolved of it in the regular way, or, (what is more probable) breaks it outright as well as the head of his father confessor. At all events, Scheherazade, who, being, lineally descended from Eve, fell heir, perhaps, to the whole seven baskets of talk which the latter lady, we all know, picked up from under the trees in the garden of Eden – Scheherazade, I say, finally triumphed, and the tariff upon beauty was repealed.

Now, this conclusion (which is that of the story as we have it upon record) is, no doubt, excessively proper and pleasant – but, alas! like a great many pleasant things, is more pleasant than true; and I am indebted altogether to the 'Isitsoörnot' for the means of correcting the error. '*Le mieux*', says a French proverb, '*est l'ennemi du bien*,' and, in mentioning that Scheherazade had inherited the seven baskets of talk, I should have added that she put them out at compound interest until they amounted to seventy-seven.

'My dear sister,' said she, on the thousand-and-second night, [I quote the language of the 'Isitsoörnot', at this point, *verbatim*,] 'my dear sister,' said she, 'now that all this little difficulty about the bowstring has blown over, and that this odious tax is so happily repealed, I feel that I have been guilty of great indiscretion in withholding from you and the king (who, I am sorry to say, snores – a thing no gentleman would do) the full conclusion of the history of Sinbad the sailor. This person went through numerous other and more interesting adventures than those which I related; but the truth is, I felt sleepy on the particular night of their narration, and so was seduced into cutting them short – a grievous piece of misconduct, for which I only trust that Allah will forgive me. But even yet it is not too late to remedy my great neglect, and as soon as I have given the king a pinch or two in order to wake him up so far that he may stop making that horrible noise, I will forthwith entertain you (and him if he pleases,) with the sequel of this very remarkable story.'

Hereupon the sister of Scheherazade, as I have it from the 'Isitsoörnot', expressed no very particular intensity of gratification; but the king having been sufficiently pinched, at length ceased snoring, and finally said 'hum!' and then 'hoo!' when the queen understanding these words, (which are no doubt Arabic) to signify that he was all attention, and would do his best not to snore any more, – the queen, I say, having arranged these matters to her satisfaction, re-entered thus, at once, into the history of Sinbad the sailor.

' "At length in my old age," [these are the words of Sinbad himself, as retailed by Scheherazade,] – "at length, in my old age, and after enjoying many years of tranquility at home, I became once more possessed with a desire of visiting foreign countries,[3] and one day, without acquainting any of my family with my design, I packed up some bundles of such merchandize as was most precious and least bulky, and, engaging a porter to carry them, went with him down to the seashore, to await the arrival of any chance vessel that might convey me out of the kingdom into some region which I had not as yet explored.

' "Having deposited the packages upon the sands, we sat down beneath some trees and looked out into the ocean in the hope of perceiving a ship, but during several hours we saw none whatever. At length I fancied that I could hear a singular buzzing or humming sound, and the porter, after listening awhile, declared that he also could distinguish it. Presently it grew louder, and then still louder, so that we could have no doubt that the object which caused it was approaching us. At length, on the edge of the horizon, we discovered a black speck, which rapidly increased in size [4] until we made it out to be a vast monster, swimming with a great part of its body above the surface of the sea. It came towards us with inconceivable swiftness, throwing up huge waves of foam around its breast, and illuminating all that part of the sea through which it passed, with a long line of fire that extended far off into the distance.

' "As the thing drew near we saw it very distinctly. Its length was equal to that of three of the loftiest trees that grow, and it was as wide as the great hall of audience in your palace, O most sublime and munificent of the Caliphs. Its body, which was unlike that of ordinary fishes, was as solid as a rock, and of a jetty blackness throughout all that portion of it which floated above the water, with the exception of a narrow blood-red streak that completely begirdled it. The belly, which floated beneath the surface, and of which we could get only a glimpse now and then as the monster rose and fell with the billows, was entirely covered with metallic scales, of a colour like that of the moon in misty weather. The back was flat and nearly white, and from it there extended upwards six spines, about half the length of the whole body.

' "This horrible creature had no mouth that we could perceive; but, as if to make up for this deficiency, it was provided with at least four score of eyes, that protruded from their sockets like those of the green dragonfly, and were arranged all around the body in two rows, one above the other, and parallel to the blood-red streak, which seemed to answer the purpose of an eyebrow. Two or three of these dreadful eyes were much larger than the others, and had the appearance of solid gold.

' "Although this beast approached us, as I have before said, with the greatest rapidity, it must have been moved altogether by necromancy – for it had neither fins like a fish nor web-feet like a duck, nor wings like the sea-shell which is blown along in the manner of a vessel; nor yet did it writhe itself forward as do the eels. Its head and its tail were shaped precisely alike, only, not far from the latter, were two small holes that served for nostrils, and through which the monster puffed out its thick breath with prodigious violence, and with a shrieking disagreeable noise.

' "Our terror at beholding this hideous thing was very great; but it was even surpassed by our astonishment when, upon getting a nearer look, we perceived upon the creature's back a vast number of animals about the size and shape of men, and altogether much resembling them, except that they wore no garments (as men do), being supplied (by nature no doubt) with an ugly, uncomfortable covering, a good deal like cloth, but fitting so tight to the skin as to render the poor wretches laughably awkward and put them apparently to severe pain. On the very tips of their heads were certain square-looking boxes, which, at first sight, I thought might have been intended to answer as turbans, but I soon discovered that they were excessively heavy and solid, and I therefore concluded they were contrivances designed, by their great weight, to keep the heads of the animals steady and safe upon their shoulders. Around the necks of the creatures were fastened black collars, (badges of servitude, no doubt,) such as we keep on our dogs, only much wider and infinitely stiffer, so that it was quite impossible for these poor victims to move their heads in any direction without moving the body at the same time; and thus they were doomed to perpetual contemplation of their noses – a view puggish and snubby in a wonderful, if not positively in an awful degree.

' "When the monster had nearly reached the shore where we stood, it suddenly pushed out one of its eyes to a great extent, and emitted from it a terrible flash of fire, accompanied by a dense cloud of smoke and a noise that I can compare to nothing but thunder. As the smoke cleared away, we saw one of the odd man-animals standing near the head of the large beast with a trumpet in his hand, through which (putting it to his mouth) he presently addressed us in loud, harsh and disagreeable accents, that, perhaps, we should have mistaken for language had they not come altogether through the nose.

' "Being thus evidently spoken to, I was at a loss how to reply, as I could in no manner understand what was said; and in this difficulty I turned to the porter, who was near swooning through affright, and demanded of him his opinion as to what species of monster it was, what it wanted, and what kind of creatures those were that so swarmed upon its back. To this the porter replied, as well as he could for trepidation, that he had once before heard of this sea-beast; that it was a cruel demon, with bowels of sulphur and blood of fire, created by evil genii as the means of inflicting misery upon mankind; that the things upon its back were vermin, such as sometimes infest cats and dogs, only a little larger and more savage; and that these vermin had their uses, however evil – for, through the torture they caused the beast by their nibblings and stingings, it was goaded into that degree of wrath which was requisite to make it roar and commit ill, and so fulfil the vengeful and malicious designs of the wicked genii.

' "This account determined me to take to my heels, and, without once even looking behind me, I ran at full speed up into the hills, while the porter ran equally fast, although nearly in an opposite direction, so that, by these means, he finally made his escape with my bundles, of which I have no doubt he took excellent care – although this is a point I cannot determine, as I do not remember that I ever beheld him again.

' "For myself, I was so hotly pursued by a swarm of the men-vermin (who had come to the shore in boats) that I was very soon overtaken, bound hand and foot, and conveyed to the beast, which immediately swam out again into the middle of the sea.

' "I now bitterly repented my folly in quitting a comfortable home[5] to peril my life in such adventures as this; but regret being useless, I made the best of my condition and exerted myself to secure the good-will of the man-animal that owned the trumpet, and who appeared to exercise authority over his fellows. I succeeded so well in this endeavour that, in a few days, the creature bestowed upon me various tokens of its favour, and, in the end, even went to the trouble of teaching me the rudiments of what it was vain enough to denominate its language; so that, at length, I was enabled to converse with it readily, and came to make it comprehend the ardent desire I had of seeing the world.

' "*Washish squashish squeak, Sinbad, hey-diddle diddle, grunt unt grumble, hiss, fiss, whiss,*' said he to me, one day after dinner – but I beg a thousand pardons, I had forgotten that your majesty is not conversant with the dialect of the Cock-neighs, (so the man-animals were called; I presume because their language formed the connecting link between that of the horse and that of the rooster). With your permission, I will translate. "*Washish squashish*", and so forth : – that is to say, "I am happy to find, my dear Sinbad, that you are really a very excellent fellow; we are now about doing a thing which is called circumnavigating the globe; and since you are so desirous of seeing the world, I will strain a point and give you a free passage upon the back of the beast." '

When the Lady Scheherazade had proceeded thus far, relates the 'Isitsoörnot', the king turned over from his left side to his right, and said –

'It is, in fact, *very* surprising, my dear queen, that you omitted, hitherto, these latter adventures of Sinbad. Do you know I think them exceedingly entertaining and strange?'

The king having thus expressed himself, we are told, the fair Scheherazade resumed her history in the following words : –

'Sinbad went on in this manner, with his narrative to the caliph – "I thanked the man-animal for its kindness, and soon found myself very much at home on the beast, which swam at a prodigious rate through the ocean; although the surface of the latter is, in that part of the world, by no means flat, but round like a pomegranate, so that we went – so to say – either up hill or down hill all the time." '

'That, I think, was very singular,' interrupted the king.

'Nevertheless, it is quite true,' replied Scheherazade.

'I have my doubts,' rejoined the king; 'but, pray, be so good as to go on with the story.'

'I will,' said the queen. ' "The beast," continued Sinbad to the caliph, "swam, as I have related, up hill and down hill, until, at length, we arrived at an island, many hundreds of miles in circumference, but which, nevertheless, had been built in the middle of the sea by a colony of little things like caterpillars." ' *

'Hum !' said the king.

' "Leaving this island," said Sinbad – (for Scheherazade, it must be understood, took no notice of her husband's ill-mannered ejaculation) – "leaving this island, we came to another where the forests were of solid stone, and so hard that they shivered to pieces the finest-tempered axes with which we endeavoured to cut them down." ' †

---

* The coralites.

† 'One of the most remarkable natural curiosities in Texas is a petrified forest, near the head of Pasigno river. It consists of several hundred trees, in an erect position, all turned to stone. Some trees, now growing, are partly petrified. This is a startling fact for natural philosophers, and must cause them to modify the existing theory of petrifaction.' – *Kennedy*. [*Texas*, 1, page 120.]

This account, at first discredited, has since been corroborated by the discovery of a completely petrified forest, near the head waters of the Chayenne, or Chienne river, which has its source in the Black Hills of the Rocky chain.

There is scarcely, perhaps, a spectacle on the surface of the globe more remarkable, either in a geological or picturesque point of view, than that presented by the petrified forest, near Cairo. The traveller, having passed the tombs of the caliphs, just beyond the gates of the city, proceeds to the southward, nearly at right angles to the road across the desert to Suez, and after having travelled some ten miles up a low barren valley, covered with sand, gravel, and sea shells, fresh as if the tide had retired but yesterday, crosses a low range of sandhills, which has for some distance run parallel to his path. The scene now presented to him is beyond conception singular and desolate. A mass of fragments of trees, all converted into stone, and when struck by his horse's hoof ringing like cast iron, is seen to extend itself for miles and miles around him, in the form of a decayed and prostrate forest. The wood is of a dark brown hue, but retains its form in perfection, the pieces being from one to fifteen feet in length, and from half a foot to three feet in thickness, strewed so closely together, as far as the eye can reach, that an Egyptian donkey can scarcely thread its way through amongst them, and so natural that, were it in Scotland or Ireland, it might pass without remark for some enormous drained bog, on which the exhumed trees lay rotting in the sun. The roots and rudiments of the branches are, in many cases, nearly perfect, and in some the worm-holes eaten under the bark are readily recognisable. The most delicate of the sap vessels, and all the finer portions of the centre of the wood, are perfectly entire, and bear to be examined with the strongest magnifiers. The whole are so thoroughly silicified as to scratch glass and be capable of receiving the highest polish. – *Asiatic Magazine*. [III. p. 359: Third Series.]

'Hum!' said the king, again; but Scheherazade, paying him no attention, continued in the language of Sinbad.

' "Passing beyond this last island, we reached a country where there was a cave that ran to the distance of thirty or forty miles within the bowels of the earth, and that contained a greater number of far more spacious and more magnificent palaces than are to be found in all Damascus and Bagdad. From the roofs of these palaces there hung myriads of gems, like diamonds, but larger than men; and in among the streets of towers and pyramids and temples, there flowed immense rivers as black as ebony and swarming with fish that had no eyes." ' *

'Hum!' said the king.

' "We then swam into a region of the sea where we found a lofty mountain, down whose sides there streamed torrents of melted metal, some of which were twelve miles wide and sixty miles long; † while from an abyss on the summit, issued so vast a quantity of ashes that the sun was entirely blotted out from the heavens, and it became darker than the darkest midnight; so that, when we were even at the distance of a hundred and fifty miles from the mountain, it was impossible to see the whitest object, however close we held it to our eyes." ' ‡

'Hum!' said the king.

' "After quitting this coast, the beast continued his voyage until we met with a land in which the nature of things seemed reversed – for we here saw a great lake, at the bottom of which, more than a hundred feet beneath the surface of the water,

* The Mammoth Cave of Kentucky.

† In Iceland, 1783.

‡ 'During the eruption of Hecla, in 1766, clouds of this kind produced such a degree of darkness that, at Glaumba, which is more than fifty leagues from the mountain, people could only find their way by groping. During the eruption of Vesuvius, in 1794, at Caserta, four leagues distant, people could only walk by the light of torches. On the first of May, 1812, a cloud of volcanic ashes and sand, coming from a volcano in the island of St Vincent, covered the whole of Barbadoes, spreading over it so intense a darkness that, at mid-day, in the open air, one could not perceive the trees or other objects near him, or even a white handkerchief placed at the distance of six inches from the eye.' – *Murray*, p. 215, *Phil. edit.* [1. Encyclopaedia of Geography.]

there flourished in full leaf a forest of tall and luxuriant trees." ' *

'Hoo!' said the king.

' "Some hundred miles farther on brought us to a climate where the atmosphere was so dense as to sustain iron or steel, just as our own does feathers." ' †

'Fiddle de dee,' said the king.

' "Proceeding still in the same direction, we presently arrived at the most magnificent region in the whole world. Through it there meandered a glorious river for several thousands of miles. This river was of unspeakable depth, and of a transparency richer than that of amber. It was from three to six miles in width; and its banks, which arose on either side to twelve hundred feet in perpendicular height, were crowned with ever-blossoming trees and perpetual sweet-scented flowers that made the whole territory one gorgeous garden; but the name of this luxuriant land was the kingdom of Horror, and to enter it was inevitable death." ' ‡

'Humph!' said the king.

' "We left this kingdom in great haste, and, after some days, came to another, where we were astonished to perceive myriads of monstrous animals with horns resembling scythes upon their heads. These hideous beasts dig for themselves vast caverns in the soil, of a funnel shape, and line the sides of them with rocks, so disposed one upon the other that they fall instantly, when trodden upon by other animals, thus precipitating them into the monsters' dens, where their blood is immediately sucked, and their carcases afterwards hurled contemptuously out to an immense distance from the caverns of death." ' ¶

* 'In the year 1790, in the Caraccas, during an earthquake, a portion of the granite soil sank and left a lake eight hundred yards in diameter, and from eighty to a hundred feet deep. It was a part of the Forest of Aripao which sank, and the trees remained green for several months under the water.' – *Murray*, p. 221. [Encyc. of Geog.]

† The hardest steel ever manufactured may, under the action of a blow-pipe, be reduced to an impalpable powder, which will float readily in the atmospheric air.

‡ The region of the Niger. See *Simmond*'s '*Colonial Magazine*'.

¶ The *Myrmeleon* – lion-ant. The term 'monster' is equally applicable to

'Pooh!' said the king.

'"Continuing our progress, we perceived a district abounding with vegetables that grew not upon any soil but in the air.* There were others that sprang from the substance of other vegetables;† others that derived their sustenance from the bodies of living animals;‡ and then, again, there were others that glowed all over with intense fire;¶ others that moved from place to place [6] at pleasure,§ and what is still more wonderful, we discovered flowers that lived and breathed and moved their limbs at will, and had, moreover, the detestable passion of mankind for enslaving other creatures, and confining them in horrid and solitary prisons until the fulfilment of appointed tasks." '**

---

small abnormal things and to great, while such epithets as 'vast' are merely comparative. The cavern of the myrmeleon is *vast* in comparison with the hole of the common red ant. A grain of silex is, also, a 'rock'.

*The *Epidendron, Flos Aeris*, of the family of the *Orchideæ*, grows with merely the surface of its roots attached to a tree or other object, from which it derives no nutriment – subsisting altogether upon air.

†The *Parasites*, such as the wonderful *Rafflesia Arnoldi*.

‡*Schouw* advocates a class of plants that grow upon living animals – the *Plantæ Epizoæ*. Of this class are the *Fuci* and *Algæ*.

Mr J. B. Williams, of Salem, Mass., presented the 'National Institute', with an insect from New Zealand, with the following description : – ' "*The Hotte*", a decided caterpillar, or worm, is found growing at the foot of the *Rata* tree, with a plant growing out of its head. This most peculiar and most extraordinary insect travels up both the *Rata* and *Puriri* trees, and entering into the top, eats its way, perforating the trunk of the tree until it reaches the root, it then comes out of the root, and dies, or remains dormant, and the plant propagates out of its head; the body remains perfect and entire, of a harder substance than when alive. From this insect the natives make a coloring for tattooing.'

¶In mines and natural caves we find a species of cryptogamous *fungus* that emits an intense phosphorescence.

§The orchis, scabius and vallisneria.

**'The corolla of this flower, (*Aristolochia Clematitis*,) which is tubular, but terminating upwards in a ligulate limb, is inflated into a globular figure at the base. The tubular part is internally beset with stiff hairs, pointing downwards. The globular part contains the pistil, which consists merely of a germen and stigma, together with the surrounding stamens. But the stamens, being shorter than even the germen, cannot discharge the pollen so as to throw it upon the stigma, as the flower stands always upright till after impregnation. And hence, without some additional and peculiar aid,

'Pshaw!' said the king.

' "Quitting this land, we soon arrived at another in which the bees and the birds are mathematicians of such genius and erudition, that they gave daily instructions in the science of geometry to the wise men of the empire. The king of the place having offered a reward for the solution of two very difficult problems, they were solved upon the spot – the one by the bees, and the other by the birds; but the king keeping their solutions a secret, it was only after the most profound researches and labor, and the writing of an infinity of big books, during a long series of years, that the men-mathematicians at length arrived at the identical solutions which had been given upon the spot by the bees and by the birds." ' *

'Oh my!' said the king.

---

the pollen must necessarily fall down to the bottom of the flower. Now, the aid that Nature has furnished in this case, is that of the *Tipula Pennicornis*, a small insect, which entering the tube of the corolla in quest of honey, descends to the bottom, and rummages about till it becomes quite covered with pollen; but, not being able to force its way out again, owing to the downward position of the hairs, which converge to a point like the wires of a mouse-trap, and being somewhat impatient of its confinement, it brushes backwards and forwards, trying every corner, till, after repeatedly traversing the stigma, it covers it with pollen sufficient for its impregnation, in consequence of which the flower soon begins to droop and the hairs to shrink to the side of the tube, effecting an easy passage for the escape of the insect.' – *Rev. P. Keith* – '*System of Physiological Botany*'.

* The bees – ever since bees were – have been constructing their cells with just such sides, in just such number, and at just such inclinations, as it has been demonstrated (in a problem involving the profoundest mathematical principles) are the very sides, in the very number, and at the very angles which will afford the creatures the most room that is compatible with the greatest stability of structure.

During the latter part of the last century, the question arose among mathematicians – 'to determine the best form that can be given to the sails of a windmill, according to their varying distances from the revolving vanes, and likewise from the centres of revolution.' This is an excessively complex problem; for it is, in other words, to find the best possible position at an infinity of varied distances, and at an infinity of points on the arm. There were a thousand futile attempts to answer the query on the part of the most illustrious mathematicians; and when, at length, an undeniable solution was discovered, men found that the wings of a bird had given it with absolute precision, ever since the first bird had traversed the air.

' "We had scarcely lost sight of this empire when we found ourselves close upon another, from whose shores there flew over our heads a flock of fowls a mile in breadth and two hundred and forty miles long; so that, although they flew a mile during every minute, it required no less than four hours for the whole flock to pass over us – in which there were several millions of millions of fowls." ' *

'Oh fy !' said the king.

' "No sooner had we got rid of these birds, which occasioned us great annoyance, than we were terrified by the appearance of a fowl of another kind, and infinitely larger than even the rocs which I met in my former voyages; for it was bigger than the biggest of the domes upon your seraglio, oh, most Munificent of Caliphs. This terrible fowl had no head that we could perceive, but was fashioned entirely of belly, which was of a prodigious fatness and roundness, of a soft looking substance, smooth, shining and striped with various colors. In its talons, the monster was bearing away to his eyrie in the heavens, a house from which it had knocked off the roof, and in the interior of which we distinctly saw human beings, who, beyond doubt, were in a state of frightful despair at the horrible fate which awaited them. We shouted with all our might, in the hope of frightening the bird into letting go of its prey; but it merely gave a snort or puff, as if of rage, and then let fall upon our heads a heavy sack which proved to be filled with sand." '

'Stuff !' said the king.

' "It was just after this adventure that we encountered a continent of immense extent and of prodigious solidity, but which, nevertheless, was supported entirely upon the back of a sky-blue cow that had no fewer than four hundred horns." '†

'*That,* now, I believe,' said the king, 'because I have read something of the kind before, in a book.'

* He observed a flock of pigeons passing betwixt Frankfort and the Indiana territory, one mile at least in breadth; it took up four hours in passing; which, at the rate of one mile per minute, gives a length of 240 miles; and, supposing three pigeons to each square yard, gives 2,230,272,000 pigeons. '*Travels in Canada and the United States*', by Lieut. F. Hall.

† 'The earth is upheld by a cow of a blue color, having horns four hundred in number.' – *Sale*'s *Koran*.

' "We passed immediately beneath this continent, (swimming in between the legs of the cow,) and, after some hours, found ourselves in a wonderful country indeed, which, I was informed by the man-animal, was his own native land, inhabited by things of his own species. This elevated the man-animal very much in my esteem; and in fact, I now began to feel ashamed of the contemptuous familiarity with which I had treated him; for I found that the man-animals in general were a nation of the most powerful magicians, who lived with worms in their brains,* which, no doubt, served to stimulate them by their painful writhings and wrigglings to the most miraculous efforts of imagination." '

'Nonsense!' said the king.

' "Among the magicians, were domesticated several animals of very singular kinds; for example, there was a huge horse whose bones were iron and whose blood was boiling water. In place of corn, he had black stones for his usual food; and yet, in spite of so hard a diet, he was so strong and swift that he would drag a load more weighty than the grandest temple in this city, at a rate surpassing that of the flight of most birds." '†

'Twattle!' said the king.

' "I saw, also, among these people a hen without feathers, but bigger than a camel; instead of flesh and bone she had iron and brick; her blood, like that of the horse, (to whom in fact she was nearly related,) was boiling water; and like him she ate nothing but wood or black stones. This hen brought forth very frequently, a hundred chickens in the day; and, after birth, they took up their residence for several weeks within the stomach of their mother." '‡

'Fal lal!' said the king.

' "One of this nation of mighty conjurors created a man out of brass and wood, and leather, and endowed him with such ingenuity that he would have beaten at chess, all the race of

---

* 'The *Entozoa*, or intestinal worms, have repeatedly been observed in the muscles, and in the cerebral substance of men.' – See *Wyatt's Physiology*, p. 143.

† On the great Western Railway, between London and Exeter, a speed of 71 miles per hour has been attained. A train weighing 90 tons was whirled from Paddington to Didcot (53 miles,) in 51 minutes.

** The Daguerreotype.

mankind with the exception of the great Caliph, Haroun Alraschid.* Another of these magi constructed (of like material) a creature that put to shame even the genius of him who made it; for so great were its reasoning powers that, in a second, it performed calculations of so vast an extent that they would have required the united labor of fifty thousand fleshly men for a year.† But a still more wonderful conjuror fashioned for himself a mighty thing that was neither man nor beast, but which had brains of lead intermixed with a black matter like pitch, and fingers that it employed with such incredible speed and dexterity that it would have had no trouble in writing out twenty thousand copies of the Koran in an hour; and this was so exquisite a precision, that in all the copies there should not be found one to vary from another by the breadth of the finest hair. This thing was of prodigious strength, so that it erected or overthrew the mightiest empires at a breath; but its power was exercised equally for evil and for good." '

'Ridiculous !' said the king.

' "Among this nation of necromancers there was also one who had in his veins the blood of the salamanders; for he made no scruple of sitting down to smoke his chibouc in a red-hot oven until his dinner was thoroughly roasted upon its floor.‡ Another had the faculty of converting the common metals into gold, without even looking at them during the process.¶ Another had such delicacy of touch that he made a wire so fine as to be invisible.§ Another had such quickness of perception that he counted all the separate motions of an elastic body, while it was springing backwards and forwards at the rate of nine hundred millions of times in a second." '**

'Absurd !' said the king.

*Maelzel's Automaton Chess-player.[8]
† Babbage's Calculating Machine.[9]
‡ *Chabert*, and since him, a hundred others.[10]
¶ The Electrotype.
§ *Wollaston* made of platinum for the field of views in a telescope a wire one eighteen-thousandth part of an inch in thickness. It could be seen only by means of the microscope.
** Newton demonstrated that the retina beneath the influence of the violet ray of the spectrum, vibrated 900,000,000 of times in a second.

' "Another of these magicians, by means of a fluid that no-body ever yet saw, could make the corpses of his friends brandish their arms, kick out their legs, fight, or even get up and dance at his will.* Another had cultivated his voice to so great an extent that he could have made himself heard from one end of the earth to the other.† Another had so long an arm that he could sit down in Damascus and indite a letter at Bagdad – or indeed at any distance whatsoever.‡ Another commanded the lightning to come down to him out of the heavens, and it came at his call; and served him for a plaything when it came. Another took two loud sounds and out of them made a silence. Another constructed a deep darkness out of two brilliant lights.¶ [11] Another made ice in a red-hot furnace.§ Another directed the sun to paint his portrait, and the sun did.** Another took this luminary with the moon and the planets, and having first weighed them with scrupulous accuracy, probed into their depths and found out the solidity of the substance of which they are made. But the

* The Voltaic pile.

† The Electro Telegraph transmits intelligence instantaneously – at least so far as regards any distance upon the earth.

‡ The Electro Telegraph Printing Apparatus.

¶ Common experiments in Natural Philosophy. If two red rays from two luminous points be admitted into a dark chamber so as to fall on a white surface, and differ in their length by 0.0000258 of an inch, their intensity is doubled. So also if the difference in length be any whole-number multiple of that fraction. A multiple by $2\frac{1}{4}$, $3\frac{1}{4}$, &c., gives an intensity equal to one ray only; but a multiple by $2\frac{1}{2}$, $3\frac{1}{2}$, &c., gives the result of total darkness. In violet rays similar effects arise when the difference in length is 0.000157 of an inch; and with all other rays the results are the same – the difference varying with a uniform increase from the violet to the red.

Analogous experiments in respect to sound produce analogous results.

§ Place a platina crucible over a spirit lamp, and keep it a red heat; pour in some sulphuric acid, which, though the most volatile of bodies at a common temperature, will be found to become completely fixed in a hot crucible, and not a drop evaporates – being surrounded by an atmosphere of its own, it does not, in fact touch the sides. A few drops of water are now introduced, when the acid immediately coming in contact with the heated sides of the crucible, flies off in sulphurous acid vapor, and so rapid is its progress, that the caloric of the water passes off with it, which falls a lump of ice to the bottom; by taking advantage of the moment before it is allowed to re-melt, it may be turned out a lump of ice from a red-hot vessel.

** The Daguerreotype.

whole nation is, indeed, of so surprising a necromantic ability, that not even their infants, nor their commonest cats and dogs have any difficulty in seeing objects that do not exist at all, or that for twenty thousand years before the birth of the nation itself, had been blotted out from the face of creation." '*

'Preposterous!' said the king.

' "The wives and daughters of these incomparably great and wise magi," ' continued Scheherazade, without being in any manner disturbed by these frequent and most ungentlemanly interruptions on the part of her husband – ' "the wives and daughters of these eminent conjurors are everything that is accomplished and refined; and would be everything that is interesting and beautiful, but for an unhappy fatality that besets them, and from which not even the miraculous powers of their husbands and fathers has, hitherto, been adequate to save. Some fatalities come in certain shapes, and some in others – but this of which I speak, has come in the shape of a crotchet." '

'A what?' said the king.

' "A crotchet," ' said Scheherazade. ' "One of the evil genii who are perpetually upon the watch to inflict ill, has put it into the heads of these accomplished ladies that the thing which we describe as personal beauty, consists altogether in the protuberance of the region which lies not very far below the small of the back. – Perfection of loveliness, they say, is in the direct ratio of the extent of this hump. Having been long possessed of this idea, and bolsters being cheap in that country, the days have long gone by since it was possible to distinguish a woman from a dromedary –" '

* Although light travels 200,000 miles in a second, the distance of what we suppose to be the nearest fixed star (Sireus) is so inconceivably great, that its rays would require *at least* three years to reach the earth. For stars beyond this 20 – or even 1000 years – would be a moderate estimate. Thus, if they had been annihilated 20 or 1000 years ago, we might still see them to-day, by the light which *started* from their surfaces, 20 or 1000 years in the past time. That many which we see daily are really extinct, is not impossible – not even improbable.

The elder Herschel maintains that the light of the faintest nebulæ seen through his great telescope, must have taken 3,000,000 years in reaching the earth. Some, made visible by Lord Ross' instrument must, then, have required at least 20,000,000.

'Stop!' said the king, – 'I can't stand that, and I won't. You have already given me a dreadful headache with your lies. The day, too, I perceive, is beginning to break. How long have we been married? – my conscience is getting to be troublesome again. And then that dromedary touch – do you take me for a fool? Upon the whole you might as well get up and be throttled.'

These words, as I learn from the 'Isitsoörnot', both grieved and astonished Scheherazade; but, as she knew the king to be a man of scrupulous integrity, and quite unlikely to forfeit his word, she submitted to her fate with a good grace. She derived, however, great consolation, (during the tightening of the bowstring,) from the reflection that much of the history remained still untold, and that the petulance of her brute of a husband had reaped for him a most righteous reward, in depriving him of many inconceivable adventures.

Some Words with a Mummy

THE symposium of the preceding evening had been a little too much for my nerves. I had a wretched head-ache, and was desperately drowsy. Instead of going out, therefore, to spend the evening as I had proposed, it occurred to me that I could not do a wiser thing than just eat a mouthful of supper and go immediately to bed.

A *light* supper of course. I am exceedingly fond of Welsh rabbit. More than a pound at once, however, may not at all times be advisable. Still, there can be no material objection to two. And really between two and three, there is merely a single unit of difference. I ventured, perhaps, upon four. My wife will have it five; – but, clearly, she has confounded two very distinct affairs. The abstract number, five, I am willing to admit; but, concretely, it has reference to bottles of Brown Stout, without which, in the way of condiment, Welsh rabbit is to be eschewed.

Having thus concluded a frugal meal, and donned my nightcap, with the serene hope of enjoying it till noon the next day, I placed my head upon the pillow, and through the aid of a capital conscience, fell into a profound slumber forthwith.

But when were the hopes of humanity fulfilled? I could not have completed my third snore when there came a furious ringing at the street-door bell, and then an impatient thumping at the knocker, which awakened me at once. In a minute afterward and while I was still rubbing my eyes, my wife thrust in my face a note from my old friend, Doctor Ponnonner. It ran thus :

Come to me by all means, my dear good friend, as soon as you receive this. Come and help us to rejoice. At last, by long persevering diplomacy, I have gained the assent of the Directors of the City Museum, to my examination of the Mummy – you know the one I mean. I have permission to unswathe it and open it, if desirable. A few friends only will be present – you, of course. The Mummy is now at my house, and we shall begin to unroll it at eleven to-night.

Yours ever

PONNONNER

By the time I had reached the 'Ponnonner', it struck me that I was as wide awake as a man need be. I leaped out of bed in an ecstacy, overthrowing all in my way; dressed myself with a rapidity truly marvellous; and set off, at the top of my speed, for the Doctor's.

There I found a very eager company assembled. They had been awaiting me with much impatience; the Mummy was extended upon the dining table; and the moment I entered, its examination was commenced.

It was one of a pair brought, several years previously, by Captain Arthur Sabretash, a cousin of Ponnonner's, from a tomb near Eleithias, in the Lybian Mountains,[1] a considerable distance above Thebes on the Nile. The grottoes at this point, although less magnificent than the Theban sepulchres, are of higher interest, on account of affording more numerous illustrations of the private life of the Egyptians. The chamber from which our specimen was taken, was said to be very rich in such illustrations; the walls being completely covered with fresco paintings and bas-reliefs, while statues, vases, and Mosaic work of rich patterns, indicated the vast wealth of the deceased.

The treasure had been deposited in the Museum precisely in the same condition in which Captain Sabretash had found it; – that is to say, the coffin had not been disturbed. For eight years it had thus stood, subject only externally to public inspection. We had now, therefore, the complete Mummy at our disposal; and to those who are aware how very rarely the unransacked antique reaches our shores, it will be evident, at once, that we had great reason to congratulate ourselves upon our good fortune.

Approaching the table, I saw on it a large box, or case, nearly seven feet long, and perhaps three feet wide, by two feet and a half deep. It was oblong – not coffin-shaped. The material was at first supposed to be the wood of the sycamore (*platanus*), but, upon cutting into it, we found it to be pasteboard, or more properly, *papier mâché*, composed of papyrus. It was thickly ornamented with paintings, representing funeral scenes, and other mournful subjects, interspersed among which in every variety of position, were certain series of hieroglyphical characters intended, no doubt, for the name of the departed. By good luck,

Mr Gliddon formed one of our party;[2] and he had no difficulty in translating the letters, which were simply phonetic, and represented the word, *Allamistakeo.*

We had some difficulty in getting this case open without injury, but, having at length accomplished the task, we came to a second, coffin-shaped, and very considerably less in size than the exterior one, but resembling it precisely in every other respect. The interval between the two was filled with resin, which had, in some degree, defaced the colors of the interior box.

Upon opening this latter (which we did quite easily,) we arrived at a third case, also coffin-shaped, and varying from the second one in no particular, except in that of its material, which was cedar, and still emitted the peculiar and highly aromatic odor of that wood. Between the second and the third case there was no interval; the one fitting accurately within the other.

Removing the third case, we discovered and took out the body itself. We had expected to find it, as usual, enveloped in frequent rolls, or bandages, of linen, but, in place of these, we found a sort of sheath, made of papyrus, and coated with a layer of plaster, thickly gilt and painted. The paintings represented subjects connected with the various supposed duties of the soul, and its presentation to different divinities, with numerous identical human figures, intended, very probably, as portraits of the persons embalmed. Extending from head to foot, was a columnar, or perpendicular inscription in phonetic hieroglyphics, giving again his name and titles, and the names and titles of his relations.

Around the neck thus ensheathed, was a collar of cylindrical glass beads, diverse in color, and so arranged as to form images of deities, of the scarabæus, etc., with the winged globe. Around the small of the waist was a similar collar, or belt.

Stripping off the papyrus, we found the flesh in excellent preservation, with no perceptible odor. The color was reddish. The skin was hard, smooth and glossy. The teeth and hair were in good condition. The eyes (it seemed) had been removed, and glass ones substituted, which were very beautiful and wonderfully life-like, with the exception of somewhat too determined a stare. The finger and toe nails were brilliantly gilded.

Mr Gliddon was of opinion, from the redness of the epidermis, that the embalmment had been effected altogether by asphaltum; but, on scraping the surface with a steel instrument, and throwing into the fire some of the powder thus obtained, the flavor of camphor and other sweet-scented gums became apparent.

We searched the corpse very carefully for the usual openings through which the entrails are extracted, but, to our surprise, we could discover none. No member of the party was at that period aware that entire or unopened mummies are not unfrequently met. The brain it was customary to withdraw through the nose; the intestines through an incision in the side; the body was then shaved, washed, and salted; then laid aside for several weeks, when the operation of embalming, properly so called, began.

As no trace of an opening could be found, Doctor Ponnonner was preparing his instruments for dissection, when I observed that it was then past two o'clock. Hereupon it was agreed to postpone the internal examination until the next evening; and we were about to separate for the present, when some one suggested an experiment or two with the Voltaic pile.

The application of electricity to a Mummy three or four thousand years old at the least, was an idea, if not very sage, still sufficiently original,[3] and we all caught at it at once. About one tenth in earnest and nine tenths in jest, we arranged a battery in the Doctor's study, and conveyed thither the Egyptian.

It was only after much trouble that we succeeded in laying bare some portions of the temporal muscle which appeared of less stony rigidity than other parts of the frame, but which, as we had anticipated, of course, gave no indication of galvanic susceptibility when brought in contact with the wire. This the first trial, indeed, seemed decisive, and, with a hearty laugh at our own absurdity, we were bidding each other good night, when my eyes, happening to fall upon those of the Mummy, were there immediately riveted in amazement. My brief glance, in fact, had sufficed to assure me that the orbs which we had all supposed to be glass, and which were originally noticeable for a certain wild stare, were now so far covered by the lids that only a small portion of the *tunica albuginea* remained visible.

With a shout I called attention to the fact, and it became immediately obvious to all.

I cannot say that I was *alarmed* at the phenomenon, because 'alarmed' is, in my case, not exactly the word. It is possible, however, that, but for the Brown Stout, I might have been a little nervous. As for the rest of the company, they really made no attempt at concealing the downright fright which possessed them. Doctor Ponnonner was a man to be pitied. Mr Gliddon, by some peculiar process, rendered himself invisible. Mr Silk Buckingham, I fancy, will scarcely be so bold as to deny that he made his way, upon all fours, under the table.[4]

After the first shock of astonishment, however, we resolved, as a matter of course, upon farther experiment forthwith. Our operations were now directed against the great toe of the right foot. We made an incision over the outside of the exterior *os sesamoideum pollicis pedis*,[5] and thus got at the root of the *abductor* muscle. Re-adjusting the battery, we now applied the fluid to the bisected nerves – when, with a movement of exceeding life-likeness, the Mummy first drew up its right knee so as to bring it nearly in contact with the abdomen, and then, straightening the limb with inconceivable force, bestowed a kick upon Doctor Ponnonner, which had the effect of discharging that gentleman, like an arrow from a catapult, through a window into the street below.

We rushed out *en masse* to bring in the mangled remains of the victim, but had the happiness to meet him upon the staircase, coming up in an unaccountable hurry, brimfull of the most ardent philosophy, and more than ever impressed with the necessity of prosecuting our experiments with rigor and with zeal.

It was by his advice, accordingly, that we made, upon the spot, a profound incision into the tip of the subject's nose, while the Doctor himself, laying violent hands upon it, pulled it into vehement contact with the wire.

Morally and physically – figuratively and literally – was the effect electric. In the first place, the corpse opened its eyes and winked very rapidly for several minutes, as does Mr Barnes in the pantomime;[6] in the second place, it sneezed; in the third, it sat upon end; in the fourth, it shook its fist in Doctor Ponnonner's face; in the fifth, turning to Messieurs Gliddon and Buckingham, it addressed them, in very capital Egyptian, thus :

'I must say, gentlemen, that I am as much surprised as I am mortified, at your behaviour. Of Doctor Ponnonner nothing better was to be expected. He is a poor little fat fool who *knows* no better. I pity and forgive him. But you, Mr Gliddon – and you, Silk – who have travelled and resided in Egypt until one might imagine you to the manor born – you, I say, who have been so much among us that you speak Egyptian fully as well, I think, as you write your mother tongue – you, whom I have always been led to regard as the firm friend of the mummies –I really did anticipate more gentlemanly conduct from *you*. What am I to think of your standing quietly by and seeing me thus unhandsomely used? What am I to suppose by your permitting Tom, Dick and Harry to strip me of my coffins, and my clothes, in this wretchedly cold climate? In what light (to come to the point) am I to regard your aiding and abetting that miserable little villain, Doctor Ponnonner, in pulling me by the nose?'

It will be taken for granted, no doubt, that upon hearing this speech under the circumstances, we all either made for the door, or fell into violent hysterics, or went off in a general swoon. One of these three things was, I say, to be expected. Indeed each and all of these lines of conduct might have been very plausibly pursued. And, upon my word, I am at a loss to know how or why it was that we pursued neither the one or the other. But, perhaps, the true reason is to be sought in the spirit of the age, which proceeds by the rule of contraries altogether, and is now usually admitted as the solution of everything in the way of paradox and impossibility. Or, perhaps, after all, it was only the Mummy's exceedingly natural and matter-of-course air that divested his words of the terrible. However this may be, the facts are clear, and no member of our party betrayed any very particular trepidation, or seemed to consider that any thing had gone very especially wrong.

For my part I was convinced it was all right, and merely step-

ped aside, out of the range of the Egyptian's fist. Doctor Ponnonner thrust his hands into his breeches' pockets, looked hard
at the Mummy, and grew excessively red in the face. Mr Gliddon
stroked his whiskers and drew up the collar of his shirt. Mr
Buckingham hung down his head, and put his right thumb
into the left corner of his mouth.

The Egyptian regarded him with a severe countenance for
some minutes, and at length, with a sneer, said:

'Why don't you speak, Mr Buckingham? Did you hear what
I asked you, or not? *Do* take your thumb out of your mouth!'

Mr Buckingham, hereupon, gave a slight start, took his right
thumb out of the left corner of his mouth, and, by way of in-
demnification, inserted his left thumb in the right corner of the
aperture above-mentioned.

Not being able to get an answer from Mr B., the figure turned
peevishly to Mr Gliddon, and, in a peremptory tone, demanded
in general terms what we all meant.

Mr Gliddon replied at great length, in phonetics; and but for
the deficiency of American printing-offices in hieroglyphical
type, it would afford me much pleasure to record here, in the
original, the whole of his very excellent speech.

I may as well take this occasion to remark, that all the subsequent conversation in which the Mummy took a part, was carried on in primitive Egyptian, through the medium (so far as
concerned myself and other untravelled members of the company) – through the medium, I say, of Messieurs Gliddon and
Buckingham, as interpreters. These gentlemen spoke the
mother-tongue of the mummy with inimitable fluency and grace;
but I could not help observing that (owing, no doubt, to the
introduction of images entirely modern, and, of course, entirely
novel to the stranger,) the two travellers were reduced, occasionally, to the employment of sensible forms for the purpose of conveying a particular meaning. Mr Gliddon, at one period, for
example, could not make the Egyptian comprehend the term
'politics', until he sketched upon the wall, with a bit of charcoal,
a little carbuncle-nosed gentleman, out at elbows, standing upon
a stump, with his left leg drawn back, his right arm thrown

forward, with the fist shut, the eyes rolled up toward Heaven, and the mouth open at an angle of ninety degrees. Just in the same way Mr Buckingham failed to convey the absolutely modern idea, 'wig', until, (at Doctor Ponnonner's suggestion,) he grew very pale in the face, and consented to take off his own.

It will be readily understood that Mr Gliddon's discourse turned chiefly upon the vast benefits accruing to science from the unrolling and disembowelling of mummies; apologizing, upon this score, for any disturbance that might have been occasioned *him*, in particular, the individual Mummy called Allamistakeo; and concluding with a mere hint, (for it could scarcely be considered more,) that, as these little matters were now explained, it might be as well to proceed with the investigation intended. Here Doctor Ponnonner made ready his instruments.

In regard to the latter suggestions of the orator, it appears that Allamistakeo had certain scruples of conscience, the nature of which I did not distinctly learn; but he expressed himself satisfied with the apologies tendered, and, getting down from the table, shook hands with the company all round.

When this ceremony was at an end, we immediately busied ourselves in repairing the damages which our subject had sustained from the scalpel. We sewed up the wound in his temple, bandaged his foot, and applied a square inch of black plaster to the tip of his nose.

It was now observed that the Count, (this was the title, it seems, of Allamistakeo,) had a slight fit of shivering – no doubt from the cold. The doctor immediately repaired to his wardrobe, and soon returned with a black dress coat, made in Jennings' best manner, a pair of sky-blue plaid pantaloons with straps, a pink gingham *chemise*, a flapped vest of brocade, a white sack overcoat, a walking cane with a hook, a hat with no brim, patent-leather boots, straw-colored kid gloves, an eye-glass, a pair of whiskers, and a waterfall cravat. Owing to the disparity of size between the Count and the doctor, (the proportion being as two to one,) there was some little difficulty in adjusting these habiliments upon the person of the Egyptian; but when all was arranged, he might have been said to be dressed. Mr Gliddon, therefore, gave him his arm, and led him to a comfortable chair by the fire, while the doctor rang the bell upon the spot and ordered a supply of cigars and wine.

The conversation soon grew animated. Much curiosity was, of course, expressed in regard to the somewhat remarkable fact of Allamistakeo's still remaining alive.

'I should have thought,' observed Mr Buckingham, 'that it is high time you were dead.'

'Why,' replied the Count, very much astonished, 'I am little more than seven hundred years old! My father lived a thousand, and was by no means in his dotage when he died.'

Here ensued a brisk series of questions and computations, by means of which it became evident that the antiquity of the Mummy had been grossly misjudged. It had been five thousand and fifty years, and some months, since he had been consigned to the catacombs at Eleithias.

'But my remark,' resumed Mr Buckingham, 'had no reference to your age at the period of interment; (I am willing to grant, in fact, that you are still a young man,) and my allusion was to the immensity of time during which, by your own showing, you must have been done up in asphaltum.'

'In what?' said the Count.

'In asphaltum,' persisted Mr B.

'Ah, yes; I have some faint notion of what you mean; it might be made to answer, no doubt, – but in my time we employed scarcely anything else than the Bichloride of Mercury.' [7]

'But what we are especially at a loss to understand,' said Doctor Ponnonner, 'is how it happens that, having been dead and buried in Egypt five thousand years ago, you are here to-day all alive, and looking so delightfully well.'

'Had I been, as you say, *dead*,' replied the Count, 'it is more than probable that dead I should still be; for I perceive you are yet in the infancy of Galvanism, and cannot accomplish with it what was a common thing among us in the old days. But the fact is, I fell into catalepsy, and it was considered by my best friends that I was either dead or should be; they accordingly embalmed me at once – I presume you are aware of the chief principle of the embalming process?'

'Why, not altogether.'

'Ah, I perceive; – a deplorable condition of ignorance! Well, I cannot enter into details just now: but it is necessary to explain that to embalm, (properly speaking,) in Egypt, was to arrest indefinitely *all* the animal functions subjected to the process. I use the word 'animal' in its widest sense, as including the physical not more than the moral and *vital* being. I repeat that the leading principle of embalmment consisted, with us, in the immediately arresting, and holding in perpetual *abeyance*, *all* the animal functions subjected to the process. To be brief, in whatever condition the individual was, at the period of embalmment, in that condition he remained. Now, as it is my good fortune to be of the blood of the Scarabæus, I was embalmed *alive*, as you see me at present.'

'The blood of the Scarabæus!' exclaimed Doctor Ponnonner.

'Yes. The Scarabæus was the *insignium*, or the "arms", of a very distinguished and a very rare patrician family. To be "of the blood of the Scarabæus", is merely to be one of that family of which the Scarabæus is the *insignium*. I speak figuratively.'

'But what has this to do with your being alive?'

'Why it is the general custom, in Egypt, to deprive a corpse, before embalmment, of its bowels and brains; the race of the Scarabæi alone did not coincide with the custom. Had I not been a Scarabæus, therefore, I should have been without bowels and brains; and without either it is inconvenient to live.'

'I perceive that;' said Mr Buckingham, 'and I presume that all the *entire* mummies that come to hand are of the race of Scarabæi.'

'Beyond doubt.'

'I thought,' said Mr Gliddon very meekly, 'that the Scarabæus was one of the Egyptian gods.'

'One of the Egyptian *what*?' exclaimed the Mummy, starting to its feet.

'Gods!' repeated the traveler.

'Mr Gliddon I really am astonished to hear you talk in this style,' said the Count, resuming his chair. 'No nation upon the face of the earth has ever acknowledged more than *one god*. The Scarabæus, the Ibis, etc., were with us, (as similar creatures have been with others) the symbols, or *media*, through which we offered worship to the Creator too august to be more directly approached.'

There was here a pause. At length the colloquy was renewed by Doctor Ponnonner.

'It is not improbable, then, from what you have explained,' said he, 'that among the catacombs near the Nile, there may exist other mummies of the Scarabæus tribe, in a condition of vitality.'

'There can be no question of it,' replied the Count; 'all the Scarabæi embalmed accidentally while alive, are alive now. Even some of those *purposely* so embalmed, may have been overlooked by their executors, and still remain in the tombs.'

'Will you be kind enough to explain,' I said, 'what you mean by "purposely so embalmed?" '

'With great pleasure,' answered the Mummy, after surveying me leisurely through his eye-glass – for it was the first time I had ventured to address him a direct question.

'With great pleasure,' said he. 'The usual duration of man's life, in my time, was about eight hundred years. Few men died, unless by most extraordinary accident, before the age of six hundred; few lived longer than a decade of centuries; but eight were considered the natural term. After the discovery of the embalming principle, as I have already described it to you, it occurred to our philosophers that a laudable curiosity might be gratified, and, at the same time, the interests of science much advanced, by living this natural term in instalments. In the case of history, indeed, experience demonstrated that something of this kind was indispensable. An historian, for example, having attained the age of five hundred, would write a book with great labor and then get himself carefully embalmed; leaving instructions to his executors *pro tem.*, that they should cause him to be revivified after the lapse of a certain period – say five or six hundred years. Resuming existence at the expiration of this time, he would invariably find his great work converted into a species of hap-hazard note-book – that is to say, into a kind of literary arena for the conflicting guesses, riddles, and personal squabbles of whole herds of exasperated commentators. These guesses, etc., which passed under the name of annotations or emendations, were found so completely to have enveloped, distorted, and overwhelmed the text, that the author had to go about with a lantern to discover his own book. When discovered, it was never worth the trouble of the search. After rewriting it throughout, it was regarded as the bounden duty of the historian to set himself to work, immediately, in correcting from his own private knowledge and experience, the traditions of the day concerning the epoch at which he had originally lived. Now this process of re-scription and personal rectification, pursued by various individual sages, from time to time, had the effect of preventing our history from degenerating into absolute fable.'

'I beg your pardon,' said Doctor Ponnonner at this point, laying his hand gently upon the arm of the Egyptian – 'I beg your pardon, sir, but may I presume to interrupt you for one moment?'

'By all means, *sir*,' replied the Count, drawing up.

'I merely wished to ask you a question,' said the Doctor. 'You mentioned the historian's personal correction of *traditions* respecting his own epoch. Pray, sir, upon an average, what proportion of these Kabbala were usually found to be right?'

'The Kabbala, as you properly term them, sir, were generally discovered to be precisely on a par with the facts recorded in the un-re-written histories themselves; – that is to say, not one individual iota of either, was ever known, under any circumstances, to be not totally and radically wrong.'

'But since it is quite clear,' resumed the Doctor, 'that at least five thousand years have elapsed since your entombment, I take it for granted that your histories at that period, if not your traditions, were sufficiently explicit on that one topic of universal interest, the Creation, which took place, as I presume you are aware, only about ten centuries before.'

'Sir !' said Count Allamistakeo.

The Doctor repeated his remarks, but it was only after much additional explanation, that the foreigner could be made to comprehend them. The latter at length said, hesitatingly :

'The ideas you have suggested are to me, I confess, utterly novel. During my time I never knew any one to entertain so singular a fancy as that the universe (or this world if you will have it so) ever had a beginning at all. I remember, once, and once only, hearing something remotely hinted, by a man of many speculations, concerning the origin *of the human race*; and by this individual the very word *Adam,* (or Red Earth)[8] which you make use of, was employed. He employed it, however, in a generical sense, with reference to the spontaneous germination from rank soil (just as a thousand of the lower *genera* of creatures are germinated) – the spontaneous germination, I say, of five vast hordes of men, simultaneously upspringing in five distinct and nearly equal divisions of the globe.'

Here, in general, the company shrugged their shoulders, and one or two of us touched our foreheads with a very significant air. Mr Silk Buckingham, first glancing slightly at the occiput and then at the sinciput of Allamistakeo, spoke as follows : –

'The long duration of human life in your time, together with the occasional practice of passing it, as you have explained, in instalments, must have had, indeed, a strong tendency to the general development and conglomeration of knowledge. I presume, therefore, that we are to attribute the marked inferiority of the old Egyptians in all particulars of science, when compared with the moderns, and more especially with the Yankees, altogether to the superior solidity of the Egyptian skull.'

'I confess again,' replied the Count with much suavity, 'that I am somewhat at a loss to comprehend you; pray, to what particulars of science do you allude?'

Here our whole party, joining voices, detailed, at great length, the assumptions of phrenology and the marvels of animal magnetism.

Having heard us to an end, the Count proceeded to relate a few anecdotes, which rendered it evident that prototypes of Gall and Spurzheim had flourished and faded in Egypt so long ago as to have been nearly forgotten, and that the manœuvres of Mesmer[9] were really very contemptible tricks when put in collation with the positive miracles of the Theban *savans*, who created lice and a great many other similar things.

I here asked the Count if his people were able to calculate eclipses. He smiled rather contemptuously, and said they were.

This put me a little out, but I began to make other inquiries in regard to his astronomical knowledge, when a member of the company, who had never as yet opened his mouth, whispered in my ear that, for information on this head, I had better consult Ptolemy, (whoever Ptolemy is)[10] as well as one Plutarch *de facie lunæ*.[11]

I then questioned the Mummy about burning-glasses and lenses, and, in general, about the manufacture of glass; but I had not made an end of my queries before the silent member again touched me quietly on the elbow, and begged me for God's sake to take a peep at Diodorus Siculus.[12] As for the Count, he merely asked me, in the way of reply, if we moderns possessed any such microscopes as would enable us to cut cameos in the style of the Egyptians. While I was thinking how I should answer this question, little Doctor Ponnoner committed himself in a very extraordinary way.

'Look at our architecture!' he exclaimed, greatly to the indignation of both the travelers, who pinched him black and blue to no purpose.

'Look,' he cried with enthusiasm, 'at the Bowling-Green Fountain in New York!'[13] or if this be too vast a contemplation, regard for a moment the Capitol at Washington, D. C.!' – and the good little medical man went on to detail very minutely the proportions of the fabric to which he referred. He explained that the portico alone was adorned with no less than four and twenty columns, five feet in diameter, and ten feet apart.

The Count said that he regretted not being able to remember, just at that moment, the precise dimensions of any one of the principal buildings of the city of Aznac,[14] whose foundations were laid in the night of Time, but the ruins of which were still standing, at the epoch of his entombment, in a vast plain of sand to the westward of Thebes. He recollected, however, (talking of porticoes) that one affixed to an inferior palace in a kind of suburb called Carnac, consisted of a hundred and forty-four columns, thirty-seven feet each in circumference, and twenty-five feet apart. The approach of this portico, from the Nile, was through an avenue two miles long, composed of sphinxes, statues and obelisks, twenty, sixty, and a hundred feet in height. The palace itself (as well as he could remember) was, in one direction, two miles long, and might have been, altogether, about seven in circuit. Its walls were richly painted all over, within and without, with hieroglyphics. He would not pretend to *assert* that even fifty or sixty of the Doctor's Capitols might have been built within these walls, but he was by no means sure that two or three hundred of them might not have been squeezed in with some trouble. That palace at Carnac was an insignificant little building after all. He, (the Count) however, could not conscientiously refuse to admit the ingenuity, magnificence, and superiority of the Fountain at the Bowling-Green, as described by the Doctor. Nothing like it, he was forced to allow, had ever been seen in Egypt or elsewhere.

I here asked the Count what he had to say to our rail-roads.

'Nothing,' he replied, 'in particular.' They were rather slight, rather ill-conceived, and clumsily put together. They could not be compared, of course, with the vast, level, direct, iron-grooved causeways, upon which the Egyptians conveyed entire temples and solid obelisks of a hundred and fifty feet in altitude.

I spoke of our gigantic mechanical forces.

He agreed that we knew something in that way, but inquired how I should have gone to work in getting up the imposts on the lintels of even the little palace at Carnac.

This question I concluded not to hear, and demanded if he had any idea of Artesian wells; but he simply raised his eyebrows; while Mr Gliddon, winked at me very hard, and said, in a low tone, that one had been recently discovered by the engineers employed to bore for water in the Great Oasis.

I then mentioned our steel; but the foreigner elevated his nose, and asked me if our steel could have executed the sharp carved work seen on the obelisks, and which was wrought altogether by edge-tools of copper.

This disconcerted us so greatly that we thought it advisable to vary the attack to Metaphysics. We sent for a copy of a book called the 'Dial',[15] and read out of it a chapter or two about something which is not very clear, but which the Bostonians call the Great Movement or Progress.

The Count merely said that Great Movements were awfully

common things in his day, and as for Progress it was at one time quite a nuisance, but it never progressed.

We then spoke of the great beauty and importance of Democracy, and were at much trouble in impressing the Count with a due sense of the advantages we enjoyed in living where there was suffrage *ad libitum*, and no king.

He listened with marked interest, and in fact seemed not a little amused. When we had done, he said that, a great while ago, there had occurred something of a very similar sort. Thirteen Egyptian provinces determined all at once to be free, and so set a magnificent example to the rest of mankind. They assembled their wise men, and concocted the most ingenious constitution it is possible to conceive. For a while they managed remarkably well; only their habit of bragging was prodigious. The thing ended, however, in the consolidation of the thirteen states, with some fifteen or twenty others, in the most odious and insupportable despotism that ever was heard of upon the face of the Earth.

I asked what was the name of the usurping tyrant.

As well as the Count could recollect, it was *Mob*.

Not knowing what to say to this, I raised my voice, and deplored the Egyptian ignorance of steam.

The Count looked at me with much astonishment, but made no answer. The silent gentleman, however, gave me a violent nudge in the ribs with his elbows – told me I had sufficiently exposed myself for once – and demanded if I was really such a fool as not to know that the modern steam engine is derived from the invention of Hero, through Solomon de Caus.[16]

We were now in imminent danger of being discomfited; but, as good luck would have it, Doctor Ponnonner, having rallied, returned to our rescue, and inquired if the people of Egypt would seriously pretend to rival the moderns in the all-important particular of dress.

The Count, at this, glanced downward to the straps of his pantaloons, and then, taking hold of the end of one of his coat-tails, held it up close to his eyes for some minutes. Letting it fall, at last, his mouth extended itself very gradually from ear to ear; but I do not remember that he said anything in the way of reply.

Hereupon we recovered our spirits, and the Doctor, approaching the Mummy with great dignity, desired it to say candidly, upon its honor as a gentleman, if the Egyptians had comprehended, at *any* period, the manufacture of either Ponnonner's lozenges, or Brandreth's pills.[17]

We looked, with profound anxiety, for an answer; – but in vain. It was not forthcoming. The Egyptian blushed and hung down his head. Never was triumph more consummate; never was defeat borne with so ill a grace. Indeed I could not endure the spectacle of the poor Mummy's mortification. I reached my hat, bowed to him stiffly, and took leave.

Upon getting home I found it past four o'clock, and went immediately to bed. It is now ten, A. M. I have been up since seven, penning these memoranda for the benefit of my family and of mankind. The former I shall behold no more. My wife is a shrew. The truth is, I am heartily sick of this life and of the nineteenth century in general. I am convinced that every thing is going wrong. Besides, I am anxious to know who will be President in 2045. As soon, therefore, as I shave and swallow a cup of coffee, I shall just step over to Ponnonner's and get embalmed for a couple of hundred years.

The Power of Words

Oinos. Pardon, Agathos, the weakness of a spirit new-fledged with immortality ! [1]

Agathos. You have spoken nothing, my Oinos, for which pardon is to be demanded. Not even here is knowledge a thing of intuition. For wisdom ask of the angels freely, that it may be given !

Oinos. But in this existence, I dreamed that I should be at once cognizant of all things, and thus at once happy in being cognizant of all.

Agathos. Ah, not in knowledge is happiness, but in the acquisition of knowledge ! In for ever knowing, we are for ever blessed; but to know all were the curse of a fiend.

Oinos. But does not The Most High know all?

Agathos. *That* (since he is The Most Happy) must be still the *one* thing unknown even to HIM.

Oinos. But, since we grow hourly in knowledge, must not *at last* all things be known?

Agathos. Look down into the abysmal distances ! – attempt to force the gaze down the multitudinous vistas of the stars, as we sweep slowly through them thus – and thus – and thus ! Even the spiritual vision, is it not at all points arrested by the continuous golden walls of the universe? – the walls of the myriads of the shining bodies that mere number has appeared to blend into unity?

Oinos. I clearly perceive that the infinity of matter is no dream.

Agathos. There are *no* dreams in Aidenn [2] – but it is here whispered that, of this infinity of matter, the *sole* purpose is to afford infinite springs, at which the soul may allay the thirst *to know* which is for ever unquenchable within it – since to quench it would be to extinguish the soul's self. Question me then, my Oinos, freely and without fear. Come ! we will leave to the left the loud harmony of the Pleiades,[3] and swoop outward from the throne into the starry meadows beyond Orion, where, for pansies and violets, and heart's-ease, are the beds of the triplicate and triple-tinted suns.[4]

Oinos. And now, Agathos, as we proceed, instruct me! speak to me in the earth's familiar tones! I understood not what you hinted to me, just now, of the modes or of the methods of what, during mortality, we were accustomed to call Creation. Do you mean to say that the Creator is not God?

Agathos. I mean to say that the Deity does not create.

Oinos. Explain!

Agathos. In the beginning *only*, he created. The seeming creatures which are now, throughout the universe, so perpetually springing into being, can only be considered as the mediate or indirect, not as the direct or immediate results of the Divine creative power.

Oinos. Among men, my Agathos, this idea would be considered heretical in the extreme.

Agathos. Among angels, my Oinos, it is seen to be simply true.

Oinos. I can comprehend you thus far – that certain operations of what we term Nature, or the natural laws, will, under certain conditions, give rise to that which has all the *appearance* of creation. Shortly before the final overthrow of the earth, there were, I well remember, many very successful experiments in what some philosophers were weak enough to denominate the creation of animalculæ.

Agathos. The cases of which you speak were, in fact, instances of the secondary creation – and of the *only* species of creation which has ever been, since the first word spoke into existence the first law.

Oinos. Are not the starry worlds that, from the abyss of nonentity, burst hourly forth into the heavens – are not these stars, Agathos, the immediate handiwork of the King?

Agathos. Let me endeavor, my Oinos, to lead you, step by step, to the conception I intend. You are well aware that, as no thought can perish, so no act is without infinite result.[5] We moved our hands, for example, when we were dwellers on the earth, and, in so doing, we gave vibration to the atmosphere which engirdled it. This vibration was indefinitely extended, till it gave impulse to every particle of the earth's air, which thenceforward, *and for ever*, was actuated by the one movement of the hand. This fact the mathematicians of our globe well knew. They made the special effects, indeed, wrought in the fluid by special impulses, the subject of exact calculation – so that it became easy to determine in what precise period an impulse of given extent would engirdle the orb, and impress (for ever) every atom of the atmosphere circumambient. Retrograding, they found no difficulty, from a given effect, under given conditions, in determining the value of the original impulse. Now the mathematicians who saw that the results of any given impulse were absolutely endless – and who saw that a portion of these results were accurately traceable through the agency of algebraic analysis – who saw, too, the facility of the retrogradation – these men saw, at the same time, that this species of analysis itself, had within itself a capacity for indefinite progress – that there were no bounds conceivable to its advancement and applicability, except within the intellect of him who advanced or applied it. But at this point our mathematicians paused.

Oinos. And why, Agathos, should they have proceeded?

Agathos. Because there were some considerations of deep interest, beyond. It was deducible from what they knew, that to a being of infinite understanding – one to whom the *perfection* of the algebraic analysis lay unfolded – there could be no difficulty in tracing every impulse given the air – and the ether through the air – to the remotest consequences at any even infinitely remote epoch of time. It is indeed demonstrable that every such impulse *given the air*, must, *in the end,* impress every individual thing that exists *within the universe*; – and the being of infinite understanding – the being whom we have imagined – might trace the remote undulations of the impulse – trace them upward and onward in their influences upon all particles of all matter – upward and onward for ever in their modifications of old forms – or in other words *in their creation of new* – until he found them reflected – unimpressive *at last* – back from the throne of the Godhead. And not only could such a being do this, but at any epoch, should a given result be afforded him – should one of these numberless comets, for example, be presented to his inspection – he could have no difficulty in determining, by the analytic retrogradation, to what original impulse it was due. This power of retrogradation in its absolute fulness and perfection – this faculty of referring at *all* epochs, *all* effects to *all* causes – is of course the prerogative of the Deity alone – but in every variety of degree, short of the absolute perfection, is the power itself exercised by the whole host of the Angelic Intelligences.

Oinos. But you speak merely of impulses upon the air.

Agathos. In speaking of the air, I referred only to the earth : – but the general proposition has reference to impulses upon the ether – which, since it pervades, and alone pervades all space, is thus the great medium of *creation*.

Oinos. Then all motion, of whatever nature, creates?

Agathos. It must : but a true philosophy has long taught that the source of all motion is thought – and the source of all thought is —

Oinos. God.[6]

Agathos. I have spoken to you, Oinos, as to a child of the fair Earth which lately perished – of impulses upon the atmosphere of the Earth.

Oinos. You did.

Agathos. And while I thus spoke, did there not cross your mind some thought of the *physical power of words*? Is not every word an impulse on the air?

Oinos. But why, Agathos, do you weep? – and why – oh why do your wings droop as we hover above this fair star – which is the greenest and yet most terrible[7] of all we have encountered in our flight? Its brilliant flowers look like a fairy dream – but its fierce volcanoes like the passions of a turbulent heart.

Agathos. They *are* ! – they *are* ! This wild star – it is now three centuries since with clasped hands, and with streaming eyes, at the feet of my beloved – I spoke it – with a few passionate sentences – into birth. Its brilliant flowers *are* the dearest of all unfulfilled dreams, and its raging volcanoes *are* the passions of the most turbulent and unhallowed of hearts.

The System of Dr Tarr and Prof. Fether

DURING the autumn of 18—, while on a tour through the extreme Southern provinces of France, my route led me within a few miles of a certain *Maison de Santé*, or private Mad-House, about which I had heard much, in Paris, from my medical friends. As I had never visited a place of the kind, I thought the opportunity too good to be lost; and so proposed to my traveling companion, (a gentleman with whom I had made casual acquaintance, a few days before,) that we should turn aside, for an hour or so, and look through the establishment. To this he objected – pleading haste, in the first place, and, in the second, a very usual horror at the sight of a lunatic. He begged me, however, not to let any mere courtesy toward himself interfere with the gratification of my curiosity, and said that he would ride on leisurely, so that I might overtake him during the day, or, at all events, during the next. As he bade me good-bye, I bethought me that there might be some difficulty in obtaining access to the premises, and mentioned my fears on this point. He replied that, in fact, unless I had personal knowledge of the superintendent, Monsieur Maillard, or some credential in the way of a letter, a difficulty might be found to exist, as the regulations of these private mad-houses were more rigid than the public hospital laws. For himself, he added, he had, some years since, made the acquaintance of Maillard, and would so far assist me as to ride up to the door and introduce me; although his feelings on the subject of lunacy would not permit of his entering the house.

I thanked him, and, turning from the main-road, we entered a grass-grown by-path, which, in half an hour, nearly lost itself in a dense forest, clothing the base of a mountain. Through this dank and gloomy wood we rode some two miles, when the *Maison de Santé* came in view. It was a fantastic *château*, much dilapidated, and indeed scarcely tenantable through age and neglect. Its aspect inspired me with absolute dread, and, checking my horse, I half resolved to turn back. I soon, however, grew ashamed of my weakness, and proceeded.

As we rode up to the gate-way, I perceived it slightly open, and the visage of a man peering through. In an instant afterward, this man came forth, accosted my companion by name, shook him cordially by the hand, and begged him to alight. It was Monsieur Maillard himself. He was a portly, fine-looking gentleman of the old school, with a polished manner, and a certain air of gravity, dignity, and authority which was very impressive.

My friend, having presented me, mentioned my desire to inspect the establishment, and received Monsieur Maillard's assurance that he would show me all attention, now took leave, and I saw him no more.

When he had gone, the superintendent ushered me into a small and exceedingly neat parlor, containing, among other indications of refined taste, many books, drawings, pots of flowers, and musical instruments. A cheerful fire blazed upon the hearth. At a piano, singing an aria from Bellini, sat a young and very beautiful woman, who, at my entrance, paused in her song, and received me with graceful courtesy. Her voice was low, and her whole manner subdued. I thought, too, that I perceived the traces of sorrow in her countenance, which was excessively, although, to my taste, not unpleasingly pale. She was attired in deep mourning, and excited in my bosom a feeling of mingled respect, interest, and admiration.

I had heard, at Paris, that the institution of Monsieur Maillard was managed upon what is vulgarly termed the 'system of soothing' [1] – that all punishments were avoided – that even confinement was seldom resorted to – that the patients, while secretly watched, were left much apparent liberty, and that most of them were permitted to roam about the house and grounds, in the ordinary apparel of persons in right mind.

Keeping these impressions in view, I was cautious in what I said before the young lady; for I could not be sure that she was sane; and, in fact, there was a certain restless brilliancy about her eyes which half led me to imagine she was not. I confined my remarks, therefore, to general topics, and to such as I thought would not be displeasing or exciting even to a lunatic. She replied in a perfectly rational manner to all that I said; and even her original observations were marked with the soundest good sense; but a long acquaintance with the metaphysics of *mania*, had taught me to put no faith in such evidence of sanity, and I continued to practice, throughout the interview, the caution with which I commenced it.

Presently a smart footman in livery brought in a tray with fruit, wine, and other refreshments, of which I partook, the lady soon afterwards leaving the room. As she departed I turned my eyes in an inquiring manner toward my host.

'No,' he said, 'oh, no – a member of my family – my niece, and a most accomplished woman.'

'I beg a thousand pardons for the suspicion,' I replied, 'but of course you will know how to excuse me. The excellent administration of your affairs here is well understood in Paris, and I thought it just possible, you know –'

'Yes, yes – say no more – or rather it is myself who should thank you for the commendable prudence you have displayed. We seldom find so much of forethought in young men; and, more than once, some unhappy *contre-temps* has occurred in consequence of thoughtlessness on the part of our visiters. While my former system was in operation, and my patients were permitted the privilege of roaming to and fro at will, they were often aroused to a dangerous frenzy by injudicious persons who called to inspect the house. Hence I was obliged to enforce a rigid system of exclusion; and none obtained access to the premises upon whose discretion I could not rely.'

'While your *former* system was in operation !' I said, repeating his words – 'do I understand you, then, to say that the "soothing system" of which I have heard so much, is no longer in force?'

'It is now,' he replied, 'several weeks since we have concluded to renounce it forever.'

'Indeed ! you astonish me !'

'We found it, sir,' he said, with a sigh, 'absolutely necessary to return to the old usages. The *danger* of the soothing system was, at all times, appalling; and its advantages have been much overrated. I believe, sir, that in this house it has been given a fair trial, if ever in any. We did every thing that rational humanity could suggest. I am sorry that you could not have paid us a visit at an earlier period, that you might have judged for yourself. But I presume you are conversant with the soothing practice – with its details.'

'Not altogether. What I have heard has been at third or fourth hand.'

'I may state the system then, in general terms, as one in which the patients were *menagés*, humored. We contradicted *no* fancies which entered the brains of the mad. On the contrary, we not only indulged but encouraged them; and many of our most permanent cures have been thus effected. There is no argument which so touches the feeble reason of the madman as the *argumentum ad absurdum*. We have had men, for example, who fancied themselves chickens. The cure was, to insist upon the thing as a fact – to accuse the patient of stupidity in not sufficiently perceiving it to be a fact – and thus to refuse him any other diet for a week than that which properly appertains to a chicken. In this manner a little corn and gravel were made to perform wonders.'

'But was this species of acquiescence all?'

'By no means. We put much faith in amusements of a simple kind, such as music, dancing, gymnastic exercises generally, cards, certain classes of books, and so forth. We affected to treat each individual as if for some ordinary physical disorder; and the word "lunacy" was never employed. A great point was to set each lunatic to guard the actions of all the others. To repose confidence in the understanding or discretion of a madman, is to gain him body and soul. In this way we were enabled to dispense with an expensive body of keepers.'

'And you had no punishments of any kind?'

'None.'

'And you never confined your patients?'

'Very rarely. Now and then, the malady of some individual growing to a crisis, or taking a sudden turn of fury, we conveyed him to a secret cell, lest his disorder should infect the rest, and there kept him until we could dismiss him to his friends – for

with the raging maniac we have nothing to do. He is usually removed to the public hospitals.'

'And you have now changed all this – and you think for the
better?'

'Decidedly. The system had its disadvantages, and even its
dangers. It is now, happily, exploded throughout all the *Maisons
de Santé* of France.'

'I am very much surprised,' I said, 'at what you tell me; for
I made sure that, at this moment, no other method of treatment
for mania existed in any portion of the country.'

'You are young yet, my friend,' replied my host, 'but the time
will arrive when you will learn to judge for yourself of what is
going on in the world, without trusting to the gossip of others.
Believe nothing you hear, and only one half that you see. Now,
about our *Maisons de Santé*, it is clear that some ignoramus has
misled you. After dinner, however, when you have sufficiently
recovered from the fatigue of your ride, I will be happy to take
you over the house, and introduce to you a system which, in my
opinion, and in that of every one who has witnessed its operation,
is incomparably the most effectual as yet devised.'

'Your own?' I inquired – 'one of your own invention?'

'I am proud,' he replied, 'to acknowledge that it is – at least in
some measure.'

In this manner I conversed with Monsieur Maillard for an
hour or two, during which he showed me the gardens and con-
servatories of the place.

'I cannot let you see my patients,' he said, 'just at present. To a
sensitive mind there is always more or less of the shocking in
such exhibitions; and I do not wish to spoil your appetite for
dinner. We will dine. I can give you some veal *à la Menehoult*,
with cauliflowers in *velouté* sauce – after that a glass of *Clos de
Vougeot* – then your nerves will be sufficiently steadied.'

At six, dinner was announced; and my host conducted me into
a large *salle à manger*, where a very numerous company were
assembled – twenty-five or thirty in all. They were, apparently,
people of rank – certainly of high breeding – although their
habiliments, I thought, were extravagantly rich, partaking some-

what too much of the ostentatious finery of the *vieille cour*. I noticed that at least two-thirds of these guests were ladies; and some of the latter were by no means accoutred in what a Parisian would consider good taste at the present day. Many females, for example, whose age could not have been less than seventy, were bedecked with a profusion of jewelry, such as rings, bracelets, and ear-rings, and wore their bosoms and arms shamefully bare. I observed, too, that very few of the dresses were well made – or, at least, that very few of them fitted the wearers. In looking about, I discovered the interesting girl to whom Monsieur Maillard had presented me in the little parlor; but my surprise was great to see her wearing a hoop and farthingale, with high-heeled shoes, and a dirty cap of Brussels lace, so much too large for her that it gave her face a ridiculously diminutive expression. When I had first seen her she was attired, most becomingly, in deep mourning. There was an air of oddity, in short, about the dress of the whole party, which, at first, caused me to recur to my original idea of the 'soothing system', and to fancy that Monsieur Maillard had been willing to deceive me until after dinner, that I might experience no uncomfortable feelings during the repast, at finding myself dining with lunatics; but I remembered having been informed, in Paris, that the southern provincialists were a peculiarly eccentric people, with a vast number of antiquated notions; and then, too, upon conversing with several members of the company, my apprehensions were immediately and fully dispelled.

The dining-room itself, although perhaps sufficiently comfortable, and of good dimensions, had nothing too much of elegance about it. For example, the floor was uncarpeted; in France, however, a carpet is frequently dispensed with. The windows, too, were without curtains; the shutters, being shut, were securely fastened with iron bars, applied diagonally, after the fashion of our ordinary shop-shutters. The apartment, I observed, formed, in itself, a wing of the *château*, and thus the windows were on three sides of the parallelogram; the door being at the other. There were no less than ten windows in all.

The table was superbly set out. It was loaded with plate, and more than loaded with delicacies. The profusion was absolutely barbaric. There were meats enough to have feasted the Anakim.[2] Never, in all my life, had I witnessed so lavish, so wasteful an expenditure of the good things of life. There seemed very little taste, however, in the arrangements; and my eyes, accustomed to quiet lights, were sadly offended by the prodigious glare of a multitude of wax candles, which, in silver *candelabra*, were deposited upon the table, and all about the room, wherever it was possible to find a place. There were several active servants in attendance; and, upon a large table, at the farther end of the apartment, were seated seven or eight people with fiddles, fifes, trombones, and a drum. These fellows annoyed me very much, at intervals, during the repast, by an infinite variety of noises, which were intended for music, and which appeared to afford much entertainment to all present, with the exception of myself.

Upon the whole, I could not help thinking that there was much of the *bizarre* about every thing I saw – but then the world is made up of all kinds of persons, with all modes of thought, and all sorts of conventional customs. I had traveled, too, so much as to be quite an adept in the *nil admirari*, so I took my seat very coolly at the right hand of my host, and, having an excellent appetite, did justice to the good cheer set before me.

The conversation, in the mean time, was spirited and general. The ladies, as usual, talked a great deal. I soon found that nearly all the company were well educated; and my host was a world of good-humored anecdote in himself. He seemed quite willing to speak of his position as superintendent of a *Maison de Santé*; and, indeed, the topic of lunacy was, much to my surprise, a favorite one with all present. A great many amusing stories were told, having reference to the *whims* of the patients.

'We had a fellow here once,' said a fat little gentleman, who sat at my right – 'a fellow that fancied himself a tea-pot; and, by the way, is it not especially singular how often this particular crotchet has entered the brain of the lunatic? There is scarcely an insane asylum in France which cannot supply a human tea-pot. *Our* gentleman was a Britannia-ware tea-pot, and was careful to polish himself every morning with buckskin and whiting.'

'And then,' said a tall man, just opposite, 'we had here, not long ago, a person who had taken it into his head that he was a donkey – which, allegorically speaking, you will say, was quite true. He was a troublesome patient; and we had much ado to keep him within bounds. For a long time he would eat nothing but thistles; but of this idea we soon cured him by insisting upon his eating nothing else. Then he was perpetually kicking out his heels – so – so –'

'Mr De Kock! I will thank you to behave yourself!' here interrupted an old lady, who sat next to the speaker. 'Please keep your feet to yourself! You have spoiled my brocade! Is it necessary, pray, to illustrate a remark in so practical a style? Our friend, here, can surely comprehend you without all this. Upon my word, you are nearly as great a donkey as the poor unfortunate imagined himself. Your acting is very natural, as I live.'

'*Mille pardons! mam'selle!*' replied Monsieur De Kock, thus addressed – 'a thousand pardons! I had no intention of offending. Mam'selle Laplace – Monsieur De Kock will do himself the honor of taking wine with you.'

Here Monsieur De Kock bowed low, kissed his hand with much ceremony, and took wine with Mam'selle Laplace.

'Allow me, *mon ami*,' now said Monsieur Maillard, addressing myself, 'allow me to send you a morsel of this veal *à la St Menehoult* – you will find it particularly fine.'

At this instant three sturdy waiters had just succeeded in depositing safely upon the table an enormous dish, or trencher, containing what I supposed to be the '*monstrum horrendum, informe, ingens, cui lumen ademptum*'.[3] A closer scrutiny assured me, however, that it was only a small calf roasted whole, and set upon its knees, with an apple in its mouth, as is the English fashion of dressing a hare.

'Thank you, no,' I replied; 'to say the truth, I am not particularly partial to veal *à la St* – what is it? – for I do not find that it altogether agrees with me. I will change my plate, however, and try some of the rabbit.'

There were several side-dishes on the table, containing what appeared to be the ordinary French rabbit – a very delicious *morceau*, which I can recommend.

'Pierre,' cried the host, 'change this gentleman's plate, and give him a side-piece of this rabbit *au-chat*.'

'This what?' said I.

'This rabbit *au-chat*.'

'Why, thank you – upon second thoughts, no. I will just help myself to some of the ham.'

There is no knowing what one eats, thought I to myself, at the tables of these people of the province. I will have none of their rabbit *au-chat* – and, for the matter of that, none of their *cat-au-rabbit* either.

'And then,' said a cadaverous looking personage, near the foot of the table, taking up the thread of the conversation where it had been broken off – 'and then, among other oddities, we had a patient, once upon a time, who very pertinaciously maintained himself to be a Cordova cheese, and went about, with a knife in his hand, soliciting his friends to try a small slice from the middle of his leg.'

'He was a great fool, beyond doubt,' interposed some one, 'but not to be compared with a certain individual whom we all know, with the exception of this strange gentleman. I mean the man who took himself for a bottle of champagne, and always went off with a pop and a fizz, in this fashion.'

Here the speaker, very rudely, as I thought, put his right thumb in his left cheek, withdrew it with a sound resembling the popping of a cork, and then, by a dexterous movement of the tongue upon the teeth, created a sharp hissing and fizzing, which lasted for several minutes, in imitation of the frothing of champagne. This behavior, I saw plainly, was not very pleasing to Monsieur Maillard; but that gentleman said nothing, and the conversation was resumed by a very lean little man in a big wig.

'And then there was an ignoramus,' said he, 'who mistook himself for a frog; which, by the way, he resembled in no little degree. I wish you could have seen him, sir' – here the speaker addressed myself – 'it would have done your heart good to see the natural airs that he put on. Sir, if that man was *not* a frog, I can only observe that it is a pity he was not. His croak thus – o-o-o-o-gh – o-o-o-o-gh! was the finest note in the world – B flat; and when he put his elbows upon the table thus – after taking a glass or two of wine – and distended his mouth, thus, and rolled up his eyes, thus, and winked them, with excessive rapidity, thus, why then, sir, I take it upon myself to say, positively, that you would have been lost in admiration of the genius of the man.'

'I have no doubt of it,' I said.

'And then,' said somebody else, 'then there was Petit Gaillard, who thought himself a pinch of snuff, and was truly distressed because he could not take himself between his own finger and thumb.'

'And then there was Jules Desoulières, who was a very singular genius, indeed, and went mad with the idea that he was a pumpkin. He persecuted the cook to make him up into pies – a thing which the cook indignantly refused to do. For my part, I am by no means sure that a pumpkin pie à la Desoulières, would not have been very capital eating, indeed !'

'You astonish me !' said I; and I looked inquisitively at Monsieur Maillard.

'Ha ! ha ! ha !' said that gentleman – 'he ! he ! he ! – hi ! hi ! hi ! – ho ! ho ! ho ! – hu ! hu ! hu ! – very good indeed ! You must not be astonished, *mon ami*; our friend here is a wit – a *drôle* – you must not understand him to the letter.'

'And then,' said some other one of the party, 'then there was Bouffon Le Grand – another extraordinary personage in his way. He grew deranged through love, and fancied himself possessed of two heads. One of these he maintained to be the head of Cicero; the other he imagined a composite one, being Demosthenes' from the top of the forehead to the mouth, and Lord Brougham from the mouth[4] to the chin. It is not impossible that he was wrong; but he would have convinced you of his being in the right; for he was a man of great eloquence. He had an absolute passion for oratory, and could not refrain from display. For example, he used to leap upon the dinner-table, thus, and – and –'

Here a friend, at the side of the speaker, put a hand upon his shoulder, and whispered a few words in his ear; upon which he ceased talking with great suddenness, and sank back within his chair.

'And then,' said the friend, who had whispered, 'there was Boullard, the tee-totum. I call him the tee-totum, because, in fact, he was seized with the droll, but not altogether irrational crotchet, that he had been converted into a tee-totum. You would have roared with laughter to see him spin.[5] He would turn round upon one heel by the hour, in this manner – so –'

Here the friend whom he had just interrupted by a whisper, performed an exactly similar office for himself.

'But then,' cried an old lady, at the top of her voice, 'your Monsieur Boullard was a madman, and a very silly madman at best; for who, allow me to ask you, ever heard of a human tee-totum? The thing is absurd. Madame Joyeuse was a more sensible person, as you know. She had a crotchet, but it was instinct with common sense, and gave pleasure to all who had the honor of her acquaintance. She found, upon mature deliberation, that, by some accident, she had been turned into a chicken-cock; but, as such, she behaved with propriety. She flapped her wings with prodigious effect – so – so – so – and, as for her crow, it was delicious! Cock-a-doodle-doo! – cock-a-doodle-doo! – cock-a-doodle-de-doo-doo-dooo-do-o-o-o-o-o-o-!'

'Madame Joyeuse, I will thank you to behave yourself!' here interrupted our host, very angrily. 'You can either conduct yourself as a lady should do, or you can quit the table forthwith – take your choice.'

The lady, (whom I was much astonished to hear addressed as Madame Joyeuse, after the description of Madame Joyeuse she had just given,) blushed up to the eye-brows, and seemed exceedingly abashed at the reproof. She hung down her head, and said not a syllable in reply. But another and younger lady resumed the theme. It was my beautiful girl of the little parlor!

'Oh, Madame Joyeuse *was* a fool!' she exclaimed; 'but there was really much sound sense, after all, in the opinion of Eugénie Salsafette. She was a very beautiful and painfully modest young lady, who thought the ordinary mode of habiliment indecent, and wished to dress herself, always, by getting outside, instead of inside of her clothes. It is a thing very easily done, after all. You have only to do so – and then so – so – so – and then so – so – so – and then– '

'Mon dieu! Mam'selle Salsafette!' here cried a dozen voices at once. 'What *are* you about? – forbear! – that is sufficient! – we see, very plainly, how it is done! – hold! hold!' and several persons were already leaping from their seats to withhold Mam'selle Salsafette from putting herself upon a par with the Medicean Venus, when the point was very effectually and suddenly accomplished by a series of loud screams, or yells, from some portion of the main body of the château.

My nerves were very much affected, indeed, by these yells; but the rest of the company I really pitied. I never saw any set of reasonable people so thoroughly frightened in my life. They all grew as pale as so many corpses, and, shrinking within their seats, sat quivering and gibbering with terror, and listening for a repetition of the sound. It came again – louder and seemingly nearer – and then a third time *very* loud, and then a fourth time with a vigor evidently diminished. At this apparent dying away of the noise, the spirits of the company were immediately regained, and all was life and anecdote as before. I now ventured to inquire the cause of the disturbance.

'A mere *bagatelle*,' said Monsieur Maillard. 'We are used to these things, and care really very little about them. The lunatics, every now and then, get up a howl in concert; one starting another, as is sometimes the case with a bevy of dogs at night. It occasionally happens, however, that the *concerto* yells are succeeded by a simultaneous effort at breaking loose; when, of course, some little danger is to be apprehended.'

'And how many have you in charge?'

'At present, we have not more than ten, altogether.'

'Principally females, I presume?'

'Oh, no – every one of them men, and stout fellows, too, I can tell you.'

'Indeed! I have always understood that the majority of lunatics were of the gentler sex.'

'It is generally so, but not always. Some time ago, there were about twenty-seven patients here; and, of that number, no less than eighteen were women; but, lately, matters have changed very much, as you see.'

'Yes – have changed very much, as you see,' here interrupted the gentleman who had broken the shins of Mam'selle Laplace.

'Yes – have changed very much, as you see!' chimed in the whole company at once.

'Hold your tongues, every one of you!' said my host, in a great rage. Whereupon the whole company maintained a dead silence for nearly a minute. As for one lady, she obeyed Monsieur Maillard to the letter, and thrusting out her tongue, which was an excessively long one, held it very resignedly, with both hands, until the end of the entertainment.

'And this gentlewoman,' said I, to Monsieur Maillard, bending over and addressing him in a whisper – 'this good lady who has just spoken, and who gives us the cock-a-doodle-de-doo – she, I presume, is harmless – quite harmless, eh?'

'Harmless!' ejaculated he, in unfeigned surprise, 'why – why what *can* you mean?'

'Only slightly touched?' said I, touching my head. 'I take it for granted that she is not particularly – not dangerously affected, eh?'

'*Mon Dieu!* what *is* it you imagine? This lady, my particular old friend, Madame Joyeuse, is as absolutely sane as myself. She has her little eccentricities, to be sure – but then, you know, all old women – all *very* old women are more or less eccentric!'

'To be sure,' said I – 'to be sure – and then the rest of these ladies and gentlemen –'

'Are my friends and keepers,' interrupted Monsieur Maillard, drawing himself up with *hauteur* – 'my very good friends and assistants.'

'What! all of them?' I asked – 'the women and all?'

'Assuredly,' he said – 'we could not do at all without the women; they are the best lunatic-nurses in the world; they have a way of their own, you know; their bright eyes have a marvellous effect; – something like the fascination of the snake, you know.'

'To be sure,' said I – 'to be sure! They behave a little odd, eh? – they are a little *queer*, eh? – don't you think so?'

'Odd! – queer! – why, do you *really* think so? We are not very prudish, to be sure, here in the South – do pretty much as we please – enjoy life, and all that sort of thing, you know –'

'To be sure,' said I – 'to be sure.'

'And then, perhaps, this *Clos de Vougeot* is a little heady, you know – a little *strong* – you understand, eh?'

'To be sure,' said I – 'to be sure. By-the-bye, monsieur, did I understand you to say that the system you have adopted, in place of the celebrated soothing system, was one of very rigorous severity?'

'By no means. Our confinement is necessarily close; but the treatment – the medical treatment, I mean – is rather agreeable to the patients than otherwise.'

'And the new system is one of your own invention?'

'Not altogether. Some portions of it are referable to Professor Tarr, of whom you have, necessarily, heard; and, again, there are modifications in my plan which I am happy to acknowledge as belonging of right to the celebrated Fether, with whom, if I mistake not, you have the honor of an intimate acquaintance.'

'I am quite ashamed to confess,' I replied, 'that I have never even heard the name of either gentleman before.'

'Good Heavens!' ejaculated my host, drawing back his chair abruptly, and uplifting his hands. 'I surely do not hear you aright! You did not intend to say, eh? that you had never *heard* either of the learned Doctor Tarr, or of the celebrated Professor Fether?'

'I am forced to acknowledge my ignorance,' I replied; 'but the truth should be held inviolate above all things. Nevertheless, I feel humbled to the dust, not to be acquainted with the works of these no doubt extraordinary men. I will seek out their writings forthwith, and peruse them with deliberate care. Monsieur Maillard, you have really – I must confess it – you have *really* made me ashamed of myself!'

And this was the fact.

'Say no more, my good young friend,' he said kindly, pressing my hand – 'join me now in a glass of Sauterne.'

We drank. The company followed our example, without stint. They chatted – they jested – they laughed – they perpetrated a thousand absurdities – the fiddles shrieked – the drum row-de-dowed – the trombones bellowed like so many brazen bulls of Phalaris[6] – and the whole scene, growing gradually worse and worse, as the wines gained the ascendancy, became at length a sort of Pandemonium *in petto*.[7] In the meantime, Monsieur Maillard and myself, with some bottles of Sauterne and Vougeot between us, continued our conversation at the top of the voice. A word spoken in an ordinary key stood no more chance of being heard than the voice of a fish from the bottom of Niagara Falls.

'And, sir,' said I, screaming in his ear, 'you mentioned something, before dinner, about the danger incurred in the old system of soothing. How is that?'

'Yes,' he replied, 'there was, occasionally, very great danger, indeed. There is no accounting for the caprices of madmen; and, in my opinion, as well as in that of Doctor Tarr and Professor Fether, it is *never* safe to permit them to run at large unattended. A lunatic may be "soothed", as it is called, for a time, but, in the end, he is very apt to become obstreperous. His cunning, too, is proverbial, and great. If he has a project in view, he conceals his design with a marvellous wisdom; and the dexterity with which he counterfeits sanity, presents, to the metaphysician, one of the most singular problems in the study of mind. When a madman appears *thoroughly* sane, indeed, it is high time to put him in a strait-jacket.'

'But the *danger*, my dear sir, of which you were speaking – in your own experience – during your control of this house – have you had practical reason to think liberty hazardous, in the case of a lunatic?'

'Here? – in my own experience? – why, I may say, yes. For example: – no *very* long while ago, a singular circumstance occurred in this very house. The "soothing system", you know, was then in operation, and the patients were at large. They behaved remarkably well – especially so – any one of sense might have known that some devilish scheme was brewing from that particular fact, that the fellows behaved so *remarkably* well. And, sure enough, one fine morning the keepers found themselves pinioned hand and foot, and thrown into the cells, where they were attended, as if *they* were the lunatics, by the lunatics themselves, who had usurped the offices of the keepers.'

'You don't tell me so! I never heard of anything so absurd in my life!'

'Fact – it all came to pass by means of a stupid fellow – a lunatic – who, by some means, had taken it into his head that he had invented a better system of government than any ever heard of before – of lunatic government, I mean. He wished to give his invention a trial, I suppose – and so he persuaded the rest of the patients to join him in a conspiracy for the overthrow of the reigning powers.'

'And he really succeeded?'

'No doubt of it. The keepers and kept were soon made to exchange places. Not that exactly either – for the madmen had been free, but the keepers were shut up in cells forthwith, and treated, I am sorry to say, in a very cavalier manner.'

'But I presume a counter revolution was soon effected. This condition of things could not have long existed. The country people in the neighborhood – visiters coming to see the establishment – would have given the alarm.'

'There you are out. The head rebel was too cunning for that. He admitted no visiters at all – with the exception, one day, of a very stupid-looking young gentleman of whom he had no reason to be afraid. He let him in to see the place – just by way of variety – to have a little fun with him. As soon as he had gammoned him sufficiently,[8] he let him out, and sent him about his business.'

'And *how* long, then, did the madmen reign?'

'Oh, a very long time, indeed – a month certainly – how much longer I can't precisely say. In the mean time, the lunatics had a jolly season of it – that you may swear. They doffed their own shabby clothes, and made free with the family wardrobe and jewels. The cellars of the *château* were well stocked with wine; and these madmen are just the devils that know how to drink it. They lived well, I can tell you.'

'And the treatment – what was the particular species of treatment which the leader of the rebels put into operation?'

'Why, as for that, a madman is not necessarily a fool, as I have already observed; and it is my honest opinion that his treatment was a much better treatment than that which it superseded. It was a very capital system, indeed – simple – neat – no trouble at all – in fact it was delicious – it was –'

Here my host's observations were cut short by another series of yells, of the same character as those which had previously disconcerted us. This time, however, they seemed to proceed from persons rapidly approaching.

'Gracious Heavens!' I ejaculated – 'the lunatics have most undoubtedly broken loose.'

'I very much fear it is so,' replied Monsieur Maillard, now becoming excessively pale. He had scarcely finished the sentence, before loud shouts and imprecations were heard beneath the windows; and, immediately afterward, it became evident that some persons outside were endeavoring to gain entrance into the room. The door was beaten with what appeared to be a sledgehammer, and the shutters were wrenched and shaken with prodigious violence.

A scene of the most terrible confusion ensued. Monsieur Maillard, to my excessive astonishment, threw himself under the sideboard. I had expected more resolution at his hands. The members of the orchestra, who, for the last fifteen minutes, had been seemingly too much intoxicated to do duty, now sprang all at once to their feet and to their instruments, and, scrambling upon their table, broke out, with one accord, into 'Yankee Doodle', which they performed, if not exactly in tune, at least with an energy superhuman, during the whole of the uproar.

Meantime, upon the main dining-table, among the bottles and glasses, leaped the gentleman who, with such difficulty, had been restrained from leaping there before. As soon as he fairly settled himself, he commenced an oration, which, no doubt, was a very capital one, if it could only have been heard. At the same moment, the man with the tee-totum predilections, set himself to spinning around the apartment, with immense energy, and with arms outstretched at right angles with his body; so that he had all the air of a tee-totum in fact, and knocked every body down that happened to get in his way. And now, too, hearing an incredible popping and fizzing of champagne, I discovered, at length, that it proceeded from the person who performed the bottle of that delicate drink during dinner. And then, again, the frog-man croaked away as if the salvation of his soul depended upon every note that he uttered. And, in the midst of all this, the continuous braying of a donkey arose over all. As for my old friend, Madame Joyeuse, I really could have wept for the poor lady, she appeared so terribly perplexed. All she did, however, was to stand up in a corner, by the fire-place, and sing out incessantly, at the top of her voice, 'Cock-a-doodle-de-dooooooh !'

And now came the climax – the catastrophe of the drama. As no resistance, beyond whooping and yelling and cock-a-doodle-ing, was offered to the encroachments of the party without, the ten windows were very speedily, and almost simultaneously, broken in. But I shall never forget the emotions of wonder and horror with which I gazed, when, leaping through these windows, and down among us *péle-méle*, fighting, stamping, scratching, and howling, there rushed a perfect army of what I took to be Chimpanzees, Ourang-Outangs, or big black baboons of the Cape of Good Hope.

I received a terrible beating – after which I rolled under a sofa, and lay still. After lying there some fifteen minutes, however, during which time I listened with all my ears to what was going on in the room, I came to some satisfactory *dénouement* of this tragedy. Monsieur Maillard, it appeared, in giving me the account of the lunatic who had excited his fellows to rebellion, had been merely relating his own exploits. This gentleman had, indeed, some two or three years before, been the superintendent of the establishment; but grew crazy himself, and so became a patient. This fact was unknown to the traveling companion who introduced me. The keepers, ten in number, having been suddenly overpowered, were first well tarred, then carefully feathered, and then shut up in underground cells. They had been so imprisoned for more than a month, during which period Monsieur Maillard had generously allowed them not only the tar and feathers (which constituted his 'system') but some bread, and abundance of water. The latter was pumped on them daily. At length, one escaping through a sewer, gave freedom to all the rest.

The 'soothing system', with important modifications, has been resumed at the *château*; yet I cannot help agreeing with Monsieur Maillard, that his own 'treatment' was a very capital one of its kind. As he justly observed, it was 'simple – neat – and gave no trouble at all – not the least'.

I have only to add that, although I have searched every library in Europe for the works of Dr *Tarr* and Professor *Fether*, I have, up to the present day, utterly failed in my endeavors at procuring an edition.

The Facts in the Case of M. Valdemar

OF course I shall not pretend to consider it any matter for wonder, that the extraordinary case of M. Valdemar has excited discussion. It would have been a miracle had it not – especially under the circumstances. Through the desire of all parties concerned, to keep the affair from the public, at least for the present, or until we had farther opportunities for investigation – through our endeavors to effect this – a garbled or exaggerated account made its way into society, and became the source of many unpleasant misrepresentations, and, very naturally, of a great deal of disbelief.

It is now rendered necessary that I give the *facts* – as far as I comprehend them myself. They are, succinctly, these :

My attention, for the last three years, had been repeatedly drawn to the subject of Mesmerism; and, about nine months ago, it occurred to me, quite suddenly, that in the series of experiments made hitherto, there had been a very remarkable and most unaccountable omission : – no person had as yet been mesmerized *in articulo mortis*. It remained to be seen, first, whether, in such condition, there existed in the patient any susceptibility to the magnetic influence; secondly, whether, if any existed, it was impaired or increased by the condition; thirdly, to what extent, or for how long a period, the encroachments of Death might be arrested by the process. There were other points to be ascertained, but these most excited my curiosity – the last in especial, from the immensely important character of its consequences.

In looking around me for some subject by whose means I might test these particulars, I was brought to think of my friend, M. Ernest Valdemar, the well-known compiler of the 'Bibliotheca Forensica', and author (under the *nom de plume* of Issachar Marx)[1] of the Polish versions of 'Wallenstein' and 'Gargantua'. M. Valdemar, who has resided principally at Harlaem, N.Y., since the year 1839, is (or was) particularly noticeable for the extreme spareness of his person – his lower limbs much resembling those of John Randolph;[2] and, also, for the whiteness of his whiskers, in violent contrast to the blackness of his hair – the latter, in consequence, being very generally mistaken for a wig. His temperament was markedly nervous, and rendered him a good subject for mesmeric experiment. On two or three occasions I had put him to sleep with little difficulty, but was disappointed in other results which his peculiar constitution had naturally led me to anticipate. His will was at no period positively, or thoroughly, under my control, and in regard to *clairvoyance*, I could accomplish with him nothing to be relied upon. I always attributed my failure at these points to the disordered state of his health. For some months previous to my becoming acquainted with him, his physicians had declared him in a confirmed phthisis. It was his custom, indeed, to speak calmly of his approaching dissolution, as of a matter neither to be avoided nor regretted.

When the ideas to which I have alluded first occurred to me, it was of course very natural that I should think of M. Valdemar. I knew the steady philosophy of the man too well to apprehend any scruples from *him*; and he had no relatives in America who would be likely to interfere. I spoke to him frankly upon the subject; and, to my surprise, his interest seemed vividly excited. I say to my surprise; for, although he had always yielded his person freely to my experiments, he had never before given me any tokens of sympathy with what I did. His disease was of that character which would admit of exact calculation in respect to the epoch of its termination in death; and it was finally arranged between us that he would send for me about twenty-four hours before the period announced by his physicians as that of his decease.

It is now rather more than seven months since I received, from M. Valdemar himself, the subjoined note:

MY DEAR P——,
    You may as well come *now*. D—— and F—— are agreed that I cannot hold out beyond to-morrow midnight; and I think they have hit the time very nearly.

                                                            VALDEMAR

I received this note within half an hour after it was written, and in fifteen minutes more I was in the dying man's chamber. I had not seen him for ten days, and was appalled by the fearful alteration which the brief interval had wrought in him. His face wore a leaden hue; the eyes were utterly lustreless; and the emaciation was so extreme that the skin had been broken through by the cheek-bones. His expectoration was excessive. The pulse was barely perceptible. He retained, nevertheless, in a very remarkable manner, both his mental power and a certain degree of physical strength. He spoke with distinctness – took some palliative medicines without aid – and, when I entered the room, was occupied in penciling memoranda in a pocket-book. He was propped up in the bed by pillows. Doctors D— and F— were in attendance.

After pressing Valdemar's hand, I took these gentlemen aside, and obtained from them a minute account of the patient's condition. The left lung had been for eighteen months in a semi-osseous or cartilaginous state, and was, of course, entirely useless for all purposes of vitality. The right, in its upper portion, was also partially, if not thoroughly, ossified, while the lower region was merely a mass of purulent tubercles, running one into another. Several extensive perforations existed; and, at one point, permanent adhesion to the ribs had taken place. These appearances in the right lobe were of comparatively recent date. The ossification had proceeded with very unusual rapidity; no sign of it had been discovered a month before, and the adhesion had only been observed during the three previous days. Independently of the phthisis, the patient was suspected of aneurism of the aorta; but on this point the osseous symptoms rendered an exact diagnosis impossible.[3] It was the opinion of both physicians that M. Valdemar would die about midnight on the morrow (Sunday). It was then seven o'clock on Saturday evening.

On quitting the invalid's bed-side to hold conversation with myself, Doctors D— and F— had bidden him a final farewell. It had not been their intention to return; but, at my request, they agreed to look in upon the patient about ten the next night.

When they had gone, I spoke freely with M. Valdemar on the subject of his approaching dissolution, as well as, more particularly, of the experiment proposed. He still professed himself quite willing and even anxious to have it made, and urged me to commence it at once. A male and a female nurse were in attendance; but I did not feel myself altogether at liberty to engage in a task of this character with no more reliable witnesses than these people, in case of sudden accident, might prove. I therefore postponed operations until about eight the next night, when the arrival of a medical student with whom I had some acquaintance, (Mr Theodore L—l,) relieved me from farther embarrassment. It had been my design, originally, to wait for the physicians; but I was induced to proceed, first, by the urgent entreaties of M. Valdemar, and secondly, by my conviction that I had not a moment to lose, as he was evidently sinking fast.

Mr L—l was so kind as to accede to my desire that he would take notes of all that occurred; and it is from his memoranda that what I now have to relate is, for the most part, either condensed or copied *verbatim*.

It wanted about five minutes of eight when, taking the patient's hand, I begged him to state, as distinctly as he could, to Mr L—l, whether he (M. Valdemar) was entirely willing that I should make the experiment of mesmerizing him in his then condition.

He replied feebly, yet quite audibly, 'Yes, I wish to be mesmerized' – adding immediately afterwards, 'I fear you have deferred it too long.'

While he spoke thus, I commenced the passes which I had already found most effectual in subduing him. He was evidently influenced with the first lateral stroke of my hand across his forehead; but although I exerted all my powers, no farther perceptible effect was induced until some minutes after ten o'clock, when Doctors D— and F— called, according to appointment. I explained to them, in a few words, what I designed, and as they opposed no objection, saying that the patient was already in the death agony, I proceeded without hesitation – exchanging, however, the lateral passes for downward ones, and directing my gaze entirely into the right eye of the sufferer.

By this time his pulse was imperceptible and his breathing was stertorous, and at intervals of half a minute.

This condition was nearly unaltered for a quarter of an hour. At the expiration of this period, however, a natural although a very deep sigh escaped the bosom of the dying man, and the stertorous breathing ceased – that is to say, its stertorousness was no longer apparent; the intervals were undiminished. The patient's extremities were of an icy coldness.

At five minutes before eleven I perceived unequivocal signs of the mesmeric influence. The glassy roll of the eye was changed for that expression of uneasy *inward* examination which is never seen except in cases of sleep-waking, and which it is quite impossible to mistake. With a few rapid lateral passes I made the lids quiver, as in incipient sleep, and with a few more I closed them altogether. I was not satisfied, however, with this, but continued the manipulations vigorously, and with the fullest exertion of the will, until I had completely stiffened the limbs of the slumberer, after placing them in a seemingly easy position. The legs were at full length; the arms were nearly so, and reposed on the bed at a moderate distance from the loins. The head was very slightly elevated.

When I had accomplished this, it was fully midnight, and I requested the gentlemen present to examine M. Valdemar's condition. After a few experiments, they admitted him to be in an unusually perfect state of mesmeric trance. The curiosity of both the physicians was greatly excited. Dr D— resolved at once to remain with the patient all night, while Dr F— took leave with a promise to return at daybreak. Mr L—l and the nurses remained.

We left M. Valdemar entirely undisturbed until about three o'clock in the morning, when I approached him and found him in precisely the same condition as when Dr F— went away – that is to say, he lay in the same position; the pulse was imperceptible; the breathing was gentle (scarcely noticeable, unless through the application of a mirror to the lips); the eyes were closed naturally; and the limbs were as rigid and as cold as marble. Still, the general appearance was certainly not that of death.

As I approached M. Valdemar I made a kind of half effort to influence his right arm into pursuit of my own, as I passed the latter gently to and fro above his person. In such experiments with this patient I had never perfectly succeeded before, and assuredly I had little thought of succeeding now; but to my astonishment, his arm very readily, although feebly, followed every direction I assigned it with mine. I determined to hazard a few words of conversation.

'M. Valdemar,' I said, 'are you asleep?' He made no answer, but I perceived a tremor about the lips, and was thus induced to repeat the question, again and again. At its third repetition, his whole frame was agitated by a very slight shivering; the eyelids unclosed themselves so far as to display a white line of the ball; the lips moved sluggishly, and from between them, in a barely audible whisper, issued the words:

'Yes; – asleep now. Do not wake me! – let me die so!'

I here felt the limbs and found them as rigid as ever. The right arm, as before, obeyed the direction of my hand. I questioned the sleep-waker again:

'Do you still feel pain in the breast, M. Valdemar?'

The answer now was immediate, but even less audible than before.

'No pain – I am dying.'

I did not think it advisable to disturb him farther just then, and nothing more was said or done until the arrival of Dr F—, who came a little before sunrise, and expressed unbounded astonishment at finding the patient still alive. After feeling the pulse and applying a mirror to the lips, he requested me to speak to the sleep-waker again. I did so, saying:

'M. Valdemar, do you still sleep?'

As before, some minutes elapsed ere a reply was made; and during the interval the dying man seemed to be collecting his energies to speak. At my fourth repetition of the question, he said very faintly, almost inaudibly:

'Yes; still asleep – dying.'

It was now the opinion, or rather the wish, of the physicians, that M. Valdemar should be suffered to remain undisturbed in his present apparently tranquil condition, until death should supervene – and this, it was generally agreed, must now take place within a few minutes. I concluded, however, to speak to him once more, and merely repeated my previous question.

While I spoke, there came a marked change over the countenance of the sleep-waker. The eyes rolled themselves slowly open, the pupils disappearing upwardly; the skin generally assumed a cadaverous hue, resembling not so much parchment as white paper; and the circular hectic spots which, hitherto, had been strongly defined in the centre of each cheek, *went out* at once. I use this expression, because the suddenness of their departure put me in mind of nothing so much as the extinguishment of a candle by a puff of the breath. The upper lip, at the same time, writhed itself away from the teeth, which it had previously covered completely; while the lower jaw fell with an audible jerk, leaving the mouth widely extended, and disclosing in full view the swollen and blackened tongue. I presume that no member of the party then present had been unaccustomed to death-bed horrors; but so hideous beyond conception was the appearance of M. Valdemar at this moment, that there was general shrinking back from the region of the bed.

I now feel that I have reached a point of this narrative at which every reader will be startled into positive disbelief. It is my business, however, simply to proceed.

There was no longer the faintest sign of vitality in M. Valdemar; and concluding him to be dead, we were consigning him to the charge of the nurses, when a strong vibratory motion was observable in the tongue. This continued for perhaps a minute. At the expiration of this period, there issued from the distended and motionless jaws a voice – such as it would be madness in me to attempt describing. There are, indeed, two or three epithets which might be considered as applicable to it in part; I might say, for example, that the sound was harsh, and broken and hollow; but the hideous whole is indescribable, for the simple reason that no similar sounds have ever jarred upon the ear of humanity. There were two particulars, nevertheless, which I thought then, and still think, might fairly be stated as characteristic of the intonation – as well adapted to convey some idea of its unearthly peculiarity. In the first place, the voice seemed to reach our ears – at least mine – from a vast distance, or from some deep cavern within the earth. In the second place, it impressed me (I fear, indeed, that it will be impossible to make myself comprehended) as gelatinous or glutinous matters impress the sense of touch.

I have spoken both of 'sound' and of 'voice'. I mean to say that the sound was one of distinct – of even wonderfully, thrillingly distinct – syllabification. M. Valdemar *spoke* – obviously in reply to the question I had propounded to him a few minutes before. I had asked him, it will be remembered, if he still slept. He now said :

'Yes; – no; – I *have been* sleeping – and now – now – *I am dead*.'

No person present even affected to deny, or attempted to repress, the unutterable, shuddering horror which these few words, thus uttered, were so well calculated to convey. Mr L—l (the student) swooned. The nurses immediately left the chamber, and could not be induced to return. My own impressions I would not pretend to render intelligible to the reader. For nearly an hour, we busied ourselves, silently – without the utterance of a word – in endeavors to revive Mr L—l. When he came to himself, we addressed ourselves again to an investigation of M. Valdemar's condition.

It remained in all respects as I have last described it, with the exception that the mirror no longer afforded evidence of respiration. An attempt to draw blood from the arm failed. I should mention, too, that this limb was no farther subject to my will. I endeavored in vain to make it follow the direction of my hand. The only real indication, indeed, of the mesmeric influence, was now found in the vibratory movement of the tongue, whenever I addressed M. Valdemar a question. He seemed to be making an effort to reply, but had no longer sufficient volition. To queries put to him by any other person than myself he seemed utterly insensible – although I endeavored to place each member of the company in mesmeric *rapport* with him. I believe that I have now related all that is necessary to an understanding of the sleep-waker's state at this epoch. Other nurses were procured; and at ten o'clock I left the house in company with the two physicians and Mr L—l.

In the afternoon we all called again to see the patient. His condition remained precisely the same. We had now some discussion as to the propriety and feasibility of awakening him; but we had little difficulty in agreeing that no good purpose would be served by so doing. It was evident that, so far, death (or what is usually termed death) had been arrested by the mesmeric process. It seemed clear to us all that to awaken M. Valdemar would be merely to insure his instant, or at least his speedy dissolution.

From this period until the close of last week – *an interval of nearly seven months* – we continued to make daily calls at M. Valdemar's house, accompanied, now and then, by medical and other friends. All this time the sleep-waker remained *exactly* as I have last described him. The nurses' attentions were continual.

It was on Friday last that we finally resolved to make the experiment of awakening, or attempting to awaken him; and it is the (perhaps) unfortunate result of this latter experiment which has given rise to so much discussion in private circles – to so much of what I cannot help thinking unwarranted popular feeling.

For the purpose of relieving M. Valdemar from the mesmeric trance, I made use of the customary passes. These, for a time, were unsuccessful. The first indication of revival was afforded by a partial descent of the iris. It was observed, as especially remarkable, that this lowering of the pupil was accompanied by the profuse out-flowing of a yellowish ichor (from beneath the lids) of a pungent and highly offensive odor.

It was now suggested that I should attempt to influence the patient's arm, as heretofore. I made the attempt and failed. Dr F— then intimated a desire to have me put a question. I did so, as follows :

'M. Valdemar, can you explain to us what are your feelings or wishes now?'

There was an instant return of the hectic circles on the cheeks; the tongue quivered, or rather rolled violently in the mouth (although the jaws and lips remained rigid as before;) and at length the same hideous voice which I have already described, broke forth :

'For God's sake! – quick! – quick! – put me to sleep – or, quick! – waken me! – quick! – I *say to you that I am dead!*'

I was thoroughly unnerved, and for an instant remained undecided what to do. At first I made an endeavor to re-compose the patient; but, failing in this through total abeyance of the will, I retraced my steps and as earnestly struggled to awaken him. In this attempt I soon saw that I should be successful – or at least I soon fancied that my success would be complete – and I am sure that all in the room were prepared to see the patient awaken.

For what really occurred, however, it is quite impossible that any human being could have been prepared.

As I rapidly made the mesmeric passes,[4] amid ejaculations of 'dead! dead!' absolutely *bursting* from the tongue and not from the lips of the sufferer, his whole frame at once – within the space of a single minute, or even less, shrunk – crumbled – absolutely *rotted* away beneath my hands. Upon the bed, before that whole company, there lay a nearly liquid mass of loathsome – of detestable putridity.[5]

EUREKA

A Prose Poem

With Very Profound Respect,
This Work is Dedicated
to
Alexander Von Humboldt[1]

Preface

To the few who love me and whom I love – to those who feel rather than to those who think – to the dreamers and those who put faith in dreams as in the only realities – I offer this Book of Truths, not in its character of Truth-Teller, but for the Beauty that abounds in its Truth; constituting it true. To these I present the composition as an Art-Product alone : – let us say as a Romance; or, if I be not urging too lofty a claim, as a Poem.

What I here propound is true : – therefore it cannot die : – or if by any means it be now trodden down so that it die, it will 'rise again to the Life Everlasting'.

Nevertheless it is as a Poem only that I wish this work to be judged after I am dead.

E.A.P.

Eureka

An Essay on the Material and Spiritual Universe

It is with humility really unassumed – it is with a sentiment even of awe – that I pen the opening sentence of this work; for of all conceivable subjects I approach the reader with the most solemn – the most comprehensive – the most difficult – the most august.

What terms shall I find sufficiently simple in their sublimity – sufficiently sublime in their simplicity – for the mere enunciation of my theme?

I design to speak of the *Physical, Metaphysical and Mathematical – of the Material and Spiritual Universe*; – *of its Essence, its Origin, its Creation, its Present Condition and its Destiny*. I shall be so rash, moreover, as to challenge the conclusions, and thus, in effect, to question the sagacity, of many of the greatest and most justly reverenced of men.

In the beginning, let me as distinctly as possible announce – not the theorem which I hope to demonstrate – for, whatever the mathematicians may assert, there is, in this world at least, *no such thing* as demonstration – but the ruling idea which, throughout this volume, I shall be continually endeavoring to suggest.

My general proposition, then, is this : – *In the Original Unity of the First Thing lies the Secondary Cause of All Things, with the Germ of their Inevitable Annihilation.*

In illustration of this idea, I propose to take such a survey of the Universe that the mind may be able really to receive and to perceive an individual impression.

He who from the top of Ætna casts his eyes leisurely around, is affected chiefly by the *extent* and *diversity* of the scene. Only by a rapid whirling on his heel could he hope to comprehend the panorama in the sublimity of its *oneness*. But as, on the summit of Ætna, *no* man has thought of whirling on his heel, so no man has ever taken into his brain the full uniqueness of the prospect; and so, again, whatever considerations lie involved in this uniqueness, have as yet no practical existence for mankind.

I do not know a treatise in which a survey of the *Universe* – using the word in its most comprehensive and only legitimate acceptation – is taken at all : – and it may be as well here to mention that by the term 'Universe', wherever employed without qualification in this essay, I mean in most cases to designate *the utmost conceivable expanse of space, with all things, spiritual and material, that can be imagined to exist within the compass of that expanse*. In speaking of what is *ordinarily* implied by the expression, 'Universe', I shall in most cases, again take a phrase of limitation – 'the Universe of Stars'. Why this distinction is considered necessary, will be seen in the sequel.

But even of treatises on the really limited, although always assumed as the *un*limited, Universe of *Stars*, I know none in which a survey, even of this limited Universe, is so taken as to warrant deductions from its *individuality*. The nearest approach to such a work is made in the 'Cosmos' of Alexander Von Humboldt. He presents the subject, however, *not* in its individuality but in its generality. His theme, in its last result, is the law of *each* portion of the merely physical Universe, as this law is related to the laws of *every other* portion of this merely physical Universe. His design is simply synœretical.[2] In a word, he discusses the universality of material relation, and discloses to the eye of Philosophy whatever inferences have hitherto lain hidden *behind* this universality. But however admirable be the succinctness with which he has treated each particular point of his topic, the mere multiplicity of these points occasions, necessarily, an amount of detail, and thus an involution of idea, which preclude all *individuality* of impression.

It seems to me that, in aiming at this latter effect, and, through it, at the consequences – the conclusions – the suggestions – the speculations – or, if nothing better offer itself, the mere guesses which may result from it – we require something like a mental gyration on the heel. We need so rapid a revolution of all things about the central point of sight that, while the minutiæ vanish altogether, even the more conspicuous objects become blended into one. Among the vanishing minutiæ, in a survey of this kind, would be all exclusively terrestrial matters. The Earth would be considered in its planetary relations alone. A man, in this view, becomes Mankind; Mankind a member of the cosmical family of Intelligences.

And now, before proceeding to our subject proper, let me beg the reader's attention to an extract or two from a somewhat remarkable letter, which appears to have been found corked in a bottle and floating on the *Mare Tenebrarum* – an ocean well described by the Nubian geographer, Ptolemy Hephestion,[3] but little frequented in modern days unless by the Transcendentalists and some other divers for crotchets. The date of this letter, I confess, surprises me even more particularly than its contents; for it seems to have been written in the year *two* thousand eight hundred and forty-eight. As for the passages I am about to transcribe, they, I fancy, will speak for themselves.

'Do you know, my dear friend,' says the writer, addressing, no doubt, a contemporary – 'Do you know that it is scarcely more than eight or nine hundred years ago since the metaphysicians first consented to relieve the people of the singular fancy that there exist *but two practicable roads to Truth*? Believe it if you can! It appears, however, that long, long ago, in the night of Time, there lived a Turkish philosopher called Aries and surnamed Tottle.'[4] [Here, possibly, the letter-writer means Aristotle; the best names are wretchedly corrupted in two or three thousand years.] 'The fame of this great man depended mainly on his demonstration that sneezing is a natural provision, by means of which over-profound thinkers are enabled to expel superfluous ideas through the nose; but he obtained a scarcely less valuable celebrity as the founder, or at all events as the principal propagator, of what was termed the *de*ductive or *à priori* philosophy. He started with what he maintained to be axioms, or self-evident truths : – and the now well-understood fact that *no* truths are *self*-evident, really does not make in the slightest degree against his speculations : – it was sufficient for his purpose that the truths in question were evident at all. From axioms he proceeded, logically, to results. His most illustrious disciples were one Tuclid, a geometrician,' [meaning Euclid] 'and one Kant,[5] a Dutchman, the originator of that species of Transcendentalism which, with the change merely of a C for a K, now bears his peculiar name.

'Well, Aries Tottle flourished supreme, until the advent of one Hog, surnamed "the Ettrick shepherd",[6] who preached an entirely different system, which he called the *à posteriori* or *inductive*. His plan referred altogether to sensation. He proceeded by observing, analyzing, and classifying facts – *instantiæ Naturæ*, as they were somewhat affectedly called – and arranging them into general laws. In a word, while the mode of Aries rested on *noumena*, that of Hog depended on *phenomena*; and so great was the admiration excited by this latter system that, at its first introduction, Aries fell into general disrepute. Finally, however, he recovered ground, and was permitted to divide the empire of Philosophy with his more modern rival : – the savans contenting themselves with proscribing all *other* competitors, past, present, and to come; putting an end to all controversy on the topic by the promulgation of a Median law, to the effect that the Aristotelian and Baconian roads[7] are, and of right ought to be, the sole possible avenues to knowledge : – "Baconian", you must know, my dear friend,' adds the letter-writer at this point, 'was an adjective invented as equivalent to Hog-ian, while more dignified and euphonious.

'Now I do assure you most positively' – proceeds the epistle – 'that I represent these matters fairly; and you can easily understand how restrictions so absurd on their very face must have operated, in those days, to retard the progress of true Science, which makes its most important advances – as all History will show – by seemingly intuitive *leaps*. These ancient ideas confined investigation to crawling; and I need not suggest to you that crawling, among varieties of locomotion, is a very capital thing of its kind; – but because the snail is sure of foot, for this reason must we clip the wings of the eagles? For many centuries, so great was the infatuation, about Hog especially, that a virtual stop was put to all thinking, properly so called. No man dared utter a truth for which he felt himself indebted to his soul alone. It mattered not whether the truth was even demonstrably such;

for the dogmatizing philosophers of that epoch regarded only *the road* by which it professed to have been attained. The end, with them, was a point of no moment, whatever: – "the means!" they vociferated – "let us look at the means!" – and if, on scrutiny of the means, it was found to come neither under the category Hog, nor under the category Aries (which means ram), why then the savans went no farther, but, calling the thinker "a fool" and branding him a "theorist", would never, thenceforward, have any thing to do either with *him* or with his truths.

'Now, my dear friend,' continues the letter-writer, 'it cannot be maintained that by the crawling system, exclusively adopted, men would arrive at the maximum amount of truth, even in any long series of ages; for the repression of imagination was an evil not to be counterbalanced even by *absolute* certainty in the snail processes. But their certainty was very far from absolute. The error of our progenitors was quite analogous with that of the wiseacre who fancies he must necessarily see an object the more distinctly, the more closely he holds it to his eyes. They blinded themselves, too, with the impalpable, titillating Scotch snuff of *detail*;[8] and thus the boasted facts of the Hog-ites were by no means always facts – a point of little importance but for the assumption that they always *were*. The vital taint, however, in Baconianism – its most lamentable fount of error – lay in its tendency to throw power and consideration into the hands of merely perceptive men – of those inter-Tritonic minnows, the microscopical savans – the diggers and pedlers of minute *facts*, for the most part in physical science – facts all of which they retailed at the same price on the highway; their value depending, it was supposed, simply upon the *fact of their fact*, without reference to their applicability or inapplicability in the development of those ultimate and only legitimate facts, called Law.

'Than the persons' – the letter goes on to say – 'than the persons thus suddenly elevated by the Hog-ian philosophy into a station for which they were unfitted – thus transferred from the sculleries into the parlors of Science – from its pantries into its pulpits – than these individuals a more intolerant – a more intolerable set of bigots and tyrants never existed on the face of the earth. Their creed, their text and their sermon were, alike, the one word "*fact*" – but, for the most part, even of this one word, they knew not even the meaning. On those who ventured to *disturb* their facts with the view of putting them in order and to use, the disciples of Hog had no mercy whatever. All attempts at generalization were met at once by the words "theoretical", "theory", "theorist" – all *thought*, to be brief, was very properly resented as a personal affront to themselves. Cultivating the natural sciences to the exclusion of Metaphysics, the Mathematics, and Logic, many of these Bacon-engendered philosophers – one-idead, one-sided and lame of a leg – were more wretchedly helpless – more miserably ignorant, in view of all the comprehensible objects of knowledge, than the veriest unlettered hind who proves that he knows something at least, in admitting that he knows absolutely nothing.

'Nor had our forefathers any better right to talk about *certainty*, when pursuing, in blind confidence, the *à priori* path of axioms, or of the Ram. At innumerable points this path was scarcely as straight as a ram's-horn. The simple truth is, that the Aristotelians erected their castles on a basis far less reliable than air; *for no such things as axioms ever existed or can possibly exist at all*. This they must have been very blind, indeed, not to see, or at least to suspect; for, even in their own day, many of their long-admitted "axioms" had been abandoned : – "*ex nihilo nihil fit*",[9] for example, and a "thing cannot act where it is not", and "there cannot be antipodes", and "darkness cannot proceed from light". These and numerous similar propositions formerly accepted, without hesitation, as axioms, or undeniable truths, were, even at the period of which I speak, seen to be altogether untenable : – how absurd in these people, then, to persist in relying upon a basis, as immutable, whose mutability had become so repeatedly manifest!

'But, even through evidence afforded by themselves against themselves, it is easy to convict these *à priori* reasoners of the grossest unreason – it is easy to show the futility – the impalpability of their axioms in general. I have now lying before me' – it will be observed that we still proceed with the letter – 'I have now lying before me a book printed about a thousand years ago. Pundit assures me that it is decidedly the cleverest ancient work on its topic, which is "Logic".[10] The author, who was much esteemed in his day, was one Miller or Mill; and we find it recorded of him, as a point of some importance, that he rode a mill-horse whom he called Jeremy Bentham : – but let us glance at the volume itself!

'Ah! – "Ability or inability to conceive," says Mr Mill very properly, "is *in no case* to be received as a criterion of axiomatic truth." Now, that this is a palpable truism no one in his senses will deny. *Not* to admit the proposition, is to insinuate a charge of variability in Truth itself, whose very title is a synonym of the Steadfast. If ability to conceive be taken as a criterion of Truth, then a truth to *David* Hume would very seldom be a truth to *Joe*;[11] and ninety-nine hundredths of what is undeniable in Heaven would be demonstrable falsity upon Earth. The proposition of Mr Mill, then, is sustained. I will not grant it to be an *axiom*; and this merely because I am showing that *no* axioms exist; but, with a distinction which could not have been cavilled at even by Mr Mill himself, I am ready to grant that, *if* an axiom *there be*, then the proposition of which we speak has the fullest right to be considered an axiom – that no *more* absolute axiom *is* – and, consequently, that any subsequent proposition which shall conflict with this one primarily advanced, must be either a falsity in itself – that is to say no axiom – or, if admitted axiomatic, must at once neutralize both itself and its predecessor.

'And now, by the logic of their own propounder, let us proceed to test any one of the axioms propounded. Let us give Mr Mill the fairest of play. We will bring the point to no ordinary issue. We will select for investigation no common-place axiom – no axiom of what, not the less preposterously because only impliedly, he terms his secondary class – as if a positive truth by definition could be either more or less positively a truth : – we will select, I say, no axiom of an unquestionability so questionable as is to be found in Euclid. We will not talk, for example, about such propositions as that two straight lines cannot enclose a space, or that the whole is greater than any one of its parts. We will afford the logician *every* advantage. We will come at once to a proposition which he regards as the acme of the unquestionable – as the quintessence of axiomatic undeniability. Here it is : –

"Contradictions cannot *both* be true – that is, cannot cöexist in nature." Here Mr Mill means, for instance, – and I give the most forcible instance conceivable – that a tree must be either a tree or *not* a tree – that it cannot be at the same time a tree *and* not a tree : – all which is quite reasonable of itself and will answer remarkably well as an axiom, until we bring it into collation with an axiom insisted upon a few pages before – in other words – words which I have previously employed – until we test it by the logic of its own propounder. "A tree," Mr Mill asserts, "must be either a tree or *not* a tree." Very well : – and now let me ask him, *why*. To this little query there is but one response : – I defy any man living to invent a second. The sole answer is this : – "Because we find it *impossible to conceive* that a tree can be anything else than a tree or not a tree." This, I repeat, is Mr Mill's sole answer : – he will not *pretend* to suggest another : – and yet, by his own showing, his answer is clearly no answer at all; for has he not already required us to admit, *as an axiom*, that ability or inability to conceive is *in no case* to be taken as a criterion of axiomatic truth? Thus all – absolutely *all* his argumentation is at sea without a rudder. Let it not be urged that an exception from the general rule is to be made, in cases where the "impossibility to conceive" is so peculiarly great as when we are called upon to conceive a tree *both* a tree and *not* a tree. Let no attempt, I say, be made at urging this sotticism; for, in the first place, there are no *degrees* of "impossibility", and thus no one impossible conception can be *more* peculiarly impossible than another impossible conception : – in the second place, Mr Mill himself, no doubt after thorough deliberation, has most distinctly, and most rationally, excluded all opportunity for exception, by the emphasis of his proposition, that, *in no case*, is ability or inability to conceive, to be taken as a criterion of axiomatic truth : – in the third place, even were exceptions admissible at all, it remains to be shown how any exception is admissible *here*. That a tree can be both a tree and not a tree, is an idea which the angels, or the devils, *may* entertain, and which no doubt many an earthly Bedlamite, or Transcendentalist, *does*.

'Now I do not quarrel with these ancients,' continues the letter-writer, '*so much* on account of the transparent frivolity of their logic – which, to be plain, was baseless, worthless and fantastic altogether – as on account of their pompous and infatuate proscription of all *other* roads to Truth than the two narrow and crooked paths – the one of creeping and the other of crawling – to which, in their ignorant perversity, they have dared to confine the Soul – the Soul which loves nothing so well as to soar in those regions of illimitable intuition which are utterly incognizant of "*path*".

'By the bye, my dear friend, is it not an evidence of the mental slavery entailed upon those bigoted people by their Hogs and Rams, that in spite of the eternal prating of their savans about *roads* to Truth, none of them fell, even by accident, into what we now so distinctly perceive to be the broadest, the straightest and most available of all mere roads – the great thoroughfare – the majestic highway of the *Consistent*? Is it not wonderful that they should have failed to deduce from the works of God the vitally momentous consideration that *a perfect consistency can be nothing but an absolute truth*? How plain – how rapid our progress since the late announcement of this proposition! By its means, investigation has been taken out of the hands of the ground-moles, and given as a duty, rather than as a task, to the true – to the *only* true thinkers – to the generally-educated men of ardent imagination. These latter – our Keplers – our Laplaces – "speculate" – "theorize" – these are the terms – can you not fancy the shout of scorn with which they would be received by our progenitors, were it possible for them to be looking over my shoulders as I write? The Keplers, I repeat, speculate – theorize – and their theories are merely corrected – reduced – sifted – cleared, little by little, of their chaff of inconsistency – until at length there stands apparent an unencumbered *Consistency* – a consistency which the most stolid admit – because it *is* a consistency – to be an absolute and unquestionable *Truth*.

'I have often thought, my friend, that it must have puzzled these dogmaticians of a thousand years ago, to determine, even, by which of their two boasted roads it is that the cryptographist attains the solution of the more complicated cyphers – or by which of them Champollion guided mankind to those important and innumerable truths which, for so many centuries, have lain entombed amid the phonetical hieroglyphics of Egypt.[12] In especial, would it not have given these bigots some trouble to determine by which of their two roads was reached the most momentous and sublime of *all* their truths – the truth – the fact of *gravitation*? Newton deduced it from the laws of Kepler. Kepler admitted that these laws he *guessed* – these laws whose investigation disclosed to the greatest of British astronomers that principle, the basis of all (existing) physical principle, in going behind which we enter at once the nebulous kingdom of Metaphysics. Yes! – these vital laws Kepler *guessed* – that it is to say, he *imagined* them. Had he been asked to point out either the *de*ductive or *in*ductive route by which he attained them, his reply might have been – "I know nothing about *routes* – but I *do* know the machinery of the Universe. Here it is. I grasped it with *my soul* – I reached it through mere dint of *intuition*." Alas, poor ignorant old man! Could not any metaphysician have told him that what he called "intuition" was but the conviction resulting from *de*ductions or *in*ductions of which the processes were so shadowy as to have escaped his consciousness, eluded his reason, or bidden defiance to his capacity of expression? How great a pity it is that some "moral philosopher" had not enlightened him about all this! How it would have comforted him on his death-bed to know that, instead of having gone intuitively and thus unbecomingly, he had, in fact, proceeded decorously and legitimately – that is to say Hog-ishly, or at least Ram-ishly – into the vast halls where lay gleaming, untended, and hitherto untouched by mortal hand – unseen by mortal eye – the imperishable and priceless secrets of the Universe!

'Yes, Kepler was essentially a *theorist*; but this title, *now* of so much sanctity, was, in those ancient days, a designation of supreme contempt. It is only *now* that men begin to appreciate that divine old man – to sympathize with the prophetical and poetical rhapsody of his ever-memorable words. For *my* part,' continues the unknown correspondent, 'I glow with a sacred fire when I even think of them, and feel that I shall never grow weary of their repetition : – in concluding this letter, let me have the real pleasure of transcribing them once again : – *"I care not whether my work be read now or by posterity. I can afford to wait a century for readers*[13] *when God himself has waited six thousand years for an observer. I triumph. I have stolen the golden secret of the Egyptians. I will indulge my sacred fury."* '

Here end my quotations from this very unaccountable if not impertinent epistle; and perhaps it would be folly to comment, in any respect, upon the chimerical, not to say revolutionary, fancies of the writer – whoever he is – fancies so radically at war with the well-considered and well-settled opinions of this age. Let us proceed, then, to our legitimate thesis, *The Universe*.

This thesis admits a choice between two modes of discussion : – We may ascend or descend. Beginning at our own point of view – at the Earth on which we stand – we may pass to the other planets of our system – thence to the Sun – thence to our system considered collectively – and thence, through other systems, indefinitely outwards; or, commencing on high at some point as definite as we can make it or conceive it, we may come down to the habitation of Man. Usually – that is to say, in ordinary essays on Astronomy – the first of these two modes is, with certain reservation, adopted : – this for the obvious reason that astronomical *facts*, merely, and principles, being the object, that object is best fulfilled in stepping from the known because proximate, gradually onward to the point where all certitude becomes lost in the remote. For my present purpose, however, – that of enabling the mind to take in, as if from afar and at one glance, a distant conception of the *individual* Universe – it is clear that a descent to small from great – to the outskirts from the centre (if we could establish a centre) – to the end from the beginning (if we could fancy a beginning) would be the preferable course, but for the difficulty, if not impossibility, of presenting, in this course, to the unastronomical, a picture at all comprehensible in regard to such considerations as are involved in *quantity* – that is to say, in number, magnitude and distance.

Now, distinctness – intelligibility, at all points, is a primary feature in my general design. On important topics it is better to be a good deal prolix than even a very little obscure. But abstruseness is a quality appertaining to no subject in itself. All are alike, in facility of comprehension, to him who approaches them by properly graduated steps. It is merely because a stepping-stone, here and there, is heedlessly left unsupplied in our road to the Differential Calculus, that this latter is not altogether as simple a thing as a sonnet by Mr Solomon Seesaw.[14]

By way of admitting, then, no *chance* for misapprehension, I think it advisable to proceed as if even the more obvious facts of Astronomy were unknown to the reader. In combining the two modes of discussion to which I have referred, I propose to avail myself of the advantages peculiar to each – and very especially of the *iteration in detail* which will be unavoidable as a consequence of the plan. Commencing with a descent, I shall reserve for the return upwards those indispensable considerations of *quantity* to which allusion has already been made.

Let us begin, then, at once, with that merest of words, 'Infinity'. This, like 'God', 'spirit', and some other expressions of which the equivalents exist in nearly all languages, is by no means the expression of an idea – but of an effort at one. It stands for the possible attempt at an impossible conception. Man needed a term by which to point out the *direction* of this effort – the cloud behind which lay, forever invisible, the *object* of this attempt. A word, in fine, was demanded, by means of which one human being might put himself in relation at once with another human being and with a certain *tendency* of the human intellect. Out of this demand arose the word, 'Infinity'; which is thus the representative but of the *thought of a thought*.

As regards *that* infinity now considered – the infinity of space – we often hear it said that 'its idea is admitted by the mind – is acquiesced in – is entertained – on account of the greater difficulty which attends the conception of a limit'. But this is merely one of those *phrases* by which even profound thinkers, time out of mind, have occasionally taken pleasure in deceiving *themselves*. The quibble lies concealed in the word 'difficulty'. 'The mind,' we are told, 'entertains the idea of *limitless*, through the greater *difficulty* which it finds in entertaining that of *limited*, space.' Now, were the proposition but fairly *put*, its absurdity would become transparent at once. Clearly, there is no mere *difficulty* in the case. The assertion intended, if presented *according* to its intention and without sophistry, would run thus: –

'The mind admits the idea of limitless, through the greater *impossibility* of entertaining that of limited, space.'

It must be immediately seen that this is not a question of two statements between whose respective credibilities – or of two arguments between whose respective validities – the *reason* is called upon to decide : – it is a matter of two conceptions, directly conflicting, and each avowedly impossible, one of which the *intellect* is supposed to be capable of entertaining, on account of the greater *impossibility* of entertaining the other. The choice is *not* made between two difficulties; – it is merely *fancied* to be made between two impossibilities. Now of the former, there *are* degrees, – but of the latter, none : – just as our impertinent letter-writer has already suggested. A task *may* be more or less difficult; but it is either possible or not possible : – there are no gradations. It might be more difficult to overthrow the Andes than an ant-hill; but it can be no more *impossible* to annihilate the matter of the one than the matter of the other. A man may jump ten feet with less *difficulty* than he can jump twenty, but the *impossibility* of his leaping to the moon is not a whit less than that of his leaping to the dog-star.

Since all this is undeniable : since the choice of the mind is to be made between *impossibilities* of conception : since one impossibility cannot be greater than another : and since, thus, one cannot be preferred to another : the philosophers who not only maintain, on the grounds mentioned, man's *idea* of infinity but, on account of such supposititious idea, *infinity itself* – are plainly engaged in demonstrating one impossible thing to be possible by showing how it is that some one other thing – is impossible too. This, it will be said, is nonsense; and perhaps it is : – indeed I think it very capital nonsense – but forgo all claim to it as nonsense of mine.

The readiest mode, however, of displaying the fallacy of the philosophical argument on this question, is by simply adverting to a *fact* respecting it which has been hitherto quite overlooked – the fact that the argument alluded to both proves and disproves its own proposition. 'The mind is impelled,' say the theologians and others, 'to admit a *First Cause*, by the superior difficulty it experiences in conceiving cause beyond cause without end.' The quibble, as before, lies in the word 'difficulty' – but *here* what is it employed to sustain? A First Cause. And what is a First Cause? An ultimate termination of causes. And what is an ultimate termination of causes? Finity – the Finite. Thus the one quibble, in two processes, by God knows how many philosophers, is made to support now Finity and now Infinity – could it not be brought to support something besides? As for the quibblers – *they*, at least, are insupportable. But – to dismiss them: – what they prove in the one case is the identical nothing which they demonstrate in the other.

Of course, no one will suppose that I here contend for the absolute impossibility of *that* which we attempt to convey in the word 'Infinity'. My purpose is but to show the folly of endeavoring to prove Infinity itself, or even our conception of it, by any such blundering ratiocination as that which is ordinarily employed.

Nevertheless, as an individual, I may be permitted to say that I *cannot* conceive Infinity, and am convinced that no human being can. A mind not thoroughly self-conscious – not accustomed to the introspective analysis of its own operations – will, it is true, often deceive itself by supposing that it *has* entertained the conception of which we speak. In the effort to entertain it, we proceed step beyond step – we fancy point still beyond point; and so long as we *continue* the effort, it may be said, in fact, that we are *tending* to the formation of the idea designed; while the strength of the impression that we actually form or have formed it, is in the ratio of the period during which we keep up the mental endeavor. But it is in the act of discontinuing the endeavor – of fulfilling (as we think) the idea – of putting the finishing stroke (as we suppose) to the conception – that we overthrow at once the whole fabric of our fancy by resting upon some one ultimate and therefore definite point. This fact, however, we fail to perceive, on account of the absolute coincidence, in time, between the settling down upon the ultimate point and the act of cessation in thinking. – In attempting, on the other hand, to frame the idea of a *limited* space, we merely converse the processes which involve the impossibility.

We *believe* in a God. We may or may not *believe* in finite or in infinite space; but our belief, in such cases, is more properly designated as *faith*, and is a matter quite distinct from that belief proper – from that *intellectual* belief – which presupposes the mental conception.

The fact is, that, upon the enunciation of any one of that class of terms to which 'Infinity' belongs – the class representing *thoughts of thought* – he who has a right to say that he thinks *at all*, feels himself called on, *not* to entertain a conception, but simply to direct his mental vision toward some given point, in the intellectual firmament, where lies a nebula never to be solved. To solve it, indeed, he makes no effort; for with a rapid instinct he comprehends, not only the impossibility, but, as regards all human purposes, the *inessentiality*, of its solution. He perceives that the Deity has not *designed* it to be solved. He sees, at once, that it lies *out* of the brain of man, and even *how*, if not exactly *why*, it lies out of it. There *are* people, I am aware, who, busying themselves in attempts at the unattainable, acquire very easily, by dint of the jargon they emit, among those thinkers-that-they-think with whom darkness and depth are synonymous, a kind of cuttle-fish reputation for profundity; but the finest quality of Thought is its self-cognizance; and, with some little equivocation, it may be said that no fog of the mind can well be greater than that which, extending to the very boundaries of the mental domain, shuts out even these boundaries themselves from comprehension.

It will now be understood that, in using the phrase, 'Infinity of Space', I make no call upon the reader to entertain the impossible conception of an *absolute* infinity. I refer simply to the '*utmost conceivable expanse*' of space – a shadowy and fluctuating domain, now shrinking, now swelling, with the vacillating energies of the imagination.

Hitherto, the Universe of Stars has always been considered as coincident with the Universe proper, as I have defined it in the commencement of this Discourse. It has been always either directly or indirectly assumed – at least since the dawn of intelligible Astronomy – that, were it possible for us to attain any given point in space, we should still find, on all sides of us, an interminable succession of stars. This was the untenable idea of Pascal[15] when making perhaps the most successful attempt ever made, at periphrasing the conception for which we struggle in the word 'Universe'. 'It is a sphere,' he says, 'of which the centre is everywhere, the circumference, nowhere.' But although this intended definition is, in fact, *no* definition of the Universe of *Stars*, we may accept it, with some mental reservation, as a definition (rigorous enough for all practical purposes) of the Universe *proper* – that is to say, of the Universe of *space*. This latter, then, let us regard as '*a sphere of which the centre is everywhere, the circumference nowhere*'. In fact, while we find it impossible to fancy an end to space, we have no difficulty in picturing to ourselves any one of an infinity of beginnings.

As our starting point, then, let us adopt the *Godhead*. Of this Godhead, *in itself*, he alone is not imbecile – he alone is not impious who propounds — nothing. '*Nous ne connaissons rien*,' says the Baron de Bielfeld[16] – '*Nous ne connaissons rien de la nature ou de l'essence de Dieu: – pour savoir ce qu'il est, il faut être Dieu même.*' – 'We know absolutely *nothing* of the nature or essence of God: – in order to comprehend what he is, we should have to be God ourselves.'

'*We should have to be God ourselves!*' – With a phrase so startling as this yet ringing in my ears, I nevertheless venture to demand if this our present ignorance of the Deity is an ignorance to which the soul is *everlastingly* condemned.

By *Him*, however – *now*, at least, the Incomprehensible – by Him – assuming him as *Spirit* – that is to say, as *not Matter* – a distinction which, for all intelligible purposes, will stand well instead of a definition – by Him, then, existing as Spirit, let us content ourselves with supposing to have been *created*, or made out of Nothing, by dint of his Volition – at some point of Space which we will take as a centre – at some period into which we do not pretend to inquire, but at all events immensely remote – by Him, then again, let us suppose to have been created— *what*? This is a vitally momentous epoch in our considerations. *What* is it that we are justified – that alone we are justified in supposing to have been primarily, *created*?

We have attained a point where only *Intuition* can aid us : –

but now let me recur to the idea which I have already suggested as that alone which we can properly entertain of Intuition. It is but *the conviction arising from those inductions or deductions of which the processes are so shadowy as to escape our consciousness, elude our reason, or defy our capacity of expression*. With this understanding, I now assert – that an intuition altogether irresistible, although inexpressible, forces me to the conclusion that what God originally created – that that Matter which, by dint of his Volition, he first made from his Spirit, or from Nihility, *could* have been nothing but Matter in its utmost conceivable state of — what? of Simplicity?

This will be found the sole absolute *assumption* of my Discourse. I use the word 'assumption' in its ordinary sense; yet I maintain that even this my primary proposition, is very far indeed, from being really a mere assumption. Nothing was ever more certainly – no human conclusion was ever, in fact, more regularly – more rigorously *de*duced : – but, alas! the processes lie out of the human analysis – at all events are beyond the utterance of the human tongue. If, however, in the course of this Essay, I succeed in showing that, out of Matter in its extreme of Simplicity, all things *might* have been constructed, we reach directly the inference that they *were* thus constructed, through the impossibility of attributing supererogation to Omnipotence.

Let us now endeavor to conceive what Matter must be, when, or if, in its absolute extreme of *Simplicity*. Here the Reason flies at once to Imparticularity – to a particle – to *one* particle – a particle of *one* kind – of *one* character – of *one* nature – of *one* size – of one form – a particle, therefore, '*without* form and void' – a particle positively a particle at all points – a particle absolutely unique, individual, undivided, and not indivisible only because He who *created* it, by dint of his Will, can by an infinitely less energetic exercise of the same Will, as a matter of course, divide it.

Oneness, then, is all that I predicate of the originally created Matter; but I propose to show that this *Oneness is a principle abundantly sufficient to account for the constitution, the existing phænomena and the plainly inevitable annihilation of at least the material Universe*.

The willing into being the primordial Particle, has completed the act, or more properly the *conception*, of Creation. We now proceed to the ultimate purpose for which we are to suppose the Particle created – that is to say, the ultimate purpose so far as our considerations *yet* enable us to see it – the constitution of the Universe from it, the Particle.

This constitution has been effected by *forcing* the originally and therefore normally *One* into the abnormal condition of *Many*. An action of this character implies reäction. A diffusion from Unity, under the conditions, involves a tendency to return into Unity – a tendency ineradicable until satisfied. But on these points I will speak more fully hereafter.

The assumption of absolute Unity in the primordial Particle includes that of infinite divisibility. Let us conceive the Particle, then, to be only not totally exhausted by diffusion into Space. From the one Particle, as a centre, let us suppose to be radiated spherically – in all directions – to immeasurable but still to definite distances in the previously vacant Space – a certain inexpressibly great yet limited number of unimaginably yet not infinitely minute atoms.

Now, of these atoms, thus diffused, or on diffusion, what conditions are we permitted – not to assume, but to infer, from consideration as well of their source as of the character of the design apparent in their diffusion? *Unity* being their source, and *difference from Unity* the character of the design manifested in their diffusion, we are warranted in supposing this character to be at least generally preserved throughout the design, and to form a portion of the design itself : – that is to say, we shall be warranted in conceiving continual differences at all points from the uniquity and simplicity of the origin. But, for these reasons, shall we be justified in imagining the atoms heterogeneous, dissimilar, unequal, and inequidistant? More explicitly – are we to consider no two atoms as, at their diffusion, of the same nature, or of the same form, or of the same size? – and, after fulfilment of their diffusion into Space, is absolute inequidistance, each from each, to be understood of all of them? In such arrangement, under such conditions, we most easily and immediately comprehend the subsequent most feasible carrying out to completion of any such design as that which I have suggested – the design of multiplicity out of unity – diversity out of sameness – heterogeneity out of homogeneity – complexity out of simplicity – in a word, the utmost possible multiplicity of *relation* out of the emphatically irrelative One. Undoubtedly, therefore, we *should* be warranted in assuming all that has been mentioned, but for the reflection, first, that supererogation is not presumable of any Divine Act; and, secondly, that the object supposed in view, appears as feasible when some of the conditions in question are dispensed with, in the beginning, as when all are understood immediately to exist. I mean to say that some are involved in the rest, or so instantaneous a consequence of them as to make the distinction inappreciable. Difference of *size*, for example, will at once be brought about through the tendency of one atom to a second, in preference to a third, on account of particular inequidistance; which is to be comprehended as *particular inequidistances between centres of quantity, in neighboring atoms of different form* – a matter not at all interfering with the generally-equable distribution of the atoms. Difference of *kind*, too, is easily conceived to be merely a result of differences in size and form, taken more or less conjointly : – in fact, since the *Unity* of the Particle Proper implies absolute homogeneity, we cannot imagine the atoms, at their diffusion, differing in kind, without imagining, at the same time, a special exercise of the Divine Will, at the emission of each atom, for the purpose of effecting, in each, a change of its essential nature : – and so fantastic an idea is the less to be indulged, as the object proposed is seen to be thoroughly attainable without such minute and elaborate interposition. We perceive, therefore, on the whole, that it would be supererogatory, and consequently unphilosophical, to predicate of the atoms, in view of their purposes, any thing more than *difference of form* at their dispersion, with particular inequidistance after it – all other differences arising at once out of these, in the very first processes of mass-constitution : – We thus establish the Universe on a purely *geometrical* basis. Of course, it is by no means necessary to assume absolute difference, even of form, among *all* the atoms radiated – any more than absolute particular inequidistance of each from each. We are required to

conceive merely that no *neighboring* atoms are of similar form –
no atoms which can ever approximate, until their inevitable
rëunition at the end.

Although the immediate and perpetual *tendency* of the disunited atoms to return into their normal Unity, is implied, as I
have said, in their abnormal diffusion; still it is clear that this
tendency will be without consequence – a tendency and no more
– until the diffusive energy, in ceasing to be exerted, shall leave *it*,
the tendency, free to seek its satisfaction. The Divine Act, however, being considered as determinate, and discontinued on fulfilment of the diffusion, we understand, at once, a *rëaction* – in
other words, a *satisfiable* tendency of the disunited atoms to return into *One*.

But the diffusive energy being withdrawn, and the rëaction
having commenced in furtherance of the ultimate design – *that
of the utmost possible Relation* – this design is now in danger of
being frustrated, in detail, by reason of that very tendency to
return which is to effect its accomplishment in general. *Multiplicity* is the object; but there is nothing to prevent proximate
atoms, from lapsing *at once*, through the now satisfiable tendency
– *before* the fulfilment of any ends proposed in multiplicity – into
absolute oneness among themselves : – there is nothing to impede
the aggregation of various *unique* masses, at various points of
space : – in other words, nothing to interfere with the accumula-
tion of various masses, each absolutely One.

For the effectual completion of the general design, we thus
see the necessity for a repulsion of limited capacity – a separate
something which, on withdrawal of the diffusive Volition, shall
at the same time allow the approach, and forbid the junction, of
the atoms; suffering them infinitely to approximate, while denying them positive contact; in a word, having the power – *up to a
certain epoch* – of preventing their *coalition*, but no ability to
interfere with their *coalescence* in any respect *or degree*. The repulsion, already considered as so peculiarly limited in other
regards, must be understood, let me repeat, as having power to
prevent absolute coalition, *only up to a certain epoch*. Unless we
are to conceive that the appetite for Unity among the atoms
is doomed to be satisfied *never*; – unless we are to conceive that

what had a beginning is to have no end – a conception which cannot *really* be entertained, however much we may talk or dream of entertaining it – we are forced to conclude that the repulsive influence imagined, will, finally – under pressure of the Uni-tendency *collectively* applied, but never and in no degree *until*, on fulfilment of the Divine purposes, such collective application shall be naturally made – yield to a force which, at that ultimate epoch, shall be the superior force precisely to the extent required, and thus permit the universal subsidence into the inevitable, because original and therefore normal, *One*. The conditions here to be reconciled are difficult indeed : – we cannot even comprehend the possibility of their conciliation; – nevertheless, the apparent impossibility is brilliantly suggestive.

That the repulsive something actually exists, *we see*. Man neither employs, nor knows, a force sufficient to bring two atoms into contact. This is but the well-established proposition of the impenetrability of matter. All Experiment proves – all Philosophy admits it. The *design* of the repulsion – the necessity for its existence – I have endeavored to show; but from all attempt at investigating its nature have religiously abstained; this on account of an intuitive conviction that the principle at issue is strictly spiritual – lies in a recess impervious to our present understanding – lies involved in a consideration of what now – in our human state – is *not* to be considered – in a consideration of *Spirit in itself*. I feel, in a word, that here the God has interposed, and here only, because here and here only the knot demanded the interposition of the God.

In fact, while the tendency of the diffused atoms to return into Unity, will be recognized, at once, as the principle of the Newtonian Gravity, what I have spoken of as a repulsive influence prescribing limits to the (immediate) satisfaction of the tendency, will be understood as *that* which we have been in the practice of designating now as heat, now as magnetism, now as *electricity*;[17] displaying our ignorance of its awful character in the vacillation of the phraseology with which we endeavor to circumscribe it.

Calling it, merely for the moment, electricity, we know that all experimental analysis of electricity has given, as an ultimate

result, the principle, or seeming principle, *heterogeneity*. *Only*
where things differ is electricity apparent; and it is presumable
that they *never* differ where it is not developed at least, if not
apparent. Now, this result is in the fullest keeping with that
which I have reached unempirically. The design of the repulsive
influence I have suggested to be that of preventing immediate
Unity among the diffused atoms; and these atoms are represented
as different each from each. *Difference* is their character – their
essentiality – just as *no-difference* was the essentiality of their
course. When we say, then, that an attempt to bring any two of
these atoms together would induce an effort, on the part of the
repulsive influence, to prevent the contact, we may as well use
the strictly convertible sentence that an attempt to bring together
any two differences will result in a development of electricity.
All existing bodies, of course, are composed of these atoms in
proximate contact, and are therefore to be considered as mere
assemblages of more or fewer differences; and the resistance
made by the repulsive spirit, on bringing together any two such
assemblages, would be in the ratio of the two sums of the differences in each: – an expression which, when reduced, is equivalent to this: – *The amount of electricity developed on the approximation of two bodies, is proportional with the difference
between the respective sums of the atoms of which the bodies are
composed*. That *no* two bodies are absolutely alike, is a simple
corollary from all that has been here said. Electricity, therefore,
existing always, is *developed* whenever *any* bodies, but *manifested* only when bodies of appreciable difference, are brought
into approximation.

To electricity – so, for the present, continuing to call it – we
may not be wrong in referring the various physical appearances
of light, heat and magnetism; but far less shall we be liable to
err in attributing to this strictly spiritual principle the more important phænomena of vitality, consciousness and *Thought*. On
this topic, however, I need pause *here* merely to suggest that
these phænomena, whether observed generally or in detail, seem
to proceed *at least in the ratio of the heterogeneous*.

Discarding now the two equivocal terms, 'gravitation' and
'electricity', let us adopt the more definite expressions, *'Attrac-*

tion' and 'Repulsion'.[18] The former is the body; the latter the soul: the one is the material; the other the spiritual, principle of the Universe. *No other principles exist. All* phænomena are referable to one, or to the other, or to both combined. So rigorously is this the case – so thoroughly demonstrable is it that Attraction and Repulsion are the *sole* properties through which we perceive the Universe – in other words, by which Matter is manifested to Mind – that, for all merely argumentative purposes, we are fully justified in assuming that Matter *exists* only as Attraction and Repulsion – that Attraction and Repulsion *are* matter: – there being no conceivable case in which we may not employ the term 'Matter' and the terms 'Attraction' and 'Repulsion', taken together, as equivalent, and therefore convertible, expressions in Logic.

I said, just now, that what I have described as the tendency of the diffused atoms to return into their original Unity, would be understood as the principle of the Newtonian law of Gravity: and, in fact, there can be but little difficulty in such an understanding, if we look at the Newtonian Gravity in a merely general view, as a force impelling Matter to seek Matter; that is to say, when we pay no attention to the known *modus operandi* of the Newtonian force. The general coincidence satisfies us; but, on looking closely, we see, in detail, much that appears *in*coincident, and much in regard to which no coincidence, at least, is established. For example; the Newtonian Gravity, when we think of it in certain moods, does *not* seem to be a tendency to *oneness* at all, but rather a tendency of all bodies in all directions – a phrase apparently expressive of a tendency to diffusion. Here, then, is an *in*coincidence. Again; when we reflect on the mathematical *law* governing the Newtonian tendency, we see clearly that no coincidence has been made good, in respect of the *modus operandi*, at least, between Gravity as known to exist and that seemingly simple and direct tendency which I have assumed.

In fact, I have attained a point at which it will be advisable to strengthen my position by reversing my processes. So far, we have gone on *à priori*, from an abstact consideration of *Simplicity*, as that quality most likely to have characterized the original action of God. Let us now see whether the established facts of the Newtonian Gravitation may not afford us, *à posteriori*, some legitimate inductions.

What does the Newtonian law declare? – That all bodies attract each other with forces proportional with their quantities of matter and inversely proportional with the squares of their distances. Purposely, I have here given, in the first place, the vulgar version of the law; and I confess that in this, as in most other vulgar versions of great truths, we find little of a suggestive character. Let us now adopt a more philosophical phraseology : – *Every atom, of every body, attracts every other atom, both of its own and of every other body, with a force which varies inversely as the squares of the distances between the attracting and attracted atom*. – Here, indeed, a flood of suggestion bursts upon the mind.

But let us see distinctly what it was that Newton *proved* – according to the grossly irrational definitions of *proof* prescribed by the metaphysical schools. He was forced to content himself with showing how thoroughly the motions of an imaginary Universe, composed of attracting and attracted atoms obedient to the law he announced, coincide with those of the actually existing Universe so far as it comes under our observation. This was the amount of his *demonstration* – that is to say, this was the amount of it, according to the conventional cant of the 'philosophies'. His successors added proof multiplied by proof – such proof as a sound intellect admits – but the *demonstration* of the law itself, persist the metaphysicians, had not been strengthened in any degree. '*Ocular, physical proof*', however, of Attraction, here upon Earth, in accordance with the Newtonian theory, was, at length, much to the satisfaction of some intellectual grovellers, afforded. This proof arose collaterally and incidentally (as nearly all important truths have arisen) out of an attempt to ascertain the mean density of the Earth. In the famous Maskelyne, Cavendish and Bailly experiments [19] for this purpose, the attraction of the mass of a mountain* was seen, felt, measured, and found to be mathematically consistent with the theory of the British astronomer.

* Schehallien, in Wales. [20]

But in spite of this confirmation of that which needed none –
in spite of the so-called corroboration of the 'theory' by the so-
called 'ocular and physical proof' – in spite of the *character* of
this corroboration – the ideas which even really philosophical
men cannot help imbibing of Gravity – and, especially, the ideas
of it which ordinary men get and contentedly maintain, are *seen*
to have been derived, for the most part, from a consideration of
the principle as they find it developed – *merely in the planet on
which they stand*.

Now, to what does so partial a consideration tend – to what
species of error does it give rise? On the Earth we *see* and *feel*,
only that Gravity impels all bodies towards the *centre* of the
Earth. No man in the common walks of life could be *made* to
see or feel anything else – could be made to perceive that anything, anywhere, has a perpetual, gravitating tendency in any
other direction than to the centre of the Earth; yet (with an exception hereafter to be specified) it is a fact that every earthly
thing (not to speak now of every heavenly thing) has a tendency
not *only* to the Earth's centre but in every conceivable direction
besides.

Now, although the philosophic cannot be said to *err with* the
vulgar in this matter, they nevertheless permit themselves to be
influenced, without knowing it, by the *sentiment* of the vulgar
idea. 'Although the Pagan fables are not believed,' says Bryant,
in his very erudite 'Mythology',[21] 'yet we forget ourselves continually and make inferences from them as from existing realities.'
I mean to assert that the merely *sensitive perception* of Gravity
as we experience it on Earth, beguiles mankind into the fancy of
concentralization or *especiality* respecting it – has been continually biasing towards this fancy even the mightiest intellects –
perpetually, although imperceptibly, leading them away from the
real characteristics of the principle; thus preventing them, up to
this date, from ever getting a glimpse of that vital truth which
lies in a diametrically opposite direction – behind the principle's
essential characteristics – those, *not* of concentralization or especiality – but of *universality* and *diffusion*. This 'vital truth' is
Unity as the *source* of the phænomenon.

Let me now repeat the definition of Gravity : – *Every atom, of every body, attracts every other atom, both of its own and of every other body,* with a force which varies inversely as the squares of the distances of the attracting and attracted atom.

Here let the reader pause with me, for a moment, in contemplation of the miraculous – of the ineffable – of the altogether unimaginable complexity of relation involved in the fact that *each atom attracts every other atom* – involved merely in this fact of the Attraction, without reference to the law or mode in which the Attraction is manifested – involved *merely* in the fact that each atom attracts every other atom *at all*, in a wilderness of atoms so numerous that those which go to the composition of a cannon-ball, exceed, probably, in mere point of number, all the stars which go to the constitution of the Universe.

Had we discovered, simply, that each atom tends to some one point, a favorite with all – to some especially attractive atom – we should still have fallen upon a discovery which, in itself, would have sufficed to overwhelm the mind: – but what is it that we are actually called on to comprehend? That each atom attracts – sympathizes with the most delicate movements of every other atom, and with each and with all at the same time, and forever, and according to a determinate law of which the complexity, even considered by itself solely, is utterly beyond the grasp of the imagination. If I propose to ascertain the influence of one mote in a sunbeam on its neighboring mote,[22] I cannot accomplish my purpose without first counting and weighing all the atoms in the Universe and defining the precise positions of all at one particular moment. If I venture to displace, by even the billionth part of an inch, the microscopical speck of dust which lies now on the point of my finger, what is the character of that act upon which I have adventured? I have done a deed which shakes the Moon in her path,[23] which causes the Sun to be no longer the Sun, and which alters forever the destiny of the multitudinous myriads of stars that roll and glow in the majestic presence of their Creator.

These ideas – conceptions such as *these* – unthought-like thoughts – soul-reveries rather than conclusions or even considerations of the intellect: – ideas, I repeat, such as these, are such as we can alone hope profitably to entertain in any effort at grasping the great principle, *Attraction*.

But now, – *with* such ideas – with such a *vision* of the marvellous complexity of Attraction fairly in his mind – let any person competent of thought on such topics as these, set himself to the task of imagining a *principle* for the phænomena observed – a condition from which they sprang.

Does not so evident a brotherhood among the atoms point to a common parentage? Does not a sympathy so omniprevalent, so ineradicable, and so thoroughly irrespective, suggest a common paternity as its source? Does not one extreme impel the reason to the other? Does not the infinitude of division refer to the utterness of individuality? Does not the entireness of the complex hint at the perfection of the simple? It is *not* that the atoms, as we see them, are divided or that they are complex in their relations – but that they are inconceivably divided and unutterably complex: – it is the extremeness of the conditions to which I now allude, rather than to the conditions themselves. In a word, not because the atoms were, at some remote epoch of time, even *more than together* – is it not because originally, and therefore normally, they were *One* – that now, in all circumstances – at all points – in all directions – by all modes of approach – in all relations and through all conditions – they struggle *back* to this absolutely, this irrelatively, this unconditionally *One*?

Some person may here demand : – 'Why – since it is to the *One* that the atoms struggle back – do we not find and define Attraction "as merely general tendency to a centre?" – why, in especial, do not *your* atoms – the atoms which you describe as having been radiated from a centre – proceed at once, rectilinearly, back to the central point of their origin?'

I reply that *they do*; as will be distinctly shown; but that the cause of their so doing is quite irrespective of the centre *as such*. They all tend rectilinearly towards a centre, because of the sphericity with which they have been radiated into space. Each atom, forming one of a generally uniform globe of atoms, finds more atoms in the direction of the centre, of course, than in any other, and in that direction, therefore, is impelled – but is *not* thus impelled because the centre is *the point of its origin*. It is not to any *point* that the atoms are allied. It is not any *locality*, either in the concrete or in the abstract, to which I suppose them bound. Nothing like *location* was conceived as their origin. Their source lies in the principle, *Unity*. *This* is their lost parent. *This* they seek always – immediately – in all directions – wherever it is even partially to be found; thus appeasing, in some measure, the ineradicable tendency, while on the way to its absolute satisfaction in the end. It follows from all this, that any principle which shall be adequate to account for the *law*, or *modus operandi*, of the attractive force in general, will account for this law in particular : – that is to say, any principle which will show why the atoms should tend to their *general centre of radiation* with forces inversely proportional with the squares of the distances, will be admitted as satisfactorily accounting, at the same time, for the tendency, according to the same law, of these atoms each to each : – *for* the tendency to the centre *is* merely the tendency each to each, and not any tendency to a centre as such. – Thus it will be seen, also, that the establishment of my propositions would involve no *necessity* of modification in the terms of the Newtonian definition of Gravity, which declares that each atom attracts each other atom and so forth, and declares this merely; but (always under the supposition that what I propose be, in the end, admitted) it seems clear that some error might occasionally be avoided, in the future processes of Science, were a more ample phraseology adopted : – for instance : – 'Each atom tends to every other atom &c. with a force &c. : *the general result being a tendency of all, with a similar force, to a general centre*.'

The reversal of our processes has thus brought us to an identical result; but, while in the one process *Intuition* was the starting-point, in the other it was the goal. In commencing the former journey I could only say that, with an irresistible Intuition, I *felt* Simplicity to have been the characteristic of the original action of God : – in ending the latter I can only declare that, with an irresistible intuition, I perceive Unity to have been the source of the observed phænomena of the Newtonian Gravity. Thus, according to the schools, I *prove* nothing. So be it : – I design but to suggest – and to *convince* through the suggestion. I am proudly aware that there exist many of the most profound and cautiously discriminative intellects which cannot *help* being abundantly content with my – suggestions. To these intellects – as to my own – there is no mathematical demonstration which *could* bring the least additional *true proof* of the great *Truth* which I have advanced – *the truth of Original Unity as the source – as the principle of the Universal Phænomena.* For my part, I am not sure that I speak and see – I am not so sure that my heart beats and that my soul lives : – of the rising of to-morrow's sun – a probability that as yet lies in the Future – I do not pretend to be one thousandth part as sure – as I am of the irretrievably by-gone *Fact* that All Things and All Thoughts of Things, with all their ineffable Multiplicity of Relation, sprang at once into being from the primordial and irrelative *One*.

Referring to the Newtonian Gravity, Dr Nichol, the eloquent author of 'The Architecture of the Heavens',[24] says:–'In truth we have no reason to suppose this great Law, as now revealed, to be the ultimate or simplest, and therefore the universal and all-comprehensive, form of a great Ordinance. The mode in which its intensity diminishes with the element of distance, has not the aspect of an ultimate *principle*; which always assumes the simplicity and self-evidence of those axioms which constitute the basis of Geometry.'

Now, it is quite true that 'ultimate principles', in the common understanding of the words, always assume the simplicity of geometrical axioms – (as for 'self-evidence', there is no such thing) – but these principles are clearly *not* 'ultimate'; in other terms what we are in the habit of calling principles are no principles, properly speaking – since there can be but one *principle*, the Volition of God. We have no right to assume, then, from what we observe in rules that we choose foolishly to name 'principles', anything at all in respect to the characteristics of a principle proper. The 'ultimate principles' of which Dr Nichol speaks as having geometrical simplicity, may and do have this geometrical turn, as being part and parcel of a vast geometrical system, and thus a system of simplicity itself – in which, nevertheless, the *truly* ultimate principle is, *as we know*, the consummation of the complex – that is to say, of the unintelligible – for is it not the Spiritual Capacity of God?

I quoted Dr Nichol's remark, however, not so much to question its philosophy, as by way of calling attention to the fact that, while all men have admitted *some* principle as existing behind the Law of Gravity, no attempt has been yet made to point out what this principle in particular *is* : – if we except, perhaps, occasional fantastic efforts at referring it to Magnetism, or Mesmerism, or Swedenborgianism, or Transcendentalism, or some other equally delicious *ism* of the same species, and invariably patronized by one and the same species of people. The great mind of Newton, while boldly grasping the Law itself, shrank from the principle of the Law. The more fluent and comprehensive at least, if not the more patient and profound, sagacity of Laplace, had not the courage to attack it. But hesitation on the part of these two astronomers it is, perhaps, not so very difficult to understand. They, as well as all the first class of mathematicians, were mathematicians *solely* : – their intellect, at least, had a firmly-pronounced mathematico-physical tone. What lay not distinctly within the domain of Physics, or of Mathematics, seemed to them either Non-Entity or Shadow. Nevertheless, we may well wonder that Leibnitz, who was a marked exception to the general rule in these respects, and whose mental temperament was a singular admixture of the mathematical with the physico-metaphysical, did not at once investigate and establish the point at issue. Either Newton or Laplace, seeking a principle and discovering none *physical*, would have rested contentedly in the conclusion that there was absolutely none; but it is almost impossible to fancy, of Leibnitz, that, having exhausted in his search the physical dominions, he would not have stepped at once, boldly and hopefully, amid his old familiar haunts in the kingdom of Metaphysics. Here, indeed, it is clear that he *must* have adventured in search of the treasure : – that he did not find it after all, was, perhaps, because his fairy guide, Imagination, was not sufficiently well-grown, or well-educated, to direct him aright.

I observed, just now, that, in fact, there had been certain vague attempts at referring Gravity to some very uncertain *isms.*

These attempts, however, although considered bold and justly so considered, looked no farther than to the generality – the merest generality – of the Newtonian Law. Its *modus operandi* has never, to my knowledge, been approached in the way of an effort at explanation. It is, therefore, with no unwarranted fear of being taken for a madman at the outset, and before I can bring my propositions fairly to the eye of those who alone are competent to decide on them, that I here declare the *modus operandi* of the Law of Gravity to be an exceedingly simple and perfectly explicable thing [25] – that is to say, when we make our advances towards it in just gradations and in the true direction – when we regard it from the proper point of view.

Whether we reach the idea of absolute *Unity* as the source of All Things, from a consideration of Simplicity as the most probable characteristic of the original action of God; – whether we arrive at it from an inspection of the universality of relation in the gravitating phænomena; – or whether we attain it as a result of the mutual corroboration afforded by both processes; – still, the idea itself, if entertained at all, is entertained in inseparable connection with another idea – that of the condition of the Universe of Stars as we *now* perceive it – that is to say, a condition of immeasurable *diffusion* through space. Now a connection between these two ideas – unity and diffusion – cannot be established unless through the entertainment of a third idea – that of *radiation*. Absolute Unity being taken as a centre, then the existing Universe of Stars is the result of *radiation* from that centre.

Now, the laws of radiation are *known*. They are part and parcel of the *sphere*. They belong to the class of indisputable geometrical properties. We say of them, 'they are true – they are evident'. To demand *why* they are true, would be to demand why the axioms are true upon which their demonstration is based. Nothing is demonstrable, strictly speaking; but if anything *be*, then the properties – the laws in question are demonstrated.

But these laws – what do they declare? Radiation – how – by what steps does it proceed outwardly from a centre?

From a *luminous* centre, *Light* issues by radiation; and the quantities of light received upon any given plane, supposed to be shifting its position so as to be now nearer the centre and now farther from it, will be diminished in the same proportion as the squares of the distances of the plane from the luminous body, are increased; and will be increased in the same proportion as these squares are diminished.

The expression of the law may be thus generalized: – the number of light-particles (or, if the phrase be preferred, the number of light-impressions) received upon the shifting plane, will be *inversely* proportional with the squares of the distances of the plane. Generalizing yet again, we may say that the diffusion – the scattering – the radiation, in a word – is *directly* proportional with the squares of the distances.

For example: at the distance B, from the luminous centre A, a certain number of particles are so diffused as to occupy the surface B. Then at double the distance – that is to say

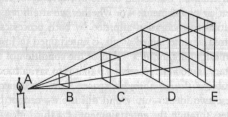

at C – they will be so much farther diffused as to occupy four such surfaces: – at treble the distance, or at D, they will be so much farther separated as to occupy nine such surfaces : – while, at quadruple the distance, or at E, they will have become so scattered as to spread themselves over sixteen such surfaces – and so on forever.

In saying, generally, that the radiation proceeds in direct proportion with the squares of the distances, we use the term radiation to express *the degree of the diffusion* as we proceed outwardly from the centre. Conversing the idea, and employing the word 'concentralization' to express *the degree of the drawing together* as we come back toward the centre from an outward position, we may say that concentralization proceeds *inversely* as the squares of the distances. In other words, we have reached the conclusion that, on the hypothesis that matter was originally radiated from a centre and is now returning to it, the concentralization, in the return, proceeds *exactly as we know the force of gravitation to proceed*.

Now here, if we could be permitted to assume that concentralization exactly represents the *force of the tendency to the centre* – that the one is exactly proportional with the other, and that the two proceed together – we should have shown all that is required. The sole difficulty existing, then, is to establish a direct proportion between 'concentralization' and the *force* of concentralization; and this is done, of course, if we establish such proportion between 'radiation' and the *force* of radiation.

A very slight inspection of the Heavens assures us that the stars have a certain general uniformity, equability, or equidistance, of distribution through that region of space in which, collectively, and in a roughly globular form, they are situated : – this species of very general, rather than absolute, equability, being in full keeping with my deduction of inequidistance, within certain limits, among the originally diffused atoms, as a corollary from the design of infinite complexity of relation out of irrelation. I started, it will be remembered, with the idea of a generally uniform but particularly *un*uniform distribution of the atoms; – an idea, I repeat, which an inspection of the stars, as they exist, confirms.

But even in the merely general equability of distribution, as regards the atoms, there appears a difficulty which, no doubt, has already suggested itself to those among my readers who have borne in mind that I suppose this equability of distribution effected through *radiation from a centre*. The very first glance at the idea, radiation, forces us to the entertainment of the hitherto unseparated and seemingly inseparable idea of agglomeration about a centre, with dispersion as we recede from it – the idea, in a word, of *in*equability of distribution in respect to the matter radiated.

Now, I have elsewhere* observed[26] that it is by just such difficulties as the one now in question – such peculiarities – such roughness – such protuberances above the plane of the ordinary

* '*Murders in the Rue Morgue*'.

– that Reason feels her way, if at all, in her search for the True. By the difficulty – the 'peculiarity' – now presented, I leap at once to *the* secret – a secret which I might never have attained *but* for the peculiarity and the inferences which, *in its mere character of peculiarity*, it affords me.

The process of thought, at this point, may be thus roughly sketched : – I say to myself – 'Unity, as I have explained it, is a truth – I feel it. Diffusion is a truth – I see it. Radiation, by which alone these two truths are reconciled, is a consequent truth – I perceive it. *Equability* of diffusion, first deduced *à priori* and then corroborated by the inspection of phænomena, is also a truth – I fully admit it. So far all is clear around me : – there are no clouds behind which *the* secret – the great secret of the gravitating *modus operandi* – can possibly lie hidden; – but this secret lies *hereabouts*, most assuredly; and *were* there but a cloud in view, I should be driven to suspicion of that cloud.' And now, just as I say this, there actually comes a cloud into view. This cloud is the seeming impossibility of reconciling my truth, *radiation*, with my truth, *equability of diffusion*. I say now : – 'Behind this *seeming* impossibility is to be found what I desire.' I do not say *'real* impossibility', for invincible faith in my truths assures me that it is a mere difficulty after all – but I go on to say, with unflinching confidence, that, *when* this *difficulty* shall be solved, we shall find, *wrapped up in the process of solution*, the key to the secret at which we aim. Moreover – I *feel* that we shall discover *but one* possible solution of the difficulty; this for the reason that, were there two, one would be supererogatory – would be fruitless – would be empty – would contain no key – since no duplicate key can be needed to any secret of Nature.

And now, let us see : – Our usual notions of radiation – in fact *all* our distinct notions of it – are caught merely from the process as we see it exemplified in *Light*. Here there is a *continuous* outpouring of *ray-streams*, and *with a force which we have at least no right to suppose varies at all*. Now, in any such radiation *as this* – continuous and of unvarying force – the regions nearer the centre must *inevitably* be always more crowded with the radiated matter than the regions more remote. But I have assumed *no* such radiation *as this*. I assumed no *continuous* radiation; and for the simple reason that such an assumption would have involved, first, the necessity of entertaining a conception which I have shown no man *can* entertain, and which (as I will more fully explain hereafter) all observation of the firmament refutes – the conception of the absolute infinity of the Universe of Stars – and would have involved, secondly, the impossibility of understanding a rëaction – that is, gravitation – as existing now – since, while an act is continued, no rëaction, of course, can take place. My assumption, then – or rather my inevitable deduction from just premises – was that of a *determinate* radiation – one finally *dis*continued.

Let me now describe the sole possible mode in which it is conceivable that matter could have been diffused through space, so as to fulfil the conditions at once of radiation and of generally equable distribution.

For convenience of illustration, let us imagine, in the first place, a hollow sphere of glass, or of anything else, occupying the space throughout which the universal matter is to be thus equally diffused, by means of radiation, from the absolute, irrelative, unconditional Particle, placed in the centre of the sphere.

Now, a certain exertion of the diffusive power (presumed to be the Divine Volition) – in other words, a certain *force* – whose measure is the quantity of matter – that is to say, the number of atoms – emitted; emits, by radiation, this certain number of atoms; forcing them in all directions outwardly from the centre –their proximity to each other diminishing as they proceed – until, finally, they are distributed, loosely, over the interior surface of the sphere.

When these atoms have attained this position, or while proceeding to attain it, a second and inferior exercise of the same force – or a second and inferior force of the same character – emits, in the same manner – that is to say, by radiation as before – a second stratum of atoms which proceeds to deposit itself upon the first; the number of atoms, in this case as in the former, being of course the measure of the force which emitted them; in other words the force being precisely adapted to the purpose it effects – the force and the number of atoms sent out by the force, being *directly proportional*.

When this second stratum has reached its destined position – or while approaching it – a third still inferior exertion of the force, or a third inferior force of a similar character – the number of atoms emitted being in *all* cases the measure of the force – proceeds to deposit a third stratum upon the second : – and so on, until these concentric strata, growing gradually less and less, come down at length to the central point; and the diffusive matter, simultaneously with the diffusive force, is exhausted.

We have now the sphere filled, through means of radiation, with atoms equably diffused. The two necessary conditions – those of radiation and of equable diffusion – are satisfied; and by the *sole* process in which the possibility of their simultaneous satisfaction is conceivable.* For this reason, I confidently expect to find, lurking in the present condition of the atoms as distributed throughout the sphere, the secret of which I am in search – the all-important principle of the *modus operandi* of the Newtonian law. Let us examine, then, the actual condition of the atoms.

They lie in a series of concentric strata. They are equably diffused throughout the sphere.

The atoms being *equably* distributed, the greater the superficial extent of any of these concentric strata, or spheres, the more atoms will lie upon it. In other words, the number of atoms lying upon the surface of any one of the concentric spheres, is directly proportional with the extent of that surface.

But, in any series of concentric spheres, the surfaces are directly proportional with the squares of the distances from the centre.†

Therefore the number of atoms in any stratum is directly proportional with the square of that stratum's distance from the centre.

But the number of atoms in any stratum is the measure of the force which emitted that stratum – that is to say, is *directly proportional* with the force.

* Here describe the whole process as one instantaneous flash.[27]
† Succinctly – The surfaces of spheres are as the squares of their radii.

Therefore the force which radiated any stratum is directly proportional with the square of that stratum's distance from the centre: – or, generally,

The force of the radiation has been directly proportional with the squares of the distances: – or, particularly, *The force by which any individual atom was sent to its position in the sphere, was directly proportional with the square of that atom's distance while in that position, from the centre of the sphere.*

Now, Rëaction, as far as we know any thing of it, is Action conversed. The *general* principle of Gravity being, in the first place, understood as the rëaction of an act – as the expression of a desire on the part of Matter, while existing in a state of diffusion, to return into the Unity whence it was diffused; and, in the second place, the mind being called on to determine the *character* of the desire – the manner in which it would, naturally, be manifested; in other words, being called on to conceive a probable law, or *modus operandi*, for the return; could not well help arriving at the conclusion that this law of return would be precisely the converse of the law of departure. That such would be the case, any one, at least, would be abundantly justified in taking for granted, until such time as some person should suggest something like a plausible reason why it should *not* be the case – until such a period as a law of return shall be imagined which the intellect can consider as preferable.

Matter, then, radiated into space with a force varying as the squares of the distances, might, *à priori*, be supposed to return towards its centre of radiation with a force varying *inversely* as the squares of the distances : and I have already shown * that any principle which will explain why the atoms should tend, according to any law, to the general centre, must be admitted as satisfactorily explaining, at the same time, why, according to the same law, they should tend each to each. For, in fact, the tendency to the general centre is not to a centre as such, but because of its being a point in tending towards which each atom tends most directly to its real and essential centre, *Unity* – the absolute and final Union of all.

The consideration here involved presents to my own mind no

* Page 238.

embarrassment whatever – but this fact does not blind me to the possibility of its being obscure to those who may have been less in the habit of dealing with abstractions : – and, on the whole, it may be as well to look at the matter from one or two other points of view.

The absolute, irrelative particle primarily created by the Volition of God, must have been in a condition of positive *normality*, or rightfulness – for wrongfulness implies *relation*. Right is positive; wrong is negative – is merely the negation of right; as cold is the negation of heat – darkness of light. That a thing may be wrong, it is necessary that there be some other thing in *relation* to which it *is* wrong – some condition which it fails to satisfy; some law which it violates; some being whom it aggrieves. If there be no such being, law, or condition, in respect to which the thing is wrong – and, still more especially, if no beings, laws, or conditions exist at all – then the thing can*not* be wrong and consequently must be *right*.

Any deviation from normality involves a tendency to return to it. A difference from the normal – from the right – from the just – can be understood as effected only by the overcoming a difficulty; and if the force which overcomes the difficulty be not infinitely continued, the ineradicable tendency to return will at length be permitted to act for its own satisfaction. On withdrawal of the force, the tendency acts. This is the principle of rëaction as the inevitable consequence of finite action. Employing a phraseology of which the seeming affectation will be pardoned for its expressiveness, we may say that Rëaction is the return from the condition of *as it is and ought not to be* into the condition of *as it was, originally, and therefore ought to be* : – and let me add here that the *absolute* force of Rëaction would no doubt be always found in direct proportion with the reality – the truth – the absoluteness – of the *originality* – if ever it were possible to measure this latter : – and, consequently, the greatest of all conceivable rëactions must be that manifested in the tendency which we now discuss – the tendency to return into the *absolutely* original – into the *supremely* primitive. Gravity, then, *must be the strongest of forces* – an idea reached *à priori* and abundantly confirmed by induction. What use I make of the idea, will be seen in the sequel.

The atoms, now, having been diffused from their normal condition of Unity, seek to return to — what? Not to any particular *point*, certainly; for it is clear that if, on the diffusion, the whole Universe of matter had been projected, collectively, to a distance from the point of radiation, the atomic tendency to the general centre of the sphere would not have been disturbed in the least: – the atoms would not have sought the point *in absolute space* from which they were originally impelled. It is merely the *condition*, and not the point or locality at which this condition took its rise, that these atoms seek to re-establish; – it is merely *that condition which is their normality*, that they desire. 'But they seek a centre,' it will be said, 'and a centre is a point.' True; but they seek this point not in its character of point – (for, were the whole sphere moved from its position, they would seek, equally, the centre; and the centre *then* would be a *new* point) – but because it so happens, on account of the form in which they collectively exist – (that of the sphere) – that only *through* the point in question – the sphere's centre – they can attain their true object, Unity. In the direction of the centre each atom perceives more atoms than in any other direction. Each atom is impelled towards the centre because along the straight line joining it and the centre and passing on to the surface beyond, there lie a greater number of atoms than along any other straight line joining it, the atom, with any point of the sphere – a greater number of objects that seek it, the individual atom – a greater number of tendencies to Unity – a greater number of satisfactions for its own tendency to Unity – in a word, because in the direction of the centre lies the utmost possibility of satisfaction, generally, for its own individual appetite. To be brief, the *condition*, Unity, is all that is really sought; and if the atoms *seem* to seek the centre of the sphere, it is only impliedly – through implication – because such centre happens to imply, to include, or to involve, the only essential centre, Unity. But *on account of* this implication or involution, there is no possibility of practically separating the tendency to Unity in the abstract, from the tendency to the concrete centre. Thus the tendency of the atoms to the general centre *is*, to all practical intents and for all logical purposes, the tendency each to each; and the tendency each to each *is* the tendency to the centre; and the one tendency may be assumed *as* the other; whatever will apply to the one must be thoroughly applicable to the other; and, in conclusion, whatever principle will satisfactorily explain the one, cannot be questioned as an explanation of the other.

In looking carefully around me for rational objection to what I have advanced, I am able to discover nothing; – but of that class of objections usually urged by the doubters for Doubt's sake, I very readily perceive *three*; and proceed to dispose of them in order.

It may be said, first: 'The proof that the force of radiation (in the case described) is directly proportional with the squares of the distances, depends on an unwarranted assumption – that of the number of atoms in each stratum being the measure of the force with which they are emitted.'

I reply, not only that I am warranted in such assumption, but that I should be utterly *un*warranted in any other. What I assume is, simply, that an effect is the measure of its cause – that every exercise of the Divine Will will be proportional with that which demands the exertion – that the means of Omnipotence, or of Omniscience, will be exactly adapted to its purposes. Neither can a deficiency nor an excess of cause bring to pass any effect. Had the force which radiated any stratum to its position, been either more or less than was needed for the purpose – that is to say, not *directly proportional* with the purpose – then to its position that stratum could not have been radiated. Had the force which, with a view to general equability of distribution, emitted the proper number of atoms for each stratum, been not *directly proportional* with the number, then the number would *not* have been the number demanded for the equable distribution.

The second supposable objection is somewhat better entitled to an answer.

It is an admitted principle in Dynamics that every body, on receiving an impulse, or disposition to move, will move onward in a straight line, in the direction imparted by the impelling force, until deflected, or stopped, by some other force. How then, it may be asked, is my first or external stratum of atoms to be understood as discontinuing their movement at the surface of the imaginary glass sphere, when no second force, of more than an imaginary character, appears, to account for the discontinuance?

I reply that the objection, in this case, actually does arise out of 'an unwarranted assumption' – on the part of the objector – the assumption of a principle, in Dynamics, at an epoch when *no* 'principles', in *anything*, exist : [28] – I use the word 'principle', of course, in the objector's understanding of the word.

'In the beginning' we can admit – indeed we can comprehend – but one *First Cause* – the truly ultimate *Principle* – the Volition of God. The primary *act* – that of Radiation from Unity – must have been independent of all that which the world now calls 'principle' – because all that we so designate is but a consequence of the rëaction of that primary act : – I say '*primary*' act; for the creation of the absolute material Particle is more properly to be regarded as a *conception* than as an '*act*' in the ordinary meaning of the term. Thus, we must regard the primary act as an act for the establishment of what we now call 'principles'. But this primary act itself is to be considered as *continuous Volition*. The Thought of God is to be understood as originating the Diffusion – as proceeding with it – as regulating it – and, finally, as being withdrawn from it on its completion. *Then* commences Rëaction, and through Rëaction, 'Principle', as we employ the word. It will be advisable, however, to limit the application of this word to the two *immediate* results of the discontinuance of the Divine Volition – that is, to the two agents, *Attraction* and *Repulsion*. Every other Natural agent depends, either more or less immediately, on these two, and therefore would be more conveniently designated as *sub*-principle.

It may be objected, thirdly, that, in general, the peculiar mode of distribution which I have suggested for the atoms, is 'an hypothesis and nothing more'.

Now, I am aware that the word 'hypothesis' is a ponderous sledge-hammer, grasped immediately, if not lifted, by all very diminutive thinkers, on the first appearance of any proposition wearing, in any particular, the garb of *a theory*. But 'hypothesis' cannot be wielded *here* to any good purpose, even by those who succeed in lifting it – little men or great.

I maintain, first, that *only* in the mode described is it conceivable that Matter could have been diffused so as to fulfil at once the conditions of radiation and of generally equable distribution. I maintain, secondly, that these conditions themselves have been imposed upon me, as necessities, in a train of ratiocination as rigorously logical as that which establishes any demonstration in Euclid; and I maintain, thirdly, that even if the charge of 'hypothesis' were as fully sustained as it is, in fact, unsustained and untenable, still the validity and indisputability of my result would not, even in the slightest particular, be disturbed.

To explain : – The Newtonian Gravity – a law of Nature – a law whose existence as such no one out of Bedlam questions – a law whose admission as such enables us to account for nine-tenths of the Universal phænomena – a law which, merely because it does so enable us to account for these phænomena, we are perfectly willing, without reference to any other considerations, to admit, and cannot help admitting, as a law – a law, nevertheless, of which neither the principle nor the *modus operandi* of the principle, has ever yet been traced by the human analysis – a law, in short, which, neither in its detail nor in its generality, has been found susceptible of explanation *at all* – is at length seen to be at every point thoroughly explicable, provided we only yield our assent to — what? To an hypothesis? Why, *if* an hypothesis – if the merest hypothesis – if an hypothesis for whose assumption – as in the case of that *pure* hypothesis the Newtonian law itself – no shadow of *à priori* reason could be assigned – if an hypothesis, even so absolute as all this implies, would enable us to perceive a principle for the Newtonian law – would enable us to understand as satisfied, conditions so miraculously – so ineffably complex and seemingly irreconcileable as those involved in the relations of which Gravity tells us, – what rational being *could* so expose his fatuity as to call even this absolute hypothesis an hypothesis any longer – unless, indeed, he were to persist in so calling it, with the understanding that he did so, simply for the sake of consistency *in words*?

But what is the true state of our present case? What is *the fact*? Not only that it is *not* an hypothesis which we are required *to adopt*, in order to admit the principle at issue explained, but that it *is* a logical conclusion which we are requested *not* to adopt if we can avoid it – which we are simply invited to *deny if we can* : – a conclusion of so accurate a logicality that to dispute it would be the effort – to doubt its validity beyond our power : – a conclusion from which we see no mode of escape, turn as we will; a result which confronts us either at the end of an *in*ductive journey from the phænomena of the very Law discussed, or at the close of a *de*ductive career from the most rigorously simple of all conceivable assumptions – *the assumption, in a word, of Simplicity itself.*

And if here, it be urged, that although my starting-point is, as I assert, the assumption of absolute Simplicity, yet Simplicity, considered merely in itself, is no axiom; and that only deductions from axioms are indisputable – it is thus that I reply :

Every other science than Logic is the science of certain concrete relations. Arithmetic, for example, is the science of the relations of number – Geometry, of the relations of form – Mathematics in general, of the relations of quantity in general – of whatever can be increased or diminished. Logic, however, is the science of Relation in the abstract – of absolute Relation – of Relation considered solely in itself. An axiom in any particular science other than Logic is, thus, merely a proposition announcing certain concrete relations which seem to be too obvious for dispute – as when we say, for instance, that the whole is greater than its part : – and, thus again, the principle of the *Logical* axiom – in other words, of an axiom in the abstract – is, simply, *obviousness of relation*. Now, it is clear, not only that what is obvious to one mind may not be obvious to another, but that what is obvious to one mind at one epoch, may be anything but obvious, at another epoch, to the same mind. It is clear, moreover, that what, today, is obvious even to the majority of mankind, or to the majority of the best intellects of mankind, may to-morrow be, to either majority, more or less obvious, or in no respect obvious at all. It is seen, then, that the *axiomatic principle* itself is susceptible of variation,[29] and of course that axioms are susceptible of similar change. Being mutable, the 'truths' which grow out of them are necessarily mutable too; or, in other words, are never to be positively depended on as truths at all – since Truth and Immutability are one.

It will now be readily understood that no axiomatic idea – no idea founded in the fluctuating principle, obviousness of relation – can possibly be so secure – so reliable a basis for any structure erected by the Reason, as *that* idea – (whatever it is, wherever we can find it, or *if* it be practicable to find it anywhere) – which is *ir*relative altogether – which not only presents to the understanding *no obviousness* of relation, either greater or less, to be considered, but subjects the intellect, not in the slightest degree, to the necessity of even looking at *any relation at all*. If such an idea be not what we too heedlessly term 'an axiom', it is at least preferable, as a logical basis, to any axiom ever propounded, or to all imaginable axioms combined : – and such, precisely, is the idea with which my deductive process, so thoroughly corroborated by induction, commences. My *Particle Proper* is but *Absolute Radiation*.

To sum up what has been advanced : – As a starting point I have taken it for granted, simply, that the Beginning had nothing behind it or before it – that it was a Beginning in fact – that it was a Beginning and nothing different from a Beginning – in short, that this Beginning was – *that which it was*. If this be a 'mere assumption' then a 'mere assumption' let it be.

To conclude this branch of the subject : – I am fully warranted in announcing that *the Law which we call Gravity exists on account of Matter's having been radiated, at its origin, atomically, into a limited * sphere of Space, from one, individual, unconditional, irrelative, and absolute Particle Proper, by the sole process in which it was possible to satisfy, at the same time, the two conditions, radiation and equable distribution throughout the sphere – that is to say, by a force varying in direct proportion*

---

* A sphere is *necessarily* limited. I prefer tautology to a chance of misconception.

*with the squares of the distances between the radiated atoms,
respectively, and the Particular centre of Radiation.*

I have already given my reasons for presuming Matter to have
been diffused by a determinate rather than by a continuous or
infinitely continued force. Supposing a continuous force, we
should be unable, in the first place, to comprehend a rëaction at
all; and we should be required, in the second place, to entertain
the impossible conception of an infinite extension of Matter. Not
to dwell upon the impossibility of the conception, the infinite
extension of Matter is an idea which, if not positively disproved,
is at least not in any respect warranted by telescopic observation
of the stars – a point to be explained more fully hereafter; and
this empirical reason for believing in the original finity of Matter
is unempirically confirmed. For example: – Admitting, for the
moment, the possibility of understanding Space as *filled* with the
radiated atoms – that is to say, admitting, as well as we can, for
argument's sake, that the succession of the atoms had absolutely
no end – then it is clear that, even when the Volition of God had
been withdrawn from them, and thus the tendency to return into
Unity permitted (abstractly) to be satisfied, this permission would
have been nugatory and invalid – practically valueless and of no
effect whatever. No Rëaction could have taken place; no movement toward Unity could have been made; no Law of Gravity
could have obtained.

To explain: – Grant the *abstract* tendency of any one atom
to any one other as the inevitable result of diffusion from the
normal Unity : – or, what is the same thing, admit any given
atom as *proposing* to move in any given direction – it is clear
that, since there is an *infinity* of atoms on all sides of the atom
proposing to move, it never can actually move toward the satisfaction of its tendency in the direction given, on account of a
precisely equal and counter-balancing tendency in the direction
diametrically opposite. In other words, exactly as many tendencies to Unity are behind the hesitating atom as before it; for
it is mere folly to say that one infinite line is longer or shorter
than another infinite line, or that one infinite number is greater
or less than another number that is infinite. Thus the atom in
question must remain stationary forever. Under the impossible

circumstances which we have been merely endeavoring to conceive for argument's sake, there could have been no aggregation of Matter – no stars – no worlds – nothing but a perpetually atomic and inconsequential Universe. In fact, view it as we will, the whole idea of unlimited Matter is not only untenable, but impossible and preposterous.

With the understanding of a *sphere* of atoms, however, we perceive, at once, a *satisfiable* tendency to union. The general result of the tendency each to each, being a tendency of all to the centre, the *general* process of condensation, or approximation, commences immediately, by a common and simultaneous movement, on withdrawal of the Divine Volition; the *individual* approximations, or coalescences of atom with atom, being subject to almost infinite variations of time, degree, and condition, on account of the excessive multiplicity of relation, arising from the differences of form assumed as characterizing the atoms at the moment of their quitting the Particle Proper; as well as from the subsequent particular inequidistance, each from each.

What I wish to impress upon the reader is the certainty of there arising, at once, (on withdrawal of the diffusive force, or Divine Volition,) out of the condition of the atoms as described, at innumerable points throughout the Universal sphere, innumerable agglomerations, characterized by innumerable specific differences of form, size, essential nature, and distance each from each. The development of Repulsion (Electricity) must have commenced, of course, with the very earliest particular efforts at Unity, and must have proceeded constantly in the ratio of coalescence – that is to say, *in that of Condensation*, or, again, of Heterogeneity.

Thus the two Principles Proper, *Attraction* and *Repulsion* – the Material and the Spiritual – accompany each other, in the strictest fellowship, forever. Thus *The Body and The Soul walk hand in hand*.

If now, in fancy, we select any one of the agglomerations considered as in their primary stages throughout the Universal sphere, and suppose this incipient agglomeration to be taking place at that point where the centre of our Sun exists – or rather where it *did* exist originally; for the Sun is perpetually shifting his position – we shall find ourselves met, and borne onward for a time at least, by the most magnificent of theories – by the Nebular Cosmogony of Laplace:[30] – although 'Cosmogony' is far too comprehensive a term for what he really discusses – which is the constitution of our solar system alone – of one among the myriad of similar systems which make up the Universe of Stars.

Confining himself to an *obviously limited* region – that of our solar system with its comparatively immediate vicinity – and *merely* assuming – that is to say, assuming without any basis whatever – *much* of what I have been just endeavoring to place upon a more stable basis than assumption; assuming, for example, matter as diffused (without pretending to account for the diffusion) throughout, and somewhat beyond, the space occupied by our system – diffused in a state of heterogeneous nebulosity and obedient to that omniprevalent law of Gravity at whose principle he ventured to make no guess : – assuming all this (which is quite true, although he had no logical right to its assumption) Laplace has shown, dynamically and mathematically, that the results in such case necessarily ensuing, are those and those alone which we find manifested in the actually existing condition of the system itself.

To explain: – Let us conceive *that* particular agglomeration of which we have just spoken – the one at the point designated by our Sun's centre – to have so far proceeded that a vast quantity of nebulous matter has here assumed a roughly globular form; its centre being, of course, coincident with what is now, or rather was originally, the centre of our Sun; and its surface extending out beyond the orbit of Neptune, the most remote of our planets : – in other words, let us suppose the diameter of this rough sphere to be some 6000 millions of miles. For ages, this mass of matter has been undergoing condensation, until at length it has become reduced into the bulk we imagine; having proceeded gradually, of course, from its atomic and imperceptible state, into what we understand of appreciable nebulosity.

Now, the condition of this mass implies a rotation about an imaginary axis – a rotation which, commencing with the absolute incipiency of the aggregation, has been ever since acquiring velocity. The very first two atoms which met, approaching each other from points not diametrically opposite, would, in rushing partially past each other, form a nucleus for the rotary movement described. How this would increase in velocity, is readily seen. The two atoms are joined by others: – an aggregation is formed. The mass continues to rotate while condensing. But any atom at the surface has, of course, a more rapid motion than one nearer the centre. The outer atom, however, with its superior velocity, approaches the centre; carrying this superior velocity with it as it goes. Thus every atom, proceeding inwardly, and finally attaching itself to the condensed centre, adds something to the original velocity of that centre – that is to say, increases the rotary movement of the mass.

Let us now suppose this mass so far condensed that it occupies *precisely* the space circumscribed by the orbit of Neptune, and that the velocity with which the surface of the mass moves, in the general rotation, is precisely that velocity with which Neptune now revolves about the Sun. At this epoch, then, we are to understand that the constantly increasing centrifugal force, having gotten the better of the non-increasing centripetal, loosened and separated the exterior and least condensed stratum, or a few of the exterior and least condensed strata, at the equator of the sphere, where the tangential velocity predominated; so that these strata formed about the main body an independent ring encircling the equatorial regions: – just as the exterior portion thrown off, by excessive velocity of rotation, from a grindstone, would form a ring about the grindstone, but for the solidity of the superficial material: were this caoutchouc, or anything similar in consistency, precisely the phænomenon I describe would be presented.

The ring thus whirled from the nebulous mass, *revolved*, of course, *as* a separate ring, with just that velocity with which, while the surface of the mass, it *rotated*. In the meantime, condensation still proceeding, the interval between the discharged ring and the main body continued to increase, until the former was left at a vast distance from the latter.

Now, admitting the ring to have possessed, by some seemingly accidental arrangement of its heterogeneous materials, a constitution nearly uniform, then this ring, *as* such, would never have ceased revolving about its primary; but, as might have been anticipated, there appears to have been enough irregularity in the disposition of the materials, to make them cluster about centres of superior solidity; and thus the annular form was destroyed.* No doubt, the band was soon broken up into several portions, and one of these portions, predominating in mass, absorbed the others into itself; the whole settling, spherically, into a planet. That this latter, *as* a planet, continued the revolutionary movement which characterized it while a ring, is sufficiently clear; and that it took upon itself, also, an additional movement in its new condition of sphere, is readily explained. The ring being understood as yet unbroken, we see that its exterior, while the whole revolves about the parent body, moves more rapidly than its interior. When the rupture occurred, then, some portion in each fragment must have been moving with greater velocity than the others. The superior movement prevailing, must have whirled each fragment round – that is to say, have caused it to rotate; and the direction of the rotation must, of course, have been the direction of the revolution whence it arose. *All* the fragments having become subject to the rotation described, must, in coalescing, have imparted it to the one planet constituted by their coalescence. – This planet was Neptune. Its material continuing to undergo condensation, and the centrifugal force generated in its rotation getting, at length, the better of the centripetal, as before in the case of the parent orb, a ring was whirled also from the equatorial surface of this planet: this ring, having been un-uniform in its constitution, was broken up, and its several fragments, being absorbed by the most massive, were collectively spherified into a moon. Subsequently, the operation was repeated, and a second moon was the result. We thus account for the planet Neptune, with the two satellites which accompany him.†

---

* Laplace assumed his nebulosity heterogeneous, merely that he might be thus enabled to account for the breaking up of the rings; for had the nebulosity been homogeneous, they would not have broken. I reach the same result – heterogeneity of the secondary masses immediately resulting from the atoms – purely from an *à priori* consideration of their general design – *Relation*.

† When this book went to press the *ring* of Neptune had not been positively determined.

In throwing off a ring from its equator, the Sun reestablished that equilibrium between its centripetal and centrifugal forces which had been disturbed in the process of condensation; but, as this condensation still proceeded, the equilibrium was again immediately disturbed, through the increase of rotation. By the time the mass had so far shrunk that it occupied a spherical space just that circumscribed by the orbit of Uranus, we are to understand that the centrifugal force had so far obtained the ascendency that new relief was needed: a second equatorial band was, consequently, thrown off, which, proving ununiform, was broken up, as before in the case of Neptune; the fragments settling into the planet Uranus; the velocity of whose actual revolution about the Sun indicates, of course, the rotary speed of that Sun's equatorial surface at the moment of the separation. Uranus, adopting a rotation from the collective rotations of the fragments composing it, as previously explained, now threw off ring after ring; each of which, becoming broken up, settled into a moon : – three moons, at different epochs, having been formed, in this manner, by the rupture and general spherification of as many distinct ununiform rings.

By the time the Sun had shrunk until it occupied a space just that circumscribed by the orbit of Saturn, the balance, we are to suppose, between its centripetal and centrifugal forces had again become so far disturbed, through increase of rotary velocity, the result of condensation, that a third effort at equilibrium became necessary; and an annular band was therefore whirled off, as twice before; which, on rupture through ununiformity, became consolidated into the planet Saturn. This latter threw off, in the first place, seven ununiform bands, which, on rupture, were spherified respectively into as many moons; but, subsequently, it appears to have discharged, at three distinct but not very distant epochs, three rings whose equability of constitution was, by apparent accident, so considerable as to present no occasion for their rupture; thus they continue to revolve as rings. I use the phrase '*apparent* accident'; for of accident in the ordinary sense there was, of course, nothing : – the term is properly applied only to the result of indistinguishable or not immediately traceable *law*.

Shrinking still farther, until it occupied just the space circumscribed by the orbit of Jupiter, the Sun now found need of farther effort to restore the counterbalance of its two forces, continually disarranged in the still continued increase of rotation. Jupiter, accordingly, was now thrown off; passing from the annular to the planetary condition; and, on attaining this latter, threw off in its turn, at four different epochs, four rings, which finally resolved themselves into so many moons.

Still shrinking, until its sphere occupied just the space defined by the orbit of the Asteroids, the Sun now discarded a ring which appears to have had nine centres of superior solidity, and, on breaking up, to have separated into nine fragments no one of which so far predominated in mass as to absorb the others.* All therefore, as distinct although comparatively small planets, proceeded to revolve in orbits whose distances, each from each, may be considered as in some degree the measure of the force which drove them asunder : – all the orbits, nevertheless, being so closely coincident as to admit of our calling them *one*, in view of the other planetary orbits.

Continuing to shrink, the Sun, on becoming so small as just to fill the orbit of Mars, now discharged this planet – of course by the process repeatedly described. Since he has no moon, however, Mars could have thrown off no ring. In fact, an epoch had now arrived in the career of the parent body, the centre of the system. The *de*crease of its nebulosity, which is the *in*crease of its density, and which again is the *de*crease of its condensation, out of which latter arose the constant disturbance of equilibrium – must, by this period, have attained a point at which the efforts for restoration would have been more and more ineffectual just in proportion as they were less frequently needed. Thus the processes of which we have been speaking would everywhere show signs of exhaustion – in the planets, first, and secondly, in the original mass. We must not fall into the error of supposing the decrease of interval observed among the planets as we approach the Sun, to be in any respect indicative of an increase of frequency in the periods at which they were discarded. Exactly the converse is to be understood. The longest interval of time must

* Another asteroid discovered since the work went to press.

have occurred between the discharges of the two interior; the shortest, between those of the two exterior, planets. The decrease of the interval of space is, nevertheless, the measure of the density, and thus inversely of the condensation, of the Sun, throughout the processes detailed.

Having shrunk, however, so far as to fill only the orbit of our Earth, the parent sphere whirled from itself still one other body – the Earth – in a condition so nebulous as to admit of this body's discarding, in its turn, yet another, which is our Moon; – but here terminated the lunar formations.

Finally, subsiding to the orbits first of Venus and then of Mercury, the Sun discarded these two interior planets; neither of which has given birth to any moon.

Thus from his original bulk – or, to speak more accurately, from the condition in which we first considered him – from a partially spherified nebular mass, *certainly* much more than 5,600 millions of miles in diameter – the great central orb and origin of our solar-planetary-lunar system, has gradually descended, by condensation, in obedience to the law of Gravity, to a globe only 882,000 miles in diameter; but it by no means follows, either that its condensation is yet complete, or that it may not still possess the capacity of whirling from itself another planet.

I have here given – in outline of course, but still with all the detail necessary for distinctness – a view of the Nebular Theory as its author himself conceived it. From whatever point we regard it, we shall find it *beautifully true*. It is by far too beautiful, indeed, *not* to possess Truth [31] as its essentiality – and here I am very profoundly serious in what I say. In the revolution of the satellites of Uranus, there does appear something seemingly inconsistent with the assumptions of Laplace; but that *one* inconsistency can invalidate a theory constructed from a million of intricate consistencies, is a fancy fit only for the fantastic. In prophecying, confidently, that the apparent anomaly to which I refer, will, sooner or later, be found one of the strongest possible corroborations of the general hypothesis, I pretend to no especial spirit of divination. It is a matter which the only difficulty seems *not* to foresee.*

* I am prepared to show that the anomalous revolution of the satellites of

The bodies whirled off in the processes described, would exchange, it has been seen, the superficial *rotation* of the orbs whence they originated, for a *revolution* of equal velocity about these orbs as distant centres; and the revolution thus engendered must proceed, so long as the centripetal force, or that with which the discarded body gravitates toward its parent, is neither greater nor less than that by which it was discarded; that is, than the centrifugal, or, far more properly, than the tangential, velocity. From the unity, however, of the origin of these two forces, we might have expected to find them as they are found – the one accurately counterbalancing the other. It has been shown, indeed, that the act of whirling-off is, in every case, merely an act for the preservation of the counterbalance.

After referring, however, the centripetal force to the omniprevalent law of Gravity, it has been the fashion with astronomical treatises, to seek beyond the limits of mere Nature – that is to say, of *Secondary* Cause – a solution of the phænomenon of tangential velocity. This latter they attribute directly to a *First* Cause – to God. The force which carries a stellar body around its primary they assert to have originated in an impulse given immediately by the finger – this is the childish phraseology employed – by the finger of Deity itself. In this view, the planets, fully formed, are conceived to have been hurled from the Divine hand, to a position in the vicinity of the suns, with an impetus mathematically adapted to the masses, or attractive capacities, of the suns themselves. An idea so grossly unphilosophical, although so supinely adopted, could have arisen only from the difficulty of otherwise accounting for the absolutely accurate adaptation, each to each, of two forces so seemingly independent, one of the other, as are the gravitating and tangential. But it should be remembered that, for a long time, the coincidence between the moon's rotation and her sidereal revolution – two matters seemingly far more independent than those now considered – was looked upon as positively miraculous; and there was a strong disposition, even among astronomers, to attribute

---

Uranus is a simply perspective anomaly arising from the *bouleversement* of the axis of the planet.

the marvel to the direct and continual agency of God – who, in this case, it was said, had found it necessary to interpose, specially, among his general laws, a set of subsidiary regulations, for the purpose of forever concealing from mortal eyes the glories, or perhaps the horrors, of the other side of the Moon – of that mysterious hemisphere which has always avoided, and must perpetually avoid, the telescopic scrutiny of mankind. The advance of Science, however, soon demonstrated – what to the philosophical instinct needed *no* demonstration – that the one movement is but a portion – something more, even, than a consequence – of the other.

For my part, I have no patience with fantasies at once so timorous, so idle, and so awkward. They belong to the veriest cowardice of thought. That Nature and the God of Nature are distinct, no thinking being can long doubt. By the former we imply merely the laws of the latter. But with the very idea of God, omnipotent, omniscient, we entertain, also, the idea of *the infallibility* of his laws. With Him there being neither Past nor Future – with Him all being *Now* – do we not insult him in supposing his laws so contrived as not to provide for every possible contingency? – or, rather, what idea *can* we have of *any* possible contingency, except that it is at once a result and a manifestation of his laws? He who, divesting himself of prejudice, shall have the rare courage to think absolutely for himself, cannot fail to arrive, in the end, at the condensation of *laws* into *Law* – cannot fail of reaching the conclusion that *each law of Nature is dependent at all points upon all other laws*, and that all are but consequences of one primary exercise of the Divine Volition. Such is the principle of the Cosmogony which, with all necessary deference, I here venture to suggest and to maintain.

In this view, it will be seen that, dismissing as frivolous, and even impious, the fancy of the tangential force having been imparted to the planets immediately by 'the finger of God', I consider this force as originating in the rotation of the stars : – this rotation as brought about by the in-rushing of the primary atoms, towards their respective centres of aggregation : – this in-rushing as the consequence of the law of Gravity : – this law as but the mode in which is necessarily manifested the tendency of the atoms to return into imparticularity: – this tendency as but the inevitable rëaction of the first and most sublime of Acts – that act by which a God, self-existing and alone existing, became all things at once, through dint of his volition, while all things were thus constituted a portion of God.

The radical assumptions of this Discourse suggest to me, and in fact imply, certain important *modifications* of the Nebular Theory as given by Laplace. The efforts of the repulsive power I have considered as made for the purpose of preventing contact among the atoms, and thus as made in the ratio of the approach to contact – that is to say, in the ratio of condensation.* In other words, *Electricity*, with its involute phænomena, heat, light and magnetism, is to be understood as proceeding as condensation proceeds, and, of course, inversely as density proceeds, or the *cessation to condense*. Thus the Sun, in the process of its consolidation, must soon, in developing repulsion, have become excessively heated – incandescent: and we can perceive how the operation of discarding its rings must have been materially assisted by the slight encrustation of its surface consequent on cooling. Any common experiment shows us how readily a crust of the character suggested, is separated, through heterogeneity, from the interior mass. But, on every successive rejection of the crust, the new surface would appear incandescent as before; and the period at which it would again become so far encrusted as to be readily loosened and discharged, may well be imagined as exactly coincident with that at which a new effort would be needed, by the whole mass, to restore the equilibrium of its two forces, disarranged through condensation. In other words : – by the time the electric influence (Repulsion) has prepared the surface for rejection, we are to understand that the gravitating influence (Attraction) is precisely ready to reject it. Here, then, as everywhere, *the Body and the Soul walk hand in hand*.

These ideas are empirically confirmed at all points. Since condensation can never, in any body, be considered as absolutely at an end, we are warranted in anticipating that, whenever we have an opportunity of testing the matter, we shall find indications of resident luminosity in *all* the stellar bodies – moons and planets

*See page 256.

as well as suns. That our Moon is self-luminous,[32] we see at her every total eclipse, when, if not so, she would disappear. On the dark part of the satellite, too, during her phases, we often observe flashes like our own Auroras; and that these latter, with our various other so-called electrical phænomena, without reference to any more steady radiance, must give our Earth a certain appearance of luminosity to an inhabitant of the Moon, is quite evident. In fact, we should regard all the phænomena referred to, as mere manifestations, in different moods and degrees, of the Earth's feebly-continued condensation.

If my views are tenable, we should be prepared to find the newer planets – that is to say, those nearer the Sun – more luminous than those older and more remote : – and the extreme brilliancy of Venus (on whose dark portions, during her phases, the Auroras are frequently visible) does not seem to be altogether accounted for by her mere proximity to the central orb. She is no doubt vividly self-luminous, although less so than Mercury : while the luminosity of Neptune may be comparatively nothing.

Admitting what I have urged, it is clear that, from the moment of the Sun's discarding a ring, there must be a continuous diminution both of his heat and light, on account of the continuous encrustation of his surface; and that a period would arrive – the period immediately previous to a new discharge – when a *very material* decrease of both light and heat, must become apparent. Now, we know that tokens of such changes are distinctly recognizable. On the Melville islands – to adduce merely one out of a hundred examples – we find traces of *ultra-tropical* vegetation [33] – of plants that never could have flourished without immensely more light and heat than are at present afforded by our Sun to any portion of the surface of the Earth. Is such vegetation referable to an epoch immediately subsequent to the whirling-off of Venus? At this epoch must have occurred to us our greatest access of solar influence; and, in fact, this influence must then have attained its maximum : – leaving out of view, of course, the period when the Earth itself was discarded – the period of its mere organization.

Again : – we know that there exist *non-luminous suns* – that is to say, suns whose existence we determine through the movements of others, but whose luminosity is not sufficient to impress us. Are these suns invisible merely on account of the length of time elapsed since their discharge of a planet? And yet again: – may we not – at least in certain cases – account for the sudden appearances of suns where none had been previously suspected, by the hypothesis that, having rolled with encrusted surfaces throughout the few thousand years of our astronomical history, each of these suns, in whirling off a new secondary, has at length been enabled to display the glories of its still incandescent interior? – To the well-ascertained fact of the proportional increase of heat as we descend into the Earth, I need of course, do nothing more than refer : – it comes in the strongest possible corroboration of all that I have said on the topic now at issue.

In speaking, not long ago, of the repulsive or electrical influence, I remarked that 'the important phænomena of vitality, consciousness, and thought, whether we observe them generally or in detail, seem to proceed *at least in the ratio of the heterogeneous*'.* I mentioned, too, that I would recur to the suggestion : – and this is the proper point at which to do so. Looking at the matter, first, in detail, we perceive that not merely the *manifestation* of vitality, but its importance, consequences, and elevation of character, keep pace, very closely, with the heterogeneity, or complexity, of the animal structure. Looking at the question, now, in its generality, and referring to the first movements of the atoms towards mass-constitution, we find that heterogeneousness, brought about directly through condensation, is proportional with it forever. We thus reach the proposition that *the importance of the development of the terrestrial vitality proceeds equably with the terrestrial condensation*.

Now this is in accordance with what we know of the succession of animals on the Earth. As it has proceeded in its condensation, superior and still superior races have appeared. Is it impossible that the successive geological revolutions which have attended, at least, if not immediately caused, these successive elevations of vitalic character – is it improbable that these revolutions have themselves been produced by the successive planetary discharges from the Sun – in other words, by the successive varia-

* Page 232.

tions in the solar influence on the Earth? Were this idea tenable, we should not be unwarranted in the fancy that the discharge of yet a new planet, interior to Mercury, may give rise to yet a new modification of the terrestrial surface – a modification from which may spring a race both materially and spiritually superior to Man. These thoughts impress me with all the force of truth – but I throw them out, of course, merely in their obvious character of suggestion.

The Nebular Theory of Laplace has lately received far more confirmation than it needed, at the hands of the philosopher, Comte.[34] These two have thus together shown – *not*, to be sure, that Matter at any period actually existed as described, in a state of nebular diffusion, but that, admitting it so to have existed throughout the space and much beyond the space now occupied by our solar system, *and to have commenced a movement towards a centre* – it must gradually have assumed the various forms and motions which are now seen, in that system, to obtain. A demonstration such as this – a dynamical and mathematical demonstration, as far as demonstration can be and one empirically confirmed – a demonstration unquestionable and unquestioned – unless, indeed, by that unprofitable and disreputable tribe, the professional questioners – the mere madmen who deny the Newtonian law of Gravity on which the results of the French mathematicians are based – a demonstration, I say, such as this, would to most intellects be conclusive – and I confess that it is so to mine – of the validity of the nebular hypothesis upon which the demonstration depends.

That the demonstration does not *prove* the hypothesis, according to the common understanding of the word 'proof', I admit, of course. To show that certain existing results – that certain established facts – may be, even mathematically, accounted for by the assumption of a certain hypothesis, is by no means to establish the hypothesis itself. In other words: – to show that, certain data being given, a certain existing result might, or even *must*, have ensued, will fail to prove that this result *did* ensue, *from the data,* until such time as it shall be also shown that there are, *and can be,* no other data from which the result in question might *equally* have ensued. But, in the case now discussed, although all must admit the deficiency of what we are in the habit of term-ing 'proof', still there are many intellects, and those of the loftiest order, to which *no* proof could bring one iota of additional *con-viction*. Without going into details which might impinge upon the Cloud-Land of Metaphysics,[35] I may as well here observe that the force of conviction, in cases such as this, will always, with the right-thinking, be proportional with the amount of *complexity* intervening between the hypothesis and the result. To be less abstract: – The greatness of the complexity found existing among cosmical conditions, by rendering great in the same proportion the difficulty of accounting for all these condi-tions *at once*, strengthens, also in the same proportion, our faith in that hypothesis which does, in such manner, satisfactorily account for them : – and as *no* complexity can well be conceived greater than that of the astronomical conditions, so no conviction can be stronger – to *my* mind at least – than that with which I am impressed by an hypothesis that not only reconciles these con-ditions, with mathematical accuracy, and reduces them into a consistent and intelligible whole, but is, at the same time, the *sole* hypothesis by means of which the human intellect has been ever enabled to account for them *at all*.

A most unfounded opinion has been latterly current in gos-siping and even in scientific circles – the opinion that the so-called Nebular Cosmogony has been overthrown. This fancy has arisen from the report of late observations made, among what hitherto have been termed the 'nebulæ', through the large telescope of Cincinnati, and the world-renowned instrument of Lord Rosse. Certain spots in the firmament which presented, even to the most powerful of the old telescopes, the appearance of nebulosity, or haze, had been regarded for a long time as confirming the theory of Laplace. They were looked upon as stars in that very process of condensation which I have been attempting to describe. Thus it was supposed that we 'had ocular evidence' – an evidence, by the way, which has always been found very questionable – of the truth of the hypothesis; and, although certain telescopic improvements, every now and then, enabled us to perceive that a spot, here and there, which we had been classing among the nebulæ, was, in fact, but a cluster of stars deriving its nebular

character only from its immensity of distance – still it was
thought that no doubt could exist as to the actual nebulosity of
numerous other masses, the strong-holds of the nebulists, bidding
defiance to every effort at segregation. Of these latter the most
interesting was the great 'nebula' in the constellation Orion : –
but this, with innumerable other miscalled 'nebulæ', when
viewed through the magnificent modern telescopes, has become
resolved into a simple collection of stars.[36] Now this fact has
been very generally understood as conclusive against the Nebular
Hypothesis of Laplace; and, on announcement of the discoveries in question, the most enthusiastic defender and most eloquent
popularizer of the theory, Dr Nichol, went so far as to 'admit
the necessity of abandoning' an idea which had formed the
material of his most praiseworthy book.*

Many of my readers will no doubt be inclined to say that the
result of these new investigations *has* at least a strong *tendency*
to overthrow the hypothesis; while some of them, more thought-
ful, will suggest that, although the theory is by no means disproved through the segregation of the particular 'nebulæ' alluded to, still a *failure* to segregate them, with such telescopes,
might well have been understood as a triumphant *corroboration*
of the theory : – and this latter class will be surprised, perhaps, to
hear me say that even with *them* I disagree. If the propositions
of this Discourse have been comprehended, it will be seen that,
in my view, a failure to segregate the 'nebulæ' would have tended
to the refutation, rather than to the confirmation, of the Nebular Hypothesis.

Let me explain : – The Newtonian Law of Gravity we may,
of course, assume as demonstrated. This law, it will be remem-

* '*Views of the Architecture of the Heavens*'. A letter, purporting to be
from Dr Nichol to a friend in America, went the rounds of our newspapers,
about two years ago, I think, admitting 'the necessity' to which I refer. In a
subsequent Lecture, however, Dr N. appears in some manner to have
gotten the better of the necessity, and does not quite *renounce* the theory,
although he seems to wish that he could sneer at it as 'a purely hypothetical one'. What else was the Law of Gravity before the Maskelyne experiments? and who questioned the Law of Gravity, even then? The late experiments of Comte, however, are to the Laplacian theory what those of Maskelyne were to the Newtonian.

bered, I have referred to the rëaction of the first Divine Act – to the rëaction of an exercise of the Divine Volition temporarily overcoming a difficulty. This difficulty is that of forcing the normal into the abnormal – of impelling that whose originality, and therefore whose rightful condition, was *One*, to take upon itself the wrongful condition of *Many*. It is only by conceiving this difficulty as *temporarily* overcome, that we can comprehend a rëaction. There could have been no rëaction had the act been infinitely continued. So long as the act *lasted*, no rëaction, of course, could commence; in other words, no *gravitation* could take place – for we have considered the one as but the manifestation of the other. But gravitation *has* taken place; therefore the act of Creation has ceased : and gravitation has long ago taken place; therefore the act of Creation has long ago ceased. We can no more expect, then, to observe *the primary processes* of Creation; and to these primary processes the condition of nebulosity has already been explained to belong.

Through what we know of the propagation of light, we have direct proof that the more remote of the stars have existed, under the forms in which we now see them, for an inconceivable number of years. So far back *at least*, then, as the period when these stars underwent condensation, must have been the epoch at which the mass-constitutive processes began. That we may conceive these processes, then, as still going on in the case of certain 'nebulæ', while in all other cases we find them thoroughly at an end, we are forced into assumptions for which we have really *no* basis whatever – we have to thrust in, again, upon the revolting Reason, the blasphemous idea of special interposition – we have to suppose that, in the particular instances of these 'nebulæ', an unerring God found it necessary to introduce certain supplementary regulations – certain improvements of the general law – certain retouchings and emendations, in a word, which had the effect of deferring the completion of these individual stars for centuries of centuries beyond the æra during which all the other stellar bodies had time, not only to be fully constituted, but to grow hoary with an unspeakable old age.

Of course, it will be immediately objected that since the light by which we recognize the nebulæ now, must be merely that which left their surfaces a vast number of years ago, the processes at present observed, or supposed to be observed, are, in fact, *not* processes now actually going on, but the phantoms of processes completed long in the Past – just as I maintain all these mass-constitutive processes *must* have been.

To this I reply that neither is the now-observed condition of the condensed stars their actual condition, but a condition completed long in the Past; so that my argument drawn from the *relative* condition of the stars and the 'nebulæ', is in no manner disturbed. Moreover, those who maintain the existence of nebulæ, do *not* refer the nebulosity to extreme distance; they declare it a real and not merely a perspective nebulosity. That we may conceive, indeed, a nebular mass as visible at all, we must conceive it as *very near us* in comparison with the condensed stars brought into view by the modern telescopes. In maintaining the appearances in question, then, to be really nebulous, we maintain their comparative vicinity to our point of view. Thus, their condition, as we see them now, must be referred to an epoch *far less remote* than that to which we may refer the now-observed condition of at least the majority of the stars. – In a word, should Astronomy ever demonstrate a 'nebula', in the sense at present intended, I should consider the Nebular Cosmogony – *not*, indeed, as corroborated by the demonstration – but as thereby irretrievably overthrown.

By way, however, of rendering unto Cæsar *no more* than the things that are Cæsar's, let me here remark that the assumption of the hypothesis which led him to so glorious a result, seems to have been suggested to Laplace in great measure by a misconception – by the very misconception of which we have just been speaking – by the generally prevalent misunderstanding of the character of the nebulæ, so mis-named. These he supposed to be, in reality, what their designation implies. The fact is, this great man had, very properly, an inferior faith in his own merely *perceptive* powers. In respect, therefore, to the actual existence of nebulæ – an existence so confidently maintained by his telescopic contemporaries – he depended less upon what he saw than upon what he heard.

It will be seen that the only valid objections to his theory, are those made to its hypothesis *as* such – to what suggested it – not to what it suggests; to its propositions rather than to its results. His most unwarranted assumption was that of giving the atoms a movement towards a centre, in the very face of his evident understanding that these atoms, in unlimited succession, extended throughout the Universal space. I have already shown that, under such circumstances, there could have occurred no movement at all; and Laplace, consequently, assumed one on no more philosophical ground than that something of the kind was necessary for the establishment of what he intended to establish.

His original idea seems to have been a compound of the true Epicurean atoms with the false nebulæ of his contemporaries; and thus his theory presents us with the singular anomaly of absolute truth deduced, as a mathematical result, from a hybrid datum of ancient imagination intertangled with modern inacumen. Laplace's real strength lay, in fact, in an almost miraculous mathematical instinct: – on this he relied; and in no instance did it fail or deceive him: – in the case of the Nebular Cosmogony, it led him, blindfolded, through a labyrinth of Error, into one of the most luminous and stupendous temples of Truth.

Let us now fancy – merely fancy – for the moment, that the ring first thrown off by the Sun – that is to say, the ring whose breaking-up constituted Neptune – did not, in fact, break up until the throwing-off of the ring out of which Uranus arose; that this latter ring, again, remained perfect until the discharge of that out of which sprang Saturn; that this later, again, remained entire until the discharge of that from which originated Jupiter – and so on. Let us imagine, in a word, that no dissolution occurred among the rings until the final rejection of that which gave birth to Mercury. We thus paint to the eye of the mind a series of cöexistent concentric circles; and looking as well at *them* as at the processes by which, according to Laplace's hypothesis, they were constructed, we perceive at once a very singular analogy with the atomic strata and the process of the original radiation as I have described it. Is it impossible that, on measuring the *forces*, respectively, by which each successive planetary circle was thrown off – that is to say, on measuring the successive excesses of rotation over gravitation which occasioned the successive discharges – we should find the analogy in question more decidedly confirmed? *Is it improbable that we shall discover these forces to have varied – as in the original radiation – proportionally with the squares of the distances?*

Our solar system, consisting, in chief, of one sun, with seventeen planets certainly, and possibly a few more, revolving about it at various distances, and attended by seventeen moons assuredly, but *very* probably by several others – is now to be considered as *an example* of the innumerable agglomerations which proceeded to take place throughout the Universal Sphere of atoms on withdrawal of the Divine Volition. I mean to say that our solar system is to be understood as affording a *generic instance* of these agglomerations, or, more correctly, of the ulterior conditions at which they arrived. If we keep our attention fixed on the idea of *the utmost possible Relation* as the Omnipotent design, and on the precautions taken to accomplish it through difference of form, among the original atoms, and particular inequidistance, we shall find it impossible to suppose for a moment that even any two of the incipient agglomerations reached precisely the same result in the end. We shall rather be inclined to think that *no two stellar* bodies in the Universe – whether suns, planets or moons – are particularly, while *all* are generally, similar. Still less, then, can we imagine any two *assemblages* of such bodies – any two 'systems' – as having more than a general resemblance.* Our telescopes, at this point, thoroughly confirm our deductions. Taking our own solar system, then, as merely a loose or general type of all, we have so far proceeded in our subject as to survey the Universe of Stars under the aspect of a spherical space, throughout which, dispersed with merely general equability, exist a number of but generally similar *systems*.

Let us now, expanding our conceptions, look upon each of

---

*It is not *impossible* that some unlooked-for optical improvement may disclose to us, among innumerable varieties of systems, a luminous sun, encircled by luminous and non-luminous rings, within and without and between which, revolve luminous and non-luminous planets, attended by moons having moons – and even these latter again having moons.

these systems as in itself an atom; which in fact it is, when we consider it as but one of the countless myriads of systems which constitute the Universe. Regarding all, then, as but colossal atoms, each with the same ineradicable tendency to Unity which characterizes the actual atoms of which it consists – we enter at once on a new order of aggregations. The smaller systems, in the vicinity of a larger one, would, inevitably, be drawn into still closer vicinity. A thousand would assemble here; a million there – perhaps here, again, even a billion – leaving, thus, immeasurable vacancies in space. And if, now, it be demanded why, in the case of these systems – of these merely Titanic atoms – I speak, simply, of an 'assemblage', and not, as in the case of the actual atoms, of a more or less consolidated agglomeration : – if it be asked, for instance, why I do not carry what I suggest to its legitimate conclusion, and describe, at once, these assemblages of system-atoms as rushing to consolidation in spheres – as each becoming condensed into one magnificent sun – my reply is that μέλλοντα ταῦτα [37] – I am but pausing, for a moment, on the awful threshold of *the Future*. For the present, calling these assemblages 'clusters', we see them in the incipient stages of their consolidation. Their *absolute* consolidation is *to come*.

We have now reached a point from which we behold the Universe of Stars as a spherical space, interspersed, *unequably*, with *clusters*. It will be noticed that I here prefer the adverb 'unequably' to the phrase 'with a merely general equability', employed before. It is evident, in fact, that the equability of distribution will diminish in the ratio of the agglomerative processes – that is to say, as the things distributed diminish in number. Thus the increase of *in*equability – an increase which must continue until, sooner or later, an epoch will arrive at which the largest agglomeration will absorb all the others – should be viewed as, simply, a corroborative indication of the *tendency to One*.

And here, at length, it seems proper to inquire whether the ascertained *facts* of Astronomy confirm the general arrangement which I have thus, deductively, assigned to the Heavens. Thoroughly, they *do*. Telescopic observation, guided by the laws of perspective, enables us to understand that the perceptible Universe exists as *a roughly spherical cluster of clusters, irregularly disposed*.

The 'clusters' of which this Universal '*cluster of clusters*' consists, are merely what we have been in the practice of designating 'nebulæ' and, of these 'nebulæ', *one* is of paramount interest to mankind. I allude to the Galaxy, or Milky Way. This interests us, first and most obviously, on account of its great superiority in apparent size, not only to any one other cluster in the firmament, but to all the other clusters taken together. The largest of these latter occupies a mere point, comparatively, and is distinctly seen only with the aid of a telescope. The Galaxy sweeps throughout the Heaven and is brilliantly visible to the naked eye. But it interests man chiefly, although less immediately, on account of its being his home; the home of the Earth on which he exists; the home of the Sun about which this Earth revolves; the home of that 'system' of orbs of which the Sun is the centre and primary – the Earth one of seventeen secondaries, or planets – the Moon one of seventeen tertiaries, or satellites. The Galaxy, let me repeat, is but one of the *clusters* which I have been describing – but one of the mis-called 'nebulæ' revealed to us – by the telescope alone, sometimes – as faint hazy spots in various quarters of the sky. We have no reason to suppose the Milky Way *really* more extensive than the least of these 'nebulæ'. Its vast superiority in size is but an apparent superiority arising from our position in regard to it – that is to say, from our position in its midst. However strange the assertion may at first appear to those unversed in Astronomy, still the astronomer himself has no hesitation in asserting that we are *in the midst* of that inconceivable host of stars – of suns – of systems – which constitute the Galaxy. Moreover, not only have *we* – not only has *our* Sun a right to claim the Galaxy as its own especial cluster, but, with slight reservation, it may be said that all the distinctly visible stars of the firmament – all the stars visible to the naked eye – have equally a right to claim it as *their* own.

There has been a great deal of misconception in respect to the *shape* of the Galaxy; which, in nearly all our astronomical treatises, is said to resemble that of a capital Y. The cluster in question has, in reality, a certain general – *very* general resemblance to the planet Saturn, with its encompassing triple ring. Instead of the solid orb of that planet, however, we must picture to ourselves a lenticular star-island, or collection of stars; our Sun lying excentrically – near the shore of the island – on that side of it which is nearest the constellation of the Cross and farthest from that of Cassiopeia. The surrounding ring, where it approaches our position, has in it a longitudinal *gash*, which does, in fact, cause *the ring, in our vicinity*, to assume, loosely, the appearance of a capital Y.

We must not fall into the error, however, of conceiving the somewhat indefinite girdle as at all *remote*, comparatively speaking, from the also indefinite lenticular cluster which it surrounds; and thus, for mere purpose of explanation, we may speak of our Sun as actually situated at that point of the Y where its three component lines unite; and, conceiving this letter to be of a certain solidity – of a certain thickness, very trivial in comparison with its length – we may even speak of our position as *in the middle* of this thickness. Fancying ourselves thus placed, we shall no longer find difficulty in accounting for the phænomena presented – which are perspective altogether. When we look upward or downward – that is to say, when we cast our eyes in the direction of the letter's *thickness* – we look through fewer stars than when we cast them in the direction of its *length*, or *along* either of the three component lines. Of course, in the former case, the stars appear scattered – in the latter, crowded. – To reverse this explanation: – An inhabitant of the Earth, when looking, as we commonly express ourselves, *at* the Galaxy, is then beholding it in some of the directions of its length – is looking *along* the lines of the Y – but when, looking out into the general Heaven, he turns his eyes *from* the Galaxy, he is then surveying it in the direction of the letter's thickness; and on this account the stars seem to him scattered; while, in fact, they are as close together, on an average, as in the mass of the cluster. *No* consideration could be better adapted to convey an idea of this cluster's stupendous extent.

If, with a telescope of high space-penetrating power, we carefully inspect the firmament, we shall become aware of *a belt of clusters* – of what we have hitherto called 'nebulæ' – a *band*, of varying breadth, stretching from horizon to horizon, at right angles to the general course of the Milky Way. This band is the ultimate *cluster of clusters*. This belt is *The Universe of Stars*. Our Galaxy is but one, and perhaps one of the most inconsiderable, of the clusters which go to the constitution of this ultimate, Universal *belt* or *band*. The appearance of this cluster of clusters, to our eyes, *as* a belt or band, is altogether a perspective phænomenon of the same character as that which causes us to behold our own individual and roughly-spherical cluster, the Galaxy, under guise also of a belt, traversing the Heavens at right angles to the Universal one. The shape of the all-inclusive cluster is, of course *generally*, that of each individual cluster which it includes. Just as the scattered stars which, on looking *from* the Galaxy, we see in the general sky, are, in fact, but a portion of that Galaxy itself, and as closely intermingled with it as any of the telescopic points in what seems the densest portion of its mass – so are the scattered 'nebulæ' which, on casting our eyes *from* the Universal *belt*, we perceive at all points of the firmament – so, I say, are these scattered 'nebulæ' to be understood as only perspectively scattered, and as but a portion of the one supreme and Universal *sphere*.

No astronomical fallacy is more untenable, and none has been more pertinaciously adhered to, than that of the absolute *illimitation* of the Universe of Stars.[38] The reasons for limitation, as I have already assigned them, *à priori*, seem to me unanswerable; but, not to speak of these, *observation* assures us that there is, in numerous directions around us, certainly, if not in all, a positive limit – or, at the very least, affords us no basis whatever for thinking otherwise. Were the succession of stars endless, then the background of the sky would present us an uniform luminosity, like that displayed by the Galaxy – since there could be absolutely no point, in all that background, at which would not exist a star. The only mode, therefore, in which, under such a state of affairs, we could comprehend the *voids* which our telescopes find in innumerable directions, would be by supposing the distance of the invisible background so immense that no ray from it has yet been able to reach us at all. That this *may* be so, who shall venture to deny? I maintain, simply, that we have not even the shadow of a reason for believing that it *is* so.

When speaking of the vulgar propensity to regard all bodies on the Earth as tending merely to the Earth's centre, I observed that, 'with certain exceptions to be specified hereafter, every body on the Earth tends not only to the Earth's centre, but in every conceivable direction besides'.* The 'exceptions' refer to those frequent gaps in the Heavens, where our utmost scrutiny can detect not only no stellar bodies, but no indications of their existence: – where yawning chasms, blacker than Erebus, seem to afford us glimpses, through the boundary walls of the Universe of Stars, into the illimitable Universe of Vacancy, beyond. Now as any body, existing on the Earth, chances to pass, either through its own movement or the Earth's, into a line with any one of these voids, or cosmical abysses, it clearly is no longer attracted *in the direction of that void*, and for the moment, consequently, is 'heavier' than at any period, either after or before. Independently of the consideration of these voids, however, and looking only at the generally unequable distribution of the stars, we see that the absolute tendency of bodies on the Earth to the Earth's centre, is in a state of perpetual variation.

We comprehend, then, the insulation of our Universe. We perceive the isolation of *that* – of *all* that which we grasp with the senses. We know that there exists one cluster of clusters – a collection around which, on all sides, extend the immeasurable wildernesses of a Space *to all human perception* untenanted. But *because* on the confines of this Universe of Stars we are compelled to pause, through want of farther evidence from the senses, is it right to conclude that, in fact, there *is* no material point beyond that which we have thus been permitted to attain? Have we, or have we not, an analogical right to the inference that this perceptible Universe – that this cluster of clusters – is but one of *a series* of clusters of clusters, the rest of which are invisible through distance – through the diffusion of their light being so excessive, ere it reaches us, as not to produce upon our retinas a light-impression – or from there being no such emanation as light at all, in those unspeakably distant worlds – or,

* Page 235.

lastly, from the mere interval being so vast, that the electric tidings of their presence in Space, have not yet – through the lapsing myriads of years – been enabled to traverse that interval?

Have we any right to inferences – have we any ground whatever for visions such as these? If we have a right to them in *any* degree, we have a right to their infinite extension.

The human brain has obviously a leaning to the '*Infinite*', and fondles the phantom of the idea. It seems to long with a passionate fervor for this impossible conception, with the hope of intellectually believing it when conceived. What is general among the whole race of Man, of course no individual of that race can be warranted in considering abnormal; nevertheless, there *may* be a class of superior intelligences, to whom the human bias alluded to may wear all the character of monomania.

My question, however, remains unanswered : – Have we any right to infer – let us say, rather, to imagine – an interminable succession of the 'clusters of clusters', or of 'Universes' more or less similar?

I reply that the 'right', in a case such as this, depends absolutely on the hardihood of that imagination which ventures to claim the right. Let me declare, only, that, as an individual, I myself feel impelled to the *fancy* – without daring to call it more – that there *does* exist a *limitless* succession of Universes, more or less similar to that of which we have cognizance – to that of which *alone* we shall ever have cognizance – at the very least until the return of our own particular Universe into Unity. *If* such clusters of clusters exist, however – *and they do* – it is abundantly clear that, having had no part in our origin, they have no portion in our laws. They neither attract us, nor we them. Their material – their spirit is not ours – is not that which obtains in any part of our Universe. They can not impress our senses or our souls. Among them and us – considering all, for the moment, collectively – there are no influences in common. Each exists, apart and independently, *in the bosom of its proper and particular God*.[39]

In the conduct of this Discourse, I am aiming less at physical than at metaphysical order. The clearness with which even material phænomena are presented to the understanding, depends very little, I have long since learned to perceive, upon a merely natural, and almost altogether upon a moral, arrangement. If then I seem to step somewhat too discursively from point to point of my topic, let me suggest that I do so in the hope of thus the better keeping unbroken that chain of *graduated impression* by which alone the intellect of Man can expect to encompass the grandeurs of which I speak, and, in their majestic totality, to comprehend them.

So far, our attention has been directed, almost exclusively, to a general and relative grouping of the stellar bodies in space. Of specification there has been little; and whatever ideas of *quantity* have been conveyed – that is to say, of number, magnitude, and distance – have been conveyed incidentally and by way of preparation for more definitive conceptions. These latter let us now attempt to entertain.

Our solar system, as has been already mentioned, consists, in chief, of one sun and seventeen planets certainly, but in all probability a few others, revolving around it as a centre, and attended by seventeen moons of which we know, with possibly several more of which as yet we know nothing. These various bodies are not true spheres, but oblate spheroids – spheres flattened at the poles of the imaginary axes about which they rotate : – the flattening being a consequence of the rotation. Neither is the Sun absolutely the centre of the system; for this Sun itself, with all the planets, revolves about a perpetually shifting point of space, which is the system's general centre of gravity. Neither are we to consider the paths through which these different spheroids move – the moons about the planets, the planets about the Sun, or the Sun about the common centre – as circles in an accurate sense. They are, in fact, *ellipses – one of the foci being the point about which the revolution is made.* An ellipse is a curve, returning into itself, one of whose diameters is longer than the other. In the longer diameter are two points, equidistant from the middle of the line, and so situated otherwise that if, from each of them a straight line be drawn to any one point of the curve, the two lines, taken together, will be equal to the longer diameter itself. Now let us conceive such an ellipse. At one of the points mentioned, which are the *foci*, let us fasten an orange. By an elastic thread let us connect this orange with a pea; and let us place this latter on the circumference of the ellipse. Let us now move the pea continuously around the orange – keeping always on the circumference of the ellipse. The elastic thread, which, of course, varies in length as we move the pea, will form what in geometry is called a *radius vector*. Now, if the orange be understood as the Sun, and the pea as a planet revolving about it, then the revolution should be made at such a rate – with the velocity so varying – that the *radius vector* may pass over *equal areas of space in equal times*. The progress of the pea *should be* – in other words, the progress of the planet *is*, of course, – slow in proportion to its distance from the Sun – swift in proportion to its proximity. Those plants, moreover, move the more slowly which are the farther from the Sun; *the squares of their periods of revolution having the same proportion to each other, as have to each other the cubes of their mean distances from the Sun.*

The wonderfully complex laws of revolution here described, however, are not to be understood as obtaining in our system alone. They *everywhere* prevail where Attraction prevails. They control *the Universe of Stars*. Every shining speck in the firmament is, no doubt, a luminous sun, resembling our own, at least in its general features, and having in attendance upon it a greater or less number of planets, greater or less, whose still lingering luminosity is not sufficient to render them visible to us at so vast a distance, but which, nevertheless, revolve, moon-attended, about their starry centres, in obedience to the principles just detailed – in obedience to the three omniprevalent laws of revolution – the three immortal laws *guessed* by the imaginative Kepler, and but subsequently demonstrated and accounted for by the patient and mathematical Newton. Among a tribe of philosophers who pride themselves excessively upon matter-of-fact, it is far too fashionable to sneer at all speculation under the comprehensive *sobriquet*, 'guess-work'. The point to be considered is, *who* guesses. In guessing with Plato, we spend our time to better purpose, now and then, than in hearkening to a demonstration by Alcmæon.[40]

In many works on Astronomy I find it distinctly stated that the laws of Kepler are *the basis* of the great principle, Gravitation. This idea must have arisen from the fact that the suggestion of these laws by Kepler, and his proving them *à posteriori* to have an actual existence, led Newton to account for them by the hypothesis of Gravitation, and, finally, to demonstrate them *à priori*, as necessary consequences of the hypothetical principle. Thus so far from the laws of Kepler being the basis of Gravity, Gravity is the basis of these laws – as it is, indeed, of all the laws of the material Universe which are not referable to Repulsion alone.

The mean distance of the Earth from the Moon – that is to say, from the heavenly body in our closest vicinity – is 237,000 miles. Mercury, the planet nearest the Sun, is distant from him 37 millions of miles. Venus, the next, revolves at a distance of 68 millions : – the Earth, which comes next, at a distance of 95 millions : – Mars, then, at a distance of 144 millions. Now come the nine Asteroids [41] (Ceres, Juno, Vesta, Pallas, Astræa, Flora, Iris, Hebe and   ) at an average distance of about 250 millions. Then we have Jupiter, distant 490 millions; then Saturn, 900 millions; then Uranus, 19 hundred millions; finally Neptune, lately discovered, and revolving at a distance, say of 28 hundred millions. Leaving Neptune out of the account – of which as yet we know little accurately [42] and which is, possibly, one of a system of Asteroids – it will be seen that, within certain limits, there exists an *order of interval* among the planets. Speaking loosely, we may say that each outer planet is twice as far from the Sun as is the next inner one. May not the *order* here mentioned – *may not the law of Bode* [43] – *be deduced from consideration of the analogy suggested by me as having place between the solar discharge of rings and the mode of the atomic radiation?*

The numbers hurriedly mentioned in this summary of distance, it is folly to attempt comprehending, unless in the light of abstract arithmetical facts. They are not practically tangible ones. They convey no precise ideas. I have stated that Neptune, the planet farthest from the Sun, revolves about him at a distance of 28 hundred millions of miles. So far good : – I have stated a mathematical fact; and, without comprehending it in the least, we may put it to use – mathematically. But in mentioning, even, that the Moon revolves about the Earth at the comparatively trifling distance of 237,000 miles, I entertained no expectation of giving any one to understand – to know – to feel – how far from the Earth the Moon actually *is*. 237,000 *miles*! There are, perhaps, few of my readers who have not crossed the Atlantic ocean; yet how many of them have a distinct idea of even the 3,000 miles intervening between shore and shore? I doubt, indeed, whether the man lives who can force into his brain the most remote conception of the interval between one milestone and its next neighbor upon the turnpike. We are in some measure aided, however, in our consideration of distance, by combining this consideration with the kindred one of velocity. Sound passes through 1100 feet of space in a second of time. Now were it possible for an inhabitant of the Earth to see the flash of a cannon discharged in the Moon, and to hear the report, he would have to wait, after perceiving the former, more than 13 entire days and nights before getting any intimation of the latter.

However feeble be the impression, even thus conveyed, of the Moon's real distance from the Earth, it will, nevertheless, effect a good object in enabling us more clearly to see the futility of attempting to grasp such intervals as that of the 28 hundred millions of miles between our Sun and Neptune; or even that of the 95 millions between the Sun and the Earth we inhabit. A cannon-ball, flying at the greatest velocity with which a ball has ever been known to fly, could not traverse the latter interval in less than 20 years; while for the former it would require 590.

Our Moon's real diameter is 2160 miles; yet she is comparatively so trifling an object that it would take nearly 50 such orbs to compose one as great as the Earth.

The diameter of our own globe is 7912 miles – but from the enunciation of these numbers what positive idea do we derive?

If we ascend an ordinary mountain [44] and look around us from its summit, we behold a landscape stretching, say 40 miles, in every direction; forming a circle 250 miles in circumference; and including an area of 5000 square miles. The extent of such a prospect, on account of the *successiveness* with which its portions necessarily present themselves to view, can be only very feebly and very partially appreciated: – yet the entire panorama would comprehend no more than one 40,000th part of the mere *surface* of our globe. Were this panorama, then, to be succeeded, after the lapse of an hour, by another of equal extent; this again by a third, after the lapse of another hour; this again by a fourth after lapse of another hour – and so on, until the scenery of the whole Earth were exhausted; and were we to be engaged in examining these various panoramas for twelve hours of every day; we should nevertheless, be 9 years and 48 days in completing the general survey.

But if the mere surface of the Earth eludes the grasp of the imagination, what are we to think of its cubical contents? It embraces a mass of matter equal in weight to at least 2 sextillions, 200 quintillions of tons. Let us suppose it in a state of quiescence: and now let us endeavor to conceive of mechanical force sufficient to set it in motion! Not the strength of all the myriads of beings whom we may conclude to inhabit the planetary worlds of our system – not the combined physical strength of *all* these beings – even admitting all to be more powerful than man – would avail to stir the ponderous mass a *single inch* from its position.

What are we to understand, then, of the force, which under similar circumstances, would be required to move the *largest* of our planets, Jupiter? This is 86,000 miles in diameter, and would include within its surface more than a thousand orbs of the magnitude of our own. Yet this stupendous body is actually flying around the Sun at the rate of 29,000 miles an hour – that is to say, with a velocity 40 times greater than that of a cannon-ball! The thought of such a phænomenon cannot well be said to *startle* the mind: – it palsies and appals it. Not unfrequently we task our imagination in picturing the capacities of an angel. Let us fancy such a being at a distance of some hundred miles from Jupiter – a close eye-witness of this planet as it speeds on its annual revolution. Now *can* we, I demand, fashion for ourselves any conception so distinct of this ideal being's spiritual exaltation, as *that* involved in the supposition that, even by this immeasurable mass of matter, whirled immediately before his eyes, with a velocity so unutterable, he – an angel – angelic though he be – is not at once struck into nothingness and overwhelmed?

At this point, however, it seems proper to suggest that, in fact, we have been speaking of comparative trifles. Our Sun – the central and controlling orb of the system to which Jupiter belongs, is not only greater than Jupiter, but greater by far than all the planets of the system taken together. This fact is an essential condition, indeed, of the stability of the system itself. The diameter of Jupiter has been mentioned : – it is 86,000 miles : – that of the Sun is 882,000 miles. An inhabitant of the latter, travelling 90 miles a day, would be more than 80 years in going round its circumference. It occupies a cubical space of 681 quadrillions, 472 trillions of miles. The Moon, as has been stated, revolves about the Earth at a distance of 237,000 miles – in an orbit, consequently, of nearly a million and a half. Now, were the Sun placed upon the Earth, centre over centre, the body of the former would extend, in every direction, not only to the line of the Moon's orbit, but beyond it, a distance of 200,000 miles.

And here, once again, let me suggest that, in fact, we have *still* been speaking of comparative trifles. The distance of the planet Neptune from the Sun has been stated : – it is 28 hundred millions of miles; its orbit, therefore, is about 17 billions. Let this be borne in mind while we glance at some one of the brightest stars. Between this and the star of *our* system, (the Sun,) there is a gulf of space, to convey any idea of which we should need the tongue of an archangel. From *our* system, then, and from *our* Sun, or star, the star at which we suppose ourselves glancing is a thing altogether apart : – still, for the moment, let us imagine it placed upon our Sun, centre over centre, as we just now imagined this Sun itself placed upon the Earth. Let us now conceive the particular star we have in mind, extending, in every direction, beyond the orbit of Mercury – of Venus – of the Earth : – still *on*, beyond the orbit of Mars – of the asteroids – of Jupiter – of Saturn – of Uranus – until, finally, we fancy it filling the circle – *17 billions of miles in circumference* – which is described by the revolution of Leverrier's planet. When we have conceived all this, we shall have entertained no extravagant conception. There is the very best reason for believing that many of the stars are even far larger than the one we have imagined. I mean to say that we have the very best *empirical* basis for such belief : – and, in looking back at the original, atomic arrangements for *diversity*, which have been assumed as a part of the Divine plan in the constitution of the Universe, we shall be enabled easily to understand, and to credit, the existence of even far vaster disproportions in stellar size than any to which I have hitherto alluded. The largest orbs, of course, we must expect to find rolling through the widest vacancies of Space.

I remarked, just now, that to convey an idea of the interval between our Sun and any one of the other stars, we should require the eloquence of an archangel. In so saying, I should not be accused of exaggeration; for, in simple truth, these are topics on which it is scarcely possible to exaggerate. But let us bring the matter more distinctly before the eye of the mind.

In the first place, we may get a general, *relative* conception of the interval referred to, by comparing it with the inter-planetary spaces. If, for example, we suppose the Earth, which is, in reality, 95 millions of miles from the Sun, to be only *one foot* from that luminary; then Neptune would be 40 feet distant; *and the star Alpha Lyræ, at the very least, 159.*

Now I presume that, in the termination of my last sentence, few of my readers have noticed anything especially objectionable – particularly wrong. I said that the distance of the Earth from the Sun being taken at *one foot,* the distance of Neptune would be 40 feet, and that of Alpha Lyræ, 159. The proportion between one foot and 159, has appeared, perhaps, to convey a sufficiently definite impression of the proportion between the two intervals – that of the Earth from the Sun and that of Alpha Lyræ from the same luminary. But my account of the matter should, in reality, have run thus : – The distance of the Earth from the Sun being taken at one foot, the distance of Neptune would be 40 feet, and that of Alpha Lyræ, 159 — *miles* : – that is to say, I had assigned to Alpha Lyræ, in my first statement of the case, only the 5280*th part* of that distance which is the *least distance possible* at which it can actually lie.

To proceed : – However distant a mere *planet* is, yet when we look at it through a telescope, we see it under a certain form – of a certain appreciable size. Now I have already hinted at the probable bulk of many of the stars; nevertheless, when we view any one of them, even through the most powerful telescope, it is found to present us with *no form*, and consequently with *no magnitude* whatever. We see it as a point and nothing more.

Again; – Let us suppose ourselves walking, at night, on a highway. In a field on one side of the road, is a line of tall objects, say trees, the figures of which are distinctly defined against the background of the sky. This line of objects extends at right angles to the road, and from the road to the horizon. Now, as we proceed along the road, we see these objects changing their positions, respectively, in relation to a certain fixed point in that portion of the firmament which forms the background of the view. Let us suppose this fixed point – sufficiently fixed for our purpose – to be the rising moon. We become aware, at once, that while the tree nearest us so far alters its position in respect to the moon, as to seem flying behind us, the tree in the extreme distance has scarcely changed at all its relative position with the satellite. We then go on to perceive that the farther the objects are from us, the less they alter their positions; and the converse. Then we begin, unwittingly, to estimate the distances of individual trees by the degrees in which they evince the relative alteration. Finally, we come to understand how it might be possible to ascertain the actual distance of any given tree in the line, by using the amount of relative alteration as a basis in a simple geometrical problem. Now this relative alteration is what we call 'parallax'; and by parallax we calculate the distances of the heavenly bodies. Applying the principle to the trees in question, we should, of course, be very much at a loss to comprehend the distance of *that* tree, which, however far we proceeded along the road, should evince *no* parallax at all. This, in the case described, is a thing impossible; but impossible only because all distances on our Earth are trivial indeed : – in comparison with the vast cosmical quantities, we may speak of them as absolutely nothing.

Now, let us suppose the star Alpha Lyræ directly overhead; and let us imagine that, instead of standing on the Earth, we stand at one end of a straight road stretching through Space to a distance equalling the diameter of the Earth's orbit – that is to say, to a distance of *190 millions of miles*. Having observed, by means of the most delicate micrometrical instruments, the exact position of the star, let us now pass along this inconceivable road, until we reach its other extremity. Now, once again, let us look at the star. It is *precisely* where we left it. Our instruments, however delicate, assure us that its relative position is absolutely – is identically the same as at the commencement of our unutterable journey. *No* parallax – none whatever – has been found.

The fact is, that, in regard to the distance of the fixed stars – of any one of the myriads of suns glistening on the farther side of that awful chasm which separates our system from its brothers in the cluster to which it belongs – astronomical science, until very lately, could speak only with a negative certainty. Assuming the brightest as the nearest, we could say, even of *them*, only that there is a certain incomprehensible distance on the *hither* side of which they cannot be: – how far they are beyond it we had in no case been able to ascertain. We perceived, for example, that Alpha Lyræ cannot be nearer to us than 19 trillions, 200 billions of miles; but, for all we knew, and indeed for all we now know, it may be distant from us the square, or the cube, or any other power of the number mentioned. By dint, however, of wonderfully minute and cautious observations, continued, with novel instruments, for many laborious years, *Bessel*, not long ago deceased,[45] has lately succeeded in determining the distance of six or seven stars; among others, that of the star numbered 61 in the constellation of the Swan. The distance in this latter instance ascertained, is 670,000 times that of the Sun; which last it will be remembered, is 95 millions of miles. The star 61 Cygni, then, is nearly 64 trillions of miles from us – or more than three times the distance assigned, *as the least possible*, for Alpha Lyræ.

In attempting to appreciate this interval by the aid of any considerations of *velocity*, as we did in endeavoring to estimate the distance of the moon, we must leave out of sight, altogether, such nothings as the speed of a cannon ball, or of sound. Light, however, according to the latest calculations of Struve, proceeds at the rate of 167,000 miles in a second. Thought itself cannot pass through this interval more speedily – if, indeed, thought can traverse it at all. Yet, in coming from 61 Cygni to us, even at this inconceivable rate, light occupies more than *ten years*; and, consequently, were the star this moment blotted out from the Universe, still, *for ten years*, would it continue to sparkle on, undimmed in its paradoxical glory.

Keeping now in mind whatever feeble conception we may have attained of the interval between our Sun and 61 Cygni, let us remember that this interval, however unutterably vast, we are permitted to consider as but the *average* interval among the countless host of stars composing that cluster, or 'nebula', to which our system, as well as that of 61 Cygni, belongs. I have, in fact, stated the case with great moderation : – we have excellent reason for believing 61 Cygni to be one of the *nearest* stars, and thus for concluding, at least for the present, that its distance from us is *less* than the average distance between star and star in the magnificent cluster of the Milky Way.

And here, once again and finally, it seems proper to suggest that even as yet we have been speaking of trifles. Ceasing to wonder at the space between star and star in our own or in any particular cluster, let us rather turn our thoughts to the intervals between cluster and cluster, in the all comprehensive cluster of the Universe.

I have already said that light proceeds at the rate of 167,000 miles in a second – that is, about 10 millions of miles in a minute, or about 600 millions of miles in an hour: – yet so far removed from us are some of the 'nebulæ' that even light, speeding with this velocity, could not and does not reach us, from those mysterious regions, in less than 3 *millions of years*. This calculation, moreover, is made by the elder Herschel, and in reference merely to those comparatively proximate clusters within the scope of his own telescope.[46] There *are* 'nebulæ', however, which, through the magical tube of Lord Rosse, are this instant whispering in our ears the secrets of *a million of ages* by-gone. In a word, the events which we behold now – at this moment – in those worlds – are the identical events which interested their inhabitants *ten hundred thousand centuries* ago. In intervals – in distances such as this suggestion forces upon the *soul* – rather than upon the mind – we find, at length, a fitting climax to all hitherto frivolous considerations of *quantity*.

Our fancies thus occupied with the cosmical distances, let us take the opportunity of referring to the difficulty which we have so often experienced, while pursuing *the beaten path* of astronomical reflection, *in accounting* for the immeasurable voids alluded to – in comprehending why chasms so totally unoccupied and therefore apparently so needless, have been made to intervene between star and star – between cluster and cluster – in understanding, to be brief, a sufficient reason for the Titanic scale, in respect of mere *Space*, on which the Universe of Stars is seen to be constructed. A rational cause for the phænomenon, I maintain that Astronomy has palpably failed to assign : – but the considerations through which, in this Essay, we have proceeded step by step, enable us clearly and immediately to perceive that *Space and Duration are one*. That the Universe of Stars might *endure* throughout an æra at all commensurate with the grandeur of its component material portions and with the high majesty of its spiritual purposes, it was necessary that the original atomic diffusion be made to so inconceivable an extent as to be only not infinite. It was required, in a word, that the stars should be gathered into visibility from invisible nebulosity – proceed from visibility to consolidation – and so grow grey in giving birth and death to unspeakably numerous and complex variations of vitalic development : – it was required that the stars should do all this – should have time thoroughly to accomplish all these Divine purposes – *during the period* in which all things were effecting their return into Unity with a velocity accumulating in the inverse proportion of the squares of the distances at which lay the inevitable End.

Throughout all this we have no difficulty in understanding the absolute accuracy of the Divine *adaptation*. The density of the stars, respectively, proceeds, of course, as their condensation diminishes; condensation and heterogeneity keep pace with each other; through the latter, which is the index of the former, we estimate the vitalic and spiritual development. Thus, in the density of the globes, we have the measure in which their purposes are fulfilled. *As* density proceeds – *as* the divine intentions *are* accomplished – *as* less and still less remains *to be* accomplished – so – in the same ratio – should we expect to find an acceleration of *the End* : – and thus the philosophical mind will easily comprehend that the Divine designs in constituting the stars, advance *mathematically* to their fulfilment : – and more; it will readily give the advance a mathematical expression; it will decide that this advance is inversely proportional with the squares of the distances of all created things from the starting-point and goal of their creation.

Not only is this Divine adaptation, however, mathematically accurate, but there is that about it which stamps it *as divine*, in distinction from that which is merely the work of human constructiveness. I allude to the complete *mutuality* of adaptation. For example; in human constructions a particular cause has a particular effect; a particular intention brings to pass a particular object; but this is all; we see no reciprocity. The effect does not re-act upon the cause; the intention does not change relations with the object. In Divine constructions the object is either design or object as we choose to regard it – and we may take at any time a cause for an effect, or the converse – so that we can never absolutely decide which is which.

To give an instance : – In polar climates the human frame, to maintain its animal heat, requires, for combustion in the capillary system, an abundant supply of highly azotized food, such as train oil. But again : – in polar climates nearly the sole food afforded man is the oil of abundant seals and whales. Now, whether is oil at hand because imperatively demanded, or the only thing demanded because the only thing to be obtained? It is impossible to decide. There is an absolute *reciprocity of adaptation*.

The pleasure which we derive from any display of human ingenuity is in the ratio of *the approach* to this species of reciprocity. In the construction of *plot*, for example, in fictitious literature,[47] we should aim at so arranging the incidents that we shall not be able to determine, of any one of them, whether it depends from any one other or upholds it. In this sense, of course, perfection of plot is really, or practically, unattainable – but only because it is a finite intelligence that constructs. The plots of God are perfect. The Universe is a plot of God.

And now we have reached a point at which the intellect is

forced, again, to struggle against its propensity for analogical inference – against its monomaniac grasping at the infinite. Moons have been seen *revolving* about planets; planets about stars; and the poetical instinct of humanity – its instinct of the symmetrical, even if the symmetry be but a symmetry of surface: – this *instinct*, which the Soul, not only of Man but of all created beings, took up, in the beginning, from the *geometrical* basis of the Universal radiation – impels us to the fancy of an endless extension of this system of *cycles*. Closing our eyes equally to *de*duction and *in*duction, we insist upon imagining a *revolution* of all the orbs of the Galaxy about some gigantic globe which we take to be the central pivot of the whole. Each cluster in the great cluster of clusters is imagined, of course, to be similarly supplied and constructed; while, that the 'analogy' may be wanting at no point, we go on to conceive these clusters themselves, again, as *revolving* about some still more august sphere; – this latter, still again, *with* its encircling clusters, as but one of a yet more magnificent series of agglomerations, *gyrating* about yet another orb central *to them* – some orb still more unspeakably sublime – some orb, let us rather say, of infinite sublimity endlessly multiplied by the infinitely sublime. Such are the conditions, continued in perpetuity, which the voice of what some people term 'analogy' calls upon the Fancy to depict and the Reason to contemplate, if possible, without becoming dissatisfied with the picture. Such, *in general*, are the interminable gyrations beyond gyration which we have been instructed by Philosophy to comprehend and to account for – at least in the best manner we can. Now and then, however, a philosopher proper – one whose frenzy takes a very determinate turn – whose genius, to speak more reverentially, has a strongly-pronounced washer-womanish bias, doing every thing up by the dozen – enables us to see *precisely* that point out of sight, at which the revolutionary processes in question do, and of right ought to, come to an end.

It is hardly worth while, perhaps, even to sneer at the reveries of Fourier [48] – but much has been said, latterly, of the hypothesis of Mädler [49] – that there exists, in the centre of the Galaxy, a

stupendous globe about which all the systems of the cluster revolve. The *period* of our own, indeed, has been stated – 117
millions of years.

That our Sun has a motion in space, independently of its rotation, and revolution about the system's centre of gravity, has
long been suspected. This motion, granting it to exist, would be
manifested perspectively. The stars in that firmamental region
which we were leaving behind us, would, in a very long series of
years, become crowded; those in the opposite quarter, scattered.
Now, by means of astronomical History, we ascertain, cloudily,
that some such phænomena have occurred. On this ground it has
been declared that our system is moving to a point in the heavens
diametrically opposite the star Zeta Herculis : – but this inference is, perhaps, the maximum to which we have any logical
right. Mädler, however, has gone so far as to designate a particular star, Alcyone in the Pleiades, as being at or about the very
spot around which a general *revolution* is performed.

Now, since by 'analogy' we are led, in the first instance, to
these dreams, it is no more than proper that we should abide by
analogy, at least in some measure, during their development; and
that analogy which suggests the revolution, suggests at the same
time a central orb about which it should be performed : – so far
the astronomer was consistent. This central orb, however, should,
dynamically, be greater than all the orbs, taken together, which
surround it. Of these there are about 100 millions. 'Why, then,'
it was of course demanded, 'do we not *see* this vast central sun –
at least equal in mass to 100 millions of such suns as ours – why
do we not *see* it – *we*, especially, who occupy the mid region of
the cluster – the very locality *near* which, at all events, must be
situated this incomparable star?' The reply was ready – 'It must
be non-luminous, as are our planets.' Here, then, to suit a purpose, analogy is suddenly let fall. 'Not so,' it may be said – 'we
know that non-luminous suns actually exist.' It is true that we
have reason at least for supposing so; but we have certainly no
reason whatever for supposing that the non-luminous suns in
question are encircled by *luminous* suns, while these again are
surrounded by non-luminous planets : – and it is precisely all
this with which Mädler is called upon to find any thing analo-

gous in the heavens – for it is precisely all this which he imagines in the case of the Galaxy. Admitting the thing to be so, we cannot help here picturing to ourselves how sad a puzzle the *why is it so* must prove to all *à priori* philosophers.

But granting, in the very teeth of analogy and of every thing else, the non-luminosity of the vast central orb, we may still inquire how this orb, so enormous, could fail of being rendered visible by the flood of light thrown upon it from the 100 millions of glorious suns glaring in all directions about it. On the urging of this question, the idea of an actually solid central sun appears, in some measure, to have been abandoned; and speculation proceeded to assert that the systems of the cluster perform their revolutions merely about an immaterial centre of gravity common to all. Here again then, to suit a purpose, analogy is let fall. The planets of our system revolve, it is true, about a common centre of gravity; but they do this in connexion with, and in consequence of, a material sun whose mass more than counterbalances the rest of the system.

The mathematical circle is a curve composed of an infinity of straight lines. But this idea of the circle – an idea which, in view of all ordinary geometry, is merely the mathematical, as contradistinguished from the practical, idea – is, in sober fact, the *practical* conception which alone we have any right to entertain in regard to the majestic circle with which we have to deal, at least in fancy, when we suppose our system revolving about a point in the centre of the Galaxy. Let the most vigorous of human imaginations attempt but to take a single step towards the comprehension of a sweep so ineffable! It would scarcely be paradoxical to say that a flash of lightning itself, travelling *forever* on the circumference of this unutterable circle, would still, *forever*, be travelling in a straight line. That the path of our Sun in such an orbit would, to any human perception, deviate in the slightest degree from a straight line, even in a million of years, is a proposition not to be entertained : – yet we are required to believe that a curvature has become apparent during the brief period of our astronomical history – during the mere point – during the utter nothingness of two or three thousand years.

It may be said that Mädler *has* really ascertained a curvature in the direction of our system's now well-established progress through Space. Admitting, if necessary, this fact to be in reality such, I maintain that nothing is thereby shown except the reality of this fact – the fact of a curvature. For its *thorough* determination, ages will be required; and, when determined, it will be found indicative of some binary or other multiple relation between our Sun and some one or more of the proximate stars. I hazard nothing, however, in predicting that, after the lapse of many centuries, all efforts at determining the path of our Sun through Space, will be abandoned as fruitless. This is easily conceivable when we look at the infinity of perturbation it must experience, from its perpetually-shifting relations with other orbs, in the common approach of all to the nucleus of the Galaxy.

But in examining other 'nebulæ' than that of the Milky Way – in surveying, generally, the clusters which overspread the heavens – do we or do we not find confirmation of Mädler's hypothesis? We do *not*. The forms of the clusters are exceedingly diverse when casually viewed; but on close inspection, through powerful telescopes, we recognize the sphere, very distinctly, as at least the proximate form of all : – their constitution, in general, being at variance with the idea of revolution about a common centre.

'It is difficult,' says Sir John Herschel,[50] 'to form any conception of the dynamical state of such systems. On one hand, without a rotary motion and a centrifugal force, it is hardly possible not to regard them as in a state of *progressive collapse*. On the other, granting such a motion and such a force, we find it no less difficult to reconcile their forms with the rotation of the whole system [meaning cluster] around any single axis, without which internal collision would appear to be inevitable.'

Some remarks lately made about the 'nebulæ' by Dr Nichol, in taking quite a different view of the cosmical conditions from any taken in this Discourse – have a very peculiar applicability to the point now at issue. He says :

'When our greatest telescopes are brought to bear upon them, we find that those which were thought to be irregular, are not so; they approach nearer to a globe. Here is one that looked oval; but Lord Rosse's telescope brought it into a circle. . . . Now there occurs a very remarkable circumstance in reference to these comparatively sweeping circular masses of nebulæ. We find they are not entirely circular, but the reverse; and that all around them, on every side, there are volumes of stars, *stretching out apparently as if they were rushing towards a great central mass in consequence of the action of some great power.*' *

Were I to describe, in my own words, what must necessarily be the existing condition of each nebula, on the hypothesis that all matter is, as I suggest, now returning to its original Unity, I should simply be going over, nearly verbatim, the language here employed by Dr Nichol, without the faintest suspicion of that stupendous truth which is the key to these nebular phæ-nomena.

And here let me fortify my position still farther, by the voice of a greater than Mädler – of one, moreover, to whom all the data of Mädler have long been familiar things, carefully and thoroughly considered. Referring to the elaborate calculations of Argelander[51] – the very researches which form Mädler's basis – *Humboldt*, whose generalizing powers have never, perhaps, been equalled, has the following observation :

'When we regard the real, proper, or non-perspective motions of the stars, we find *many groups of them moving in opposite directions*; and the data as yet in hand render it not necessary, at least, to conceive that the systems composing the Milky Way, or the clusters, generally, composing the Universe, are revolving about any particular centre unknown, whether luminous or non-luminous. It is but Man's longing for a fundamental First Cause, that impels both his intellect and fancy to the adoption of such an hypothesis.' †

---

* I must be understood as denying, *especially*, only the *revolutionary* por-tion of Mädler's hypothesis. Of course, if no great central orb exists *now* in our cluster, such will exist hereafter. Whenever existing, it will be merely the *nucleus* of the consolidation.

† Betrachtet man die nicht perspectivischen[52] eigenen Bewegungen der Sterne, so scheinen viele gruppenweise in ihrer Richtung entgegengesetzt; und die bisher gesammelten Thatsachen machen es auf's wenigste nicht nothwendig, anzunehmen, dass alle Theile unserer Sternenschicht oder gar der gesammten Sterneninseln, welche den Weltraum füllen, sich um einen grossen, unbekannten, leuchtenden oder dunkeln Centralkörper bewegen.

The phænomenon here alluded to – that of 'many groups moving in opposite directions' – is quite inexplicable by Mädler's idea; but arises, as a necessary consequence, from 'that which forms the basis of this Discourse. While the *merely general direction* of each atom – of each moon, planet, star, or cluster – would, on my hypothesis, be, of course, absolutely rectilinear; while the *general* path of all bodies would be a right line leading to the centre of all; it is clear, nevertheless, that this general rectilinearity would be compounded of what, with scarcely any exaggeration, we may term an infinity of particular curves – an infinity of local deviations from rectilinearity – the result of continuous differences of relative position among the multitudinous masses, as each proceeds on its own proper journey to the End.

I quoted, just now, from Sir John Herschel, the following words, used in reference to the clusters : – 'On one hand, without a rotary motion and a centrifugal force, it is hardly possible not to regard them as in a state of *progressive collapse*.' The fact is, that, in surveying the 'nebulæ' with a telescope of high power, we shall find it quite impossible, having once conceived this idea of 'collapse', not to gather, at all points, corroboration of the idea. A nucleus is always apparent, in the direction of which the stars seem to be precipitating themselves; nor can these nuclei be mistaken for merely perspective phænomena : – the clusters are *really* denser near the centre – sparser in the regions more remote from it. In a word, we see every thing as we *should* see it were a collapse taking place; but, in general, it may be said of these clusters, that we can fairly entertain, while looking at them, the idea of *orbitual movement about a centre*, only by admitting the *possible* existence, in the distant domains of space, of dynamical laws with which *we* are unacquainted.

On the part of Herschel, however, there is evidently *a reluctance* to regard the nebulæ as in 'a state of progressive collapse'. But if facts – if even appearances justify the supposition of their

---

Das Streben nach den letzten höchsten Grundursachen macht freilich die reflectirende Thätigkeit des Menschen, wie seine Phantasie, zu einer solchen Annahme geneigt.

being in this state, *why*, it may well be demanded, is he disinclined to admit it? Simply on account of a prejudice; – merely because the supposition is at war with a preconceived and utterly baseless notion – that of the endlessness – that of the eternal stability of the Universe.

If the propositions of this Discourse are tenable, the 'state of progressive collapse' is *precisely* that state in which alone we are warranted in considering All Things; and, with due humility, let me here confess that, for my part, I am at a loss to conceive how any *other* understanding of the existing condition of affairs, could ever have made its way into the human brain. 'The tendency to collapse' and 'the attraction of gravitation' are convertible phrases. In using either, we speak of the rëaction of the First Act. Never was necessity less obvious than that of supposing Matter imbued with an ineradicable *quality* forming part of its material nature – a quality, or instinct, *forever* inseparable from it, and by dint of which inalienable principle every atom is *perpetually* impelled to seek its fellow-atom. Never was necessity less obvious than that of entertaining this unphilosophical idea. Going boldly behind the vulgar thought, we have to conceive, metaphysically, that the gravitating principle appertains to Matter *temporarily* – only while diffused – only while existing as Many instead of as One – appertains to it by virtue of its state of radiation alone – appertains, in a word, altogether to its *condition*, and not in the slightest degree to *itself*. In this view, when the radiation shall have returned into its source – when the rëaction shall be completed – the gravitating principle will no longer exist. And, in fact, astronomers, without at any time reaching the idea here suggested, seem to have been approximating it, in the assertion that 'if there were but one body in the Universe, it would be impossible to understand how the principle, Gravity, could obtain' : – that is to say, from a consideration of Matter as they find it, they reach a conclusion at which I deductively arrive. That so pregnant a suggestion as the one quoted should have been permitted to remain so long unfruitful, is, nevertheless, a mystery which I find it difficult to fathom.

It is, perhaps, in no little degree, however, our propensity for the continuous – for the analogical – in the present case more particularly for the symmetrical – which has been leading us astray. And, in fact, the sense of the symmetrical is an instinct which may be depended on with an almost blindfold reliance. It is the poetical essence of the Universe – *of the Universe* which, in the supremeness of its symmetry, is but the most sublime of poems. Now symmetry and consistency are convertible terms : – thus Poetry and Truth are one. A thing is consistent in the ratio of its truth – true in the ratio of its consistency. *A perfect consistency, I repeat, can be nothing but an absolute truth.* We may take it for granted, then, that Man cannot long or widely err, if he suffer himself to be guided by his poetical, which I have maintained to be his truthful, in being his symmetrical, instinct. He must have a care, however, lest, in pursuing too heedlessly the superficial symmetry of forms and motions, he leave out of sight the really essential symmetry of the principles which determine and control them.

That the stellar bodies would finally be merged in one – that, at last, all would be drawn into the substance of *one stupendous central orb already existing* – is an idea which, for some time past, seems, vaguely and indeterminately, to have held possession of the fancy of mankind. It is an idea, in fact, which belongs to the class of the *excessively obvious*. It springs, instantly, from a superficial observation of the cyclic and seemingly *gyrating*, or *vorticial* movements of those individual portions of the Universe which come most immediately and most closely under our observation. There is not, perhaps, a human being, of ordinary education and of average reflective capacity, to whom, at some period, the fancy in question has not occurred, as if spontaneously, or intuitively, and wearing all the character of a very profound and very original conception. This conception, however, so commonly entertained, has never, within my knowledge, arisen out of any abstract considerations. Being, on the contrary, always suggested, as I say, by the vorticial movements about centres, a reason for it, also, – a *cause* for the ingathering of all the orbs into one, *imagined to be already existing*, was naturally sought in the same direction – among these cyclic movements themselves.

Thus it happened that, on announcement of the gradual and perfectly regular decrease observed in the orbit of Encke's

comet,[53] at every successive revolution about our Sun, astronomers were nearly unanimous in the opinion that the cause in
question was found – that a principle was discovered sufficient to
account, physically, for that final, universal agglomeration which,
I repeat, the analogical, symmetrical or poetical instinct of Man
had predetermined to understand as something more than a
simple hypothesis.

This cause – this sufficient reason for the final ingathering –
was declared to exist in an exceedingly rare but still material
medium pervading space;[54] which medium, by retarding, in
some degree, the progress of the comet, perpetually weakened its
tangential force; thus giving a predominance to the centripetal;
which, of course, drew the comet nearer and nearer at each revolution, and would eventually precipitate it upon the Sun.

All this was strictly logical – admitting the medium or ether;
but this ether was assumed, most illogically, on the ground that
no *other* mode than the one mentioned could be discovered, of
accounting for the observed decrease in the orbit of the comet : –
as if from the fact that we could *discover* no other mode of accounting for it, it followed, in any respect, that no other mode
of accounting for it existed. It is clear that innumerable causes
might operate, in combination, to diminish the orbit, without
even a possibility of our ever becoming acquainted with even
one of them. In the meantime, it has never been fairly shown,
perhaps, why the retardation occasioned by the skirts of the
Sun's atmosphere, through which the comet passes at perihelion,
is not enough to account for the phænemenon. That Encke's
comet will be absorbed into the Sun, is probable; that all the
comets of the system will be absorbed, is more than merely possible; but, in such case, the principle of absorption must be
referred to eccentricity of orbit – to the close approximation to
the Sun, of the comets at their perihelia; and is a principle not
affecting, in any degree, the ponderous *spheres*, which are to be
regarded as the true material constituents of the Universe. –
Touching comets, in general, let me here suggest, in passing,
that we cannot be far wrong in looking upon them as the *light-
ning-flashes of the cosmical Heaven.*

The idea of a retarding ether and, through it, of a final agglo-

meration of all things, seemed at one time, however, to be confirmed by the observation of a positive decrease in the orbit of the
solid moon. By reference to eclipses recorded 2500 years ago, it
was found that the velocity of the satellite's revolution *then* was
considerably less than it is *now*; that on the hypothesis that its
motion in its orbit is uniformly in accordance with Kepler's law,
and was accurately determined *then* – 2500 years ago – it is now
in advance of the position it *should* occupy, by nearly 9000 miles.
The increase of velocity proved, of course, a diminution of orbit;
and astronomers were fast yielding to a belief in an ether, as the
sole mode of accounting for the phænomenon, when Lagrange
came to the rescue. He showed that, owing to the configurations
of the spheroids, the shorter axes of their ellipses are subject to
variation in length; the longer axes being permanent; and that
this variation is continuous and vibratory – so that every orbit is
in a state of transition, either from circle to ellipse, or from ellipse
to circle. In the case of the moon, where the shorter axis is *de*-
creasing, the orbit is passing from circle to ellipse, and, consequently, is *de*creasing too; but, after a long series of ages, the
ultimate eccentricity will be attained; then the shorter axis will
proceed to *in*crease, until the orbit becomes a circle; when the
process of shortening will again take place; – and so on forever.
In the case of the Earth, the orbit is passing from ellipse to circle.
The facts thus demonstrated do away, of course, with all necessity for supposing an ether, and with all apprehension of the
system's instability – *on the ether's account*.

It will be remembered that I have myself assumed what we
may term *an ether*. I have spoken of a subtle *influence* which we
know to be ever in attendance on matter, although becoming
manifest only through matter's heterogeneity. To this *influence* –
without daring to touch it at all in any effort at explaining its
awful *nature* – I have referred the various phænomena of electricity, heat, light, magnetism; and more – of vitality, consciousness, and thought – in a word, of spirituality. It will be seen, at
once, then, that the ether thus conceived is radically distinct
from the ether of the astronomers; inasmuch as theirs is *matter*
and mine *not*.

With the idea of material ether, seems, thus, to have departed altogether the thought of that universal agglomeration so long predetermined by the poetical fancy of mankind : – an agglomeration in which a sound Philosophy might have been warranted in putting faith, at least to a certain extent, if for no other reason than that by this poetical fancy it *had* been so predetermined. But so far as Astronomy – so far as mere Physics have yet spoken, the cycles of the Universe are perpetual – the Universe has no conceivable end. Had an end been demonstrated, however, from so purely collateral a cause as an ether, Man's instinct of the Divine *capacity to adapt,* would have rebelled against the demonstration. We should have been forced to regard the Universe with some such sense of dissatisfaction as we experience in contemplating an unnecessarily complex work of human art. Creation would have affected us as an imperfect *plot* in a romance, where the *dénoûment* is awkwardly brought about by interposed incidents external and foreign to the main subject; instead of springing out of the bosom of the thesis – out of the heart of the ruling idea – instead of arising as a result of the primary proposition – as inseparable and inevitable part and parcel of the fundamental conception of the book.

What I mean by the symmetry of mere surface will now be more clearly understood. It is simply by the blandishment of this symmetry that we have been beguiled into the general idea of which Mädler's hypothesis is but a part – the idea of the vorticial indrawing of the orbs. Dismissing this nakedly physical conception, the symmetry of *principle* sees the end of all things metaphysically involved in the thought of a beginning; seeks and finds, in this origin of all things, the *rudiment* of this end; and perceives the impiety of supposing this end likely to be brought about less simply – less directly – less obviously – less artistically – than through *the rëaction of the originating Act*.

Recurring, then, to a previous suggestion, let us understand the systems – let us understand each star, with its attendant planets – as but a Titanic atom existing in space with precisely the same inclination for Unity which characterized, in the beginning, the actual atoms after their radiation throughout the Universal sphere. As these original atoms rushed towards each other in generally straight lines, so let us conceive as at least generally rectilinear, the paths of the system-atoms towards their respective centres of aggregation : – and in this direct drawing together of the systems into clusters, with a similar and simultaneous drawing together of the clusters themselves while undergoing consolidation, we have at length attained the great *Now* – the awful Present – the Existing Condition of the Universe.

Of the still more awful Future[55] a not irrational analogy may guide us in framing an hypothesis. The equilibrium between the centripetal and centrifugal forces of each system, being necessarily destroyed on attainment of a certain proximity to the nucleus of the cluster to which it belongs, there must occur, at once, a chaotic or seemingly chaotic precipitation, of the moons upon the planets, of the planets upon the suns, and of the suns upon the nuclei; and the general result of this precipitation must be the gathering of the myriad now-existing stars of the firmament into an almost infinitely less number of almost infinitely superior spheres. In being immeasurably fewer, the worlds of that day will be immeasurably greater than our own. Then, indeed, amid unfathomable abysses, will be glaring unimaginable suns. But all this will be merely a climacic magnificence foreboding the great End. Of this End the new genesis described can be but a very partial postponement. While undergoing consolidation, the clusters themselves, with a speed prodigiously accumulative, have been rushing towards their own general centre[56] – and now, with a million-fold electric velocity, commensurate only with their material grandeur and with their spiritual passion for oneness, the majestic remnants of the tribe of Stars flash, at length, into a common embrace. The inevitable catastrophe is at hand.

But this catastrophe – what is it? We have seen accomplished the ingathering of the orbs. Henceforward, are we not to understand *one material globe of globes* as comprehending and constituting the Universe? Such a fancy would be altogether at war with every assumption and consideration of this Discourse.

I have already alluded to that absolute *reciprocity of adaptation* which is the idiosyncrasy of the Divine Art – stamping it divine. Up to this point of our reflections, we have been regarding the electrical influence as a something by dint of whose repulsion

alone Matter is enabled to exist in that state of diffusion demanded for the fulfilment of its purposes : – so far, in a word, we have
been considering the influence in question as ordained for Matter's sake – to subserve the objects of matter. With a perfectly
legitimate reciprocity, we are now permitted to look at Matter,
as created *solely for the sake of this influence* – solely to serve the
objects of this spiritual Ether. Through the aid – by the means –
through the agency of Matter, and by dint of its heterogeneity –
is this Ether manifested – is *Spirit individualized*. It is merely in
the development of this Ether, through heterogeneity, that particular masses of Matter become animate – sensitive – and in the
ratio of their heterogeneity; – some reaching a degree of sensi-
tiveness involving what we call *Thought* and thus attaining
obviously Conscious Intelligence.

In this view, we are enabled to perceive Matter as a Means –
not as an End. Its purposes are thus seen to have been comprehended in its diffusion; and with the return into Unity these
purposes cease. The absolutely consolidated globe of globes would
be *objectless* : – therefore not for a moment could it continue to
exist. Matter, created for an end, would unquestionably, on fulfilment of that end, be Matter no longer. Let us endeavor to understand that it would disappear, and that God would remain all in
all.[57]

That every work of Divine conception must cöexist and
cöexpire with its particular design, seems to me especially obvious; and I make no doubt that, on perceiving the final globe of
globes to be *objectless*, the majority of my readers will be satisfied with my '*therefore* it cannot continue to exist'. Nevertheless,
as the startling thought of its instantaneous disappearance is one
which the most powerful intellect cannot be expected readily to
entertain on grounds so decidedly abstract, let us endeavor to
look at the idea from some other and more ordinary point of
view : – let us see how thoroughly and beautifully it is corroborated in an *à posteriori* consideration of Matter as we actually
find it.

I have before said that 'Attraction and Repulsion being un-
deniably the sole properties by which Matter is manifested to
Mind, we are justified in assuming that Matter *exists* only as

Attraction and Repulsion – in other words that Attraction and Repulsion *are* Matter; there being no conceivable case in which we may not employ the term "Matter" and the terms "Attraction" and "Repulsion" taken together, as equivalent, and therefore convertible, expressions of Logic.' *

Now the very definition of Attraction implies particularity – the existence of parts, particles, or atoms; for we define it as the tendency of 'each atom &c. to every other atom', &c. according to a certain law. Of course where there are *no* parts – where there is absolute Unity – where the tendency to oneness is satisfied – there can be no Attraction : – this has been fully shown, and all Philosophy admits it. When, on fulfilment of its purposes, then, Matter shall have returned into its original condition of *One* – a condition which presupposes the expulsion of the separative Ether, whose province and whose capacity are limited to keeping the atoms apart until that great day when, this Ether being no longer needed, the overwhelming pressure of the finally collective Attraction shall at length just sufficiently predominate †
and expel it : – when, I say, Matter, finally, expelling the Ether, shall have returned into absolute Unity, – it will then (to speak paradoxically for the moment) be Matter without Attraction and without Repulsion – in other words, Matter without Matter – in other words, again, *Matter no more*. In sinking into Unity, it will sink at once into that Nothingness which, to all finite perception, Unity must be – into that Material Nihility from which alone we can conceive it to have been evoked – to have been *created* by the Volition of God.

I repeat then – Let us endeavor to comprehend that the final globe of globes will instantaneously disappear, and that God will remain all in all.

But are we here to pause? Not so. On the Universal agglomeration and dissolution, we can readily conceive that a new and perhaps totally different series of conditions may ensue – another creation and radiation, returning into itself – another action and rëaction of the Divine Will. Guiding our imaginations by that omniprevalent law of laws, the law of periodicity, are we not,

* Page 233.
† 'Gravity, therefore, must be the strongest of forces.' – See page 235 *seq*.

indeed, more than justified in entertaining a belief – let us say, rather, in indulging a hope – that the processes we have here ventured to contemplate will be renewed forever, and forever, and forever; a novel Universe swelling into existence, and then subsiding into nothingness, at every throb of the Heart Divine?

And now – this Heart Divine – what is it? *It is our own.*[58]

Let not the merely seeming irreverence of this idea frighten our souls from that cool exercise of consciousness – from that deep tranquility of self-inspection – through which alone we can hope to attain the presence of this, the most sublime of truths, and look it leisurely in the face.

The *phænomena* on which our conclusions must at this point depend, are merely spiritual shadows, but not the less thoroughly substantial.

We walk about, amid the destinies of our world-existence, encompassed by dim but ever present *Memories* of a Destiny more vast – very distant in the by-gone time, and infinitely awful.

We live out a Youth peculiarly haunted [59] by such shadows; yet never mistaking them for dreams. As Memories we *know* them. *During our Youth* the distinction is too clear to deceive us even for a moment.

So long as this Youth endures, the feeling *that we exist*, is the most natural of all feelings. We understand it *thoroughly*. That there was a period at which we did *not* exist – or, that it might so have happened that we never had existed at all – are the considerations, indeed, which *during this Youth*, we find difficulty in understanding. Why we should *not* exist, is, *up to the epoch of our Manhood*, of all queries the most unanswerable. Existence – self-existence – existence from all Time and to all Eternity – seems, up to the epoch of Manhood, a normal and unquestionable condition : *– seems, because it is.*

But now comes the period at which a conventional World-Reason awakens us from the truth of our dream. Doubt, Surprise and Incomprehensibility arrive at the same moment. They say : – 'You live and the time was when you lived not. You have been created. An Intelligence exists greater than your own; and it is only through this Intelligence you live at all.' These things we struggle to comprehend and cannot : – *cannot*, because these things, being untrue, are thus, of necessity, incomprehensible.

No thinking being lives who, at some luminous point of his life of thought, has not felt himself lost amid the surges of futile efforts at understanding, or believing, that anything exists *greater than his own soul*. The utter impossibility of any one's soul feeling itself inferior to another; the intense, overwhelming dissatisfaction and rebellion at the thought; – these, with the omni-prevalent aspirations at perfection, are but the spiritual, coincident with the material, struggles towards the original Unity – are, to my mind at least, a species of proof far surpassing what Man terms demonstration, that no one soul *is* inferior to another – that nothing is, or can be, superior to any one soul – that each soul is, in part, its own God – its own Creator : – in a word, that God – the material *and* spiritual God – *now* exists solely in the diffused Matter and Spirit of the Universe; and that the regathering of this diffused Matter and Spirit will be but the re-constitution of the *purely Spiritual* and Individual God.

In this view, and in this view alone, we comprehend the riddles of Divine Injustice – of Inexorable Fate. In this view alone the existence of Evil becomes intelligible; but in this view it becomes more – it becomes endurable. Our souls no longer rebel at a *Sorrow* which we ourselves have imposed upon ourselves, in furtherance of our own purposes – with a view – if even with a futile view – to the extension of our own *Joy*.

I have spoken of *Memories* that haunt us during our Youth. They sometimes pursue us even into our Manhood : – assume gradually less and less indefinite shapes : – now and then speak to us with low voices, saying :

'There was an epoch in the Night of Time, when a still-existent Being existed – one of an absolutely infinite number of similar Beings that people the absolutely infinite domains of the absolutely infinite space.* It was not and is not in the power of this Being – any more than it is in your own – to extend, by actual increase, the joy of his Existence; but just as it *is* in your power to expand or to concentrate your pleasures (the absolute amount

* See page 280, Paragraph commencing 'I reply that the right,' and ending 'proper and particular God.'

of happiness remaining always the same) so did and does a similar capability appertain to this Divine Being, who thus passes his
Eternity in perpetual variation of Concentrated Self and almost
Infinite Self-Diffusion. What you call The Universe of Stars is
but his present expansive existence. He now feels his life through
an infinity of imperfect pleasures – the partial and pain-inter-
tangled pleasures of those inconceivably numerous things which
you designate as his creatures, but which are really but infinite
individualizations of Himself. All these creatures – *all* – those
whom you term animate, as well as those to which you deny life
for no better reason than that you do not behold it in operation –
all these creatures have, in a greater or less degree, a capacity for
pleasure and for pain: – *but the general sum of their sensations
is precisely that amount of Happiness which appertains by right
to the Divine Being when concentrated within Himself*. These
creatures are all too, more or less, and more or less obviously,
conscious Intelligences; conscious, first, of a proper identity;
conscious, secondly and by faint indeterminate glimpses, of an
identity with the Divine Being of whom we speak – of an identity
with God. Of the two classes of consciousness, fancy that the
former will grow weaker, the latter stronger, during the long
succession of ages which must elapse before these myriads of
individual Intelligences become blended – when the bright stars
become blended – into One. Think that the sense of individual
identity will be gradually merged in the general consciousness –
that Man, for example, ceasing imperceptibly to feel himself
Man, will at length attain that awfully triumphant epoch when
he shall recognize his existence as that of Jehovah.[60] In the meantime bear in mind that all is Life – Life – Life within Life – the
less within the greater, and all within the *Spirit Divine*.[61]

*

NOTE. – The pain of the consideration that we shall lose our
individual identity, ceases at once when we further reflect that the
process, as above described, is, neither more nor less than that of
the absorption, by each individual intelligence, of all other intelligences (that is, of the Universe) into its own. That God may be
all in all, each must become God.

Mellonta Tauta[1]

ON BOARD BALLOON 'SKYLARK',[2]

April 1, 2848

Now, my dear friend – now, for your sins, you are to suffer the infliction of a long gossiping letter. I tell you distinctly that I am going to punish you for all your impertinences by being as tedious, as discursive, as incoherent and as unsatisfactory as possible. Besides, here I am, cooped up in a dirty balloon, with some one or two hundred of the *canaille*,[3] all bound on a *pleasure* excursion, (what a funny idea some people have of pleasure!) and I have no prospect of touching *terra firma* for a month at least. Nobody to talk to. Nothing to do. When one has nothing to do, then is the time to correspond with one's friends. You perceive, then, why it is that I write you this letter – it is on account of my *ennui* and your sins.

Get ready your spectacles and make up your mind to be annoyed. I mean to write at you every day during this odious voyage.

Heigho! when will any *Invention* visit the human pericranium? Are we forever to be doomed to the thousand inconveniences of the balloon? Will *nobody* contrive a more expeditious mode of progress? This jog-trot movement, to my thinking, is little less than positive torture. Upon my word we have not made more than a hundred miles the hour since leaving home! The very birds beat us – at least some of them. I assure you that I do not exaggerate at all. Our motion, no doubt, seems slower than it actually is – this on account of our having no objects about us by which to estimate our velocity, and on account of our going *with* the wind. To be sure, whenever we meet a balloon we have a chance of perceiving our rate, and then, I admit, things do not appear so very bad. Accustomed as I am to this mode of traveling, I cannot get over a kind of giddiness whenever a balloon passes us in a current directly overhead. It always seems to me like an immense bird of prey about to pounce upon us and carry us off in its claws. One went over us this morning about sunrise, and so nearly overhead that its drag rope actually brushed the net-work suspending our car, and caused us very serious apprehension. Our captain said that if the material of the bag had been the trumpery varnished 'silk' of five hundred or a thousand years ago, we should inevitably have been damaged. This silk, as he explained it to me, was a fabric composed of the entrails of a species of earthworm. The worm was carefully fed on mulberries – a kind of fruit resembling a water-melon – and, when sufficiently fat, was crushed in a mill. The paste thus arising was called *papyrus* in its primary state, and went through a variety of processes until it finally became 'silk'. Singular to relate, it was once much admired as an article of *female dress* ! Balloons were also very generally constructed from it. A better kind of material, it appears, was subsequently found in the down surrounding the seed-vessels of a plant vulgarly called *euphorbium*, and at that time botanically termed milkweed. This latter kind of silk was designated as silk-buckingham, on account of its superior durability,[4] and was usually prepared for use by being varnished with a solution of gum caoutchouc – a substance which in some respects must have resembled the *gutta percha* now in common use. This caoutchouc was occasionally called India rubber or rubber of whist, and was no doubt one of the numerous *fungi*. Never tell me again that I am not at heart an antiquarian.

Talking of drag-ropes – our own, it seems, has this moment knocked a man overboard from one of the small magnetic propellers that swarm in ocean below us – a boat of about six thousand tons, and, from all accounts, shamefully crowded. These diminutive barques should be prohibited from carrying more than a definite number of passengers. The man, of course, was not permitted to get on board again, and was soon out of sight, he and his life-preserver. I rejoice, my dear friend, that we live in an age so enlightened that no such a thing as an individual is supposed to exist. It is the mass for which the true Humanity cares. By the by, talking of Humanity, do you know that our immortal Wiggins is not so original in his views of the Social Condition and so forth, as his contemporaries are inclined to suppose? Pundit assures me[5] that the same ideas were put, nearly

in the same way, about a thousand years ago, by an Irish philosopher called Furrier, on account of his keeping a retail shop for cat-
peltries[6] and other furs. Pundit *knows*, you know; there can be
no mistake about it. How very wonderfully do we see verified,
every day, the profound observation of the Hindoo Aries Tottle
(as quoted by Pundit)[7] – 'Thus must we say that, not once or
twice, or a few times, but with almost infinite repetitions, the
same opinions come round in a circle among men.'

April 2. – Spoke to-day the magnetic cutter in charge of the
middle section of floating telegraph wires. I learn that when
this species of telegraph was first put into operation by Horse,
it was considered quite impossible to convey the wires over sea;
but now we are at a loss to comprehend where the difficulty lay !
So wags the world. *Tempora mutantur* – excuse me for quoting
the Etruscan. What *would* we do without the Atalantic telegraph? (Pundit says Atlantic was the ancient adjective.) We lay
to a few minutes to ask the cutter some questions, and learned,
among other glorious news, that civil war is raging in Africa,
while the plague is doing its good work beautifully both in
Yurope and Ayesher. Is it not truly remarkable that, before the
magnificent light shed upon philosophy by Humanity, the world
was accustomed to regard War and Pestilence as calamities? Do
you know that prayers were actually offered up in the ancient
temples to the end that these *evils* (!) might not be visited upon
mankind? Is it not really difficult to comprehend upon what
principle of interest our forefathers acted? Were they so blind
as not to perceive that the destruction of a myriad of individuals
is only so much positive advantage to the mass !

April 3. – It is really a very fine amusement to ascend the
rope-ladder leading to the summit of the balloon-bag and thence
survey the surrounding world. From the car below, you know,
the prospect is not so comprehensive – you can see little vertically.
But seated here (where I write this) in the luxuriously-cushioned
open piazza of the summit, one can see everything that is going
on in all directions. Just now, there is quite a crowd of balloons in
sight, and they present a very animated appearance, while the
air is resonant with the hum of so many millions of human
voices. I have heard it asserted that when Yellow or (as Pundit

will have it) Violet, who is supposed to have been the first æronaut,[8] maintained the practicability of traversing the atmosphere in all directions, by merely ascending or descending until a favorable current was attained, he was scarcely hearkened to at all by his contemporaries, who looked upon him as merely an ingenious sort of madman, because the philosophers (?) of the day declared the thing impossible. Really now it does seem to me *quite* unaccountable how anything so obviously feasible could have escaped the sagacity of the ancient *savans*. But in all ages the great obstacles to advancement in Art have been opposed by the so-called men of science. To be sure, *our* men of science are not quite so bigoted as those of old: – oh, I have something *so* queer to tell you on this topic. Do you know that it is not more than a thousand years ago since the metaphysicians consented to relieve the people of the singular fancy that there existed but *two possible roads for the attainment of Truth* ! Believe it if you can ! It appears that long, long ago, in the night of Time, there lived a Turkish philosopher (or Hindoo possibly) called Aries Tottle. This person introduced, or at all events propagated what was termed the deductive or *à priori* mode of investigation. He started with what he maintained to be *axioms* or 'self-evident truths', and thence proceeded 'logically' to results. His greatest disciples were one Neuclid and one Cant.[9] Well, Aries Tottle flourished supreme until the advent of one Hog, surnamed the 'Ettrick Shepherd',[10] who preached an entirely different system, which he called the *à posteriori* or *in*ductive. His plan referred altogether to Sensation. He proceeded by observing, analyzing and classifying facts – *instantiæ naturæ*, as they were affectedly called – into general laws. Aries Tottle's mode, in a word, was based on *noumena*; Hog's on *phenomena*. Well, so great was the admiration excited by this latter system that, at its first introduction, Aries Tottle fell into disrepute; but finally he recovered ground, and was permitted to divide the realm of Truth with his more modern rival. The *savans* now maintained that the Aristotelian and *Baconian* roads were the sole possible avenues to knowledge. 'Baconian', you must know, was an adjective invented as equivalent to Hog-ian and more euphonious and dignified.

Now, my dear friend, I do assure you, most positively, that I represent this matter fairly, on the soundest authority; and you can easily understand how a notion so absurd on its very face must have operated to retard the progress of all true knowledge – which makes its advances almost invariably by intuitive bounds. The ancient idea confined investigation to *crawling*; and for hundreds of years so great was the infatuation about Hog especially, that a virtual end was put to all thinking properly so called. No man dared utter a truth to which he felt himself indebted to his *Soul* alone. It mattered not whether the truth was even *demonstrably* a truth, for the bullet-headed *savans* of the time regarded only the *road* by which he had attained it. They would not even *look* at the end. 'Let us see the means,' they cried, 'the means !' If, upon investigation of the means, it was found to come neither under the category Aries (that is to say Ram) nor under the category Hog, why then the savans went no farther, but pronounced the 'theorist', a fool, and would have nothing to do with him or his truth.

Now, it cannot be maintained, even, that by the crawling system the greatest amount of truth would be attained in any long series of ages, for the repression of *imagination* was an evil not to be compensated for by any superior *certainty* in the ancient modes of investigation. The error of these Jurmains, these Vrinch, these Inglitch and these Amriccans, (the latter, by the way, were our own immediate progenitors,) was an error quite analogous with that of the wiseacre who fancies that he must necessarily see an object the better the more closely he holds it to his eyes. These people blinded themselves by details. When they proceeded Hoggishly, their 'facts' were by no means always facts – a matter of little consequence had it not been for assuming that they *were* facts and must be facts because they appeared to be such. When they proceeded on the path of the Ram, their course was scarcely as straight as a ram's horn, for they *never had* an axiom which was an axiom at all. They must have been very blind not to see this, even in their own day; for even in their own day many of the long 'established' axioms had been rejected. For example – '*Ex nihilo nihil fit*';[11] 'a body cannot act where it is not'; 'there cannot exist antipodes'; 'darkness cannot come out of light' – all these, and a dozen other similar propositions, formerly admitted without hesitation as axioms, were, even at the period of which I speak, seen to be untenable. How absurd in these people, then, to persist in putting faith in 'axioms' as 'immutable bases of Truth! But even out of the mouths of their soundest reasoners it is easy to demonstrate the futility, the impalpability of their axioms in general. Who *was* the soundest of their logicians? Let me see! I will go and ask Pundit and be back in a minute . . . Ah, here we have it! Here is a book written nearly a thousand years ago and lately translated from the Inglitch – which, by the way, appears to have been the rudiment of the Amriccan. Pundit says it is decidedly the cleverest ancient work on its topic, Logic.[12] The author (who was much thought of in his day) was one Miller, or Mill; and we find it recorded of him, as a point of some importance, that he had a mill-horse called Bentham. But let us glance at the treatise!

Ah! – 'Ability or inability to conceive,' says Mr Mill, very properly, 'is in no case to be received as a criterion of axiomatic truth.' What *modern* in his senses would ever think of disputing this truism? The only wonder with us must be, how it happened that Mr Mill conceived it necessary even to hint at any thing so obvious. So far good – but let us turn over another page. What have we here? – 'Contradictories cannot both be true – that is, cannot co-exist in nature.' Here Mr Mill means, for example, that a tree must be either a tree or not a tree – that it cannot be at the same time a tree and not a tree. Very well; but I ask him *why*. His reply is this – and never pretends to be anything else than this – 'Because it is impossible to conceive that contradictories can both be true.' But this is no answer at all, by his own showing; for has he not just admitted as a truism that 'ability or inability to conceive is *in no case* to be received as a criterion of axiomatic truth'.

Now I do not complain of these ancients so much because their logic is, by their own showing, utterly baseless, worthless and fantastic altogether, as because of their pompous and imbecile proscription of all *other* roads of Truth, of all *other* means for its attainment than the two preposterous paths – the one of creeping and the one of crawling – to which they have dared to confine the Soul that loves nothing so well as to *soar*.

By the by, my dear friend, do you not think it would have puzzled these ancient dogmaticians to have determined by *which* of their two roads it was that the most important and most sublime of *all* their truths was, in effect, attained? I mean the truth of Gravitation. Newton owed it to Kepler. Kepler admitted that his three laws were *guessed at* – these three laws of all laws which led the great Inglitch mathematician to his principle, the basis of all physical principle – to go behind which we must enter the Kingdom of Metaphysics. Kepler guessed – that is to say, *imagined*. He was essentially a 'theorist' – that word now of so much sanctity, formerly an epithet of contempt. Would it not have puzzled these old moles, too, to have explained by which of the two 'roads' a cryptographist unriddles a cryptograph of more than usual secrecy, or by which of the two roads Champollion directed mankind to those enduring and almost innumerable truths which resulted from his deciphering the Hieroglyphics?

One word more on this topic and I will be done boring you. Is it not *passing* strange that, with their eternal prating about *roads* to Truth, these bigoted people missed what we now so clearly perceive to be the great highway – that of Consistency? Does it not seem singular how they should have failed to deduce from the works of God the vital fact that a perfect consistency *must be* an absolute truth![13] How plain has been our progress since the late announcement of this proposition! Investigation has been taken out of the hands of the ground-moles and given, as a task, to the true and only true thinkers, the men of ardent imagination. These latter *theorize*. Can you not fancy the shout of scorn with which my words would be received by our progenitors were it possible for them to be now looking over my shoulder? These men, I say, *theorize*; and their theories are simply corrected, reduced, systematized – cleared, little by little, of their dross of inconsistency – until, finally, a perfect consistency stands apparent which even the most stolid admit, because it *is* a consistency, to be an absolute and an unquestionable *truth*.

April 4. The new gas is doing wonders, in conjunction with the new improvement with gutta percha. How very safe, commodious, manageable, and in every respect convenient are our modern balloons! Here is an immense one approaching us at the rate of at least a hundred and fifty miles an hour. It seems to be crowded with people – perhaps there are three or four hundred passengers[14] – and yet it soars to an elevation of nearly a mile, looking down upon poor us with sovereign contempt. Still a hundred or even two hundred miles an hour is slow traveling, after all. *Do* you remember our flight on the railroad across the Kanadaw continent? – fully three hundred miles the hour – *that* was traveling.[15] Nothing to be seen, though – nothing to be done but flirt, feast and dance in the magnificent saloons. Do you remember what an odd sensation was experienced when, by chance, we caught a glimpse of external objects while the cars were in full flight? Everything seemed unique – in one mass. For my part, I cannot say but that I preferred the traveling by the slow train of a hundred miles the hour. Here we were permitted to have glass windows – even to have them open – and something like a distinct view of the country was attainable. . . . Pundit says that *the route* for the great Kanadaw railroad must have been in some measure marked out about nine hundred years ago![16] In fact, he goes so far as to assert that actual traces of a road are still discernible – traces referable to a period quite as remote as that mentioned. The track, it appears, was *double* only; ours, you know, has twelve paths; and three or four new ones are in preparation. The ancient rails were very slight, and placed so close together as to be, according to modern notions, quite frivolous, if not dangerous in the extreme. The present width of track – fifty feet – is considered, indeed, scarcely secure enough. For my part, I make no doubt that a track of some sort *must* have existed in very remote times, as Pundit asserts; for nothing can be clearer, to my mind, than that, at some period – not less than seven centuries ago, certainly – the Northern and Southern Kanadaw continents were *united*; the Kanawdians, then, would have been driven, by necessity, to a great railroad across the continent.

April 5. – I am almost devoured by ennui. Pundit is the only conversible person on board; and he, poor soul! can speak of nothing but antiquities. He has been occupied all the day in the attempt to convince me that the ancient Amriccans *governed themselves!* – did ever anybody hear of such an absurdity? –

that they existed in a sort of every-man-for-himself confederacy, after the fashion of the 'prairie dogs' that we read of in fable. He says that they started with the queerest idea conceivable, viz: that all men are born free and equal – this in the very teeth of the laws of *gradation* so visibly impressed [17] upon all things both in the moral and physical universe. Every man 'voted', as they called it – that is to say, meddled with public affairs – until, at length, it was discovered that what is everybody's business is nobody's, and that the 'Republic' (so the absurd thing was called) was without a government at all. It is related, however, that the first circumstance which disturbed, very particularly, the self-complacency of the philosophers who constructed this 'Republic', was the startling discovery that universal suffrage gave opportunity for fraudulent schemes, by means of which any desired number of votes might at any time be polled, without the possibility of prevention or even detection, by any party which should be merely villanous enough not to be ashamed of the fraud. A little reflection upon this discovery sufficed to render evident the consequences, which were that rascality *must* predominate – in a word, that a republican government *could* never be anything but a rascally one. While the philosophers, however, were busied in blushing at their stupidity in not having foreseen these inevitable evils, and intent upon the invention of new theories, the matter was put to an abrupt issue by a fellow of the name of *Mob*,[18] who took everything into his own hands and set up a despotism, in comparison with which those of the fabulous Zeros and Hellofagabaluses [19] were respectable and delectable. This Mob (a foreigner, by the by), is said to have been the most odious of all men that ever encumbered the earth. He was a giant in stature – insolent, rapacious, filthy; had the gall of a bullock with the heart of an hyena and the brains of a peacock. He died, at length, by dint of his own energies, which exhausted him. Nevertheless, he had his uses, as everything has, however vile, and taught mankind a lesson which to this day it is in no danger of forgetting – never to run directly contrary to the natural analogies. As for Republicanism, no analogy could be found for it upon the face of the earth – unless we except the case of the 'prairie dogs', an exception which seems to demonstrate, if anything, that democracy is a very admirable form of government – for dogs.

April 6. – Last night had a fine view of Alpha Lyræ, whose disk, through our captain's spy-glass, subtends an angle of half a degree,[20] looking very much as our sun does to the naked eye on a misty day. Alpha Lyræ, although so *very* much larger than our sun, by the by, resembles him closely as regards its spots,[21] its atmosphere, and in many other particulars. It is only within the last century, Pundit tells me, that the binary relation existing between these two orbs began even to be suspected. The evident motion of our system in the heavens was (strange to say !) referred to an orbit about a prodigious star in the centre of the galaxy. About this star, or at all events about a centre of gravity common to all the globes of the Milky Way and supposed to be near Alcyone in the Pleiades, every one of these globes was declared to be revolving, our own performing the circuit in a period of 117,000,000 of years ! *We*, with our present lights, our vast telescopic improvements and so forth, of course find it difficult to comprehend *the ground* of an idea such as this. Its first propagator was one Mudler.[22] He was led, we must presume, to this wild hypothesis by mere analogy in the first instance; but, this being the case, he should have at least adhered to analogy in its development. A great central orb *was*, in fact, suggested; so far Mudler was consistent. This central orb, however, dynamically, should have been greater than all its surrounding orbs taken together. The question might then have been asked – 'Why do we not see it?' – *we*, especially, who occupy the mid region of the cluster – the very locality *near* which, at least, must be situated this inconceivable central sun. The astronomer, perhaps, at this point, took refuge in the suggestion of non-luminosity; and here analogy was suddenly let fall. But even admitting the central orb non-luminous, how did he manage to explain its failure to be rendered visible by the incalculable host of glorious suns glaring in all directions about it? No doubt what he finally maintained was merely a centre of gravity common to all the revolving orbs – but here again analogy must have been let fall. Our system revolves, it is true, about a common centre of gravity, but it does this in connection with and in consequence of a material sun whose mass more than counterbalances the rest of the system. The mathematical circle is a curve composed of an infinity of straight lines; but this idea of the circle – this idea of it which, in regard to all earthly geometry, we consider as merely the mathematical, in contradistinction from the practical, idea – is, in sober fact, the *practical* conception which alone we have any right to entertain in respect to those Titanic circles with which we have to deal, at least in fancy, when we suppose our system, with its fellows, revolving about a point in the centre of the galaxy. Let the most vigorous of human imaginations but attempt to take a single step towards the comprehension of a circuit so unutterable! It would scarcely be paradoxical to say that a flash of lightning itself, traveling *forever* upon the circumference of this inconceivable circle, would still *forever* be traveling in a straight line. That the path of our sun along such a circumference – that the direction of our system in such an orbit – would, to any human perception, deviate in the slightest degree from a straight line even in a million of years, is a proposition not to be entertained; and yet these ancient astronomers were absolutely cajoled, it appears, into believing that a decisive curvature had become apparent during the brief period of their astronomical history – during the mere point – during the utter nothingness of two or three thousand years! How incomprehensible, that considerations such as this did not at once indicate to them the true state of affairs – that of the binary revolution of our sun and Alpha Lyræ around a common centre of gravity!

April 7. – Continued last night our astronomical amusements. Had a fine view of the five Nepturian asteroids, and watched with much interest the putting up of a huge impost on a couple of lintels in the new temple at Daphnis in the moon.[23] It was amusing to think that creatures so diminutive as the lunarians, and bearing so little resemblance to humanity, yet evinced a mechanical ingenuity so much superior to our own. One finds it difficult, too, to conceive the vast masses which these people handle so easily, to be as light as our reason tells us they actually are.

April 8. – Eureka! Pundit is in his glory.[24] A balloon from

Kanadaw spoke us to-day and threw on board several late papers:
they contain some exceedingly curious information relative to
Kanawdian or rather to Amriccan antiquities. You know, I presume, that laborers have for some months been employed in
preparing the ground for a new fountain at Paradise, the emperor's principal pleasure garden.[25] Paradise, it appears, has been,
literally speaking, an island time out of mind[26] – that is to say,
its northern boundary was always (as far back as any records extend) a rivulet, or rather a very narrow arm of the sea. This
arm was gradually widened until it attained its present breadth –
a mile. The whole length of the island is nine miles; the breadth
varies materially. The entire area (so Pundit says) was, about
eight hundred years ago, densely packed with houses, some of
them twenty stories high; land (for some most unaccountable
reason) being considered as especially precious just in this vicinity. The disastrous earthquake, however, of the year 2050, so
totally uprooted and overwhelmed the town (for it was almost
too large to be called a village) that the most indefatigable of our
antiquarians have never yet been able to obtain from the site
any sufficient data (in the shape of coins, medals or inscriptions)
wherewith to build up even the ghost of a theory concerning the
manners, customs, &c. &c. &c., of the aboriginal inhabitants.
Nearly all that we have hitherto known of them is, that they
were a portion of the Knickerbocker tribe of savages[27] infesting
the continent at its first discovery by Recorder Riker, a knight of
th: Golden Fleece.[28] They were by no means uncivilized, however, but cultivated various arts and even sciences after a fashion
of their own. It is related of them that they were acute in many
respects, but were oddly afflicted with a monomania for building
what, in the ancient Amriccan, was denominated 'churches' – a
kind of pagoda instituted for the worship of two idols that went
by the names of Wealth and Fashion. In the end, it is said, the
island became, nine-tenths of it, church. The women, too, it
appears, were oddly deformed by a natural protuberance of the
region just below the small of the back – although, most unaccountably, this deformity was looked upon altogether in the
light of a beauty. One or two pictures of these singular women

have, in fact, been miraculously preserved. They look very odd, *very* – like something between a turkey-cock and a dromedary.

Well, these few details are nearly all that have descended to us respecting the ancient Knickerbockers. It seems, however, that while digging in the centre of the emperor's garden, (which, you know, covers the whole island,) some of the workmen un-earthed a cubical and evidently chiseled block of granite, weigh-ing several hundred pounds. It was in good preservation, having received, apparently, little injury from the convulsion which en-tombed it. On one of its surfaces was a marble slab with (only think of it!) *an inscription – a legible inscription.* Pundit is in ecstasies. Upon detaching the slab, a cavity appeared, containing a leaden box filled with various coins, a long scroll of names, several documents which appeared to resemble newspapers, with other matters of intense interest to the antiquarian ! There can be no doubt that all these are genuine Amriccan relics belonging to the tribe called Knickerbocker. The papers thrown on board our balloon are filled with fac-similes of the coins, MSS., typography, &c. &c. I copy for your amusement the Knickerbocker inscrip-tion on the marble slab : –

THIS CORNER STONE OF A MONUMENT TO THE
MEMORY OF
GEORGE WASHINGTON,[29]
WAS LAID WITH APPROPRIATE CEREMONIES ON THE
19TH DAY OF OCTOBER, 1847,
THE ANNIVERSARY OF THE SURRENDER OF
LORD CORNWALLIS
TO GENERAL WASHINGTON AT YORKTOWN,
A.D. 1781,
UNDER THE AUSPICES OF THE
WASHINGTON MONUMENT ASSOCIATION OF THE
CITY OF NEW YORK.

This, as I give it, is a verbatim translation done by Pundit himself, so there *can* be no mistake about it. From the few words thus preserved, we glean several important items of knowledge, not the least interesting of which is the fact that a thousand years ago *actual* monuments had fallen into disuse – as was all very proper – the people contenting themselves, as we do now, with a mere indication of the design to erect a monument at some future time; a corner-stone being cautiously laid by itself 'solitary and alone' (excuse me for quoting the great Amriccan poet Benton !)[30] as a guarantee of the magnanimous *intention*. We ascertain, too, very distinctly, from this admirable inscription, the how, as well as the where and the what, of the great surrender in question. As to the *where*, it was Yorktown (wherever that was), and as to the *what*, it was General Cornwallis (no doubt some wealthy dealer in corn). *He* was surrendered. The inscription commemorates the surrender of – what? – why, 'of Lord Cornwallis'. The only question is what could the savages wish him surrendered for. But when we remember that these savages were undoubtedly cannibals, we are led to the conclusion that they intended him for sausage. As to the *how* of the surrender, no language can be more explicit. Lord Cornwallis was surrendered (for sausage) 'under the auspices of the Washington Monument Association' – no doubt a charitable institution for the depositing of corner-stones. – But, Heaven bless me ! what is the matter? Ah ! I see – the balloon has collapsed, and we shall have a tumble into the sea. I have, therefore, only time enough to add that, from a hasty inspection of fac-similes of newspapers, &c., I find that *the* great men in those days among the Amriccans were one John, a smith, and one Zacchary, a tailor.[31]

Good bye, until I see you again. Whether you ever get this letter or not is a point of little importance, as I write altogether for my own amusement. I shall cork the MS. up in a bottle however, and throw it into the sea.

Yours everlastingly,

PUNDITA

Von Kempelen and His Discovery

AFTER the very minute and elaborate paper by Arago,[1] to say nothing of the summary in 'Silliman's Journal',[2] with the detailed statement just published by Lieutenant Maury,[3] it will not be supposed, of course, that in offering a few hurried remarks in reference to Von Kempelen's discovery, I have any design to look at the subject in a *scientific* point of view. My object is simply, in the first place, to say a few words of Von Kempelen himself (with whom, some years ago, I had the honor of a slight personal acquaintance,) since every thing which concerns him must necessarily, at this moment, be of interest; and, in the second place, to look in a general way, and speculatively, at the *results* of the discovery.

It may be as well, however, to premise the cursory observations which I have to offer, by denying, very decidedly, what seems to be a general impression (gleaned, as usual in a case of this kind, from the newspapers,) viz. : that this discovery, astounding as it unquestionably is, is *unanticipated*.

By reference to the 'Diary of Sir Humphry Davy' (Cottle and Munroe, London, pp. 150,) it will be seen at pp. 53 and 82,[4] that this illustrious chemist had not only conceived the idea now in question, but had actually made *no inconsiderable progress, experimentally*, in the very *identical analysis* now so triumphantly brought to an issue by Von Kempelen, who although he makes not the slightest allusion to it, is, *without doubt* (I say it unhesitatingly, and can prove it, if required,) indebted to the 'Diary' for at least the first hint of his own undertaking. Although a little technical, I cannot refrain from appending two passages from the 'Diary', with one of Sir Humphry's equations. [As we have not the algebraic signs necessary, and as the 'Diary' is to be found at the Athenæum Library,[5] we omit here a small portion of Mr Poe's manuscript. – ED.]

The paragraph from the 'Courier and Enquirer', which is now going the rounds of the press, and which purports to claim the invention for a Mr Kissam, of Brunswick, Maine,[6] appears to me, I confess, a little apocryphal, for several reasons; although there is nothing either impossible or very improbable in the statement made. I need not go into details. My opinion of the paragraph is founded principally upon its *manner*. It does not *look* true. Persons who are narrating *facts*, are seldom so particular as Mr Kissam seems to be, about day and date and precise location. Besides, if Mr Kissam actually *did* come upon the discovery he says he did, at the period designated – nearly eight years ago – how happens it that he took no steps, *on the instant*, to reap the immense benefits which the merest bumpkin must have known would have resulted to him individually, if not to the world at large, from the discovery? It seems to me quite incredible that any man, of common understanding, could have discovered what Mr Kissam says he did, and yet have subsequently acted so like a baby – so like an owl – as Mr Kissam *admits* that he did. By-the-way, who *is* Mr Kissam? and is not the whole paragraph in the 'Courier and Enquirer' a fabrication got up to 'make a talk'? It must be confessed that it has an amazingly moon-hoax-y air. Very little dependence is to be placed upon it, in my humble opinion; and if I were not well aware, from experience, how very easily men of science are *mystified*, on points out of their usual range of inquiry, I should be profoundly astonished at finding so eminent a chemist as Professor Draper,[7] discussing Mr Kissam's (or is it Mr Quizzem's?) pretensions to this discovery, in so serious a tone.

But to return to the 'Diary' of Sir Humphry Davy. This pamphlet was *not* designed for the public eye, even upon the decease of the writer, as any person at all conversant with authorship may satisfy himself at once by the slightest inspection of the style. At page 13, for example, near the middle, we read, in reference to his researches about the protoxide of azote :[8] 'In less than half a minute the respiration being continued, diminished gradually and *were* succeeded by analogous to gentle pressure on all the muscles.' That the *respiration* was not 'diminished', is not only clear by the subsequent context, but by the use of the plural, 'were'. The sentence, no doubt, was thus intended : 'In less than half a minute, the respiration [being continued, these feelings] diminished gradually, and were succeeded by [a sensation] analogous to gentle pressure on all the muscles.' A hundred similar instances go to show that the MS. so inconsiderately published, was merely a *rough note-book*, meant only for the writer's own eye; but an inspection of the pamphlet will convince almost any thinking person of the truth of my suggestion. The fact is, Sir Humphry Davy was about the last man in the world to *commit himself* on scientific topics. Not only had he a more than ordinary dislike to quackery, but he was morbidly afraid of *appearing* empirical; so that, however fully he might have been convinced that he was on the right track in the matter now in question, he would never have spoken *out*, until he had every thing ready for the most practical demonstration. I verily believe that his last moments would have been rendered wretched, could he have suspected that his wishes in regard to burning this 'Diary' (full of crude speculations) would have been unattended to; as, it seems, they were. I say 'his wishes', for that he meant to include this note-book among the miscellaneous papers directed 'to be burnt', I think there can be no manner of doubt. Whether it escaped the flames by good fortune or by bad, yet remains to be seen. That the passages quoted above, with the other similar ones referred to, gave Von Kempelen *the hint*, I do not in the slightest degree question; but I repeat, it yet remains to be seen whether this momentous discovery itself (*momentous* under any circumstances,) will be of service or disservice to mankind at large. That Von Kempelen and his immediate friends will reap a rich harvest, it would be folly to doubt for a moment. They will scarcely be so weak as not to '*realize*', in time, by large purchases of houses and land, with other property of *intrinsic* value.

In the brief account of Von Kempelen which appeared in the 'Home Journal', and has since been extensively copied, several misapprehensions[9] of the German original seem to have been made by the translator, who professes to have taken the passage from a late number of the Presburg 'Schnellpost'.[10] '*Viele*' has evidently been misconceived (as it often is,) and what the translator renders by 'sorrows', is probably '*Leiden*', which, in its true version, 'sufferings', would give a totally different complexion to the whole account; but, of course, much of this is merely guess, on my part.

Von Kempelen, however, is by no means 'a misanthrope', in appearance, at least, whatever he may be in fact. My acquaintance with him was casual altogether; and I am scarcely warranted in saying that I know him at all; but to have seen and conversed with a man of so *prodigious* a notoriety as he has attained, or *will* attain in a few days, is not a small matter, as times go.

'The Literary World' speaks of him, confidently,[11] as a *native* of Presburg (misled, perhaps, by the account in the 'Home Journal',) but I am pleased in being able to state *positively*, since I have it from his own lips, that he was born in Utica, in the State of New York, although both his parents, I believe, are of Presburg descent. The family is connected, in some way, with Maelzel, of Automaton-chess-player memory.[12] [If we are not mistaken, the name of the *inventor* of the chess-player was either Kempelen, Von Kempelen, or something like it. – ED.] In person, he is short and stout, with large, *fat*, blue eyes, sandy hair and whiskers, a wide but pleasing mouth, fine teeth, and I think a Roman nose. There is some defect in one of his feet. His address is frank, and his whole manner noticeable for *bonhomie*. Altogether, he looks, speaks and acts as little like 'a misanthrope' as any man I ever saw. We were fellow-sojourners for a week, about six years ago, at Earl's Hotel, in Providence, Rhode Island;[13] and I presume that I conversed with him, at various times, for some three or four hours altogether. His principal topics were those of the day; and nothing that fell from him led me to suspect his scientific attainments. He left the hotel before me, intending to go to New York, and thence to Bremen; it was in the latter city that his great discovery was first made public; or, rather, it was there that he was first suspected of having made it. This is about all that I personally know of the now immortal Von Kempelen; but I have thought that even these few details would have interest for the public.

There can be little question that most of the marvellous rumors afloat about this affair, are pure inventions, entitled to about as much credit as the story of Aladdin's lamp; and yet, in a case of this kind, as in the case of the discoveries in California, it is clear that the truth *may be* stranger than fiction. The following anecdote, at least, is so well authenticated, that we may receive it implicitly.

Von Kempelen had never been even tolerably well off during his residence at Bremen; and often, it was well known, he had been put to extreme shifts, in order to raise trifling sums. When the great excitement occurred about the forgery on the house of Gutsmuth & Co., suspicion was directed towards Von Kempelen, on account of his having purchased a considerable property in Gasperitch Lane,[14] and his refusing, when questioned, to explain how he became possessed of the purchase money. He was at length arrested, but nothing decisive appearing against him, was in the end set at liberty. The police, however, kept a strict watch upon his movements, and thus discovered that he left home frequently, taking always the same road, and invariably giving his watchers the slip in the neighborhood of that labyrinth of narrow and crooked passages known by the flash-name of the 'Dondergat'.[15] Finally, by dint of great perseverance, they traced him to a garret in an old house of seven stories, in an alley called Flatzplatz; and, coming upon him suddenly, found him, as they imagined, in the midst of his counterfeiting operations. His agitation is represented as so excessive that the officers had not the slightest doubt of his guilt. After hand-cuffing him, they searched his room, or rather rooms; for it appears he occupied all the *mansarde*.

Opening into the garret where they caught him, was a closet, ten feet by eight, fitted up with some chemical apparatus, of which the object has not yet been ascertained. In one corner of the closet was a very small furnace, with a glowing fire in it, and on the fire a kind of duplicate crucible – two crucibles connected by a tube. One of these crucibles was nearly full of *lead* in a state of fusion, but not reaching up to the aperture of the tube, which was close to the brim. The other crucible had some liquid in it, which, as the officers entered, seemed to be furiously dissipating in vapor. They relate that, on finding himself taken, Von Kempelen seized the crucibles with both hands (which were encased in gloves that afterwards turned out to be asbestic), and threw the contents on the tiled floor. It was now that they hand-cuffed him; and, before proceeding to ransack the premises, they searched his person, but nothing unusual was found about him, excepting a paper parcel, in his coat pocket, containing what was afterwards ascertained to be a mixture of antimony and some *unknown substance*, in nearly, but not quite, equal proportions. All attempts at analyzing the unknown substance have, so far, failed, but that it will ultimately be analyzed, is not to be doubted.

Passing out of the closet with their prisoner, the officers went through a sort of ante-chamber, in which nothing material was found, to the chemist's sleeping-room. They here rummaged some drawers and boxes, but discovered only a few papers, of no importance, and some good coin, silver and gold. At length, looking under the bed, they saw *a large, common hair trunk, without hinges, hasp, or lock*, and with the top lying carelessly *across* the bottom portion. Upon attempting to draw this trunk out from under the bed, they found that, with their united strength (there were three of them, all powerful men), they 'could not stir it one inch'. Much astonished at this, one of them crawled under the bed, and looking into the trunk, said :

'No wonder we could n't move it – why, it's full to the brim of old bits of brass !'

Putting his feet, now, against the wall, so as to get a good purchase, and pushing with all his force, while his companions pulled with all theirs, the trunk, with much difficulty, was slid out from under the bed, and its contents examined. The supposed brass with which it was filled was all in small, smooth pieces, varying from the size of a pea to that of a dollar; but the pieces were irregular in shape, although all more or less flat – looking, upon the whole, 'very much as lead looks when thrown upon the ground in a molten state, and there suffered to grow cool'. Now, not one of these officers for a moment suspected this metal to be anything *but* brass. The idea of its being *gold* never entered their brains, of course; how *could* such a wild fancy have entered it? And their astonishment may be well conceived, when next day it became known, all over Bremen, that the 'lot of brass' which they had carted so contemptuously to the police office, without putting themselves to the trouble of pocketing the smallest scrap, was not only gold – real gold – but gold far finer than any employed in coinage – gold, in fact, absolutely pure, virgin, without the slightest appreciable alloy !

I need not go over the details of Von Kempelen's confession (as far as it went) and release, for these are familiar to the public. That he has actually realized, in spirit and in effect, if not to the letter, the old chimera of the philosopher's stone, no sane person is at liberty to doubt. The opinions of Arago are, of course, entitled to the greatest consideration; but he is by no means infallible; and what he says of *bismuth*, in his report to the academy, must be taken *cum grano salis*. The simple truth is, that up to this period, *all* analysis has failed; and until Von Kempelen chooses to let us have the key to his own published enigma, it is more than probable that the matter will remain, for years, *in statu quo*. All that yet can fairly be said to be known, is, that '*pure gold can be made at will, and very readily, from lead, in connection with certain other substances, in kind and in proportions, unknown*'.

Speculation, of course, is busy as to the immediate and ultimate results of this discovery – a discovery which few thinking persons will hesitate in referring to an increased interest in the matter of gold generally, by the late developments in California; and this reflection brings us inevitably to another – the exceeding *inopportuneness* of Von Kempelen's analysis. If many were prevented from adventuring to California, by the mere apprehension that gold would so materially diminish in value, on account of its plentifulness in the mines there, as to render the speculation of going so far in search of it a doubtful one – what impression will be wrought *now*, upon the minds of those about to emigrate, and especially upon the minds of those actually in the mineral region, by the announcement of this astounding discovery of Von Kempelen? a discovery which declares, in so many words, that beyond its intrinsic worth for manufacturing purposes, (whatever that worth may be), gold now is, or at least soon will be (for it cannot be supposed that Von Kempelen can *long* retain his secret) of no greater *value* than lead, and of far inferior value to silver. It is, indeed, exceedingly difficult to speculate prospectively upon the consequences of the discovery; but one thing may be positively maintained – that the announcement of the discovery six months ago, would have had material influence in regard to the settlement of California.

In Europe, as yet, the most noticeable results have been a rise of two hundred per cent in the price of lead, and nearly twenty-five per cent in that of silver.

Commentary

> As poet *and* mathematician, he would reason well;
> as mere mathematician, he could not have reasoned
> at all...
>
> 'The Purloined Letter' (1845)

MS. FOUND IN A BOTTLE

First published

Baltimore Saturday Visiter (19 October 1833)

Reprinted

The People's Advocate (Newburyport, Mass., 26 October 1833)
The Gift: A Christmas and New Year's Present for 1836 (Philadelphia, 1835)
Southern Literary Messenger (December 1835)
Tales of the Grotesque and Arabesque (1840), Vol. 1
Broadway Journal (11 October 1845)

Translated

Baudelaire, 'Manuscrit trouvé dans une Bouteille', *Le Pays* (January 1855)

> *Pascal avait son gouffre, avec lui se mouvant.*
> *– Hélas! tout est abîme, – action, désir, rêve,*
> *Parole!*
>
> BAUDELAIRE, *Le Gouffre* (1862)

In July 1833 the *Baltimore Saturday Visiter* announced an open competition: with a prize of $50 for the best short story and of $25 for the best poem. Poe submitted a whole series of stories (possibly six in all) under the general title, *Tales of the Folio Club*. Not only did 'MS. Found in a Bottle' win the main prize but his entire entry received the judges' accolade:

> We cannot refrain from saying that the author owes it to his reputation, as
> well as to the gratification of the community, to publish the entire volume.

These tales are eminently distinguished by a wild, vigorous, and poetical imagination, a rich style, a fertile invention, and varied and curious learning.

His literary bottle had been miraculously retrieved. That prize marked the beginning of Poe's career.

Even then his learning, however, seemed 'various and curious', half solemn, half bantering. He had drawn on *The Rime of the Ancient Mariner* – that was clear. With its porous, worm-eaten timbers, his ghost ship too was a 'skeleton ship':

> Like vessel, like crew! Death and Life-in-Death have diced for the ship's crew, and . . . the latter winneth the ancient Mariner.
>
> Part III

But there is evidence of other debts: to Captain Adam Seaborn's *Symzonia, A Voyage of Discovery* (1820), for example, and Jane Porter's romance, *Sir Edward Seaward's Narrative of His Shipwreck* (1831). Was he then poking fun at Jane Porter and John Cleves Symmes? In part, perhaps. In part he was translating their conventional language into his own symbolic terms: where 'thoughtless touches' upon a sail spread out into the word 'DISCOVERY'; where a split narrator (half sceptic, half neurasthenic) is driven beyond the reach of mechanical reason to rapt

> sensation which will admit of no analysis, to which the lessons of by-gone times are inadequate, and for which I fear futurity itself will offer me no key . . . A new sense – a new entity is added to my soul.

This was the Edgar Allan Poe to be hailed by Dostoyevsky (of *The Double*) and Conrad (of *The Secret Sharer*). But the drive beyond reason, beyond the gadgets of mathematics and obsolete science, inevitably moves beyond intuition, beyond life itself (as the angelic dialogues will show), to 'Life-in-Death'. Announced by 'spiral exhalations', the Flying Dutchman is inevitably whirled past the polar ice, through the polar night, to that ultimate polarization of black and white – issuing in the vortex.

1. (p. 1) 'Qui n'a plus qu'un moment à vivre . . .': 'He who has but a moment to live, no longer has anything to dissimulate.' Philippe Quinault (1635–88) – a suitably obscure but prolific dramatist for Poe to quote – wrote some fourteen opera librettos for Lully. His *Atys*, a *tragédie-opéra* in five acts, was first performed on 10 January 1676.

This supplanted the original epigraph in the *Baltimore Saturday Visiter*: 'A wet sheet and a flowing sea. – Cunningham'.

2. (p. 1) *the Pyrrhonism of my opinions*: Viz, extreme scepticism as taught by Pyrrho of Elis (*c.* 300 B.C.), who argued that the 'attainment' of certain knowledge was impossible, since the contrary of every proposition can be maintained with equal plausibility.

3. (p. 1) *from the port of Batavia ... to the Archipelago of the Sunda islands*: From modern Djakarta, that is, throughout the Indonesian archipelago. The Straits of Sunda divide Java and Sumatra.

4. (p. 2) *We had ... on board coir, jaggeree, ghee*: Coco-nut fibre (for cordage), brown sugar (evaporated from palm sap) and butter (clarified from buffalo's milk). The makeweight of 'opium' was to remain a hall-mark of Poe's imaginary voyages.

5. (p. 2) *the vessel consequently crank*: Zig-zagged, twisted and turned.

6. (p. 2) *the small grabs of the Archipelago*: From Arab *ghurāb*, 'a raven': two-masted coasting vessels.

7. (p. 2) *in apprehending a Simoom*: A misapprehension, possibly, for 'typhoon'. The simoom or simoon is a dry desert wind.

8. (p. 3) *We scudded with frightful velocity before the sea*: Coleridge's *Rime of the Ancient Mariner* haunts and pervades this entire manuscript: 'How a Ship having passed the Line was driven by storms to the cold Country towards the South Pole'

> And now the STORM-BLAST came, and he
> Was tyrannous and strong:
> He struck with his o'ertaking wings,
> And chased us south along . . .

> The ship drove fast, loud roared the blast,
> And southward aye we fled.
>   Part I, lines 41–50

9. (p. 4) *we must have run down the coast of New Holland*: Yet as they scud down the Australian coast into the Antarctic night, 'farther to the southward than any previous navigators', they 'felt great amazement at not meeting with the usual impediments of ice'. For Poe had been reading not only *The Rime of the Ancient Mariner*, but *Symzonia, A Voyage of Discovery* (1820) by one Captain 'Adam Seaborn', possibly the eponymous Symmes himself.

'I declare the earth is hollow and habitable within ... that it is open at the poles' pronounced a manifesto in 1818 to 'all the world'. John Cleves Symmes, its author, had studied the confused mariners' reports of warmer water and contrary migration of birds near the poles to promote one overriding idea: that the earth, formed by rotation, consisted of five concentric spheres with access through 'holes at the Poles'.

Hollow Earthers were as vociferous in the early nineteenth century as Flat Earthers. Whether Poe really believed in 'Symmes's Hole' as it was popularly called, he liked to make play with this idea of the globe as a series of spheres with open drainage, as it were, passing from the outer rim of one down the inner side of another.

10. (p. 5) *the slumbers of the kraken*: This largest of all sea monsters was first mentioned by Erik Pontoppidan, Bishop of Bergen, in his *Natural History of Norway* (1752) – the ultimate source for *A Descent into the Maelström*.

11. (p. 5) *'See! see!' cried he ... 'Almighty God! see! see!'*: cf. the sighting of Coleridge's 'spectre-bark':

> See! see! (I cried) she tacks no more!
> Hither to work us weal;
> Without a breeze, without a tide,
> She steadies with upright keel!
> *Rime of the Ancient Mariner*, Part III, lines 167–70

'But what mainly inspired us with horror and astonishment, was that she bore up under a press of sail in the very teeth of that supernatural sea, and of that ungovernable hurricane.'

12. (p. 8) *they all bore about them the marks of a hoary old age*: This whole company of decrepit, shrivelled ancients seems a multiplication of Coleridge's one lone ancient:

> whose eye is bright,
> Whose beard with age is hoar.
> *Rime of the Ancient Mariner*, Part VII, lines 618–19

cf. Melville's ship of Eld, the *Albatross* with 'her long-bearded look-outs' (*Moby-Dick*, ch. 52).

13. (p. 9) *nearly my own height ... about five feet eight inches*: 'I have seen the captain face to face': for he is exactly Edgar Allan Poe's own height. He is the narrator's mysterious double – a theme to be more explicitly developed in *William Wilson* (1839).

14. (p. 10) *some low peevish syllables of a foreign tongue*: After the stress on 'Discovery', on 'Spanish oak', on obsolete 'mathematical instruments' and a royal 'commission' – Burton R. Pollin argued – is 'there any doubt that the language was Spanish and that this was Christopher Columbus ...?' (*Romance Notes* vol. 12 (1971), p. 336). 'His gray hairs are records of the past, and his grayer eyes are Sybils of the future ...'

15. (p. 10) *fallen columns at Balbec, and Tadmor, and Persepolis*: At Baalbek in Lebanon, at Palmyra (biblical *Tadmor*) in Syria, and at Persepolis – ceremonial capital of Darius I, Xerxes and their successors – in Persia.

16. (p. 10) *stupendous ramparts of ice ... like the walls of the universe*: cf. *The Rime of the Ancient Mariner*:

> And now there came both mist and snow,
> And it grew wondrous cold:
> And ice, mast-high, came floating by,
> As green as emerald.
>
> And through the drifts the snowy clifts
> Did send a dismal sheen:
> Nor shapes of men nor beasts we ken –
> The ice was all between.
>
> Part I, lines 51–8

17. (p. 10) *howling and shrieking ... to the southward with a velocity like the headlong dashing of a cataract*: That shriek, that 'hideous velocity' southward 'into the embraces of the cataract' – reach their fullest and final expression in *The Narrative of Arthur Gordon Pym* (1838), ch. 25.

18. (p. 10) *some exciting knowledge ... whose attainment is destruction*: cf. the end of Baudelaire's *Le Voyage*:

> *Nous voulons, tant ce feu nous brûle le cerveau,*
> *Plonger au fond du gouffre, Enfer ou Ciel, qu'importe?*
> *Au fond de l'Inconnu pour trouver du nouveau!*
>
> This fire so scorches our brain, that we wish
> To plunge into the depths of the gulf, Hell or Heaven, who cares?
> To find something *new* in the depths of the Unknown!

19. (p. 11) *we are whirling dizzily ... round and round the borders of a gigantic amphitheatre*: Though Poe, with his note on Mercator, tries to put us off the trail, this spinning, vertiginous plunge must be into 'Symmes's Hole'. According to Symmes, as it happens, access was

so wide that a voyager 'might pass from the outer side … over the rim and down upon the inner side a great distance before becoming aware of the fact at all'. But Poe's theatrical evocation (of the epigraph) is inevitably resolved in this stagey close.

20. (p. 11) *originally published in 1831*: The 'NOTE' was added in 1845. Either Poe made an error, or – more likely – was deliberately pushing this prize piece back among his twenty-two-year-old juvenilia. 'The Tale … was among the first I ever wrote', he told Beverley Tucker. 'Generally, people praise extravagantly those of which I am ashamed …' (Richmond: 1 December 1835)

Select Bibliography

JOHN C. GUILDS, JR, 'Poe's "MS. Found in a Bottle": A Possible Source', *Notes and Queries* vol. 201 (1956), p. 452

FRANZ H. LINK, ' "Discovery" und "Destruction" … "MS. Found in a Bottle" ', *Die neueren Sprachen* (1961), pp. 27–38

DONALD B. STAUFFER, 'The Two Styles of Poe's Ms. Found in a Bottle', *Style* vol. 2 (1967), pp. 107–20

BURTON R. POLLIN, 'Poe's Use of Material from Bernardin De Saint-Pierre's *Etudes*', *Romance Notes* vol. 12 (1971), pp. 331–8

THE UNPARALLELED ADVENTURE OF
ONE HANS PFAALL

First Published

Southern Literary Messenger (June 1835)

Reprinted

New York *Transcript* (2–5 September 1835), as 'Lunar Discoveries, Extraordinary Aerial Voyage by Baron Hans Phaall'
Tales of the Grotesque and Arabesque (1840), Vol. 2

Translated

Alphonse Borghers, 'L'Aéronaute hollandais',* *Revue brittanique* 1843).
(September 1852).
Baudelaire, 'Aventure sans pareille d'un certain Hans Pfaall', *Le Pays* (March–April 1855).

---

* With a gratuitous pun on Wagner's *Der fliegende Holländer* (Dresden, 1843).

The 'Unparalleled Adventure' is that of a bankrupt bellows-mender on his dream flight to escape from debt and to mangle his creditors. But the fantasy is also a private confessional. This April Fool's Day ascent is self-consciously Poe's own alcoholic send-up: of a Grub Street hack, carried off by his own hot air – in a balloon made of foolscap in the shape of a fool's cap – floating effortlessly into remote and rarified regions of speculation far removed from the clutches of his creditors.

There are two modes of discussion, he maintained, ascent and descent. We can recognize the distinction as, in some measure, respectively corresponding with the manic and the depressive phases of his imagination. Predominantly, the phase is depressive; and then the mode is descendent, a downward movement, a dying fall. Yet there are occasions when the trend veers upward . . .*

But here the very name of this dreamer who rises upward has a dying 'fall': its phallic sound suggesting both erection and detumescence.

Lucian wrote his *True History* to parody tall tales by contemporary travellers (now lost) like Ctesias, Iambulus, Antonius Diogenes; Poe would write his as a burlesque on the vogue for romantic escapades to the moon. What opens as a satirical 'grotesque', then, grows into an imaginative 'arabesque'.† Yet the hoax, inverted as the foolscap balloon with its rim of tinkling bells, cuts all ways: at the expense of the toy-town Dutch; at the expense of Sir John Herschel's algebraic equations; at the expense of George Tucker, professor at his own University (and immediate target); at the expense of all lunar exploits devoid of *'verisimilitude'* – that 'effort at *plausibility* in the details of the voyage itself'. If you accept Hans Pfaall's adventures, you are fooled. If you reject them, you must be as thick as those pipe-puffing burghers who decry

the whole business as nothing better than a hoax. But hoax, with these sort of people, is, I believe, a general term for all matters above their comprehension.

Invert 'Phaal', that other variant of his name! What sound do you hear but *'laugh'*?

---

* Harry Levin, *The Power of Blackness* (1958), ch. 4 'Journey to the End of the Night', p. 103.

† To borrow, with Poe, Sir Walter Scott's terminology: 'On the Supernatural in Fictitious Composition', *Foreign Quarterly Review* vol. 1 (July 1827), pp. 60–98.

For Poe had been a keen astronomer since earliest youth. When John Allan, his step-father, in 1825 bought a house with a two-storey portico extending along one side, the sixteen-year-old Edgar had set up his telescope on the upstairs porch to study the stars and beckoning mystery of the moon. According to John H. B. Latrobe (one of the judges of the *Saturday Visiter* prize), Poe in October 1833 was already bursting with lunar schemes:

I was seated at my desk on the Monday following the publication of the tale, when a gentleman entered and introduced himself as the writer, saying that he came to thank me as one of the committee, for the award in his favor. Of this interview, the only one I ever had with Mr Poe, my recollection is very distinct, indeed, – He was if anything, below the middle size, and yet could not be described as a small man. His figure was remarkably good, and he carried himself erect and well, as one who had been trained to it. He was dressed in black, and his frock coat was buttoned to the throat, where it met the black stock, then almost universally worn. Not a particle of white was visible. Coat, hat, boots, and gloves had evidently seen their best days, but so far as mending and brushing go, everything had been done apparently, to make them presentable. On most men his clothes would have looked shabby and seedy, but there was something about this man that prevented one from criticizing his garments, and the details I have mentioned were only recalled afterwards. The impression made, however, was that the award in Mr Poe's favor was not inopportune. *Gentleman* was written all over him. His manner was easy and quiet, and although he came to return thanks for what he regarded as deserving them, there was nothing obsequious in what he said or did. His features I am unable to describe in detail. His forehead was high, and remarkable for the great development at the temple. This was the characteristic of his head, which you noticed at once, and which I have never forgotten. The expression of his face was grave, almost sad, except when he became engaged in conversation, when it became animated and changeable. His voice I remember was very pleasing in its tone and well modulated, almost rhythmical, and his words were well chosen and unhesitating. . . . I asked him whether he was then occupied with any literary labor. He replied that he was then engaged on a voyage to the moon, and at once went into a somewhat learned disquisition upon the laws of gravity, the height of the earth's atmosphere, and capacities of balloons, warming in his speech as he proceeded. Presently, speaking in the first person, he began the voyage, after describing the preliminary arrangements, as you will find them set forth in one of his tales, called 'The Adventures of Hans Phaall', and leaving the earth, and becoming more and more animated, he described his sensation as he ascended higher and higher, until, at last, he reached the point in space where the moon's attraction overcame that of the earth, when there was a sudden *bouleversement* of the car and great confusion among its tenants. By this time the speaker had become so excited, spoke so rapidly, gesticulating much, that when the turn upside-down took place, and he clapped his hands and stamped with his foot by way of emphasis, I was carried along with him, a companion of his äerial journey ... When he had finished his description he apologized for his excitability, which he laughed at himself. The conversation then turned upon other subjects, and soon afterward he took his leave.

Latrobe's account of this interview was given in an address at the Poe Memorial gathering in Baltimore, 17 November 1875. By then he was an elderly, rather unreliable witness.* According to Poe, his inspiration derived from the American edition of Sir John Herschel's *A Treatise on Astronomy* (1834):

I had been much interested in what is there said respecting the possibility of future lunar investigations. The theme excited my fancy, and I longed to give free rein to it in depicting my day-dreams about the scenery of the moon – in short, I longed to write a story embodying these dreams.†

But the day-dreams, the gestation of 'Hans Pfaall', may well have begun before 1833. The actual writing, especially 'the application of scientific principles', seems to date to the years 1834–5. It was then, he claims, he gave up a journalistic hoax (with reports from a new super-telescope) and reluctantly 'fell back upon a style half plausible, half bantering ... resolved to give what interest I could to an actual passage from the earth to the moon, describing the lunar scenery as if surveyed and personally examined by the narrator'.

This *might* just be true. But what Poe is obviously claiming is another 'first'. He could not bear being pipped to the post! And what should appear, three weeks after the publication of 'Hans Pfaall' in the *Southern Literary Messenger*, but the first of a series of articles – 'Discoveries in the Moon' – the hoax of the century – in the New York *Sun*? Supposedly reprinted from the Edinburgh *Courant* and Edinburgh *Journal of Science*, they relayed discoveries 'Lately Made' by Sir John Herschel's new telescope 'at the Cape of Good Hope'. With a magnifying power of 42,000, it could spot objects on the moon a mere eighteen inches in diameter. On 25 August 1835, banner headlines announced Herschel's discovery of life on the moon. Reddish flora had been sighted, 'precisely similar to the *Papaver Rhoeas* or rose-poppy of our sublunary cornfields'. Huge claret-coloured gems

---

* For he patently contradicts another statement, made twenty-three years earlier: 'At my instance he called on me several times, and entered at length into the discussion of subjects on which he proposed to employ his pen ...' (December 1852).

† 'The Literati of New York', *Godey's Lady's Book*, 1846.

were seen; then bison-like creatures with adjustable eye-flaps. On 28 August came the climax: the revelation of furry winged men resembling bats! That issue sold 19,360 copies. The series ended on 31 August when Herschel's lunar observations were cut short by fire. The sun's rays, striking the great lens, had ignited his observatory.

How could Poe, that arch-hoaxer, sit quietly by? Excitedly he wrote to John P. Kennedy:

> Have you seen the 'Discoveries in the Moon'? Do you not think it altogether suggested by *Hans Phaal*? It is very singular, – but when I first purposed writing a Tale concerning the Moon, the idea of *Telescopic* discoveries suggested itself to me – but I afterwards abandoned it. I had however spoken of it freely, & from many little incidents & apparently trivial remarks in those *Discoveries* I am convinced that the idea was stolen from myself.
>
> Richmond: 11 September 1835

In public, however, he did not press the charge, giving Richard Adams Locke the credit of perpetrating a whimsical *coup*: 'decidedly the greatest *hit* in the way of *sensation* – of merely popular sensation – ever made by any similar fiction either in America or in Europe'. But again and again, in exasperation, he returned to the theme. By 1846 it even becomes the excuse for leaving his own 'Unparalleled Adventure' up in the air:

> Having read the Moon story to an end and found it anticipative of all the main points of my 'Hans Phaall', I suffered the latter to remain unfinished. The chief design in carrying my hero to the moon was to afford him an opportunity of describing the lunar scenery, but I found that he could add very little to the minute and authentic account of Sir John Herschel. The first part of 'Hans Phaall', occupying about eighteen pages of 'The Messenger', embraced merely a journal of the passage between the two orbs and a few words of general observation on the most obvious features of the satellite; the second part will most probably never appear. I did not think it advisable even to bring my voyager back to his parent earth. He remains where I left him, and is still, I believe, 'the man in the moon'.

Yet Poe was too hard on his '*jeu d'esprit*'. After the flood of recent words from Houston and Apollo spacecraft, who would not prefer another Hans Pfaall, astronaut, to his American successors? Though occasionally there have been echoes of that intense, imagined tone. Major Alfred M. Worden of Apollo 15, for one, in lunar orbit:

> My impression of living inside that vehicle, particularly the days when I was in there by myself, was one of floating free. I guess it would be almost like riding in a free air balloon, floating over the countryside. There's nothing pushing you. There is no noise, no sound . . . You have no sensation of

motion unless you look down and see the lunar landscape sweeping below you. At times, I thought of myself as a bird seemingly detached from all that is below.

The only time you're really aware of the fact that you're orbiting the moon is when you're on the front side and can see the surface. When you cross the ninth terminator, the sunset terminator – the point which divides light from darkness – and you get past it, you lose the reflective light from the earth, and it's just as black as you can imagine. In fact, you can't see anything.

The only way you know the moon is there is that its horizon cuts off the full view of the stars. So you can see a distinct difference. You can see the star field, and then you see the circular cut-out of the star field, which is the lunar horizon. And there is nothing but blackness below there. You sort of lose the sense of reality of being in lunar orbit when the moon is dark like that. You could be anywhere.

As you get close to the terminator you begin to see a few of the peaks lighted in front of you, and everything else is black. As you get closer and closer to it, you begin to see just a little more light, and a little more light, and then suddenly – bang! – everything is lit.

But then Major Worden did not fully share Colonel David R. Scott's or Colonel James B. Irwin's experience. Though circling the moon, he was no nearer those lunar Apennines than Edgar Allan Poe.

1. (p. 12) *of One Hans Phaall*: With an echo of 'fall' and 'phallus' and 'fail'. For the sound, above all, seems to matter. The spelling underwent at least four metamorphoses: 'Phaal', 'Pfaal', 'Pfaall', and 'Phaall'.

Marie Bonaparte pointed to the German root *phahl*, meaning 'stake'; Edmund Reiss, to the Latin *follis*, meaning 'bellows' (for a bellows-mender), late Latin 'windbag', French *fou*, English *fool* (for this foolscap balloon).

But a touch of sexual clowning seems also to have been intended. In 'A Tale of Jerusalem', for example, the puerile but quite legitimate name for the high priest, Abel-Shittim (*Saturday Courier*, 1832), on republication became Abel-Phittim (1836). So too in 'Lionizing' (1835) the Shandean joke on noses and inflated reputations, with its phallic innuendo, was later revised or deleted (1840). A kind of bashful obscenity is a hallmark of Poe's earliest style.

2. (p. 12) *'With a heart of furious fancies ...'*: (*Wit and Drollery*, 1661). The epigraph derived most probably from Isaac D'Israeli's chapter on 'Tom o' Bedlams' in *Curiosities of Literature* (1832). The complete stanza, properly set, reads:

> With a heart of furious fancies,
>   Whereof I am commander:
>   With a burning spear,
>   And a horse of air,
>   To the wilderness I wander;
> With a knight of ghosts and shadows,
>   I summoned am to Tourney:
>   Ten leagues beyond
>   The wide world's end;
>   Methinks it is no journey!

The stanza haunted Poe. He recalled it, fourteen years later, at the time of the California gold rush:

> And, as his strength
> Failed him at length
> He met a pilgrim shadow –
> 'Shadow,' said he,
> 'Where can it be –
> This land of Eldorado?'

> 'Over the Mountains
> Of the Moon,
> Down the Valley of the Shadow,
> Ride, boldly ride,'
> The shade replied, –
> 'If you seek for Eldorado!'
>   *Eldorado* (1849)

Insolvency and lunar escapades went hand in hand. But what once he had inflated with a zany bric-a-brac of prose burlesque was now reduced to the barest parable of the romantic dreamer on the shadow-line of death.

3. (p. 13) *not even the burgomaster Mynheer Superbus Von Underduk*: Awaiting this lunar Rip Van Winkle on his return. The Knickerbocker-type humour is heavily indebted to Washington Irving.

4. (p. 13) *sheep-bells ... to the tune of Betty Martin*: No tune, but the English proverb: 'That's all my eye, and Betty Martin!' Viz humbug, nonsense.

5. (p. 14) *vrow Grettel Pfaall*: Dutch, *vrouw*, German *Frau*: a Grettel for the absentee Hans.

6. (p.14) *He could not have been more than two feet in height*: This lunar Lilliputian has some lunatic link with the Dutch farce of 'long

speeches, and radicalism' – and thus with Jacksonian Democracy in that 'incomprehensible connection between each particular individual in the moon, with some particular individual on the earth ...' (p. 351, note 36).

See H. Allen Greer, 'Poe's "Hans Pfaall" and the Political Scene', *Emerson Society Quarterly* vol. 60 (1970), pp. 67–73.

7. (p. 14) *His feet, of course, could not be seen at all*: Though Pfaall's *alter ego*, or lunar double, was originally endowed with a diabolic tail. The 1835 text continued: 'although a horny substance of suspicious nature was occasionally protruded through a rent in the bottom of the car, or, to speak more properly, in the top of the hat'.

8. (p. 17) *written either by Professor Encke of Berlin, or by a Frenchman*: Johann Franz Encke, renowned for measurements, based on the transits of Venus, of the earth's distance from the sun. Encke's Comet (p. 28), though discovered by J. L. Pons of Marseilles in 1818, was named after the German astronomer who calculated its orbit and accurately predicted the date of its return.

There were two noted astronomers called 'Encke' at the time and a third 'of somewhat similar name', L. Hencke.

9. (p. 18) *a cousin from Nantz*: A non-existent town, whose very spelling seems deliberately non-Dutch.

10. (p. 18) *all the force, the reality ... of instinct or intuition*: The 1835 text continued:

In other words, I believed, and still do believe, that truth is frequently, of its own essence, superficial, and that, in many cases, the depth lies more in the abysses where we seek her, than in the actual situations wherein she may be found. Nature herself seemed to afford me corroboration of these ideas. In the contemplation of the heavenly bodies it struck me very forcibly that I could not distinguish a star with nearly as much precision, when I gazed upon it with earnest, direct, and undeviating attention, as when I suffered my eye only to glance in its vicinity alone. I was not, of course, at that time aware that this apparent paradox was occasioned by the centre of the visual area being less susceptible of feeble impressions of light than the exterior portions of the retina. This knowledge, and some of another kind, came afterwards in the course of an eventful period of five years, during which I have dropped the prejudices of my former humble situation in life, and forgotten the bellows-mender in far different occupations. But at the epoch of which I speak, the analogy which the casual observation of a star offered to the conclusions I had already drawn, struck me with the force of positive confirmation, and I then finally made up my mind to the course which I afterwards pursued.

Transferred to Poe's master detective Dupin, this passage became part of 'The Murders in the Rue Morgue' (1841).

11. (p. 19) *cambric muslin, very fine*: Fine linen, literally from Cambrai.

12. (p. 19) *a* particular metallic substance ... a very common acid: Poe may well be recalling *Symzonia: A Voyage of Discovery* (1820) by 'Adam Seaborn' – soon to be developed in *The Narrative of Arthur Gordon Pym*. For the Symzonians, inhabitants of the hollow earth, fly enormous cylindrical balloons filled 'with an elastic gas, which was readily made by putting a small quantity of a very dense substance into some fluid, which disengaged a vast quantity of this light gas' (p. 114).

cf. also p. 352, note 43.

13. (p. 19) a constituent of azote: Lavoisier's name for nitrogen, as 'unable to sustain life'.

14. (p. 20) *the apparatus for condensation of the atmospheric air*: Joseph Priestley's experiments were well known and illustrations of such air-pumps a commonplace in physics text books.

15. (p. 22) *so dense a hurricane of fire, and gravel, and burning wood*: The pioneer exploits of ballooning were led by a series of French spectaculars – pyrotechnic displays, hydrogen lift-offs, and manned air-probes. In 1773 the Montgolfier brothers first experimented with inverted paper bags filled with heated air. But 1783 was the *annus mirabilis*. On 5 June, near Lyons, the Montgolfier brothers lifted a linen bag, about 100 ft in diameter, into the air by burning straw; the bag drifted more than a mile in ten minutes. In September, in a demonstration before the court at Versailles, Pilâtre de Rozier made the first aerial ascent by man in a hot-air-filled captive (or tied) balloon. Soon after J. A. C. Charles in a hydrogen balloon, known as the *Charlière*, made an ascent of almost two miles (over 10,000 ft). With the Robert brothers he completed a balloon journey of twenty-seven miles.

The first ascent in Britain was made in a 'Montgolfière' a year later, from Edinburgh, by that brilliant encyclopedist and Grub Street hack (another failure like Pfaall), James Tytler. 'The schemes of transporting people through the atmosphere', he announced in the prospectus for his ascent, 'formerly thought chimerical, are realized; and it is impossible to say how far the art of aerial navigation may be improved, or with what advantages it may be attended.' (August 1784)

The more celebrated ascent by Vincenzo Lunardi in a hydrogen balloon was made from Moorfields, London, in September.

Poe was himself living in Baltimore when Charles Ferson Durant made a ballon ascent from Federal Hill on 26 September 1833, followed by a second three weeks later, on 14 October. Durant was the first professional American aeronaut. He constructed his own home-made balloon in Jersey City, trying to rouse interest in ballooning as a means of transportation. From 1830 to 1837 he made thirteen ascents in all. Six were from Castle Garden, New York City. In Chesapeake Bay he landed on the deck of the steamship *Independence*. On the last of three ascents from Boston Common, he sailed out beyond the harbour in one air current and returned on another, remaining up about two hours, at a height of 8,000 ft. No one – let alone Poe – could have missed reports of these feats, described in newspapers from New York, Boston and Philadelphia to London and Paris.

The altitude record for manned balloons, established in 1935, is 72,395 ft.

16. (p. 23) *left me dangling ... by a piece of slender cord*: The aeronaut W. W. Sadler (C. D. Laverty notes) was thrown from his car by a sudden jerk of the balloon and for a short time 'was suspended to the car by one leg' (*Scots Magazine* vol. 94, 1824, p. 631).

17. (p. 26) *Now, the mean or average interval ... is 59.9643 of the earth's equatorial* radii: About ten years later Poe was openly naming his source:

the Harpers had issued an American edition of Sir John Herschel's 'Treatise on Astronomy', and I had been much interested in what is there said respecting the possibility of future lunar investigations. The theme excited my fancy, and I longed to give free rein to it in depicting my day-dreams about the scenery of the moon . . .

'The Literati of New York: Richard Adams Locke'
Godey's Lady's Book (1846)

This whole calculation of the distance between the earth and moon, mistakes and all, is adapted from *A Treatise on Astronomy* (Philadelphia, 1834), pp. 203–5. Where Sir John errs, expressing the eccentricity of an ellipse as a fraction of 'the major semi-axis', so does Poe.

The whole of the next long paragraph too, debating a steady ratio between the height of ascent and the rarefaction of air (from 'Cotopaxi' to 'Gay-Lussac and Biot') paraphrases Herschel's *Treatise*, pp. 27–9.

18. (p. 27) *at 18,000, which is not far from the elevation of Cotopaxi*: Volcano in Ecuador, *c.* 19,344 ft.

19. (p. 27) *in the aeronautic expedition of Messieurs Gay-Lussac and Biot*: In August 1804 Joseph Louis Gay-Lussac and Jean-Baptiste Biot made a balloon ascent, but they reached a mere 3,400 metres. A few days later, alone, Gay-Lussac made a second ascent that reached a height of *c.* 7,016 metres (more than 23,000 ft). Cruising from Paris to Rouen, he tested the variations in the earth's magnetic field and the composition of the atmosphere at varying altitudes.

20. (p. 28) *The lenticular-shaped phenomenon*: Lentil-shaped, having the form of a double-convex lense. cf. of our Galaxy: 'we must picture to ourselves a lenticular star-island' (*Eureka*, p. 277). The phrase is excerpted from Herschel's *Treatise*, p. 380.

21. (p. 29) *The zodiacal light ... called Trabes*: This quotation from Pliny's *Natural History* is the first of numerous excerpts from Rees's *Cyclopaedia* (1819). See p. 350, note 32.

The account of the 'arrivals of Encke's comet at its perihelion' and M. Valz's hypothesis are again paraphrased from Herschel's *Treatise*, pp. 291 and 293.

22 (p. 30) *Mr Green, of Nassau-balloon notoriety*: cf. 'whose voyage from Dover to Weilburg in the balloon, "Nassau", occasioned so much excitement in 1837' ('The Balloon-Hoax', p. 112, introduction and p. 372, note 11). Charles Green made two high-altitude ascents: one to 19,335 ft; another to 27,146 ft.

23. (p. 32) *The convex surface of any segment of a sphere ... a sixteen-hundredth part of the whole surface of the globe*: Another piece of astronomical wizardry derived from Herschel's *Treatise*, pp. 27–8.

24. (p. 35) *The view of the earth ... was beautiful indeed*: cf. Michael Collins on Apollo 11 in 1969:

It's really a fantastic sight through that sextant. A minute ago, during that automaneuver, the reticle swept across the Mediterranean. You could see all of North Africa absolutely clear, all of Portugal, Spain, southern France, all of Italy absolutely clear. Just a beautiful sight.

Norman Mailer, *A Fire on the Moon* (1970), p. 257

25. (p. 35) *What mainly astonished me ... was the seeming concavity of the surface of the globe*: cf. Mark Twain on the extinct volcano, Haleakala, in the Hawaiian Islands:

It was curious; and not only curious, but aggravating; for it was having

348

our trouble all for nothing, to climb ten thousand feet toward heaven and then have to look *up* at our scenery . . . Formerly, when I had read an article in which Poe treated of this singular fraud perpetrated upon the eye by isolated great altitudes, I had looked upon the matter as an invention of his own fancy.

Roughing It (1872), ch. 76

26. (p. 41) *vast meadows of poppies . . . with a boundary-line of clouds*: This opium-like reverie originally continued:

And out of this melancholy water arose a forest of tall eastern trees, like a wilderness of dreams. And I bore in mind that the shadows of the trees which fell upon the lake remained not on the surface where they fell – but sunk slowly and steadily down, and commingled with the waves, while from the trunks of the trees other shadows were continually coming out, and taking the place of their brothers thus entombed. 'This, then,' I said thoughtfully, 'is the very reason why the waters of this lake grow blacker with age, and more melancholy as the hours run on.'

The passage was incorporated in 'The Island of the Fay' (1841).

27. (p. 41) *an awkward accident . . . occasioned me the loss of my little family of cats*: This perverse experiment with 'the old puss' – to be elaborated in 'The Black Cat' (1843) – are the troubled dreams of a fond cat-lover, haunted by Catterina, his own tortoiseshell.

28. (p. 46) *I undoubtedly beheld the whole of the earth's major diameter*: This is false, since from no finite distance can as much as half the surface of a sphere be surveyed.

29. (p. 47) *a circular centre . . . at all times darker than any other spot upon the visible hemisphere*: This aeronaut view of the North Pole as a black *concave* circle can only refer to John Cleves Symmes's theory of gigantic whirlpools, or holes at the Poles. According to Symmes the diameter of the North Hole was four thousand miles; that of the South, six thousand.

30. (p. 52) *covered with innumerable volcanic mountains, conical in shape*: cf. Apollo 11:

SPACECRAFT: We're about 95 degrees east, coming up on Smyth's Sea . . . Sort of hilly-looking area . . . looking back at Marginus . . . Crater Schubert and Gilbert in the centre now . . . a triple crater between the first and second, and the one at the bottom of the screen is Schubert Y . . . Zooming in now on a crater called Schubert N . . . a very conical inside wall . . . coming up on the Bombing Sea . . . Alpha 1 . . . a great bright crater. It is not a large one but an extremely bright one. It looks like a very recent and I would guess impact crater with rays streaming out in all directions . . . The crater in the centre of the screen now is Webb . . . coming back toward the bottom of the screen into the left, you can see a series of depressions. It is this type of connective craters that give us most interest . . .

CAPCOM: We are getting a beautiful picture of Langrenus now with its really conspicuous central peak.

Norman Mailer, *A Fire on the Moon* (1970), p. 307

31. (p. 52) *the Campi Phlegraei*: (in Sir John Herschel's phrase) sulphurous plain between Puteoli and Naples: the modern *Solfarata*.

Hans Pfaall tumbles on to the moon on 19 April – the very date Poe had noted in this jotting:

Ap. 19, 1787, Dr Herschel discovered 3 volcanoes in the dark part of the moon. 2 of them seemed to be almost extinct, but the 3rd showed an actual eruption of fire, or luminous matter, resembling a small piece of burning charcoal covered by a very thin coat of white ashes: it had a degree of brightness about as strong as that with which such a coal would be seen to glow in faint daylight. The adjacent parts of the mountain seemed faintly illuminated by the eruption.

'Unpublished Notes', *Works*, Vol. 16, p. 353

32. (p. 52) *certain observations of Mr Schroeter, of Lilienthal*: The scholarly reference to 'the eighty-second volume of the Philosophical Transactions' seems to indicate the source. But Poe, as usual, likes to indulge in a masquerade of learning. Most details of these observations and computations are to be found in an article by John Jerome Schroeter in the *Philosophical Transactions of the Royal Society of London* (Vol. 82, part 2, article 16). Poe himself, however, derived them – less magisterially – from Abraham Rees, *The Cyclopaedia or Universal Dictionary of Arts and Sciences, and Literature* (London, 1819), under the heading 'Moon, Nature and Furniture of the'.

Poe's notes and jottings from Rees's *Cyclopaedia*, used for the 1840 edition of 'Hans Pfaall', were mistakenly appended by James Harrison to *Eureka* (*Works*, Vol. 16, pp. 347–54). There too appear the first drafts of the footnote on Hevelius and Cassini.

33. (p. 55) *I tumbled headlong . . . into the middle of a vast crowd of ugly little people*: Thus following the example of *Somnium* (1634), that witty exposition of lunar climate and landscape as revealed by telescope. For Kepler too introduced live creatures – fur-coated primeval beings, able to bear the harsh extremes of temperature.

34. (p. 55) *gazing upwards at the earth . . . fixed immovably in the*

heavens: cf. Sir John Herschel: 'If there be inhabitants in the moon, the earth must present to them the extraordinary appearance of a moon of nearly 2° in diameter, exhibiting the same phases as we see the moon to do, but *immoveably fixed in their sky . . .*' (*A Treatise on Astronomy*, p. 220).

35 (p. 55) *I have much to say of the climate of the planet*: Though again copied word for word from Herschel's *Treatise*: 'by distillation like that *in vacuo . . .*' (pp. 218–19).

36. (p. 56) *of the incomprehensible connection between each particular individual*: What in Tucker's satiric account is a wholly comprehensible diagnosis of lunacy:

> The inhabitants of the moon resembled those of the earth, in form, stature, features, and manners, and were evidently of the same species . . . a large number of them were born without any intellectual vigour, and wandered about . . . until they were illuminated with the mental ray from some earthly brains, by means of the mysterious influence which the moon is known to exercise on our planet. But in this case the inhabitant of the earth loses what the inhabitant of the moon gains – the ordinary portion of understanding allotted to one mortal being thus divided between two; and, as might be expected, seeing that the two minds were originally the same, there is a most exact conformity between the man on the earth and his counterpart in the moon.

> > *A Voyage to the Moon* (1827), pp. 37–8

37. (p. 58) NOTE: Added in 1840 for inclusion in *Tales of the Grotesque and Arabesque*.

In his own note, Baudelaire 'analyzes' Poe's 'very strange postscript' to 'show the reader that this publication involved one of the childish aspects of this great genius':

> The reader may smile, – discovering Poe's juvenile *dadas*, I have smiled more than once myself. Will not the petty aspects of the great always be a touching spectacle for an impartial mind? It is truly strange to see a mind sometimes so profoundly Germanic and sometimes so deeply Oriental, betray on occasion the Americanism with which it is saturated.

38. (p. 58) *the celebrated 'Moon-Story' of Mr Locke*: Which rankled and rankled. Poe simply could not let the matter drop. Six years later, he again took up the charge:

> Immediately on the completion of the 'Moon story', (it was three or four days in getting finished,) I wrote an examination of its claims to credit, showing distinctly its fictitious character, but was astonished at finding that I could obtain few listeners, so really eager were all to be deceived, so magical

were the charms of a style that served as the vehicle of an exceedingly clumsy invention.

Godey's Lady's Book (1846)

39. (p. 60) *Peter Wilkins' account ... of his flying islanders*: In Robert Paltock, *The Life and Adventures of Peter Wilkins. A Cornish Man* (1751). A stage version, *Peter Wilkins' Flying Islanders*, first performed in New York in 1827, had been elaborately revived in October 1840.

40. (p. 61) *The Earl of Ross telescope, lately constructed in England*: Poe was more than up to date. Two *specula*, each 6 ft in diameter, 4 tons in weight, and of 54 ft focus, were cast after various failures, in 1842 and 1843. Mounted in his park at Parsonstown (now Birr), Eire, the Earl of Rosse's telescope was the largest of its time. Observations with it were begun in February 1845. See *Eureka*, p. 269.

41. (p. 61) *'L'Homme dans la lvne ...' of one Mr D'Avisson*: Not of a Mr Davidson, but Bishop Francis Godwin's *The Man in the Moone: or a Discourse of a Voyage thither. By Domingo Gonsales The Speedy Messenger* (London, 1638). The French translator was Jean Baudoin – J[ean] B[au] D[oin], not 'J.B.D.A.' Both Poe and Jules Verne used this 1648 edition in the belief, shared by many, that the work was French.

42. (p. 63) *That of Bergerac is utterly meaningless*: Since he ascends by the suction of dew or blast of firecrackers and descends in the arms of a spirit. Originally entitled *Histoire comique ou Voyage dans la Lune* (1650), Cyrano de Bergerac's celebrated work became *Histoire comique des Etats et Empires de la Lune* in the authorized edition of 1656.

43. (p. 64) *In the third volume of the 'American Quarterly Review' ... I forget the title of the work*: What a self-conscious clue! Poe recalls anonymous 'criticism' in the *American Quarterly Review* vol. 3 (March 1828), pp. 61–88, though the straightforward title, *A Voyage to the Moon* (1827) apparently escapes him. Yet the pseudonym 'Joseph Atterley' – whether Poe knew this or not – disguised one of his own university teachers, George Tucker, first professor of moral philosophy at the University of Virginia. Close comparison not only with the review but Tucker's book suggests that Hans Pfaall, at any rate, was aware of certain debts. His machine for the condensation of air, his use of a *'metallic substance'* (the despised *lunarium* of the original) as well as the *'bouleversement'* of his balloon on passing

from the earth's field of gravity to that of the moon – all seem to derive from Tucker.

44. (p. 64) *The 'Flight of Thomas O'Rouke'*:

In April 1786 M. Uncles made a public announcement that he was training 'four harnessed eagles, perfectly tame, and capable of flying in every direction at their master's will', to be attached to a balloon. As late as 1835, a letter written to the *Morning Advertiser* by Thomas Simmons Mackintosh continued to suggest the possibility of using hawks or eagles to direct balloons.

Marjorie Hope Nicolson, *Voyages to the Moon*, p. 70

Select Bibliography

M. N. POSEY, 'Notes on Poe's "Hans Pfaal"', *Modern Language Notes* vol. 45 (1930), pp. 501–7

MARJORIE NICOLSON, *A World in the Moon: A Study of the Changing Attitude toward the Moon in the Seventeenth and Eighteenth Centuries*, Smith College Studies in Modern Languages vol. 17 (1936), pp. 1–72

MARJORIE NICOLSON, *Voyages to the Moon* (New York: Macmillan, 1948)

J. O. BAILEY, 'Sources of Poe's *Arthur Gordon Pym*, "Hans Pfaal" and Other Pieces', *Publications of the Modern Language Association* vol. 57 (1942), pp. 513–35

C. P. WYLIE, 'Mathematical Allusions in Poe', *Science Monthly* vol. 63 (1946), pp. 227–35

EDMUND REISS, 'The Comic Setting of "Hans Pfaal"', *American Literature* vol. 29 (1957), pp. 306–9

RONALD WILKINSON, 'Poe's "Hans Pfaal" Reconsidered', *Notes and Queries* vol. 13 (1966), pp. 333–7

WILLIAM H. GRAVELY, JR, 'A Note on the Composition of Poe's Hans Pfaal', *Poe Newsletter* vol. 3 (1970), pp. 2–5

DAVID KETTERER, 'Poe's Use of the Hoax and the Unity of "Hans Pfaall"', *Criticism* vol. 13 (1971), pp. 377–85

THE CONVERSATION OF EIROS AND CHARMION

First Published

Burton's Gentleman's Magazine (December 1839)

Reprinted

Tales of the Grotesque and Arabesque (1840), Vol. 2
Saturday Museum (1 April 1843), as 'The Destruction of the World'
Tales (1845)

Translated

Isabelle Meunier, 'Fragments d'Eiros et Charmion', *La Démocratie pacifique* (July 1847)
Baudelaire, 'Entretien d'Eiros avec Charmion', *Le Pays* (July 1854)

The style is that of a Platonic dialogue, but instead of logical thrust and counter-thrust, all is speculation, pedantry, melodrama: apocalypse rationalized by equating biblical prophecy with recent advances in physics and chemistry.

1. (p. 65) *Eiros and Charmion*: The names of Cleopatra's two attendants in Shakespeare's *Antony and Cleopatra*. But Poe's source seems to be Dryden rather than Shakespeare. For in all Shakespearean texts the spelling is 'Charmian' and 'Iras'. Dryden, in *All for Love*, like Plutarch, used the correct form 'Charmion'. But why Eiros? that is the question. 'Why do you call me Eiros?'

Poe had quoted from Dryden's prologue in the introductory letter to his *Poems* (1831). He had already used the same names in recounting Cleopatra's death in his verse drama, *Politian*:

> Thus endeth the history – and her maids
> Lean over her and weep – two gentle maids
> With gentle names – Eiros and Charmion!
> Scene iv, lines 24–26

2. (p. 65) *I will bring fire to thee*: The epigraph – from Euripides, *Andromache*, 257 – was added in 1845. cf. Poe's self-conscious mockery of Greek quotations seven years earlier:

In a Blackwood article nothing makes so fine a show as your Greek. The very letters have an air of profundity about them. Only observe, madam, the astute look of that Epsilon! That Phi ought certainly to be a bishop! Was ever there a smarter fellow than that Omicron? Just twig that Tau! In short, there is nothing like Greek for a genuine sensation-paper.

'How to Write a Blackwood Article', *American Museum* (December 1838)

3. (p. 65) *Why do you call me Eiros?* : Or should it be 'Eiron', in the Greek sense of 'dissimulation'? Is this Poe, the witty hoaxer, lurking at an ironic distance, manipulating his Platonic context, elaborating his Platonic myth with the bantering εἰρωνεία of a Socrates disguised as a disembodied, angelic intelligence?

4. (p. 65) *that mad, rushing, horrible sound, like the 'voice of many waters'* : of St John the Divine's apocalyptic vision:

His head and his hairs were white like wool, as white as snow; and his eyes were as a flame of fire;

And his feet like unto fine brass, as if they burned in a furnace; and his voice as the sound of many waters.

And he had in his right hand seven stars: and out of his mouth went a sharp two-edged sword: and his countenance was as the sun shineth in his strength.

And when I saw him, I fell at his feet as dead. And he laid his right hand upon me, saying unto me, Fear not; I am the first and the last . . .

Revelation i, 14–17

5. (p. 66) *all of pain . . . which you will suffer in Aidenn*: Arabic *Adn* ('Aden', or 'Eden'), the realm of disembodied spirits. Here it is the interstellar, etherial region, literally a 'place of ether', which is also to be the setting for 'The Colloquy of Monos and Una'.

6. (p. 67) *wonders and wild fancies . . . strangely rife among mankind* : The predictions of Father Miller of the end of the world roused great excitement in the 1830s and 1840s. From 1831 on this Deist-turned-Baptist prophesied that the Second Coming would occur in 1843. Many prepared for Doomsday. Then the date was shifted to 1844.

At least 120 camp meetings were held during the summer months of 1842–4 with an estimated attendance of half a million. Signs in the heavens were reported: a meteoric shower, strange rings around the sun, crosses in the sky, a great comet at high noon that for days hung ominously overhead. Expectation became fixed on 22 October 1844. Second Adventists climbed on to their roofs and haystacks in order to be nearer heaven or assembled in cemeteries to be closer to the resurrected dead.

In 1845 Miller founded the Adventist Church. He himself outlived Poe by a dozen years.

7. (p. 67) *the announcement by astronomers of a* new *comet*: Poe, in all probability, saw Halley's Comet in August 1835. The *Edinburgh Review* had published a 47-page article on 'The Approaching Comet'; the *Quarterly Review*, a 39-page preview, 'Astronomy – the Comet'.

But he may well have been thinking of Biela's comet (discovered in 1826), of which Sir John Herschel wrote:

It is a small insignificant comet, without a tail, or any appearance of a solid nucleus whatever. Its orbit, by a remarkable coincidence, very nearly intersects that of the earth; and had the latter, at the time of its passage in 1832, been a month in advance of its actual place, it would have passed through the comet – a singular rencontre, perhaps not unattended with danger.

A Treatise on Astronomy (1834), pp. 291–2

8. (p. 69) *the character of a gigantic mantle of rare flame*: In the early morning of 13 November 1833, a rain of meteors had been visible in Baltimore. 'The intense light ... gave the sky the appearance of sunrise ...' (Col. J. Thomas Scharf, *The Chronicles of Baltimore*, 1874, pp. 465–6).

9. (p. 70) *in the proportion of twenty-one measures of oxygen, and seventy-nine of nitrogen*: These figures are broadly correct for the troposphere – the atmospheric layer closest to the earth.

But this whole passage on 'the principle of combustion' derives almost verbatim from *The Christian Philosopher* (1826) by Dr Thomas Dick. 'Dr Dick ... describes an experiment whereby combustion is seen to follow the total extraction of nitrogen from the air, saying that in all probability that was the method prophesied by the Scriptures for the fiery destruction of our world. Dr Dick suggests that by the aid of chemical apparatus, we can perform experiments "on a *small scale*, similar in kind, though infinitely inferior in degree, to the awful event under consideration"'. (Margaret Alterton, *Origins of Poe's Critical Theory*, 1925, ch. 5, pp. 140–41).

10. (p. 70) *fiery and horror-inspiring denunciations ... of the Holy Book*: cf.

should the Creator issue forth his Almighty fiat – 'Let the nitrogen of the atmosphere be completely separated from the oxygen, and let the oxygen exert its native energies without control, wherever it extends'; – from what we know of its nature, we are warranted to conclude, that instantly a universal conflagration would commence throughout all the kingdoms of nature ...'

Thomas Dick, *The Christian Philosopher*, p. 135

A DESCENT INTO THE MAELSTRÖM

First published
Graham's Lady's and Gentleman's Magazine (May 1841)

Reprinted
Tales (1845)
Boston Museum (26 May 1849)

Translated

Isabelle Meunier, 'Une Descente au Maelstrom', *La Démocratie pacifique* (September 1847)
Baudelaire, 'Une Descente dans le Maelstrom', *Le Pays* (February 1855)

We stand upon the brink of a precipice. We peer into the abyss – we grow sick and dizzy. Our first impulse is to shrink from the danger. Unaccountably we remain . . .

'The Imp of the Perverse' (1845)

This is a tale within a tale: the 'Maelström' is framed. The actual descent, that is, was made by a Norwegian fisherman; turned Ancient Mariner, he tells his tale to the narrator while poised on a great cliff above the Moskoe-ström. Like the Wedding-Guest, the narrator might cry: *

> 'I fear thee, ancient Mariner!
> I fear thy skinny hand!
> And thou art long, and lank, and brown,
> As is the ribbed sea-sand.
>
> I fear thee and thy glittering eye,
> And thy skinny hand, so brown.' –
> Fear not, fear not, thou Wedding-Guest!
> This body dropt not down.

For the vertigo of the one is juxtaposed by the descent of the other; the lure of the abyss, by the fisherman's loss of fear, his 'almost serene contemplation of the impassive Law which brought that fear about.†

---

* Coleridge, *The Rime of the Ancient Mariner*, Part IV, 224–31.
† Camille Mauclair, *Le Genie d'Edgar Poe* (Paris, 1928), p. 123.

Such is *'the well of Democritus'*, as the epigraph from Glanvill suggests. Or, put more simply, as Poe had surely read in *Rees's Cyclopaedia*:

This mode of acquiring certain knowledge he confessed to be very difficult, and, therefore, he used to say that truth lay in a deep well, from which it is the office of reason to draw it up.

1. (p. 72) *'The ways of God in Nature, as in Providence ...'*: From Joseph Glanvill, *Essays on Several Important Subjects in Philosophy and Religion* (1676), p. 15. The original reads:

The *ways* of God in *Nature* (as in *Providence*) are not as *ours* are: Nor are the Models that we frame any way commensurate to the vastness and profundity of his Works; which have a *Depth* in them greater than the *Well of Democritus*.

2. (p. 73) *The mountain upon whose top we sit is Helseggen, the Cloudy*: So too the narrator of 'Le Maelstrom', an anonymous story in *Le Magasin Universel* (April 1836), after the final plunge finds himself on the rocky shore of Mount Helseggen.

This French story (discovered by Arlin Turner) proved to be a free adaptation of a British text: 'The Maelstrom: a Fragment' in *Fraser's Magazine* (September 1834). It is this 'Fragment' (discovered by W. T. Bandy) that seems to have thrown out a challenge to Poe: how to contrive a convincing first-person narrative from such a mysterious 'escape'. It was the kind of enigma Poe could never resist.

3. (p. 73) *the Nubian geographer's account of the* Mare Tenebrarum: The Arab Idrisi, author of the *Kitab Rujjar*, or 'Book of Roger'. cf. 'They who dream by day ... penetrate, however rudderless or compassless, into the vast ocean of the "light ineffable" and again, like the adventurers of the Nubian geographer, "*agressi sunt mare tenebrarum, qui in eo esset exploraturi*".' ('*Eleonora*', 1842).

4. (p. 74) *I became aware of a loud and gradually increasing sound*: Poe may also have read a sea captain's account of the Drontheim (or Trondheim) whirlpool in *Alexander's Weekly Messenger* (10 October 1838).

5. (p. 75) *That of Jonas Ramus ... is perhaps the most circumstantial of any*: Poe's actual working source, open on his desk, was the *Encyclopaedia Britannica* (Third Edition, Edinburgh, 1797), as briefly acknowledged on p. 77. There, among other things, he found the quotation from Jonas Ramus. But what Poe did not realize was

that the whole article (quotations and all) was lifted bodily from an English translation of an original Danish source: Bishop Erik Pontoppidan, *The Natural History of Norway* (1752). It is Pontoppidan who quotes Jonas Ramus. It is Pontoppidan who raises the hypothesis of 'flux and reflux' (p. 77).

6. (p. 87) *See Archimedes*, 'De Incidentibus in Fluido'. – *lib. 2.*: This footnote was inserted in the 1845 edition of *Tales by Edgar A. Poe*. Killis Campbell has pointed out that the work contains nothing directly on the principle proposed ('Marginalia on Longfellow, Lowell, and Poe', *Modern Language Notes* vol. 42, December 1927, p. 520).

The article on 'Whirlpools' in the *Encyclopaedia Britannica* mentions cylindrical objects – specifically a cask – but suggests they be thrown overboard as a kind of decoy or plug to still the whirlpool. Far from being drawn less rapidly into the vortex, Orkney Islanders apparently argue, barrels are sucked immediately into the abyss.

Select Bibliography

ARLIN TURNER, 'Sources of Poe's "A Descent into the Maelström"', *Journal of English and Germanic Philology* vol. 46 (1947), pp. 298–301

W. T. BANDY, 'New Light on a Source of Poe's "A Descent into the Maelström"', *American Literature* vol. 24 (1953), pp. 534–7

MARGARET J. YONCE, 'The Spiritual Descent into the Maelström: A Debt to "The Rime of the Ancient Mariner"', *Poe Newsletter* vol. 2 (1969), pp. 26–9

GERARD M. SWEENEY, 'Beauty and Truth: Poe's "Descent into the Maelström"', *Poe Studies* vol. 6 (1973), pp. 22–5

THE COLLOQUY OF MONOS AND UNA

First Published
Graham's Lady's and Gentleman's Magazine (August 1841)

Reprinted
Tales (1845)

Translated
Baudelaire, 'Colloque entre Monos et Una', *Le Pays* (January 1855)

At long intervals some master-minds appeared, looking upon each advance in practical science as a retro-gradation in the true utility.

Monos, 'death-purged', is now Poe's *alter ego*. For this is Poe's flight from the modern world: that destructive trauma (as he sees it) of the split personality, that Cartesian Jekyll and Hyde of mind and spirit, where the intellect cancerously usurps the emotions till *'taste'* – the mediating faculty that alone could lead 'us gently back to Beauty, to Nature, and to Life' – withers and dies. Even the 'universal equality' of the Jacksonian era is part of the same perversion, the same infection with 'system', with 'abstraction', with 'generalities':

in the face of analogy and of God – in despite of the loud warning voice of the laws of *gradation* so visibly pervading all things in Earth and Heaven – wild attempts at an omni-prevalent Democracy were made.

Poe's education, his loyalties were wholly identified with the Southern gentry. He 'was reared not in the tradition of democratic liberalism sanctified under the names of Jefferson and Jackson, but under a powerful conservative or Whig reaction. Jeffersonianism and Jacksonianism were vulgar and frontier; the conservatism of Tidewater Virginia, especially dignified by John Marshall, was polite, urbane, and strongly anti-democratic and anti-reform.' * Below that Southern urbanity, however, what gnawing resentment! What despair!

but for the infected world at large I could anticipate no regeneration save in death. That man, as a race, should not become extinct, I saw that he must be *'born again'*.

It is a strangely paradoxical vision – anti-utilitarian, anti-industrial, anti-egalitarian – yet, for all its mystical fervour, aspiring to a *material* regeneration: an ecological Paradise Regained, purged of 'rectangular obscenities', 'rendered at length a fit dwelling-place for man'.

For individual death, too, is not a matter of moral sensibility, moral judgement, or moral regeneration: 'of moral pain or pleasure none at all'. It is a swoon rather from perception to heightened perception – a sensual progress through synaesthesia to the dissolution of identity or 'sense of being'. A sixth sense, 'a mental pendulous pulsation', leads to pure spiritual transcendence without thought, without sentience, without matter, without soul, reduced to eternal and primal 'nothingness' in space and time. Such is the passage of human consciousness from life through the veil of death to life-beyond-death: a

---

* Edward Davidson, *Poe, A Critical Study* (1957), p. 207.

centripetal reversion to that focus (the pulse divine) from which time itself and all matter originally sprang in centrifugal, fractured dispersal.

1. (p. 89) *Monos and Una*: Poe's macaronic title (conflating a Greek masculine and Latin feminine) may well be a further twist to Bulwer-Lytton's punning 'Monos and Daimonos: A Legend'. cf.:

> We have long learned to reverence the fine intellect of Bulwer . . . We feel sure of rising from the perusal a wiser if not a better man. In no instance are we deceived. From the brief tale – from the 'Monos and Daimonos' of the author – to his most ponderous and laboured novels – all is richly and glowingly intellectual – all is energetic, or astute, or brilliant, or profound.
>
> *Marginalia*, p. 174

2. (p. 89) *These things are in the future*: Sophocles, *Antigone*, 1334. Poe repeats the Greek phrase in *Eureka* (p. 275), continuing: 'I am but pausing, for a moment, on the awful threshold of *the Future*.' It became the title of one of his final stories, 'Mellonta Tauta' (1849).

3. (p. 89) *the majestic novelty of the Life Eternal*: Balzac too, Poe's contemporary, lost himself in speculations upon the nature of death. cf. *Séraphita* (1834–5), whose central character is an exalted, winged, androgynous being who appears to two young lovers. Risen above the flesh, on the point of becoming an angel, Séraphita is female to the young man, but masculine, as Séraphitus to the young woman.

Séraphita–Séraphitus, too, points the mystic way ahead, rising from sensual to heavenly love:

> The seraph lightly spread his wings to take his flight and did not look back to them – he had nothing now in common with the earth. He sprang upwards; the vast span of his dazzling pinions covered the two watchers like a beneficent shade, allowing them to raise their eyes and see him borne away in his glory, escorted by the rejoicing archangel.
>
> *Séraphita*, ch. 7

4. (p. 90) *each advance in practical science as a retro-gradation in the true utility*: cf. Poe's sonnet 'To Science':

> Science! true daughter of Old Time thou art!
> Who alterest all things with thy peering eyes.
> Why preyest thou thus upon the poet's heart,
> Vulture, whose wings are dull realities?
>
> (1829)

5. (p. 92) 'tout notre raisonnement se réduit à céder au sentiment': Pascal, *Les Pensées*, 274. Pascal continues:

Mais la fantaisie est semblable et contraire au sentiment, de sorte qu'on ne peut distinguer entre ces contraires. L'un dit que mon sentiment est fantaisie, l'autre que sa fantaisie est sentiment . . .

All our reasoning in the end gives way to feeling. But fantasy is both like and unlike feeling, so that it is impossible to disentangle their contradiction. One man says that my feeling is a matter of fantasy; another that his fantasy is a matter of feeling.

6. (p. 92) *I could anticipate no regeneration save in death*: cf. Bulwer-Lytton's 'Monos and Daimonos', where the fugitive vainly searches for solitude in the wilderness only to learn that he cannot shake off his demon.

7. (p. 94) *The senses were unusually active ... taste and smell were inextricably confounded*: Hervey Allen comments: 'The rest of the description amounts to a delineation of the symptoms of a drug addict ... There is direct evidence by Poe's cousin, Miss Herring, that, soon after he wrote this, August 1841, he was using opium to excess.' (*Israfel*, 1926, p. 413)

cf. Baudelaire:

> *Comme de longs échos qui de loin se confondent*
> *Dans une ténébreuse et profonde unité,*
> *Vaste comme la nuit et comme la clarté,*
> *Les parfums, les couleurs et les sons se répondent.*
> 'Correspondances'

> Like long-drawn echoes merging far away
> To a deep and shadowy harmony,
> Vast as the night, as vast as light,
> Scents, colours and sounds to each other reply.

8. (p. 94) *vision ... I appreciated it only as* sound: Elsewhere Poe offers a more exact example:

The orange ray of the spectrum and the buzz of the gnat (which never rises above the second A), affect me with nearly similar sensations. In hearing the gnat, I perceive the color. In perceiving the color, I seem to hear the gnat.

Which he followed by a scientific solution:

Here the vibrations of the tympanum caused by the wings of the fly, may, from within, induce abnormal vibrations of the retina, similar to those which the orange ray induces, normally, from without. By *similar*, I do not mean of equal rapidity – this would be folly; – but each millionth undulation, for example, of the retina, might accord with one of the tympanum; and I doubt whether this would not be sufficient for the effect.

'Marginalia', *Democratic Review* (November 1844)

9. (p. 96) *I measured the irregularities of the clock upon the mantel*: The association of the 'idea of *Time*' and 'that of mere *locality*' wrote Edward Hungerford, 'is startlingly suggestive when one finds that [they] were represented in phrenology by definite, primary organs. Was Poe's analysis of these psychical states caught from the science of mind? Of the organ of *Time* Gall had written: "We see persons who find amusement in a collection of watches and clocks, and must have them all go with the greatest exactness." ' ('Poe and Phrenology', *American Literature* vol. 2, 1930, p. 221)

Select Bibliography

ALLEN TATE, 'The Angelic Imagination: Poe and the Power of Words', *Kenyon Review* vol. 14 (1952), pp. 455–75; reprinted in *The Man of Letters in the Modern World: Selected Essays, 1928–1955* (New York: Meridian Books, 1955), pp. 113–45

A TALE OF THE RAGGED MOUNTAINS

First published
Godey's Lady's Book (April 1844)

Reprinted
Columbia Spy (27 April 1844)
Broadway Journal (29 November 1845)

Translated

Baudelaire, 'Une Aventure dans les Montagnes Rocheuses', *L'Illustration* (December 1852); retitled 'Les Souvenirs de M. Auguste Bedloe'

Poe seems intent on supplying both a natural and a supernatural key. Augustus Bedloe is a morphine addict who takes 'very large' doses each morning for his neuralgia. Yet his attendant, Dr Templeton, reveals intimations of his patient's dream even as he tells it, exercising a 'magnetic relation' – a kind of mental telepathy almost – by his mesmeric or hypnotic control. Which then is it: a case of transfer of traumatic experience? or of metempsychosis during that 'strange *interregnum* of the seasons'?

In the hazy 'Indian Summer' appears an 'Indian city'; the revolutionary site of Saratoga conjures up an 'insurrection' in Benares; a hallucinatory wound 'upon the right temple' prompts D. Templeton to apply poisoned leeches to 'the right temple'. Is Virginian Bedlo[e], then, really the double, or inverted *alter ego*, of British Oldeb? Has a transmigration of souls been synchronized within a single vision? Is it only in a trance, when freed by drugs from the confinements of space and time, that soul can recognize familiar soul and identities merge in the charged present?

Or is it all a hoax? Is first Bedloe, then the narrator, and so the reader, gulled by Templeton's horror-struck belief in metempsychosis? Is the patient not merely the credulous dupe, but the marked victim, of his physician's control? Is Bedloe's mind deranged, as his body is condemned, by the older man's irresponsible – possibly unscrupulous, even perversely malignant – therapy?

But the dreamer is Poe, playing at reincarnation with such typographical inversions. The Ragged Mountains lie to the south of the University of Virginia at Charlottesville. In 1827, aged eighteen, Poe himself had just gone down after two abortive terms at the University. With Freud's blessing, Marie Bonaparte knew just what to make of such dreams. 'Indeed it would be hard to think of a transference or dependence more complete than that of Bedloe on Templeton.' A 'homosexual attraction', she calls it, or 'homosexual fixation'. The shocks become erotic shocks: the poisonous snake, the 'piercing penis'; the leech, an 'impregnation by semen'. 'We have here', she concludes, 'a classic delineation, in sado-phallic terms, of a passive homosexual relation to the father, which all small boys experience at some time and which persists in many men's unconscious.' (*The Life and Works of Edgar Allan Poe, a Psycho-Analytic Interpretation*, 1933, ch. 42, p. 568)

1. (p. 99) *In moments of excitement the orbs ... seeming to emit luminous rays*:

Facial neuralgia was one of the ailments most commonly relieved not only by mesmerism, but by real galvanic current. A patient . . . could apply the electrodes from a simple galvanic pile or Cruickshank's 'crown of cups' to his temples. The 'luminous rays' from Bedloe's eyes are a further hint to the 'electromagnetic' nature of his animating force.

Doris V. Falk, 'Poe and the Power of Animal Magnetism', p. 541

2. (p. 100) *a physician ... first encountered at Saratoga*: Saratoga, of course, is a spa resort renowned for its springs. But it is also the site of General Burgoyne's surrender on 17 October 1777 – linking the first great victory of the American 'insurrection' (or revolutionary

war) with that Indian 'insurrection', Saratoga with Benares. It was General Burgoyne, paradoxically, on his return to England who managed the impeachment of Warren Hastings.

3. (p. 100) *a convert ... to the doctrines of Mesmer*: Franz Anton Mesmer (1733–1815), the German physician, whose interest in animal magnetism led to a treatment based on hypnosis. He built up a large and fashionable practice in Paris with his magnetic cures.

> When mesmerist and patient were *en rapport* they both became conductors of the magnetic fluid or, as some practitioners held, of a newly discovered 'imponderable' comparable to – or perhaps identical with – electricity, light, or electromagnetism. In fact, before he accomplished some famous 'cures' using actual magnets, Mesmer himself had considered the force to be electrical . . . Not until the 1840s did suggestion and the trance come to be regarded as the keys to the process. James Braid in his influential study, *Neurypnology, or the Rationale of Nervous Sleep* (London, 1843), coined the term 'hypnosis' and argued that all the phenomena of hypnotism-mesmerism could be accounted for by suggestion.
>
> Doris V. Falk, 'Poe and the Power of Animal Magnetism', p. 536

4. (p. 101) *the habitual use of morphine, which he swallowed in great quantity*: Like heroin, an opium derivative: with 'its customary effect – that of enduing all the external world with an intensity of interest . . . and immethodical thought'.

5. (p. 105) *Novalis errs not in saying that 'we are near waking when we dream that we dream'*: Two years earlier Poe had quoted at length in German from Novalis's *Moralische Ansichten* for his epigraph to 'The Mystery of Marie Rogêt'. But this quotation he found in Sarah Austin's *Fragments from German Prose Writers* (1841). See Novalis, *Schriften* (Jena, 1907), vol. 2, p. 141.

6. (p. 106) *the writhing creese of the Malay*: A kris, or kriss (Malay, *keris*) is a dagger with two scalloped cutting edges and serpentine blade.

7. (p. 106) *One of them struck me upon the right temple*: This whole passage derives, almost verbatim, from descriptions of the 1781 insurrection at Benares of 'Cheyte Sing' in Thomas Macaulay's review of G. R. Gleig's three-volume compilation of the *Memoirs of the Life of Warren Hastings, First Governor-General of Bengal* (*Edinburgh Review*, 1841). See Maurice Le Breton, 'Edgar Poe et Macaulay', *Revue Anglo-Americaine* vol. 13 (October 1935), pp. 38–42.

Was *Poe* attracted, by assonance, to *Bedloe*? For even the name has been traced to Macaulay's discussion of the charges brought by East India Company officials against Warren Hastings: 'in that part of the world, a very little encouragement from power will call forth, in a week, more Oatses, and Bedloes, and Dangerfields, than Westminster Hall sees in a century'. William Bedloe confirmed the false testimony of Titus Oates against the Catholics in 1678. See Burton R. Pollin, *Discoveries in Poe* (1970), ch. 2, pp. 25–7.

The name, in any case, was familiar to Poe from New York harbour. Since 1886 the Statue of Liberty has greeted immigrants from Bedloe's Island.

But he seems to have been unusually meticulous in his homework for this incident, moving on from Macaulay's essay to Gleig's *Memoirs* themselves (for the 'fatal sally'), to Warren Hastings's own *Narrative of the Insurrection*, 1782 (for the 'kiosk' or garden pavilion), as well as Sheridan's impeachment speeches. See Mukhtar Ali Isani, 'Some Sources for Poe's "Tale of the Ragged Mountains" ', pp. 38–40.

8. (p. 106) *a violent and sudden shock through my soul, as if of electricity*: Followed by a second shock 'as of a galvanic battery'. The current of animal magnetism – so charged between Templeton and Bedloe – flares to its critical flash-point: 'I had no bodily, no visible, audible, or palpable presence'. Neither Bedloe exactly, nor Oldeb now in the mesmeric bond, what is released seems to be a wholly autonomous force, a cohesive electric field within a field that pervades the animate and inanimate worlds.

9. (p. 107) *the likeness of a dead friend – a Mr Oldeb*: Yet this unlikely, and wholly unBritish, name suggests something of a hoax. Boyd Carter first pointed out that Poe's 'Indian' affray (so bizarre in the Ragged Mountains) parallels a more orthodox 'Indian' episode (of the American wilderness) in Charles Brockden Brown's *Edgar Huntly; or Memoirs of a Sleep-Walker* (1799). Both Huntly and Templeton are preoccupied by a friend's murder; in both the murder was committed by 'Indians'. Only in *Edgar Huntly* it is 'an Indian woman named *Old Deb*' who provides the solution, 'and of course the name *Oldeb* provides the "solution" for the narrator in Poe's tale' (G. R. Thompson, 'Is Poe's "A Tale of the Ragged Mountains" a Hoax?', p. 460).

10. (p. 107) *the insurrection of Cheyte Sing ... took place in 1780*: It was in August 1781 that Warren Hastings descended on Benares to extort tribute from its Rajah, Chait Singh. Rebuffed, he impetuously arrested the Rajah within the Shivala Ghat palace overlooking the

Ganges, though only two platoons of sepoys were at hand to set up guard. And they, in the confusion, were issued no ammunition.

The Rajah escaped by his rope of turbans into a waiting boat; the uprising was quickly crushed and he was exiled. But he was not forgotten. The Benares affair became one of the central counts against the Governor-General on his impeachment by Parliament.

11. (p. 108) *at the very period in which you fancied these things ... I was engaged in detailing them upon paper*: Dr Templeton's magnetic hold on his patient, that is, was so strong that Bedloe was affected even at a distance of several miles. As a physician (quoted by Sidney E. Lind) confirms: 'Magnetism can be conveyed to great distances, when persons are in perfect communication.' (*The Animal Magnetizer*, 1841)

12. (p. 108) *one of the venomous vermicular sangsues ... of Charlottesville*: That is, a bloodsucker or leech. But it was Poe, as Burton R. Pollin demonstrated, who first brazenly wormed the French term into an English text and single-handedly caused an upheaval in all subsequent dictionaries (English and American). He recalled the term, it appears, from a passage in Victor Hugo's *Notre-Dame de Paris* that was again to do service for 'The Cask of Amontillado' (1846). Needless to say there is no black and snake-like leech peculiar to Virginia; nor is such a Creole term conceivable in Virginia; nor could a single leech, of whatever species, be lethal.

13. (p. 108) *the name of the deceased had been given as Bedlo*: Thus 'a mere typographical error' confirms that palindrome that is Poe's farcical sign for the metempsychosis.

Augustus Bedloe 'certainly *seemed* young – and he made a point of speaking about his youth'. But internally the story is dated to 1827; the insurrection of Cheyte Sing 'took place in 1780'. So Bedloe was in fact forty-seven at the time of his death. Dr Templeton, 'an old gentleman, perhaps seventy years of age', must have been about twenty-three at the time of the Mutiny.

Select Bibliography

SIDNEY E. LIND, 'Poe and Mesmerism', *Publications of the Modern Language Association* vol. 62 (1947), pp. 1077–94

BOYD CARTER, 'Poe's Debt to Charles Brockden Brown', *Prairie Schooner* vol. 27 (1953), pp. 190–96

DORIS V. FALK, 'Poe and the Power of Animal Magnetism',

Publications of the Modern Language Association vol. 84 (1969), pp. 536–46

G. R. THOMPSON, 'Is Poe's "A Tale of the Ragged Mountains" a Hoax?', *Studies in Short Fiction* vol. 6 (1969), pp. 454–60

MUKHTAR ALI ISANI, 'Some Sources for Poe's "Tale of the Ragged Mountains"', *Poe Studies* vol. 5 (1972), pp. 38–40

THE BALLOON-HOAX

First Published

New York Sun (13 April 1844), as a broadside printed on one side only

Translated

Baudelaire, 'Le Canard au Ballon', *Le Pays* (January–February, 1855)

'Annexation and war with Mexico are identical,' declared Henry Clay, the Whig candidate. 'The Raven' of Texas, Sam Houston, was manoeuvring his fellow Texans into joining the United States. New England was opposed to another slave state. Then, on Saturday, 13 April 1844, the *New York Sun* published a broadside, or 'Extra page' of the midday issue, preceded by an early morning *Postscript* – as an appetizer:

BY EXPRESS

ASTOUNDING INTELLIGENCE BY PRI-
VATE EXPRESS FROM CHARLESTON
VIA NORFOLK! – THE ATLANTIC
OCEAN CROSSED IN THREE DAYS!!
– ARRIVAL AT SULLIVAN'S ISLAND
OF A STEERING BALLOON INVENTED
BY MR MONCK MASON!!

The publication created a sensation. Premium prices were paid for a copy of the newspaper and the issue was so quickly sold that Poe himself apparently was unable to obtain a copy.

The *Sun* was the first penny newspaper in New York, specializing in scoops and the sensational treatment of news. The editor, who had immediately purchased Poe's manuscript, was none other than Richard Adams Locke. Nine years earlier, in the same newspaper, he had perpetrated a similar editorial hoax, about a telescope that revealed life on the Moon. 'Discoveries in the Moon' too had taken New York by storm; and made Poe furious. 'Hans Pfaall' was only out three weeks: 'no sooner had I seen the paper than I understood the jest, which not for a moment could I doubt had been suggested by my own *jeu d'ésprit*'.* Now it was to be his turn. The memory of the New York public was fickle. This was his come-back.

He was not disappointed. For the *Columbia Spy* he wrote:

The 'Balloon-Hoax' made a far more intense sensation than anything of that character since the 'Moon-Story' of Locke. On the morning (Saturday) of its announcement, the whole square surrounding the 'Sun' building was literally besieged, blocked up – ingress and egress being alike impossible, from a period soon after sunrise until about two o'clock P. M. In Saturday's regular issue, it was stated that the news had been just received, and that an 'Extra' was then in preparation, which would be ready at ten. It was not delivered, however, until nearly noon. In the meantime I never witnessed more intense excitement to get possession of a newspaper. As soon as the few first copies made their way into the streets, they were bought up, at almost any price, from the news-boys, who made a profitable speculation beyond doubt. I saw a half-dollar given, in one instance, for a single paper, and a shilling was a frequent price. I tried, in vain, during the whole day, to get possession of a copy. It was excessively amusing, however, to hear the comments of those who had read the 'Extra'.†

(25 May 1844)

Next day the story was reprinted in the *Sunday Times*, edited by one of Poe's few Jewish friends, Major Mordecai M. Noah.

So Poe, single-handed, managed to divert his contemporaries from the raging controversy over the admission of Texas into the Union. They were mad on progress. Very well, he would give them progress. As early as 1836 Charles Green, 'of Nassau-balloon notoriety',‡ had talked of an Atlantic flight. He had even built a model of an *Atlantic Balloon*, making trial runs in 1840. It was operated by clockwork-driven propellers and had a rudder. Poe, in distant Philadelphia, was fascinated:

Some time ago, Mr Charles Green of England, published a statement of the grounds upon which he bases his assertion of the possibility of passing,

---

* 'The Literati of New York', *Godey's Lady's Book*, 1846.

† For a rather different view, of Poe perversely sabotaging his own success, see Doris V. Falk, 'Thomas Low Nichols, Poe, and the "Balloon Hoax" ', *Poe Studies* vol. 5 (1972), pp. 48–9.

‡ 'The Unparalleled Adventure of One Hans Pfaall', p. 30.

in a balloon, across the Atlantic, from New York to Europe. His facts should certainly be depended upon; for they are the result of observations made during two hundred and seventy-five ascents. For our own part, so far from gainsaying one word that the aeronaut asserts, we have for a long time past wondered why it was that our own Wise had not aeronauted himself over to Europe* – than which nothing could be a more feasible manoeuvre.

Burton's Gentleman's Magazine (March 1840)

Now, writing as it were after the event, he continued:

There is nothing put forth in the Balloon Story which is not in full keeping with the known facts of aeronautic experience – which might not really have occurred. An expedition of the kind has been long contemplated, and this *jeu d'esprit* will, beyond doubt, give the intention a new impulse. For my own part, I shall not be in the least surprised to learn, in the course of next month, or the next, that a balloon has made the actual voyage so elaborately described by the hoaxer. The trip might be made in even less time than seventy-five hours – which give only about forty miles to the hour.

Letter II, May 1844, *Doings of Gotham* (1929), p. 34

The first transatlantic balloon voyage, exactly a century later, recorded almost the same number of hours and many of the incidents in Mr Monck Mason's log.

1. (p. 110) *Mr Monck Mason's FLYING MACHINE!!!!*: Monck Mason exhibited his motor-driven dirigible balloon at the Royal Adelaide Gallery, London, in 1843. It made repeated flights around the large hall at the rate of six miles an hour.

2. (p. 110) *Arrival at Sullivan's Island*: The setting of Poe's prize-winning 'The Gold-Bug', published the previous year (1843). As Private Edgar A. Perry of Battery H of the First United States Artillery, he had served for more than a year as regimental clerk at Fort Moultrie, overlooking Sullivan's Island (1827–8).

3. (p. 111) *By the energy of an agent at Charleston, S.C.*: T. O. Mabbott discovered that in February 1844 the brig *Moon* had made the run from New York to Savannah so fast that it beat the U.S. mails by three days. That recent headline is invoked to confirm the *Sun*'s latest and even more extraordinary *coup* (Letter to the New York *Sun*, 23 January 1943).

---

* Which is precisely what he planned. On 20 December 1843, in fact, John Wise petitioned the United States Congress for permission to cross the Atlantic by balloon. A few months after 'The Balloon-Hoax' he even published a notice in the Lancaster *Intelligence* advertising the attempt, requesting help from seamen of all nations.

There was no telegraph, of course, to check such news stories. Samuel Morse had been working on the idea of an electric telegraph since 1832, but it was only in this year, 1844, that he demonstrated to Congress its practicality by transmitting messages, by code, over a wire from Washington to Baltimore. Soon after, the nomination of James K. Polk as Democratic candidate was telegraphed to Washington.

4. (p. 111) *Mr Harrison Ainsworth, author of 'Jack Sheppard', &c*: The historical novelist, at this time editor of *Ainsworth's Magazine*, and established best-seller: *Jack Sheppard* (1839), *The Tower of London* (1840), *Windsor Castle* (1843) etc.

Poe was scornful. His review of *The Tower of London* opens: 'The authorship of this work does a little, and but a little, more credit to Mr Ainsworth than that of "Jack Sheppard". It is in no spirit of cavilling that we say that it is rarely our lot to review a work more utterly destitute of every ingredient requisite to a good romance.' And concludes: 'Such libels on humanity, such provocatives to crime, such worthless, inane, disgraceful romances as "Jack Sheppard" and its successors, are a blot on our literature and a curse to our land.' (*Graham's Magazine*, March 1841). He returned to the charge, with a review of *Guy Fawkes; or the Gunpowder Treason* in the November issue.

For 'The Balloon-Hoax' is also a literary burlesque. Harrison Ainsworth, *in propria persona*, is made to parody his own melodramatic prose:

The waters give up no voice to the heavens. The immense flaming ocean writhes and is tortured uncomplainingly. The mountainous surges suggest the idea of innumerable dumb gigantic fiends struggling in impotent agony.

p. 120

Yet who but Ainsworth – romantic visionary on high – contributes that bold, creative stroke: of making a bid for North America?

5. (p. 111) *Mr Henson, the projector of the late unsuccessful flying machine*: William Samuel Henson, designer of the 'aerial steam carriage' – a monoplane, driven by a 25 horse-power steam-engine that never left the ground. As early as 1842 he lobbied Parliament for support of his newly formed *Aerial Steam Transportation Company*.

The Glasgow *Constitutional*, like Poe, saw scope for a hoax, publishing an account of an experimental flight over the Clyde that ended with a crash into the river (April 1843). The London *Times*, for one, was hoodwinked and reprinted the story.

Apart from Mason, Henson, Robert Hollond M.P., and Ainsworth, the rest of the cast (titles and all) are fictitious.

6. (p. 112) *from Dover to Weilburg in the balloon, 'Nassau'*: Indicating Poe's key source. Over a quarter of his text is appropriated from two pamphlets by Thomas Monck Mason: *Account of the Late Aeronautical Expedition from London to Weilburg, Accompanied by Robert Hollond, Esq., Monck Mason, Esq., and Charles Green, Aeronaut* (London, 1836; New York, 1837) and *Remarks on the Ellipsoidal Balloon, Propelled by the Archimedean Screw, Described as the New Aerial Machine* (London, 1843).

At 1.30 p.m. on 7 November 1836 Mason, Hollond and Green had ascended in an 82,000 cubic-foot balloon from Vauxhall Gardens, London, to descend at 7.30 a.m., next day, near Weilburg in the Duchy of Nassau – a journey of approximately 500 miles in 18 hours.

The flight broke all records and created a sensation. The *Remarks on the Ellipsoidal Balloon* was published for Mason's exhibit at the Royal Adelaide Gallery.

7. (p. 112) *the failure of Mr Henson's scheme, and of Sir George Cayley's*: Both the description of 'Mr Henson's scheme' and of Sir George Cayley's exhibit at the Polytechnic Institution derive, almost verbatim, from *Remarks on the Ellipsoidal Balloon*. As early as 1809 Sir George Cayley had proposed a theory of flight for fixed-wing model aircraft. He experimented unsuccessfully with a hybrid helicopter-cum-aeroplane: two manually operated windmills being provided for take-off, a small propeller for forward thrust.

8. (p. 112) *his own was an ellipsoid . . . in the opposite direction*: The next two paragraphs, with all their technicalities, too derive from Mason. In every detail – including the illustration on the broadside extra – Poe's 'Victoria' is modelled on Mason's model.

9. (p. 113) *oiled silk cut into gores*: Triangular wedges.

10. (p. 113) *shaped somewhat like a battledoor*: Commonly 'battledore', the racket used in playing with a shuttlecock.

11. (p. 114) *we are indebted to Mr Charles Green*: cf. an editorial (clearly by Poe) in *Burton's Gentleman's Magazine*:

Pure hydrogen must be discarded, as too subtle for our present means of retention. Balloons inflated with carburetted hydrogen (common coal gas) will retain a good inflation for a great length of time. Mr G. states that he has had gas of this kind brought in small balloons, to fill his large one, from a distance of five or six miles; and we observe (what Mr G. has not) that in Vienna, according to a simple method invented by M. F. Derionet, the gas is conveyed in hermetically sealed bags . . . from the factory to all parts of the town daily.

(March, 1840)

12. (p. 115) *for warming coffee by means of slacklime*: Lime disintegrating under moisture. Poe's neologism was coined from Mason's explanatory footnote: '. . . without the intervention of fire, by the means of slacked lime' (*Account*, p. 11).

13. (p. 115) *Mr Green's invention of the guide-rope*: cf. Mason:

By the simple contrivance of a rope of the requisite magnitude and extent, trailing on the ground beneath, (and if over the sea, with a sufficient quantity of liquid ballast contained in vessels floating on its surface,) have all these difficulties . . . been overcome.

Account, pp. 8–10

It was this gadget, Mason reckoned, that opened up the way to an ocean crossing:

Under the sway of such an instrument, the ocean, no longer the dreaded enemy of the aerial voyager, becomes at once his greatest friend . . . In his view, the Atlantic is no more than a simple canal; three days might suffice to effect its passage.

Aeronautica, or Sketches Illustrative of the Theory and Practice of Aerostation (1838)

14. (p. 117) *Wheal-Vor House . . . about a mile from Penstruthal*: This four-wheel house or caravan, that Poe swears is his 'pen's truth all' – was a supernumerary little joke inside the hoax.

15. (p. 118) *We now resolved to let off enough gas*: Repeating Monck Mason's manoeuvre, successful over the English Channel in 1836, over the Bristol Channel in 1844!

16. (p. 118) *a strong current of wind from the East*: But now a misadventure, overcome on the flight to Weilburg, becomes the pretext for continuing this mock-adventure to North America.

17. (p. 121) *an elevation equal to that of Cotopaxi*: cf. 'at 18,000, which is not far from the elevation of Cotopaxi . . .' ('Hans Pfaall', p. 348, note 18).

18. (p. 121) *absolutely and most unequivocally* concave: cf. 'What mainly astonished me, in the appearance of things below, was the seeming concavity of the surface of the globe . . .' ('Hans Pfaall',

p. 348, note 25). The explanatory *Note* derives verbatim from the earlier story.

19. (p. 123) *The grapnel caught at 2 P.M., precisely*: By Greenwich Mean Time, it appears, not Eastern Standard Time. Though Mr Forsyth (*foresight?*) – the agent who completes the British log – was surely bound to reckon by the local Charleston clock!

'As for internal evidence of falsehood,' Poe boasted, 'there is, positively, *none*.' (May 1844) Yet it looks as if Poe's hoax too cannot quite 'bear even momentary examination by the scientific' (*Doings of Gotham*, p. 34).

Select Bibliography

WALTER B. NORRIS, 'Poe's Balloon Hoax', *The Nation* vol. 91 (1910), pp. 389–90

HAROLD SCUDDER, 'Poe's "Balloon Hoax"', *American Literature* vol. 21 (1949), pp. 179–90

W. K. WIMSATT, JR, 'A Further Note on Poe's "Balloon Hoax"', *American Literature* vol. 22 (1951), pp. 491–2

RONALD WILKINSON, 'Poe's "Balloon Hoax" Once More', *American Literature* vol. 32 (1960), pp. 313–17

T. N. WEISSBUCH, 'Edgar Allan Poe: Hoaxer in the American Tradition', *New-York Historical Society Quarterly* vol. 45 (1961), pp. 291–309

MESMERIC REVELATION

First Published

Columbian Lady's and Gentleman's Magazine (August 1844)

Reprinted

New World (3 August 1844)
Saturday Museum (31 August 1844)
Tales (1845), with long insertions
Universalist Watchman (August–September 1845)
American Phrenological Journal (September 1845). Billed as 'authentic', the article was repudiated in the October issue
Star of Bethlehem (4 October 1845)
Popular Record of Modern Science, no. 35 (London: 29 November 1845), as 'The Last Conversation of a Somnambule'

Translated

Baudelaire, 'Révélation magnétique', *La Liberté de penser* (July 1848): chosen for his first published translation

Anticipating the hypnotic techniques of Charcot and the subsequent development of Freud's clinical methods, this dialogue is staged, as it were, on a psychoanalyst's couch. Vankirk's is to be the new church of mesmeric philosophy. Poe's special fascination, as always, is in this state of suspended animation (or death-in-life) which was also a kind of life-in-death or living inhumation. Their apocalyptic progress and transformation he had long ago charted in *The Narrative of Arthur Gordon Pym*; their morbid conflation was soon to be the theme of 'The Facts in the Case of M. Valdemar'.

For Poe himself was not a spiritualist. In 1845 he was to attend a series of lectures by the nineteen-year-old Andrew Jackson Davis in New York. Flanked by his own hypnotist and reporter, Davis dictated in an apparent state of trance. From the verbatim copy, he then compiled his *Principles of Nature, Her Divine Revelations, and A Voice to Mankind* (1847), a conflation of sermon with science fiction, mysticism and occult history, claiming verbal inspiration from unseen spirits. Though Davis was later to make several respectful allusions to Poe (in *The Magic Staff* and *Events in the Life of a Seer*), Poe's reaction to Davis was invariably one of contempt – from his *Marginalia* to the mock-introduction of 'my friend Martin Van Buren Mavis, (sometimes called the "Poughkeepsie Seer",)' prefixed to 'Mellonta Tauta'.

As he wrote to James Russell Lowell:

I have no belief in spirituality. I think the word a *mere* word. No one has really a conception of spirit. We cannot imagine what is not. We deceive ourselves by the idea of infinitely rarefied matter. Matter escapes the senses by degrees – a stone – a metal – a liquid – the atmosphere – a gas – the luminiferous ether. Beyond this there are other modifications more rare. But to all we attach the notion of a constitution of particles – atomic composition. For this reason only, we think spirit different; for spirit, we say is unparticled, and *therefore* is not matter. But it is clear that if we proceed sufficiently far in our ideas of rarefaction, we shall arrive at a point where the particles coalesce; for, although the particles be infinite, the infinity of littleness in the spaces between them, is an absurdity. – The unparticled matter, permeating & impelling, all things, is God. Its activity is the thought of God – which creates. Man, and other thinking beings, are individualizations of the unparticled matter. Man exists as a 'person', by being clothed with matter (the particled matter) which individualizes him. Thus habited, his life is rudimental. What we call 'death' is the painful metamorphosis. The stars are the habitations of rudimental beings. But for the necessity of the rudimental life, there would have been no worlds. At death, the worm is the butterfly – still material, but of a matter unrecognized by our organs – recognized, occasionally, perhaps, by the sleep-waker, directly – without organs – through the mesmeric medium. Thus a sleep-waker may see ghosts. Divested of the rudimental covering, the being inhabits *space* – what we suppose to be the immaterial universe – passing every where, and acting all things, by mere volition – cognizant of all secrets but that of the nature of God's volition – the motion, or activity, of the unparticled matter.

New York: 2 July 1844

Poe was doubtful what exactly to call this prelude to *Eureka*. In a letter to Professor Bush (author of *Anastasis; or, The Doctrine of the Resurrection of the Body, Rationally and Scripturally Considered*, 1844) he called it an 'article':

You will, of course, understand that the article is purely a fiction; – but I have embodied in it some thoughts which are original with myself & I am exceedingly anxious to learn if they have claim to absolute originality, and also how far they will strike you as well based.

New York: 4 January 1845

To Rufus Griswold he called it an 'Essay', insisting it be included in his projected anthology, *Prose Writers of America* (1847), 'even if something else is omitted' (24 February 1845). Griswold in the event published only 'The Fall of the House of Usher'. As always Poe wanted to have it both ways. Six months later he was crowing:

the Swedenborgians inform me that they have discovered all that I said in a magazine article, entitled 'Mesmeric Revelation', to be absolutely true, although at first they were very strongly inclined to doubt my veracity – a thing which, in that particular instance, I never dreamed of not doubting myself. The story is a pure fiction from beginning to end.

'Marginalia', *Godey's Lady's Book* (August 1845)

1. (p. 124) *the* rationale *of mesmerism, its startling* facts: All point, as Sidney E. Lind argued, to Poe's indebtedness to the Rev. Chauncey Hare Townshend's *Facts in Mesmerism* (London, 1840). Townshend too had opened with 'the fatal word Imposture' and 'Ridicule, which is *not* the test of truth'. He too 'perceived that important deductions might be drawn from' such facts; 'and that they bore upon disputed questions of the highest interest to man, connected with the three great mysteries of being – life, death, and immortality' (p. 51).

2. (p. 124) *a colloquy, occurring between a sleep-waker and myself*:

Attacking the London *Popular Record of Modern Science* for piracy, Poe added:

It had the impudence, also, to spoil the title by improving it to 'The Last Conversation of a Somnambule' – a phrase that is nothing at all to the purpose, since the person who 'converses' is not a Somnambule. He is a sleep-waker – *not* a sleep-walker; but I presume that 'The Record' thought it was only the difference of an *l*.

'Marginalia', *Graham's Lady's and Gentleman's Magazine*, Vol. 32
(March 1848)

Poe himself had learnt the distinction, it seems, from Townshend who used 'Mesmeric Sleepwaking for Induced Somnambulism' throughout his volume, 'on the ground that Somnambulism, strictly speaking, was not always, nor necessarily, an adjunct of the condition I wished to describe' (p. 10).

That condition we might call 'deep hypnosis' or 'trance'.

3. (p. 125) *advised to study Cousin*: No doubt his eclectic *Cours de l'histoire de la philosophie* (in 8 volumes, 1815–29). Since 1840 '*ministre de l'instruction publique*', Victor Cousin was at this time the supreme arbiter of educational and philosophical matters in France.

4. (p. 125) *The 'Charles Elwood' of Mr Brownson*: viz. *Charles Elwood; or, The Infidel Converted* (1840). Ex-Presbyterian, ex-Unitarian, ex-Transcendental editor of the *Boston Quarterly Review*, Orestes Augustus Brownson had entered the Roman Catholic Church in 1844.

5. (p. 125) *His end had plainly forgotten his beginning, like the government of Trinculo*: Like Gonzago's rather, in Antonio's scornful phrase: 'The latter end of his commonwealth forgets the beginning' (*The Tempest*, II, i, 154).

6. (p. 128) *The truth is, it is impossible to conceive spirit*: cf. Poe's letter to James Russell Lowell: 'No one has really a conception of spirit. We cannot imagine what is not' (2 July 1844). Or as he paraphrased his argument a week later, writing to Dr Thomas H. Chivers:

There is no such thing as spirituality. God is material. All things are material; yet the matter of God has all the qualities which we attribute to spirit: thus the difference is scarcely more than of words. There is a matter without particles – of no atomic composition: this is God. It permeates and impels all things, and thus *is* all things in itself. Its agitation is the thought of God, and creates. Man and other beings (inhabitants of stars) are portions of this unparticled matter, individualized by being incorporated in the ordinary or particled matter. Thus they exist rudimentally. Death is the painful metamorphosis.

(10 July 1844)

Thus the quarrel with New England's Transcendentalists, it turns out, hinges on a verbal quibble!

7. (p. 129) *There seems to me an insurmountable objection*: This whole scholastic debate for and against the 'absolute coalescence' of ether – P's intervention and Vankirk's reply – was inserted by Poe after first publication.

8. (p. 132) *act all things ... from the perception of the angels*: An elaborate revision of: 'pervade at pleasure the weird dominions of the infinite'. These were originally the sleep-waker's last words; his tutorial on the relativity of pain was added later.

9. (p. 134) *His brow was of the coldness of ice ... after long pressure from Azrael's hand*: (Hebrew, 'help of God'), Angel of Death in both Judaic and Muslim lore, who severed the body from the soul. The final three sentences too were added for the 1845 edition.

Select Bibliography

SIDNEY E. LIND, 'Poe and Mesmerism', *Publications of the Modern Language Association* vol. 62 (1947), pp. 1077–94

DORIS V. FALK, 'Poe and the Power of Animal Magnetism', *Publications of the Modern Language Association* vol. 84 (1969), pp. 536–46

THE THOUSAND-AND-SECOND TALE OF SCHEHERAZADE

First published
Godey's Lady's Book (February 1845)

Reprinted
Broadway Journal (25 October 1845)

Translated
Léon de Wailly, 'La 1002ᵉ Nuit', *L'Illustration* (1856)

The wonders of encyclopaedic lore defy the Arabian Nights. The real modern world beats *Gulliver's Travels* hollow. This young 'gullible' from Bagdad does not voyage east to the land of the Houyhnhnms but west to that of the 'Cock-neighs'.

Sinbad's last voyage around the world in a British armoured cruiser turns into a catalogue of western fantasy: dirigible balloons, steamboats, railways, printing-presses, daguerreotypes, electrotype and telegraph. The satiric theme is not so much the credibility gap between modern science and theology, as between the acceptance of scientific *criteria* and theological dogma. To the Caliph the Koranic 'sky-blue cow' alone is credible.

In 'The Man That Was Used Up: A Tale of the Late Bugaboo and Kickapoo Campaign' (April 1839), Poe's champion for progress and the machine age had been the Indian fighter and universally popular hero, Brevet Brigadier-General John A.B.C. Smith (alias General Winfield Scott):

'There is nothing at all like it,' he would say; 'we are a wonderful people, and live in a wonderful age. Parachutes and rail-roads – man-traps and spring-guns! Our steam-boats are upon every sea, and the Nassau balloon packet is about to run regular trips (fare either way only twenty pounds sterling) between London and Timbuctoo. And who shall calculate the immense influence upon social life – upon arts – upon commerce – upon literature – which will be the immediate result of the great principles of electromagnetics! Nor, is this all, let me assure you! There is really no end to the march of invention.'

But it is precisely this utilitarian spokesman, this hero, this darling of democracy, who is the 'man that was used up': a mass of prosthetic surgery, a mere assemblage of parts (it turns out), a mechanical illusion of artificial limbs – false teeth, false palate, false arm, padded shoulders, cork leg, glass eyes, a wig – himself the mindless product of the times he celebrates, himself an automaton for a machine age!

1. (p. 135) *like the Zohar of Simeon Jochaides*: The Cabbalistic commentary on the Pentateuch, attributed to Simon ben Yohai (of the Second Century A.D.).

2. (p. 135) *It will be remembered that, in the usual version*: cf.

Montgomery, in his lectures on *Literature* (!), has the following – 'Who does not turn with absolute contempt from the signs, and gems, and filters, and caves, and genii of Eastern Tales as from the trinkets of a toy shop, and the trumpery of a raree show?' What man of genius but must answer 'Not I'?

Pinakidia

3. (p. 138) *in my old age ... I became once more possessed with a desire of visiting foreign countries*: Like Dante's Ulysses, whom neither son, father nor wife:

> *vincer poter dentro da me l'ardore*
> *ch'i ebbi a divenir del mondo esperto,*
> *e degli vizii umani e del valore ...*
> > *Inferno*, xxvi, lines 97–9

> could conquer the ardent desire that I had
> to gain the world's experience and attain
> knowledge of human vices and of worth ...

4. (p. 139) *a black speck, which rapidly increased in size*: Isambard Kingdom Brunel's *Great Western* steamed into New York harbour on 23 April 1838, just after Poe had settled in New York.

5. (p. 141) *I now bitterly repented my folly in quitting a comfortable home*: But this Sinbad-Ulysses soon reverts to Poe's favourite boyhood hero, Robinson Crusoe.

6. (p. 146) *vegetables ... that moved from place to place*: These exotics apparently include teasel (*scabiosa*) and the Rhone water lily (*vallisneria*). The whole paragraph – *Orchideae, Parasites, Algae*, subterranean fungi and all – yet again derives from Hugh Murray, *Encyclopaedia of Geography*, revised edition (Philadelphia, 1839).

7. (p. 149) *The* Eccaleobion: (Greek, 'I invoke life'), an egg-hatching apparatus or incubator.

8. (p. 150) *Maelzel's Automaton Chess-player*: Invented by Baron Wolfgang von Kempelen in 1769, but exhibited throughout the United States by Johann Nepomuk Maelzel, the Bavarian mechanic who was himself the inventor of musical machines like the Orchestrion and the Panharmonicon. Poe, nine years earlier, had taken a leading part in exposing the hoax. (See 'Von Kempelen and His Discovery', page 425, note 12.) On Maelzel's death in 1838, the Chess-Player had been bought by Dr John K. Mitchell and stood in the Chinese Museum at Philadelphia, until destroyed by fire in 1854.

9. (p. 150) *Babbage's Calculating Machine*: Forerunner of the modern computer:

> But if these machines were ingenious, what shall we think of the calculating machine of Mr Babbage? What shall we think of an engine of wood and metal which can not only compute astronomical and navigation tables to any given extent, but render the exactitude of its operations mathematic-

ally certain through its power of correcting its possible errors? What shall we think of a machine which can not only accomplish all this, but actually print off its elaborate results, when obtained, without the slightest intervention of the intellect of man?

'Maelzel's Chess-Player', *Southern Literary Messenger* (April 1836)

10. (p. 150) Chabert, *and since him, a hundred others*: Interposing another stunt-man – not with a Turkish automaton this time but a Turkish pipe – among the engineers and scientists.

11. (p. 151) *two loud sounds ... two brilliant lights*: The wizardry with 'red rays' derives from Sir David Brewster, *Letters on Natural Magic* (1832), pp. 182–3.

SOME WORDS WITH A MUMMY

First published
American Whig Review (April 1845)

Reprinted
Broadway Journal (1 November 1845)

Translated
Baudelaire, 'Petite Discussion avec une Momie', *Le Pays* (December 1854)

It is 'all a mistake o'! The very hieroglyphs drive home the spoof, even though this is not a palpable hoax. What opens with a threat of indigestion ends with a nightmare farce of the whole indigestible modern world – its industries, its faith in 'Progress', its democratic hordes.

Joseph Priestley, author of *The History and Present State of Electricity* (1767), who had emigrated to America in 1794, wrote:

> Thus, whatever was the beginning of this world, the end will be glorious and paradisaical, beyond what our imaginations can now conceive. Extravagant as some may suppose these views to be, I think I could show them to be fairly suggested by the true theory of human nature, and to arise from the natural course of human affairs. But, for the present, I waive this subject, the contemplation of which always make me happy.
>
> 'An Essay on the First Principles of Government' (1771)

The Benthamite or Utilitarian creed, of the happiness of the majority, too was first enunciated there: 'the great standard by which everything relating to' social life 'must finally be determined'.

Poe whole-heartedly disagreed. His contempt for the Transcendentalists' view of progress he makes abundantly clear. As he wrote in his long letter to James Russell Lowell:

> I live continually in a reverie of the future. I have no faith in human perfectibility. I think that human exertion will have no appreciable effect upon humanity. Man is now only more active – not more happy – nor more wise, than he was 6000 years ago. The result will never vary – and to suppose that it will, is to suppose that the forgone man has lived in vain – that the foregone time is but the rudiment of the future – that the myriads who have perished have not been upon equal footing with ourselves –, nor are we with our posterity. I cannot agree to lose sight of man the individual, in man the mass. – I have no belief in spirituality. I think the word a *mere* word. No one has really a conception of spirit. We cannot imagine what is not . . .
>
> New York: 2 July 1844

1. (p. 155) *a tomb near Eleithias, in the Lybian Mountains*: All this Egyptian detail – the Theban sepulchres with their frescoes and bas-reliefs, the extraction of the brain before embalming, the pasteboard coffin, hieroglyphic inscription, bead collar, 'reddish' flesh and gilded nails – derives, almost verbatim as Lucille King demonstrated, from two articles in the *Encyclopaedia Americana*: on 'Mummies' (vol. 9, pp. 89–90) and on 'Embalming' (vol. 4, p. 487).

2. (p. 156) *By good luck, Mr Gliddon formed one of our party*: George Robins Gliddon (1809–57), the British Egyptologist and acting American consul in Cairo during the 1830s, became a popular lecturer on the American circuit from Boston to New York to Philadelphia in the 1840s. His *Ancient Egypt* (1843), Burton R. Pollin argues, may be the source of Allamistakeo's unruffled air of superiority:

> Men of knowledge and arts must return to Egypt to learn the origin of language and writing – of the calendar and solar motion – of the art of cutting granite with a *copper* chisel and of giving elasticity to a copper sword – of making glass with the variegated hues of the rainbow – of moving single blocks of polished syenite, 900 tons in weight, for any distance, by land and water . . .
>
> p. 34

3. (p. 157) *The application of electricity to a Mummy ... was an idea ... still sufficiently original*: Though a 'mention of the galvanic battery' one year earlier had recalled to 'memory a well-known and very extraordinary case in point, where its actions proved the means

of restoring to animation a young attorney of London, who had been interred for two days'. Apparently dead of typhus fever, the body was unearthed for a *post mortem* examination and a battery applied to one of the pectoral muscles:

A rough gash was made, and a wire hastily brought in contact, when the patient with a hurried but quite unconvulsive movement, arose from the table, stepped into the middle of the floor, gazed about him uneasily for a few seconds and then spoke. What he said was unintelligible; but the words were uttered; the syllabification was distinct. Having spoken, he fell heavily to the floor.

For some moments all were paralysed with awe – but the urgency of the case soon restored them to their presence of mind. It was seen that Mr Stapleton was alive, although in a swoon. Upon exhibition of ether he revived and was rapidly restored to health, and to the society of his friends – from whom, however, all knowledge of his resuscitation was withheld, until a relapse was no longer to be apprehended. Their wonder – their rapturous astonishment – may be conceived.

The most thrilling peculiarity of this incident, nevertheless, is involved in what Mr S. himself asserts. He declares that at no period was he altogether insensible – that, dully and confusedly he was aware of everything which happened to him, from the moment in which he was pronounced *dead* by his physicians, to that in which he fell swooning to the floor of the hospital. 'I am alive,' where the uncomprehended words which, upon recognizing the locality of the dissecting-room, he had endeavoured in his extremity to utter.

'The Premature Burial' (July 1844)

Robert Lee Rhea found just such an account of galvanic batteries used for reviving a corpse in *The Medical Repository* (January 1820). The experiment is worth quoting in full:

On the 4th of November last, various galvanic experiments were made on the body of the murderer Clydsdale, by Dr Ure, with a voltaic battery of 270 pair of four-inch plates. The results were truly appalling. On moving the rod from the hip to the heel, the knee being previously bent, the leg was thrown out with such violence as nearly to overturn one of the assistants, who in vain attempted to prevent its extension! In the second experiment the rod was applied to the phrenic nerve in the neck, when laborious breathing instantly commenced, the chest heaved and fell; the belly was protruded and collapsed, with the relaxing and retiring diaphragm; and it is thought, that but from the complete evacuation of the blood, pulsation might have occurred!! In the third experiment, the supraorbital nerve was touched, when every muscle in the murderer's face 'was thrown into fearful action'. The scene was hideous – several of the spectators left the room, and one gentleman actually fainted, from terror or sickness!! In the fourth experiment the transmitting of the electrical power from the spinal marrow to the ulnar nerve, at the elbow, the fingers were instantly put in motion, and the agitation of the arm was so great that the corpse seemed to point at the different spectators, some of whom thought it had come to life! Dr Ure appears to be of opinion, that had not incisions been made in the blood vessels of the neck, and the spinal marrow been lacerated, the criminal might have been restored to life.

Even the idea of applying electricity to a Mummy was not necessarily original. Poe's possible source, discovered by Lucille King, may be the tale 'Letter from a Revived Mummy' (New York *Evening Mirror*, 21 January 1832). There an English soldier, stunned on the battle-field, is preserved for a hundred years in a Brussels museum. The corpse is removed to New York. An attempt at resuscitation is made. When at last a galvanic battery is applied, the mummy starts to its feet, shouting 'hurrah for merry England! and darted forward as in the act of charging'.

One book certainly known to Poe was *The Mummy: A Tale of the Twenty-Second Century* (1827) by Jane Webb, centring on the resurrection of the Mummy of Cheops. In league with a Roman Catholic priest, it secures the election of a Queen of England. But the real hero is the scientist, Dr Entwerfen:

the fortunate inventor of the immortalizing snuff, one single pinch of which cures all diseases by the smell; the discoverer of the capability of caoutchouc being applied to aerial purposes; and the maker of the most compendious and powerful galvanic battery ever yet beheld by mortal.

Part 2, p. 221

A play possibly seen by Poe was *The Mummy; or, The Liquor of Life!* by William Bayle Bernard, a London farce that remained a hit on the American stage throughout the 1830s and 1840s.

4. (p. 158) *Mr Silk Buckingham . . . upon all fours, under the table*: James Silk Buckingham – tireless traveller from Asia to Canada, journalist, lecturer, teetotaller – was elsewhere scornfully pilloried by Poe. Burton R. Pollin suggests that *The Slave States of America* (1842) may have been his undoing. The vendetta long continued (see 'Mellonta Tauta', p. 311).

5. (p. 158) *the exterior* os sesamoideum pollicis pedis: One of the small bones of the big toe.

6. (p. 159) *as does Mr Barnes in the pantomime*: Comedian at the Park Theatre, father of the far more celebrated actress and playwright, Charlotte Barnes.

7. (p. 162) *in my time we employed ... the Bichloride of Mercury*:
cf. *Encyclopaedia Americana*: 'The impregnation is performed by the
injection of a strong solution, consisting of about four ounces of bichloride of mercury to a pint of alcohol, into the blood vessels' (vol.
IV, p. 487).

What the article does not mention, however, is that, far from being
Egyptian practice, this was a French discovery of the late eighteenth
century.

8. (p. 166) *the very word* Adam, (*or Red Earth*): Gliddon printed
Hebrew characters for Adam (*Adme*), as 'Red Earth or clay' (*Ancient
Egypt*, p. 29).

9. (p. 166) *prototypes of Gall and Spurzheim ... the manœuvres of
Mesmer*: Invoking the contemporary Trinity of pseudo-science. The
German Franz Joseph Gall (1758–1828) and his disciple Johan Caspar
Spurzheim (1776–1832), who died in Boston, collaborated as physicians in Vienna. On the supposition that separate attributes of the
mind must be localized in separate organs of the brain, they correlated
twenty-six faculties with bumps on different parts of the skull.

Yet Poe himself had given an enthusiastic reception to Mrs L.
Miles' *Phrenology, and the Moral Influence of Phrenology*:

> Phrenology is no longer to be laughed at. It is no longer laughed at by
> men of common understanding. It has assumed the majesty of a science,
> and, as a science ranks among the most important which can engage the
> attention of thinking beings . . .

Southern Literary Messenger (March 1836)

His own 'Literati' sketches (1846) were to be marked by phrenological
pretention.

10. (p. 167) *I had better consult Ptolemy, (whoever Ptolemy is)*: Elsewhere Poe alludes to the *Almagest*, Arab version of the *Syntaxis*, the
famous astronomical work by the Alexandrian, Claudius Ptolemy.

11. (p. 167) *one Plutarch de facie lunæ*: 'The Face in the Moon',
literally *De facie [quae] in orbe lunae [apparet]* (*Moralia* 920A–
945E). Kepler had written a Latin translation and commentary.

12. (p. 167) *a peep at Diodorus Siculus*: 'Oenopides likewise passed
some time with the priests and astrologers' of Egypt 'and learned
among other things about the orbit of the sun, that it has an oblique
course and moves in a direction opposite to that of the stars' (Diodorus Siculus, Book 1, 98.3).

Oenopides of Chios, astronomer of the fifth century B.C., is credited with the discovery of the obliquity of the ecliptic.

13. (p. 167) *Look ... at the Bowling-Green Fountain in New York!*: The Green at the foot of Broadway 'now ornamented with a fountain supplied by the Water Works of the city. The jets are made to fall upon an uncouth mass of rocks which, in the opinion of some, gives to the same a "wild and picturesque appearance".' (E. Porter Belden, *New York: Past, Present, and Future*, 1851) The water rose some seventy feet, to above the level of surrounding trees.

The *Broadway Journal* of June derided 'the hideous and distasteful' fountain, reckoning that the artist who designed the rock work went 'raving mad'.

14. (p. 167) *the city of Aznac*: A palindrome of Kansas, perhaps, modelled on 'Carnac'.

15. (p. 168) *a copy of a book called the 'Dial'*: The *Dial* (July 1840–April 1844), a quarterly of literature, philosophy and religion, was the mouthpiece of the New England Transcendentalist movement – always fair game for Poe. Since July 1842 it had been edited by Emerson.

16. (p. 169) *the invention of Hero, through Solomon de Caus*: Or Salomon de Caux (1576–1626), French engineer, whose *Les Raisons des forces mouvantes avec diverses machines* (1615) is an early exposition of the principle of steam power.

Heron, far from an ancient Egyptian, was an Alexandrian (c. 50–150 A.D.). *Called ὁ μηχανικός*, he is associated with works on *Automata-making* and the *Mechanica* (three books extant in Arabic). The *Pneumatica* describe an invention known as 'Hero's fountain', in which a jet of water is maintained by compressed air, and a steam-engine acting on the principle of Barker's Mill.

17. (p. 170) *Ponnonner's lozenges, or Brandreth's pills*: Both brand-names, presumably, of patent medicines. One of the first makers of patent medicines in the United States, Benjamin Brandreth emigrated from England in 1834.

So what began with indigestion concludes with emetics.

Select Bibliography

LUCILLE KING, 'Notes on Poe's Sources', *University of Texas Studies in English* vol. 10 (1930), pp. 128–34

ROBERT LEE RHEA, 'Some Observations on Poe's Origins', *University of Texas Studies in English* vol. 10 (1930), pp. 145–6

BURTON R. POLLIN, ' "Some Words with a Mummy" Reconsidered', *Emerson Society Quarterly* vol. 59 (1969), reprinted in *New Approaches to Poe: A Symposium*, ed. Richard P. Benton (1970), pp 60–67

THE POWER OF WORDS

First published
United States Magazine and Democratic Review (June 1845)

Reprinted
Broadway Journal (25 October 1845)

Translated
Baudelaire, 'Puissance de la Parole', *Le Pays* (August 1854)

No thought can perish. The conservation of force – whether as waves, or words – is everlasting, 'upward and onward for ever in their modifications of old forms' – that is '*in their creation of new*'.

This rhapsody is the ultimate link between the angelic dialogues and *Eureka*: the poet-creator confronting his Creator as poet. His special trial-ground is 'the very brink of sleep', 'where 'the confines of the waking world blend with those of the world of dreams'. There he must attempt to detain, control and memorize his ecstatic visions:

. . . I so regard them, through a conviction (which seems a portion of the ecstasy itself) that this ecstasy, in itself, is of a character supernal to the Human Nature – is a glimpse of the spirit's outer world; and I arrive at this conclusion – if this term is at all applicable to instantaneous intuition – by a perception that the delight experienced has, as its element, but *the absoluteness of novelty*. I say the absoluteness – for in these fancies – let me now term them psychal impressions – there is really nothing even approximate in character to impressions ordinarily received. It is as if the five senses were supplanted by five myriad others alien to mortality.

Now, so entire is my faith in the *power of words*, that, at times, I have believed it possible to embody even the evanescence of fancies such as I have attempted to describe . . . In saying this I am not to be understood as supposing that the fancies, or psychal impressions, to which I allude, are confined to my individual self – are not, in a word, common to all mankind –

for on this point it is quite impossible that I should form an opinion – but nothing can be more certain than that even a partial record of the impressions would startle the universal intellect of mankind, by the *supremeness of the novelty* of the material employed, and of its consequent suggestions. In a word – should I ever write a paper on this topic, the world will be compelled to acknowledge that, at last, I have done an original thing.

'Marginalia' no. 5, *Graham's Magazine* (March 1846)

1. (p. 171) *a spirit new-fledged with immortality!*: The weakness of *Oinos* (Greek, 'wine') is the confused intoxication of a fledgling spirit. In 'the acquisition of knowledge' angels 'are for ever blessed' (*Agathos*, 'good').

2. (p. 171) *There are no dreams in Aidenn*: As there are for Poe, bodybound on earth:

I am aware of these 'fancies' only when I am upon the very brink of sleep, with the consciousness that I am so. I have satisfied myself that this condition exists but for an inappreciable *point* of time – yet it is crowded with these 'shadows of shadows'; and for absolute *thought* there is demanded time's *endurance*.

'Marginalia' no. 5

A *cri de coeur* he was to repeat on attempting his great poem 'On the Cosmogony of the Universe':

These ideas – conceptions such as *these* – unthought-like thoughts – soul-reveries rather than conclusions or even considerations of the intellect: – ideas, I repeat, such as these, are such as we can alone hope profitably to entertain in any effort at grasping the great principle, *Attraction*.

Eureka, pp. 236-7

3. (p. 171) *the loud harmony of the Pleiades*: Centre of the universe, according to one astronomical theory (to be dismissed by Poe), and thus 'the throne' of God. cf. 'the hypothesis of Mädler – that there exists, in the centre of the Galaxy, a stupendous globe about which all the systems of the cluster revolve'. He even went 'so far as to designate a particular star, Alcyone in the Pleiades, as being at or about the very spot around which a general *revolution* is performed' (*Eureka*, p. 294).

4. (p. 172) *for pansies ... the beds of the triplicate and triple-tinted suns*: For '*pensées*' rather: '... and there is pansies, that's for thoughts.' (*Hamlet* IV, v, 176)

5. (p. 172) *as no thought can perish, so no act is without infinite result*: The idea derives from Pascal:

Le moindre mouvement importe à toute la nature; la mer entière change pour une pierre. Ainsi, dans la grâce, la moindre action importe par ses suites à tout. Donc tout est important.

En chaque action, il faut regarder, outre l'action, notre état présent, passé, futur, et des autres à qui elle importe, et voir les liaisons de toutes ces choses. Et lors on sera bien retenu.

Les Pensées, 505

The least movement affects the whole of nature; the entire sea is changed by one stone. So it is with grace: the least action affects everything in its train. Everything, then, is important.

In all we do, we must look beyond the action to our present, past and future state, as well as to others whom it affects, and perceive the interaction of all these things. And so we shall keep ourselves well in check.

A tossed pebble changes the whole sea. In our actions, then, we must consider a whole web of moral cause and effect. Thus the need for self-control. Yet Poe ignores this control. Ignoring this moral responsibility – typically enough, as Allen Tate noted – he concentrates purely on Pascal's 'physical analogy for divine grace' ('The Angelic Imagination: Poe and the Power of Words', p. 127).

Even the mathematical underpinning is delusory: 'the results of any given impulse' are not 'absolutely endless'. Though Poe was to expand on its poetic potentiality:

If I propose to ascertain the influence of one mote in a sunbeam on its neighboring mote, I cannot accomplish my purpose without first counting and weighing all the atoms in the Universe and defining the precise positions of all at one particular moment. If I venture to displace, by even the billionth part of an inch, the microscopical speck of dust which lies now on the point of my finger, what is the character of that act upon which I have adventured? I have done a deed which shakes the Moon in her path, which causes the Sun to be no longer the Sun, and which alters forever the destiny of the multitudinous myriads of stars that roll and glow in the majestic presence of their Creator.

Eureka, p. 236

6. (p. 174) *the source of all thought is – God*: Echoing *John*:

In the beginning was the Word, and the Word was with God, and the Word was God.

The same was in the beginning with God.

All things were made by him; and without him was not any thing made that was made.

i, 1–3

7. (p. 174) *this fair star – which is the greenest and yet most terrible*:

As recently as 1832 Sir John Herschel had first observed the orbits of double stars. It is the smaller of two double stars that appears greenish or blueish green.

Select Bibliography

ALLEN TATE, 'The Angelic Imagination: Poe and the Power of Words', *Kenyon Review* vol. 14 (1952), pp. 455–75; reprinted in *The Man of Letters in the Modern World: Selected Essays, 1928–1955* (New York: Meridian Books, 1955), pp. 113–45

THE SYSTEM OF DR TARR AND PROF. FETHER

First published
Graham's Lady's and Gentleman's Magazine (November 1845)

Translated
Baudelaire, 'Le Système du Docteur Goudron et du Professeur Plume', *Le Monde Illustré* (January 1865)

Not science fiction exactly, this story is included here as a psychiatrical hoax: with its dire projection of the effects of unbridled self-expression both on mentally disturbed patients and their permissive keepers.

But racial threats, too, lurk in this southern asylum. The new 'soothing system' that would *abolish* all punishments and confinements inevitably ricochets, it seems, on its progenitor, driving him mad. Once mad, moreover, he devises a second system, its diametrical opposite: that of tarring and feathering – lynching in other words, as Negroes and suspected Abolitionists were regularly lynched in the South. Thus the guardian–abolitionists of system 1, so indulgent to their childish wards, inevitably become the scapegoat–victims of system 2. But that is still not the end of this fatal cycle. Such violence too must inevitably rebound; the very keepers be degraded to stereotypes of bestial lust: 'Chimpanzees, Ourang-Outangs, or big black baboons of the Cape of Good Hope'. Howling vengeance they burst in – a leaping, lunatic mob of blacks.

This is no simple paradigm of slaves tired of slavery dispossessing their masters. Both Abolitionism and Negro slavery converge on this battlefield in lunatic terror. Such is Poe's vision of America – that asylum of the unlicensed free, mankind's last 'Good Hope': a madhouse, a lynch mob tarring and feathering to the discordant strains of 'Yankee Doodle', with wily blacks in the cellars plotting revenge. If system 1 (of the Abolitionist North) naïvely compounds the danger, system 2 (of the 'extreme' South) is suicidal.

1. (p. 176) *what is vulgarly termed the 'system of soothing'* : Poe was personally acquainted with Dr Pliny Earle who had served as resident physician at the asylum of Frankford, Pennsylvania, and Blooming-dale, New York. Both had introduced the 'Moral Treatment' that Dickens had so enthusiastically endorsed, on his visit to the State Hospital for the Insane in South Boston, as 'admirably conducted on those enlightened principles of conciliation and kindness, which twenty years ago would have been worse than heretical . . .' :

'Evince a desire to show some confidence, and repose some trust, even in mad people,' said the resident physician, as we walked along the galleries, his patients flocking round us unrestrained. Of those who deny or doubt the wisdom of this maxim after witnessing its effects, if there be such people still alive, I can only say that I hope I may never be summoned as a Juryman on a Commission of Lunacy whereof they are the subjects; for I should certainly find them out of their senses, on such evidence alone.

American Notes (1842), ch. 3

Instead of the so-called 'mechanical confinement' – of chaining and straitjackets, that is – 'Moral Treatment' was based on a system of mutual confidence and self-respect. Poe's tale was possibly conceived as a direct parody of such Dickensian good cheer: 'Besides . . . the visitor, the doctor and his relatives, the music, and the use of the "soothing system" – there is the discussion of the banquet or meal, the presiding officer's attempt to humor the deranged as the doctor humored the would-be queen in Dickens' account, and there is the ridicule of Dickens' belief that each insane person was tolerant of the fancies of all but his own' (William Whipple, p. 132).

An even closer model, however, was a private asylum at Palermo, run by 'a whimsical Sicilian Baron' in a converted castle, visited by Nathaniel Parker Willis in 1834 (Letter 69, *Pencillings by the Way*, 1835). This account was turned into a story, 'The Madhouse of Palermo' (1834, reprinted 1836), reviewed by Poe in the *Southern Literary Messenger* (August 1836). That southern retreat – a *Casa dei Pazzi* rather than a *Maison de Santé*, as Richard P. Benton in-geniously argued – may well be Poe's ultimate source.

2. (p. 181) *meats enough to have feasted the Anakim* : 'And there we

saw the giants, the sons of Anak, which come of the giants ...'
(*Numbers* xiii, 33)

3. (p. 182) *'monstrum horrendum ... cui lumen ademptum'*: Of Poly-
phemus: 'a monster fearful and hideous, vast and eyeless' (Virgil,
Aeneid III, 658).

4. (p. 184) *Demosthenes' from the top ... Lord Brougham from the
mouth*: Like a phrenological composite portrait, that is, or a living
embodiment of Lavater's *Physiognomische Fragmente* (1775).

Lord Brougham, Lord Chancellor (1830–35) – one of the founders
of the *Edinburgh Review*, of the Society for the Diffusion of Useful
Knowledge, and of the University of London – was another of Poe's
pet peeves. He had written a scathing review of his *Critical and
Miscellaneous Writings*:

> The Broughams of the human intellect are never its Newtons or its
> Bayles ... His whole design consists in an immethodical collection of the
> most *striking* and at the same time most *popularly comprehensible facts* in
> general science.
>
> *Graham's Magazine* (March 1842)

The head, then, is part oratorical genius, part versatile quack.

5. (p. 185) *the tee-totum ... You would have roared with laughter to
see him spin*: Originally '*T totum*', a small four-sided disk, having a
capital letter inscribed on each of its sides. It was twirled like a top.
The letter uppermost when it fell decided the fortune of the player.
The letters were once the initials of Latin words: T *totum*, A *aufer*,
D *depone*, N *nihil*. Later they became the initials of English words: T
take-all , H *half*, N *nothing*, P *put down*.

6. (p. 188) *bellowed like so many brazen bulls of Phalaris*: Tyrant of
Agrigentum in Sicily (*c.* 550 B.C.) who burnt his victims alive in a
brazen bull.

7. (p. 189) *a sort of Pandemonium in petto*: Literally 'in the breast',
viz. undisclosed for personal contemplation. But the Italian ran away
with Poe. What he must have meant was a 'petty Pandemonium'.

8. (p. 190) *as he had gammoned him sufficiently*: Slang, for humbug
or hoax.

Select Bibliography

WILLIAM WHIPPLE, 'Poe's Two-Edged Satiric Tale', *Nineteenth-
Century Fiction* vol. 9 (1954), pp. 121–33

RICHARD WILBUR, 'The House of Poe', 1959 (in *The Recognition of Edgar Allan Poe*, ed. Eric W. Carlson, Ann Arbor: University of Michigan Press, 1966), p. 275

RICHARD P. BENTON, 'Poe's "The System of Dr Tarr and Prof. Fether": Dickens or Willis?', *Poe Newsletter* vol. 1 (1968, pp. 7–9.

THE FACTS IN THE CASE OF M. VALDEMAR

First Published

American Whig Review (December 1845)

Reprinted

Broadway Journal (20 December 1845)
Morning Post (London: 3 January 1846), as 'Mesmerism in America'
Popular Record of Modern Science (London: 10 January 1846), as 'The Case of M. Valdemar'
Mesmerism 'In Articulo Mortis'. an Astounding and Horrifying Narration Shewing the extraordinary power of Mesmerism in arresting the Progress of Death. By Edgar A. Poe, Esq. of New York (London: Short & Co., 1846). A pamphlet, priced three pence
Boston Museum (18 August 1849)

Translated

Baudelaire, 'Mort ou vivant, cas de Mr. Valdemar', *Le Pays* (September 1854); retitled, 'La Vérité sur le cas de M. Valdemar'

This story took the world by storm. In the very month of publication a mesmerist from Boston, Robert H. Collyer, wrote to Poe:

> Your account of M. Valdemar's case has been universally copied in this city, and has created a very great sensation . . . I have not the least doubt of the *possibility* of such a phenomenon; for I did actually restore to active animation a person who died from excessive drinking of ardent spirits . . . I will give you the detailed account on your reply to this, which I require for publication, in order to put at rest the growing impression that your account is merely a *splendid creation* of your own brain, not having any truth in fact.

A year later Poe was proudly reporting to the editor, Evert A. Duyckinck, that the 'Valdemar Case' had 'fairly gone the rounds of the London Press'. It was pirated in England. It was even circulating in France. On his dedicating *The Raven and Other Poems* (1845) 'To the Noblest of her Sex – Elizabeth Barrett Browning', she replied:

there is a tale of yours which I do not find in this volume, but which is going the rounds of the newspapers, about Mesmerism ('the Valdemar Case'), throwing us all into – dreadful doubts as to whether it can be true, as the children say of ghost stories. The certain thing in the tale in question is the power of the writer, and the faculty he has of making horrible improbabilities seem near and familiar.

So generally was 'M. Valdemar' accepted as a scientific description of a real event that Poe had eventually to fend off fan letters with 'the facts'. ' "Hoax" *is* precisely the word suited to M. Valdemar's case,' he replied to a Scots admirer from Stonehaven. 'Some few persons believe it – but *I* do not – and don't you.' (30 December 1846). ' "The Valdemar Case" was a hoax, of course,' he informed a young medical student from Brunswick, Maine (11 March 1847)

1. (p. 194) *M. Ernest Valdemar* ... *(under the* nom de plume *of Issachar Marx)*: This legally-minded 'Monsieur' who lives in Harlem, translating Schiller and Rabelais under a Jewish pseudonym, seems some kind of Franco-American Pole. A kinsman of Chopin, perhaps, rehearsing his one grim nocturne. Even the name (literally *val-de-mar*) spells his doom: suspended for seven months between life and death – which is his agonizing descent into the maelström.

2. (p. 195) *resembling those of John Randolph*: John Randolph of Roanoke, a fellow Virginian, died in 1833, twelve years earlier. In his old age he had become increasingly eccentric, occasionally suffering from bouts of madness. His political stance must have appealed to Poe. 'I am an aristocrat,' he declared. 'I love liberty; I hate equality.'

3. (p. 196) *The osseous symptoms rendered an exact diagnosis impossible*: Even a modern X-ray might not expose Valdemar's internal ailments with quite such accuracy. Poe, Sidney E. Lind suggests, may have combined a number of *post mortem* reports for this living autopsy.

4. (p. 203) *As I rapidly made the mesmeric passes*: As early as 1855 the anonymous author of *Rambles and Reveries of an Art Student in Europe* pointed to the last page of Justinus Kerner, *The Seeress of Prevorst* (translated from German into English, 1845) as the source for Poe's gruesome finale:

Once, when she appeared dead, some one having uttered my name, she started into life again, and seemed unable to die – the magnetic relation between us not yet broken. She was, indeed, susceptible to magnetic influences to the last; for, when she was already cold, and her jaws stiff, her mother having made three passes over her face, she lifted her eyelids and moved her lips. At ten o'clock her sister saw a tall bright form enter the chamber, and, at the same instant, the dying woman uttered a loud cry of joy; her spirit seemed then to be set free. After a short interval, her soul also departed, leaving behind it a totally irrecognizable husk – not a single trace of her former features remaining.

5. (p. 203) *of loathsome – of detestable putridity*: 'putridity' is Poe's final manuscript correction in his own copy of the the the *Broadway Journal* in place of 'putrescence'.

Select Bibliography

SIDNEY E. LIND, 'Poe and Mesmerism', *Publications of the Modern Language Association* vol. 62 (1947), pp. 1077–94

DORIS V. FALK, 'Poe and the Power of Animal Magnetism', *Publications of the Modern Language Association* vol. 84 (1969), p. 536–46

EUREKA

First published

'Eureka: A Prose Poem' (New York: Geo. P. Putnam, June 1848)

Translated

Baudelaire, 'Eureka, poëme en prose, ou essai sur l'Univers matériel et spirituel', in four instalments, *Revue internationale mensuelle*, Geneva (October 1859 to 1860). The translation was not finally completed until 1863 (Paris: Michel Lévy, 1864)

What I have propounded will (in good time) revolutionize the world of Physical & Metaphysical Science. I say this calmly – but I say it.

To George W. Eveleth: 29 February 1848

It is no use to reason with me *now*; I must die. I have no desire to live since I have done 'Eureka'. I could accomplish nothing more.

To Maria Clemm: 7 July 1849

On 3 February 1848, Edgar Allan Poe read a two-hour lecture 'On the Cosmogony of the Universe' at the Society Library, New York. It was delivered with all the aplomb of an Edwin Booth:

He appeared inspired, and his inspiration affected the scant audience almost painfully. He wore his coat tightly buttoned across his slender chest; his eyes seemed to glow like those of his own raven . . .*

Eureka, 'A Prose Poem', was the extension and culmination of that lecture. His wife, Virginia, had died the previous year. Maria Clemm, his aunt (and mother-in-law), was now his sole support – sole audience of his 'Essay on the Material and Spiritual Universe', his *De Rerum Natura* and *Novum Organum*, or 'Book of Truths'. She later recalled:

He never liked to be alone, and I used to sit up with him, often until four o'clock in the morning, he at his desk, writing, and I dozing in my chair. When he was composing 'Eureka', we used to walk up and down the garden, his arm around me, mine around him, until I was so tired I could not walk. He would stop every few minutes and explain his ideas to me, and ask if I understood him . . .†

No doubt, Mrs Clemm – all motherliness – declared she did. For Poe insisted on an edition of 50,000, exclaiming: 'I have solved the secret of the universe.' George Putnam accepted the 'pamphlet'; he advanced a payment of fourteen dollars, extracting a receipt and signed promise 'not to ask or apply for any other loans or advance from said Putnam in any way'. For Poe it was a humiliating bargain.‡ Yet the printing of a mere 500 copies published sold very slowly.

Not that the reception of the lecture had been unfavourable. To the contrary, the *Weekly Universe* was enthusiastic. The *Evening Post* and the *Express* commented intelligently.

The work has all the completeness and oneness of plot required in a poem, with all the detail and accuracy required in a scientific lecture.

Express (4 February 1848)

His remarks on the subject were characterized by the strong analytical powers and intense capacity of imagination which distinguish him.

Tribune (4 February 1848)

. . . a nobler effort than any other Mr Poe has yet given to the world.

Courier and Enquirer (11 February 1848)

The book reviews, however, were distinctly cooler. Perhaps that

---

*Maunsell B. Field, *Memories of Many Men* (New York, 1874), p. 224.

†R. E. Shapley in a Philadelphia newspaper, quoted by George E. Woodberry (1894).

‡As he wrily informed Charles Astor Bristed, grandson of John Jacob (Fordham: 7 June 1848).

extraordinary mixture of grotesque and arabesque alone was enough to put off the 'Student of Theology' (in the *Literary World*) who so incensed Poe.* And little has changed. American and British readers have never been able to take this swan-song very seriously. They simply skip it. Until recently only the French have listened intently enough to hear in its vortices premonitions of our future. Yet the imaginative sweep, the intellectual coherence, the scientific and spiritual implications – to all who stay the course – remain stupendous.

Poe's scientific premises were threefold:

1 Keplerian physics on the elliptical orbit of planets.
2 Newtonian laws of gravity and motion.
3 Laplace's wave-theory of light and nebular hypothesis.

That is, he inherited the divinely controlled, mechanistic universe of Newton and Locke in which God, its aboriginal cause, is also the continuing source of its energy or thrust; and man, a privileged 'member of the cosmical family of Intelligences', for whose perfection the universe was created. What in Newtonian terms, however, was seen as a static 'fixed design' is now construed as a continually evolving and devolving process. Poe celebrates the organic cycles of a finite 'Universe of Stars', whose nuclear *Spirit* is immanent and identical with the creative fission itself.

The word 'scientist' had been coined only eight years earlier.† Poe, like Newton, still thought of himself as a 'natural philosopher' whose ultimate affiliations were less with research than with 'natural theology'. He wrote disdainfully:

> One thing is certain that the objections of *merely* scientific men – men, I mean, who cultivate the physical sciences to the exclusion, in a greater or less degree, of the mathematics, of metaphysics and of logic – are generally invalid except in respect to scientific *details*. Of all persons in the world, they are at the same time the most bigoted and the least capable of using, generalizing, or deciding upon the facts which they bring to light in the course of their experiments. And these are the men who chiefly write the criticisms *against* all efforts at generalization - denouncing these efforts as 'speculative' and 'theoretical'.‡

Philosophers not merely recognized God's wisdom and rationality displayed in the divine design since the creation, but revealed the key to those cryptic laws governing the operations of God. Poe's *Eureka*, as much as Emerson's *Nature* (1836), was (in Aristotle's phrase) 'the

---

* See letter to Charles Fenno Hoffman (Fordham : 20 September 1848).
† By William Whewell in *Philosophy of the Inductive Sciences* (1840).
‡ To George E. Isbell (New York : 29 February 1848).

product of wonder'. Both were cryptographers studiously deciphering the workings of nature. Both still functioned in a post-Newtonian universe.

In Newton's picture the material world basically comprised so many fixed kinds of 'solid, hard, massy Particles', whose shape, size, and number had been determined by God at the creation.* These particles were not wholly independent in their behaviour. Instead, they interacted by forces of attraction and repulsion, depending on the distances separating them; while, in addition, there were certain other 'immaterial' agencies (e.g. light, magnetism, electricity) which had something in common with the 'electric and elastic Spirit' associated with perception and volition in the human nervous system, and which were transmitted between the particles through the intermediary of a weightless 'Aether'. Of these, however, he refused to say anything on the ground that experimental knowledge was inadequate. In the very last paragraph of the *Principia Mathematica* (1687), he calls attention to a whole list of his omissions:

> I should have liked to say something of the highly subtle spirit which pervades crass bodies and lurks in them, by whose force the particles of bodies attract each other to within minute distances and cohere in this contiguity; electrical bodies act at greater distances, repelling others as well as attracting them; light is emitted, is reflected, is refracted, is inflected, and warms bodies; and sensation is excited, and the limbs of animals are moved at will, by vibrations of this spirit propagated through the solid nerve-filaments from the external sense-organs to the brain and from the brain to the muscles. But these matters cannot be expounded in a few words; nor is there a sufficiency of the experiments by which the laws of this spirit's action would have to be accurately determined and demonstrated.

Scientific developments – even in Poe's lifetime, but strikingly after his death – seemed to confirm Newton's premisses. John Dalton's concept of 'chemical atoms' (formulated in the first volume of *A New System of Chemical Philosophy*, 1808) had been applied to a table of atomic weights as early as 1803. By 1870 the physical idea of 'molecules' had been employed simultaneously by the German physicist Rudolf Clausius and James Clerk Maxwell as the foundation for their dynamical theory of heat and gases. Together Dalton's 'atoms' and Maxwell's 'molecules' seemed to provide a sure identification for Newton's 'particles'. Meanwhile Maxwell was demonstrating that light, magnetism and electricity, far from being an assorted trio of separate mysteries, were really alternative manifestations of a single

---

* The description is Stephen Toulmin's.

class of mystery (transverse waves) that conformed to a single set of mathematical equations. Maxwell's theory of electro-magnetism seemed brilliantly to cap the Newtonian system. At last Newton's mystical talk of elastic Spirits, immaterial agencies and weightless Aether had secured its authoritative, theoretical base.

But Newton had his blind spots. He could be uncritical. In the *Scholium*, appended to his definitions, he distinguished absolute time (which 'in itself and without relation to anything external flows at a uniform rate') from relative time ('measured by movement'), absolute space ('everywhere uniform and immobile') from relative space, absolute motion from relative motion – never asking why relative time, relative space, relative motion alone might not suffice for his brand of 'experimental philosophy'. He could be illogical. In the *Scholium Generale* (or general appendix) having demolished the Cartesian theory of vortices, he concludes that this in itself *proves* that space, far from being full of the subtlest matter, must be a vacuum. He could be sweeping. Having admitted his ignorance in laboratory terms of electric repulsion, electric attraction, light, physical sensation, will-power, he ascribes the whole rag-bag of these mysteries to a single phenomenon 'X', a *spiritus subtilissimus*, a force of which he can say nothing since it has totally evaded his mathematics. But were the phenomena of light consistent with his doctrine of empty space? Was the admission of an electric attraction consistent with his doctrine that mass is simply *quantity* of matter? A further complication arose with the acceptance of John Dalton's theory of 'chemical atoms'. These atoms varied from one another in mass. If the ultimate 'particles' were not uniform, but varied according to a scale of atomic weights, what became of the corpuscular theory of matter? What else was that theoretical atom – Newton's primordial 'particle' – but a unit of mass? How could *physical* quantity of itself be the key to a specific *chemical* reaction? An essential bridge between physics and chemistry was missing.

That was Poe's quandary. He inherited the Newtonian system with all its strengths and weaknesses. A critical example is his treatment of 'ether'. Of course he was not equipped with Clausius' second law of thermodynamics nor Maxwell's work on the laws of the electro-magnetic field. Yet he is no mere victim of Newton's studied vagueness on the subject of that *spiritus subtilissimus*; he stands up for his master's vacuum against the proponents of ethereal matter, proving himself as percipient in his way as Newton in his, even though the maestro at this point sadly lets him down.

For a primal energy, an 'ether', was believed to permeate all space, hung even between the minutest particles of observable matter. Sometimes called 'luminiferous ether', this was the medium through which light was transmitted from the sun, atoms were confined in their physically perceived forms, even sense data transferred from mind to mind. Once conceived as a fifth element, a quintessence, a purer form of air or fire, it was usually described by post-Newtonian physicists as a unique kind of matter: not divided into particles, uniform, homogeneous. Its function was to propagate wave-like disturbances caused by the movement of the particles. Itself stationary, all movements were movements through it. Though all-pervasive, it offered no resistance to these movements, being at once elastic and perfectly rigid.

It is surely to Poe's credit that he rejected attempts either to ascribe a corpuscular structure to this ether – that is, to conceive it as a highly rarefied gas – or to conceive light as a stream of moving particles. (Though he skirts close, mingling 'light-particles' with 'light-impressions', as if the two concepts were casually interchangeable.) For both attempts failed the experimental test. Poe echoed his master:

> To electricity – so, for the present, continuing to call it – we *may* not be wrong in referring the various physical appearances of light, heat and magnetism; but far less shall we be liable to err in attributing to this strictly spiritual principle the more important phaenomena of vitality, consciousness and *Thought*.

Or again:

> It will be remembered that I have myself assumed what we may term *an ether*. I have spoken of a subtle *influence* which we know to be ever in attendance on matter, although becoming manifest only through matter's heterogeneity. To this *influence* – without daring to touch it at all in any effort at explaining its awful *nature* – I have referred the various phaenomena of electricity, heat, light, magnetism; and more – of vitality, consciousness, and thought – in a word, of spirituality. It will be seen, at once, then, that the ether thus conceived is radically distinct from the ether of the astronomers; inasmuch as theirs is *matter* and mine *not*.

This need for a vacuum – checked by the counter-need for some elastic, immaterial ether – confounded Newton to the very end. And there the master left his disciple in the lurch.

Despite obvious scientific quirks, moreover, Poe scored some surprisingly clear-headed hits. He questioned the Euclidean assumption that the axioms of geometry are self-evident truths at the very time when the Russian Lobachevsky and Hungarian Bolyai were laying the foundations of a non-Euclidean geometry, based not on axioms but 'space definitions', which might be 'inconceivable' but were never 'inconsistent'. He recognized in light years 'the phantoms of processes completed long in the Past'. He correctly quoted the great German astronomer F. W. Bessel on his discovery of the parallax of the fixed star 61 Cygni. He correctly rejected 'the hypothesis of Mädler – that there exists, in the centre of the Galaxy, a stupendous globe about which all the systems of the cluster revolve'. He correctly dismissed 'the idea of a retarding ether' with reference to Lagrange's work on 'the configurations of the spheroids'.

But even more remarkable are his adaptations and revisions of the Newtonian system. Long before Einstein he insisted on a finite Universe of Stars:

No astronomical fallacy is more untenable, and none has been more pertinaciously adhered to, than that of the absolute *illimitation* of the Universe of Stars.

And as space is finite, he argued, so is time:

the considerations through which, in this Essay, we have proceeded step by step, enable us clearly and immediately to perceive that *Space and Duration are one.*

For the Universe of Stars is an evolutionary Universe; and the explosion of energy which at once began time and began, in time, to generate space, may even now – as R. H. Fowler first demonstrated – be in a progressive state of collapse.*

If the propositions of this Discourse are tenable, the 'state of progressive collapse' is *precisely* that state in which alone we are warranted in considering All Things; and, with due humility, let me here confess that, for my part, I am at a loss to conceive how any *other* understanding of the existing condition of affairs, could ever have made its way into the human brain. 'The tendency to collapse' and 'the attraction of gravitation' are convertible phrases.

For all matter is resolved to energy – that is, to Attraction and Repulsion:

---

* Since Einstein a wholly new vocabulary of astronomical collapse has entered the language: white dwarf, quasar, pulsar, supernova, neutron star, black hole. The concept of a 'black hole' – an assemblage of matter shrunk to a state so dense as to become invisible – would have particularly appealed to Poe. As early as 1926 R. H. Fowler proposed that a star, which has burned all its fuel, collapses upon itself to form one gigantic, dense super-molecule, or 'white dwarf'.

So rigorously is this the case – so thoroughly demonstrable is it that Attraction and Repulsion are the *sole* properties through which we perceive the Universe – in other words, by which Matter is manifested to Mind – that, for all merely argumentative purposes, we are fully justified in assuming that Matter *exists* only as Attraction and Repulsion – that Attraction and Repulsion *are* matter : – there being no conceivable case in which we may not employ the term 'Matter' and the terms 'Attraction' and 'Repulsion', taken together, as equivalent, and therefore convertible, expressions in Logic.

As modern research has shown, there is now no matter; there is only electrical energy. The inertia of the various parts of the atom – the negative 'electrons', positive 'protons' and neutral 'neutrons' – is exclusively electromagnetic in origin.

The fundamental law in Poe's Universe is 'the complete *mutuality*', 'that absolute *reciprocity of adaptation* which is the idiosyncrasy of the Divine Art . . .' For each law of nature depends at all points on all the other laws. This reciprocal dependence extends even to causality. As causality is seen as symmetrical, cause and effect can indistinguishably change their roles :

In Divine constructions the object is either design or object as we choose to regard it – and we may take at any time a cause for an effect, or the converse – so that we can never absolutely decide which is which.

So too the same symmetrical and reciprocal relationship informs matter, time, space, light and gravity. It was Paul Valéry who first associated Poe's coherence theory of truth with Einstein's theory of relativity. At their broadest synthesis, Poe's Universe and Einstein's cohere.

But Poe embraces not only physical phenomena, but life and consciousness. As everything in modern physics is stirred by deeper and deeper agitations, radiations, 'seemingly *gyrating*, or *vortical* movements', as matter dissolves layer by layer to converting charges of energy, the reciprocal law of cause and effect is seen to operate even between the scientist as observer and the objects of his observation. Nothing now, not even our central nervous system or cerebral cortex, is exempt. So only now can we begin to acknowledge the total coherence, the infinite play of mirror imagery, in Poe's design. For this absolute symmetry of the whole Universe, he claimed, inheres in the very structures of our minds. Thus his ultimate, his fundamental hypothesis : that the poetic instinct will lead undeviatingly to truth.

And, in fact, the sense of the symmetrical is an instinct which may be depended on with an almost blindfold reliance. It is the poetical essence of the Universe – *of the Universe* which, in the supremeness of its symmetry, is but the most sublime of poems. Now symmetry and consistency are convertible terms: – thus Poetry and Truth are one. A thing is consistent in the ratio of its truth – true in the ratio of its consistency. *A perfect consistency, I repeat, can be nothing but an absolute truth.* We may take it for granted, then, that Man cannot long or widely err, if he suffer himself to be guided by his poetical, which I have maintained to be his truthful, in being his symmetrical, instinct.

1. (p. 207) DEDICATED TO ALEXANDER VON HUMBOLDT: Celebrated for his journey to Central and South America (1799–1804), that laid the foundations of physical geography and meteorology. His *Kosmos* began to appear in 1845 and was only now being translated into English. So it is unlikely that Poe had read even the whole of the first volume. What he had certainly seen were the reviews. By June 1848 at least nine articles – all laudatory – had been published in Britain and America.

2. (p. 212) *His design is simply synæretical*: 'synaeretical', rather: from Greek, *synairesis*, contraction.

3. (p. 213) *the* Mare Tenebrarum ... *well described by the Nubian geographer, Ptolemy Hephestion*: A darky into the dark: the geographer is 'Nubian' only because he swept Poe's mind again and again into the Sea of Shadows that once encircled the known world. Yet only here is he identified; and that turns out to be a hoax. There was no such geographer as Ptolemy Hephestion (a conflation of two of Alexander's childhood friends and outstanding generals, Hephaestion and Ptolemy I Soter). The Arab Idrisi, or El Yrisi, was author of the *Kitab Rujjar* that mapped the *Mare Tenebrarum*. See 'A Descent into the Maelström', p. 358, note 3.

For overlapping material, to be republished in a wholly satiric context, see 'Mellonta Tauta', p. 415, introductory note.

4. (p. 213) *called Aries and surnamed Tottle*: The pun, though obvious enough, may have been suggested by Dickens's 'A Passage in the Life of Mr Watkins Tottle' (incorporated in *Sketches by Boz*). Poe's review, 'Watkins Tottle and Other Sketches', appeared in the *Southern Literary Messenger* (June 1836).

5. (p. 214) *one Tuclid ... and one Kant*: 'with the change merely of a C for a K'. It is the cant of Kant that Poe detests: that 'most detestable species of cant – the cant of *generality*' (*Graham's Magazine*, 1842).

6. (p. 214) *the advent of one Hog, surnamed 'the Ettrick shepherd'*:

A punster's joke that irrelevantly ropes in the Scot, James Hogg (1770–1835), best remembered today for *The Confessions of a Justified Sinner* (1824).

7. (p. 214) *Baconian roads*: Of Roger Bacon, that is, and more obviously Francis Bacon of the *Novum Organum* (1620).

8. (p. 215) *titillating Scotch snuff of* detail: Dismissing such Edinburgh worthies as David Hume, Adam Smith, James Mill.

9. (p. 216) 'ex nihilo nihil fit': *De nihil nihilum, in nihilum nil posse reverti* – according to Diogenes Laertius, the central concept of Epicurean physics.

10. (p. 217) *the cleverest ancient work on its topic, which is 'Logic'*: John Stuart Mill, *A System of Logic* (1843). The 'Miller', in this millennial context, is possibly the Rev. William Miller, from New York State, founder of the Adventist Church (see 'Eiros and Charmion', p. 355, note 6). Or is it Joe Miller to join *Joe* Hume, of *Joe Miller's Jests: or The Wits Vade-Mecum*, a favourite target of Poe's 'Autography'?

11. (p. 217) *a truth to* David *Hume would very seldom be a truth to* Joe: Joseph Hume, M.P., for thirty years radical leader of the House, who added 'retrenchment' to the party watchwords 'peace and reform'.

12. (p. 220) *Champollion ... amid the phonetical hieroglyphics of Egypt*: Using the Rosetta Stone, found by Napoleon's troops near the mouth of the Nile, Jean François Champollion (1790–1832) established the key for deciphering Egyptian hieroglyphs.

13. (p. 221) 'I can afford to wait a century for readers ...': Johannes Kepler in 1619, quoted by Sir David Brewster in *Martyrs to Science* (1846), p. 197. But the whole context of this mock-quotation, Margaret Alterton showed, derives from John Drinkwater Bethune's rendering of that exultant speech:

> Nothing holds me: I will indulge in my sacred fury; I will triumph over mankind by the honest confession, that I have stolen the golden vases of the Egyptians ...
>
> *Life of Kepler* (1830)

14. (p. 222) *as a sonnet by Mr Solomon Seesaw*: who simultaneously both *as*cends and *des*cends.

15. (p. 226) *This was the untenable idea of Pascal: 'C'est une sphère*

dont le centre est partout, la circonférence nulle part.' (*Les Pensées*, 348)

But the idea was not original with Pascal. Applied to God, the definition dates back to at least the early Middle Ages.

16. (p. 226) *Baron de Bielfeld* : Jacob Friedrich, Freiherr von Bielfeld (1717–1770), 'Chancellor of All the Universities in the Dominions of his Prussian Majesty', who dedicated his *Les Premiers Traits de l'Erudition Universelle* (in three volumes) to the Prince of Wales, later George IV (translated by W. Hooper, 1770, vol. 2, p. 94).

17. (p. 231) *now as heat, now as magnetism, now as* electricity : For Poe '*electricity*', in some equivocal way, is identical with 'the repulsive influence'. He was simply wrong, however. Electricity develops forces that both attract and repel. Yet his basic hypothesis – that natural forces can only originate in two ways : by electricity and by gravitation – is interesting enough. This is the modern view.

The equation for determining the resistance between two bodies as 'the ratio of the two sums of the differences in each' seems impenetrable nonsense.

18. (p. 233) *let us adopt the more definite expressions,* 'Attraction' *and* 'Repulsion': The Italian mathematician and astronomer, Ruggiero Giuseppe Boscovich (1711–87), an early advocate of Newton's theories, first introduced these terms into molecular theory. His atoms were nuclei of attractive and repulsive forces.

19. (p. 234) *In the famous Maskelyne, Cavendish and Bailly experiments* : Nevil Maskelyne (1732–1811); Henry Cavendish (1731–1810); Francis Baily (1774–1844), one of the founders of the Royal Astronomical Society, who repeated Cavendish's pendulum experiments for determining the mean density of the earth.

20. (p. 234) *Schehallien in Wales* : Meaning Mt Schiehallion in Perthshire, Scotland.

21. (p. 235) *Bryant, in his very erudite 'Mythology'* : Jacob Bryant, *A Mythological, Etymological, and Historical Dictionary: Extracted from the Analysis of Ancient Mythology* (London, 1783).

22. (p. 236) *If I propose to ascertain the influence of one mote in a sunbeam on its neighboring mote* : A role elsewhere reserved for God: 'This power of retrogradation in its absolute fulness and perfection – this faculty of referring at *all* epochs, *all* effects to *all* causes – is of course the prerogative of the Deity alone – but in every

variety of degree, short of the absolute perfection, is the power itself exercised by the whole host of the Angelic Intelligences.' ('The Power of Words', 1845)

cf. Laplace: 'an intelligent being who, at a given instant, knew all the forces animating nature and the relative positions of the beings in nature', could, 'if his intelligence were sufficiently capacious to analyse these data, include in a formula the movements of the largest bodies of the universe and those of the smallest atom. Nothing would be uncertain for him: the future as well as the past would be present to his eyes.' (*Œuvres Complètes*, 1886, vol. 7)

23. (p. 236) *I have done a deed which shakes the Moon in her path*: In Einsteinian physics this *reductio ad absurdum* in itself becomes an argument for the finitude of the material world, and so of space. For

if space is all full of fields of force, it will follow that at every point in space there are infinite forces impinging from every side upon any piece of matter situated there; and consequently, since these forces will cancel out, none of them will act on that piece of matter at all. Determinate events happen at this or that point in space only because determinate forces are at work there; and determinate means finite.

R. G. Collingwood, *The Idea of Nature* (1945), Part III, ch. 2, p. 153

24. (p. 239) *Dr Nichol, the eloquent author of 'The Architecture of the Heavens'*; A surreptitious hit at the Rev. Dr John Pringle Nichol, Regius Professor of Astronomy at the University of Glasgow, who also happened to be lecturing in New York in the very week of Poe's *Eureka* recital. Consistently Poe distorts his quotations from Nichol's lecture, at the same time implying that they derive from his *Views of the Architecture of the Heavens in a Series of Letters to a Lady*. cf. pp. 270, 296–7.

See Frederick W. Conner, 'Poe and John Nichol: Notes on a Source of *Eureka*' (in *All These to Teach*, ed. Robert A. Bryan, 1965, pp. 190–208).

25. (p. 241) *I here declare the* modus operandi *of the Law of Gravity to be an exceedingly simple and perfectly explicable thing*: A sensational challenge in view of Newton's own unceasing doubts and hesitations. 'That gravity should be innate, inherent and essential to matter,' he once wrote to Richard Bentley, 'so that one body may act upon another at a distance, through a vacuum, without the mediation of anything else through which their action may be conveyed from one to another, is to me so great an absurdity that I believe

no man who has in philosophical matters a competent faculty of thinking, can ever fall into it.' (25 February 1692/3)

26. (p. 243) *Now, I have elsewhere observed:* It is Dupin, the detective hero of 'The Murders in the Rue Morgue', not Poe, who makes this observation:

> But it is by these deviations from the plane of the ordinary, that reason feels its way, if at all, in its search for the true . . . In fact, the facility with which I shall arrive, or have arrived, at the solution of this mystery, is in the direct ratio of its apparent insolubility in the eyes of the police.
>
> (1841)

27. (p. 246) *Here describe the whole process as one instantaneous flash:* cf. Sir Arthur Eddington: 'In the beginning all the matter created was projected with a radial motion so as to disperse even faster than the present rate of dispersal of the galaxies . . .' (*The Expanding Universe*, 1933, p. 80)

28. (p. 251) *the assumption of a principle . . . at an epoch when* no '*principles*', *in* anything, *exist:* Some mathematicians have shown cautious appreciation of Poe's intuitive hits. He 'seems to have had the mind of a mathematician,' Sir Arthur Eddington wrote to Arthur Hobson Quinn, 'and consequently was not to be put off with vague phrases; and made a creditable attempt to introduce precision of thought.' (29 September 1940)

Others have been more sceptical:

> Can it be science or the work of a mathematically inclined mind when that mind alone can say when laws are operative and when they are not, when forces act and when they do not, and when criticism is stifled by the arbitrary dictum that the physical principle advanced in support of an objection was not at that time valid, although half a dozen similar laws may have been invoked previously in the construction of the argument?
>
> Clarence R. Wylie, Jr, 'Mathematical Allusions in Poe',
> *Scientific Monthly* vol. 63 (1946), p. 235

29. (p. 254) *It is seen, then, that the* axiomatic principle *itself is susceptible of variation:* Poe questioned the Euclidean assumption that the axioms of geometry are self-evident truths at the very time when the Russian Lobachevsky and Hungarian Bolyai were laying the foundation of hyperbolic non-Euclidean geometry. As Poe had argued (echoing John Stuart Mill): '*in no case* is ability or inability to conceive to be taken as a criterion of axiomatic truth'.

Yet earlier he had pressed just such an axiom for all its worth:

Now, the laws of radiation are *known*. They are part and parcel of the *sphere*. They belong to the class of indisputable geometrical properties. We say of them, 'they are true – they are evident'. To demand *why* they are true, would be to demand why the axioms are true upon which their demonstration is based.

30. (p. 257) *the most magnificent of theories ... the Nebular Cosmogony of Laplace*: Two outstanding French mathematicians, the Marquis de Laplace in collaboration with Comte Lagrange, established beyond doubt Newton's hypothesis of gravitation. Lagrange's chief work, *Mécanique Analytique,* was published in 1788. The results of Laplace's researches were published in his *Mécanique Céleste* (1799–1825), translated by the American navigator Nathaniel Bowditch (1829–39). But it was his earlier, more popular work, *Exposition du système du monde* (1796), that contained a statement of the Nebular Hypothesis, attempting to give scientific form to a theory originally propounded by Swedenborg and Kant.

I '*give Laplace's theory in full*,' Poe wrote to Charles Fenno Hoffman, 'with the expression of my firm conviction of its absolute truth *at all points*. The *ground* covered by the great French astronomer compares with that covered by my theory, as a bubble compares with the ocean on which it floats ...' (Fordham: 20 September 1848)

31. (p. 262) *It is by far too beautiful, indeed,* not *to possess Truth*: But this is no Grecian Urn; here beauty, for once, may not be truth. By 1900 Laplace's Nebular Theory was rejected in favour of new hypotheses: such as Chamberlin's and Moulton's theory of the gravitational cross-pull exerted by a passing star, with variations such as Sir James Jeans' Tidal Theory, formulated in 1918. Two key objections to the Nebular Hypothesis were, first, that such rings of gaseous material would tend to form a swarm of asteroids rather than condense into a single planet; and, second, that the angular momentum of the planet in rotation was too great in proportion to the sun to make the theory plausible.

Single stars or suns, it seems, are not very common; most stars cohere in binary or still more complex systems. This has led Dr E. M. Drobyshevski, of Leningrad, recently to vindicate Laplace – but with a revolutionary twist: that *Jupiter* was the original core of the collapsing gas cloud; that as Jupiter continued to collapse and heat, rotation condensed the dispersing gas into a ring; that this ring eventually coalesced into a star with a binary relationship to its parent, Jupiter; until the tidal exchange of gas had significantly reduced the parent's mass for a dramatic reversal of roles; the once-dominant, or primary star, becoming a burnt out planet; the secondary star, its sun.

As gas was streaming between the two stars of this proto-solar system, the heavier elements naturally condensed into small planets with dense cores; the more volatile gas condensed into the gaseous planets outside Jupiter. That is why, according to Dr Drobyshevski, the terrestrial planets (Mercury, Venus, Earth and Mars) revolve between the Sun and Jupiter. (*Nature*, 5 July 1974)

32. (p. 266) *That our Moon is self-luminous*: Which, of course, has proved nonsense.

33. (p. 266) *On the Melville islands … traces of* ultra-tropical *vegetation*: In the Timor Sea, 16 miles off the north-west coast of Australia. With memories of *Symzonia*? Or a sly dig at the best-selling author of the ultra-tropical *Typee* (1846) and *Omoo* (1847)?

34. (p. 268) *confirmation … at the hands of the philosopher, Comte*: Auguste Comte, *Cours de philosophie positive* (1830–42). Sir David Brewster – long familiar to Poe for his *Letters on Natural Magic* – had reviewed Comte's book in the *Edinburgh Review* vol. 67 (1838).

35. (p. 269) *the Cloud-Land of Metaphysics*: Another species of Nebular hypothesis!

36. (p. 270) *the great 'nebula' in the constellation Orion … resolved into a simple collection of stars*: Modern spectroscopes, far outranging Lord Rosse, have revealed 'innumerable' nebulae. Sir William Herschel's catalogue, completed by his sister in 1828, listed some 2,500. cf Thomas De Quincey, *The System of the Heavens as Revealed by Lord Rosse's Telescope*, 1846.

Though contemporary scientists accepted Lord Rosse's interpretation, a resolution of the Orion nebula into a collection of stars is now known to be impossible.

37. (p. 275) *my reply is that* μέλλοντα ταῦτα: 'These things are in the future' (Sophocles, *Antigone*, 1334). See the epigraph to 'The Colloquy of Monos and Una' (1841), and the title of that final squib, 'Mellonta Tauta' (1849).

38. (p. 278) *No astronomical fallacy is more untenable … than that of the absolute* illimitation *of the Universe of Stars*: Both the dynamic and optical objection is derived from the work of Wilhelm Olbers, the German physician and astronomer.

Lucretius had posed a naïve, yet compelling question: What would happen if you went to the edge of space and threw a spear outwards. Pascal's definition of space – as 'a sphere of which the centre is everywhere, the circumference nowhere' (p. 226) – brilliantly evades the conundrum. But Einstein directly confronts Lucretius by standing Pascal's definition, as it were, on its head: his universe is 'a sphere of which the centre is nowhere, the circumference everywhere'. In this finite sphere all possible paths along which matter or radiation can travel are curved paths 'so that they are infinite in the sense of returning infinitely upon themselves, though finite in the sense of being confined within a determinate volume which is the volume of the universe' (R. G. Collingwood, *The Idea of Nature*, Part III, ch. 2, pp. 153–4).

39. (p. 280) *Each exists* ... in the bosom of its proper and particular God: Unconsciously echoing the cosmography of the early Ionian philosopher Anaximander, who too 'declared the innumerable worlds to be gods' (Aëtius, i, 17.12) which 'have come into existence by birth, situated in the plane of the earth's equator at wide intervals' (Cicero, *De Natura Deorum*, i, 10, 25).

40. (p. 282) *In guessing with Plato ... a demonstration by Alcmæon*: cf. 'The tone metaphyiscal is also a good one. If you know any big words this is your chance for them. Talk of the Ionic and Eleatic schools – of Archytas, Gorgias and Alcmæon.' ('How To Write A Blackwood Article', 1838)

A pupil of Pythagoras, author of περὶ Φύσεως (*On Nature, c.* 500 B.C.), Alcmæon is said to have been the first Greek to operate on the eye.

41. (p. 283) *Now come the nine Asteroids*: The ninth, only discovered in 1848, was left blank in the revised text.

Today more than 1,500 are recognized. Many asteroids are about a mile or less in diameter and resemble meteorites rather than small planets. Adonis, discovered in 1936, approaches within 1,500,000 miles of the earth; Hermes, discovered in 1937, comes within 485,000 miles.

42. (p. 283) *Neptune, lately discovered ... of which as yet we know little accurately*: Because of apparent irregularities in the transit of Uranus, both J. C. Adams in England and U. J. J. Leverrier in France independently computed the hypothetical location of another planet that might be influencing it. In 1846, the following year, J. C. Galle in Berlin discovered Neptune at the exact point predicted by Adams

and Leverrier. A month later the first satellite, Triton, was also detected.

43. (p. 283) *may not the law of Bode*: Johann Elert Bode (1747–1826), founder of the *Astronomisches Jahrbuch* (1774), who by 1801 had catalogued 17,240 stars and nebulae – 12,000 more than had appeared in earlier charts. In 1772 he devised a formula to express the relative distances of the planets from the sun.

44. (p. 284) *If we ascend an ordinary mountain*: These two paragraphs, that tease our imagination with the volume and weight of the Earth, derive almost verbatim – Margaret Alterton showed – from Dr Thomas Dick, *The Christian Philosopher* (1826), pp. 17 and 20.

45. (p. 289) Bessel, *not long ago deceased*: The great German astronomer, F. W. Bessel (1784–1846). His discovery of the parallax of the fixed star 61 Cygni, announced in 1838, was officially recognized in 1841 as the first fully authenticated measurement of the distance of a star.

46. (p. 290) *the elder Herschel ... within the scope of his own telescope*: Sir William Herschel's telescope, erected at Slough in 1789, had a 48-inch mirror and a focal length of 40 ft. He concluded that the whole solar system was moving forward through space, and he could indicate the point towards which it was moving.

47. (p. 292) *In the construction of plot ... in fictitious literature*: This crucial paragraph – the matrix of Poe's critical and metaphysical theories – makes its third verbatim appearance in four years. Deriving from an earlier passage among his 'Marginalia' (*Democratic Review*, November 1844), it had been openly quoted the following year to illustrate an essay on 'The American Drama' (*American Whig Review*, August 1845).

48. (p. 293) *the reveries of Fourier*: Not the social philosopher, but John Baptiste Joseph Fourier (1768–1830), the French physicist noted for his researches on heat and numerical equations.

49. (p. 293) *the hypothesis of Mädler*: Johann Heinrich von Mädler (1794–1874), the 'Mudler' of 'Mellonta Tauta', p. 319.

50. (p. 296) *says Sir John Herschel*: In *A Treatise on Astronomy* (Philadelphia, 1834).

51. (p. 297) *the elaborate calculations of Argelander*: Friedrich Wil-

helm August Argelander (1799–1875), German astronomer, who continued Bessel's work begun at Königsberg.

52. (p. 297) *Betrachtet man die nicht perspectivischen*: Poe did not know any German. This sounding quotation and its translation may have been picked up from a review.

53. (p. 301) *observed in the orbit of Encke's comet*: Though discovered by J. L. Pons in 1818, the comet was named after Johann Franz Encke, the German astronomer who calculated its orbit and accurately predicted the date of its return. cf. 'Hans Pfaall', p. 28.

54. (p. 301) *an exceedingly rare but still material medium pervading space*: Poe can scornfully dismiss this 'retarding' medium, assured that Newton, in the *Scholium Generale*, had similarly demolished the Cartesian theory of vortices: viz. the view that space is full of a continuous and very subtle matter in constant motion revolving in eddies round every body and that the rotation of planets, for example, is caused by their floating in this subtle medium and being whirled round in the solar vortex.

55. (p. 304) *Of the still more awful Future*: Einstein's argument for the spatial finitude of the universe seems further to corroborate Poe's vision of its temporal finitude.

The spectra of the spiral nebulae have revealed facts which appear to show that they are travelling outwards from a common centre, and this has resulted in the theory that the physical universe originated at a date not infinitely remote in the past, in something resembling an explosion of energy which at once began time and began, in time, to generate space.

> R. G. Collingwood, *The Idea of Nature*, Part III, ch. 2, p. 154

56. (p. 304) *with a speed prodigiously accumulative, have been rushing towards their own general centre*:

Einstein's theory predicted that there must be enough mass within the universe to keep it from flying apart indefinitely. In other words, although all of the galaxies (or clusters of galaxies) are flying apart, as though blown asunder by some primordial 'big bang', it appears that they do not have sufficient velocity to escape one another's gravity. Their dispersal, like the flight of a ball thrown upward, seems to be slowing enough so that it must ultimately reverse itself, initiating a 'falling back' that, many theorists believe, will plunge the entire universe into a single black hole.

> Walter Sullivan, 'A Hole in the Sky', *New York Times Magazine* (14 July 1974)

A 'black hole' is an assemblage of matter so dense that its gravity is strong enough to prevent anything, including light rays, from escaping. Inside a black hole time and space (as predicted by Einstein) are interchanged. Perhaps we are even now being sucked into the very edge of such a black hole. As Kip Thorne, theorist at the California Institute of Technology, has put it, we are within a universe composed of space and time created by the explosion, 'and we are trapped inside its gravitational radius. No light can escape from the universe.'

57. (p. 305) *Matter ... would disappear, and that God would remain all in all*: So retracing his path, Poe rediscovers that goal from which in dreams he had set forth:

> By a route obscure and lonely,
> Haunted by ill angels only,
> Where an Eidolon named Night
> On a black throne reigns upright,
> I have reached these lands but newly
> From an ultimate dim Thule –
> From a wild weird clime that lieth, sublime,
> Out of Space – out of Time.
>
> *Dreamland* (1844)

58. (p. 307) *And now – this Heart Divine – what is it?* It is our own: At 'every throb', another 'Tell-Tale Heart':

And have I not told you that what you mistake for madness is but over acuteness of the senses? – now, I say, there came to my ears a low, dull, quick sound, such as a watch makes when enveloped in cotton. I knew *that* sound well, too. It was the beating of the old man's heart.

(1843/45)

59. (p. 307) *We live out a Youth peculiarly haunted*: 'Our birth is but a sleep and a forgetting ...' The full Wordsworthian note of *Intimations* was sounded in 'The Island of the Fay':

I love, indeed, to regard the dark valleys, and the grey rocks, and the waters that silently smile, and the forests that sigh in uneasy slumbers, – and the proud watchful mountains that look down upon all, – I love to regard these as themselves but the colossal members of one vast animate and sentient whole – a whole whose form (that of the sphere) is the most perfect and most inclusive of all ... whose life is eternity; whose thought is that of a god; whose enjoyment is knowledge; whose destinies are lost in immensity ...

(1841)

60. (p. 309) *that Man ... shall recognize his existence as that of Jehovah*: cf.:

The word Jehovah is not Hebrew. The Hebrews had no such letters as J and V. The word is properly Yah, Wah, compounded of *Yah*, essence, and *Wah*, existing. Its full meaning is the self-existing essence of all things.

Pinakidia (1836)

61. (p. 309) *Life within Life ... and all within the* Spirit Divine: Phrase for phrase the peroration derives from 'The Island of the Fay':

As we find cycle within cycle without end, yet all revolving around one far-distant centre which is the Godhead, may we not analogically suppose, in the same manner, life within life, the less within the greater, and all within the Spirit Divine?

So question is turned to assertion; rhetorical caution, exultantly to triumph.

Select Bibliography

PAUL VALÉRY, 'Au sujet d'*Eureka*', written as introduction to a new edition of Baudelaire's translation (Paris: Helleu et Sergent, 1923); reprinted in *La Revue Européenne* (1923) and *Variété* vol. 1 (1924), pp. 113–36; translated by Malcolm Cowley in *Leonardo, Poe, Mallarmé* (Princeton University Press, 1972), 161–76

MARGARET ALLERTON, *Origins of Poe's Critical Theory*, University of Iowa Humanistic Studies vol. 2 (1925; New York: Russell & Russell, 1965)

FLOYD STOVALL, 'Poe's debt to Coleridge', *University of Texas Studies in English* vol. 10 (1930), pp. 70–127

GEORGE NORDSTEDT, 'Poe and Einstein', *Open Court* vol. 44 (1930), pp. 173–80

MARIE BONAPARTE, *Edgar Poe, sa vie – son oeuvre: étude analytique* (Paris: Denoël et Steele, 1933); translated by John Rodker as *The Life and Works of Edgar Allan Poe, a Psycho-Analytic Interpretation* (London: Hogarth Press, 1949, 1971), ch. 44, pp. 594–636

CLAYTON HOAGLAND, 'The Universe of Eureka: a comparison of the theories of Eddington and Poe', *Southern Literary Messenger* vol. 1 (1939), pp. 307–13

ARTHUR HOBSON QUINN, *Edgar Allan Poe, A Critical Biography* (New York: Appleton-Century, 1941), ch. 17, pp. 539–61

PATRICK F. QUINN, 'Poe's *Eureka* and Emerson's *Nature*', *Emerson Society Quarterly* vol. 31 (1941), pp. 4–7

E. H. DAVIDSON, *Poe: A Critical Study* (Cambridge: Harvard University Press, 1957), ch. 8, pp. 223–53

CAROL HOPKINS MADDISON, 'Poe's *Eureka*', *Texas Studies in Literature and Language* vol 2 (1960), pp. 350–67

LOUIS BROUSSARD, *The Measure of Poe* (Norman: University of Oklahoma Press, 1969), part 2, pp. 47–104

JOHN F. LYNEN, 'The death of the present', in *The Design of the Present: Essays on Time and Form in American Literature* (New Haven: Yale University Press, 1969), pp. 205–71

HARRIET R. HOLMAN, 'Hog, Bacon, Ram and other "Savans" in *Eureka*: notes toward decoding Poe's encyclopedic satire', *Poe Newsletter* vol. 2 (1969), pp. 49–55

HARRIET R. HOLMAN, 'Splitting Poe's "Epicurean Atoms": further speculations on the literary satire of *Eureka*', *Poe Studies* vol. 5 (1972), pp. 33–7

G. R. THOMPSON, 'Unity, death, and nothingness – Poe's "romantic skepticism"', *Publications of the Modern Language Association* vol. 85 (1970), pp. 297–300

DANIEL HOFFMAN, *Poe, Poe, Poe, Poe, Poe, Poe, Poe* (New York: Doubleday, 1972), ch. 10, 'The Mind of God', pp. 278–99

MELLONTA TAUTA

First published
Godey's Lady's Book (February 1849)

Prefixed to the original publication was this letter:

To the Editor of the Lady's Book:

I have the honor of sending you, for your magazine, an article which I hope you will be able to comprehend rather more distinctly than I do myself. It is a translation, by my friend Martin Van Buren Mavis, (sometimes called the 'Poughkeepsie Seer,') of an odd-looking MS. which I found, about a year ago, tightly corked up in a jug floating in the *Mare Tenebrarum* – a sea well described by the Nubian geographer, but seldom visited, now-a-days, except by the transcendentalists and divers for crotchets.

Very Truly,

EDGAR A. POE

The exact date of recovery (February 1848) links 'Mellonta Tauta' not to *Eureka* merely, but to the first public presentation of *Eureka* in lecture form, as a spoof. For whose was the ironic mask, of this final transformation, but the very seer's whose platform style had so painfully undermined that lecture? What was Andrew Jackson Davis's

The Principles of Nature, Her Divine Revelations, and A Voice to Mankind (1847) but a mysterious transcript from a state of trance?

This final 'MS. in a Bottle', dated April Fool's Day 2848, seems a satirical offshoot of that inspired lecture then, rather than of *Eureka* where such large chunks are quoted. Intended apparently for the April 1848 issue of *Godey's Lady's Book*, the hoax was expanded to a full-scale satire of mid-Victorian America.

The eighteenth century already had its anticipations of aeroplanes, even of Anglo-German air-borne combats. Dr Johnson, in *Rambler* no. 105, allowed the possibility of submarines, but with characteristic scepticism refused to accept long-range weather forecasting or central heating. The French, in particular, had a tradition of forward projectionists that included:

SEBASTIEN MERCIER, *L'An deux mille quatre cent quarante* (Amsterdam, 1770; translated as *Memoirs of the Year 2500*, 1772; reprinted Richmond, Virginia, 1799, and Liverpool, 1802);

RESTIF DE LA BRETONNE, *L'An Deux-Mille* (1790);

BARTHELEMY ENFANTIN, *Mémoirs d'un industriel de l'an 2240* (1829).

By mid century the New York emigré paper, *Le Libertaire*, carried projections by its editor Joseph Déjacque to the year 2858. Another source, used elsewhere by Poe, was Jane Webb's *The Mummy: A Tale of the Twenty-Second Century* (1827), a projection of a mere 300 years to A.D. 2126 – to an age of mobile homes (equipped with air-conditioning), climatic control, steam-ploughing, speaking tubes, coffee machines and 'malleable glass crockery' (folding to pocket-size when not in use):

Balloons, propelled by mercury vapour, are, with aerial horses and aerial sledges, the common means of locomotion. Since the whole country is completely excavated, to fall upon the surface of the earth was like tumbling on the parchment of an immense drum . . . The post is fired in cannon balls, caught by nets and preceded by hollow whistling balls of wood . . . Quicker messages were sent by heliograph transmission of light and music.

Poe's very title had been anticipated by R. F. Williams, for a satire of British moral decline, *Eureka: A Prophecy of the Future* (1837).

But all such forecasts were still imbued with the spirit of the Enlightenment: just laws, national education, universal brotherhood, polytechnic planning and wealth. 'Where can the perfectibilty of man stop,' asked Mercier, 'armed with geometry and the mechanical arts and chemistry?' Poe had nothing but scorn for such 'human-perfectibility' spokesmen – the 'wild doctrines' of Turgot, Price, Priestley and Condorcet.* His future is totalitarian and overcrowded. The key is population control. Men as individuals are abandoned; epidemics and wars, welcomed. The sea swarms with ships; the very sky, with balloons. At hundreds of miles per hour hundreds speed by on an aimless excursion cruise. Poe's millennial 'Amricca' (*am rich, am rich, am rich*) is his final send-up – a Fool's Day calculus of suicidal, doomsday collapse.

1. (p. 310) MELLONTA TAUTA: cf. *Eureka*: 'my reply is that μέλλοντα ταῦτα – I am but pausing, for a moment, on the awful threshold of *the Future.*' (p. 275) cf. the epigraph to 'The Colloquy of Monos and Una' (p. 361, note 2). cf. H. G. Wells, *The Shape of Things To Come* (1933).

2. (p. 310) ON BOARD BALLOON 'SKYLARK': To commemorate that hopeful atheist, that visionary of intellectual beauty and 'the golden years', Percy Bysshe Shelley:

> Hail to thee, blithe Spirit!
> Bird thou never wert,
> That from Heaven, or near it,
> Pourest thy full heart
> In profuse strains of unpremeditated art.
> *To a Skylark* (1821)

3. (p. 310) *one or two hundred of the* canaille: French 'a pack of dogs': 'which seems to demonstrate ... that democracy is a very admirable form of government – for dogs' (p. 319).

4. (p. 311) *designated as silk-buckingham, on account of its superior durability*: Named after James Silk Buckingham, the Egyptologist, presumably for his 'escape from death by exposure when he was left in the desert by Bedouin marauders, while ... ascending the Nile to Nubia in 1813' (Burton R. Pollin, ' "Some Words with a Mummy" Reconsidered', p. 63).

5. (p. 311) *Pundit assures me ... Pundit* knows: Whose very name – and Pundita's, of course – plays with punning insistence on the punditry of puns.

6. (p. 312) *an Irish philosopher called Furrier, on account of his ... cat-peltries*: Charles Fourier (1772–1837), the French social philoso-

---

* See 'Lionizing' (1835) and 'The Landscape Garden' (1842).

pher, who taught that industrial communities must be reorganized as a *phalanx* (an economic commune of 1,620 people) living in a *phalanstère* (a community centre, or phalanstery). The Transcendentalist commune at Brook Farm had been converted to a phalanx in 1844 and the *Harbinger*, printed at Brook Farm, became a Fourierist weekly newspaper (1845–9).

7. (p. 312) *the Hindoo Aries Tottle (as quoted by Pundit)*: Transformed from 'a Turkish philosopher called Aries and surnamed Tottle' (*Eureka*, p. 403, note 4). For what is a 'pundit' (Hindi, *pandit*) but a learned Hindu, versed in Sanskrit and religion? What was Boston, that capital of Transcendentalists, for Poe but 'Frogpondium – the "pundits" you know' (To George W. Eveleth: 4 January 1848)? And who was the arch-Transcendentalist, the Brahmin of all pundits, but Ralph Waldo Emerson? (See Harriet R. Holman, 'Hog, Bacon, Ram', p. 50).

8. (p. 313) *when Yellow or ... Violet, who is supposed to have been the first aeronaut*: A colourful confusion over Jean Pierre Blanchard, reputed inventor of the parachute. With Dr John Jeffries of Boston, Massachusetts, he made the first sea voyage by air, crossing the English Channel by balloon in 1785. His ascent at Philadelphia in 1793 was witnessed by President Washington.

Or mix yellow with violet. What do you find but a murky 'Mr Green, of Nassau-balloon notoriety'? ('Hans Pfaall', p. 30). So Samuel Morse became 'Horse'.

9. (p. 313) *one Neuclid and one Cant*: See *Eureka*, p. 403, note 5.

10. (p. 313) *the advent of one Hog, surnamed the 'Ettrick Shepherd'*: See *Eureka*, p. 403, note 6.

11. (p. 314) *'Ex nihilo nihil fit'*: See *Eureka*, p. 404, note 9.

12. (p. 315) *the cleverest ancient work on its topic, Logic*: John Stuart Mill, *A System of Logic* (1843). His utilitarian mill-horse, of course, is Jeremy Bentham.

13. (p. 316) *a perfect consistency* must be *an absolute truth*!: To recapitulate *Eureka*:

Now symmetry and consistency are convertible terms: – thus Poetry and Truth are one. A thing is consistent in the ratio of its truth – true in the ratio of its consistency. *A perfect consistency, I repeat, can be nothing but an absolute truth*.

p. 300

14. (p. 317) *perhaps there are three or four hundred passengers*: The ancestor of this jumbo jet was first proposed in a pamphlet by Etienne Gaspard Robertson, '*La Minerve*' *vaisseau aerien, destiné aux décou-vertes* (Paris, 1820). Capable of sailing for six months and making non-stop flights across the oceans, the projected 'Minerve' was to have a capacity of sixty passengers with ladders to various parts of the balloon for observation platforms.

15. (p. 317) *fully three hundred miles the hour* – that *was traveling*: cf. Pundita's eastern *alter ego*, Scheherazade. The contemporary speed record, Poe noted, was held by the Great Western Railway: 'between London and Exeter, a speeed of 71 miles per hour has been attained' (p. 149).

16. (p. 317) the route *for the great Kanadaw railroad ... marked out about nine hundred years ago!*: Poe–Pundit erred. The Canadian Pacific Railroad spanned the continent by 1885. The *route* was marked out, not in the 1940s, but throughout the 1870s on British Columbia entering the confederacy.

17. (p. 318) *in the very teeth of the laws of* gradation *so visibly impressed*: cf.:

Among other odd ideas, that of universal equality gained ground; and in the face of analogy and of God – in despite of the loud warning voice of the laws of *gradation* so visibly pervading all things in Earth and Heaven – wild attempts at an omni-prevalent Democracy were made.
                                    'The Colloquy of Monos and Una' (1841)

18. (p. 318) *a fellow of the name of* Mob: cf. Count Allamistakeo:

I asked what was the name of the usurping tyrant. As well as the Count could recollect, it was *Mob*.
                                    'Some Words with a Mummy' (1845)

cf. a fictional fellow-Southerner, Colonel Sherburn:

The pitifulest thing out is a mob; that's what an army is – a mob; they don't fight with courage that's born in them, but with courage that's borrowed from their mass, and from their officers. But a mob without any *man* at the head of it, is *beneath* pitifulness.
                                    Twain, *Adventures of Huckleberry Finn* (1884), ch. 22

Poe's own youthful, least embittered view of democracy was framed in 1835:

Let us consider it as something akin to direct evidence that a people is not a mob, nor a mob a people, nor a mob's idol the idol of a people – that in a nation's self is the only security for a nation – and that it is absolutely necessary to model upon the *character* of the governed the machinery, whether simple or complex, of the governmental legislation.

Reviewing Bulwer-Lytton's *Rienzi*

But 'Mob' is 'a foreigner, by and by'. These bluestocking views were penned in 1848, the very Year of Revolutions.

19. (p. 318) *those of the fabulous Zeros and Hellofagabaluses*: Both Nero, who became Roman Emperor at the age of seventeen, and Heliogabalus, who became Emperor aged thirteen, were notorious for their homosexual liaisons. Especially Heliogabalus, or Elagabalus, was universally known as a 'faggot', or 'Hell of a fag'.

20. (p. 319) *Alpha Lyrae, whose disk ... subtends an angle of half a degree*: The drift of the solar system towards this star supposedly produced this result.

21. (p. 319) *resembles him closely as regards its spots*: During 1840–41 occurred the longest sun spot ever recorded by astronomers. It lasted eighteen months. Schwabe, at that time enquiring into the periodicity of sun spots, announced in 1843 an average cycle of 11.13 years. Sun spots, then, were in the news.

But that a 'binary relation' might exist between sun-spot curves and light curves of the average variable star – in other words, that our sun should be regarded as but another variable star of long period – was still a most novel and revolutionary theory to find in contemporary scientific papers – let alone a *Lady's Book*!

Alpha Lyrae (or Vega), nevertheless, does not form a binary relation with our sun. cf. *Eureka*, pp. 287–9.

22. (p. 319) *Its first propagator was one Mudler*: Johann Heinrich von Mädler (1794–1874). See *Eureka*, p. 293.

23. (p.320) *in the new temple at Daphnis in the moon*: cf. the temple-like structures sighted by Sir John Herschel, according to Richard Adams Locke's 'Discoveries in the Moon Lately Made at the Cape of Good Hope' (1835).

24. (p. 320) *Eureka! Pundit is in his glory*: Again, deliberately linking the parody of 'Mellonta Tauta' to the metaphysics of *Eureka*.

25. (p. 321) *a new fountain at ... the emperor's principal pleasure garden*: cf. Xanadu, where Kubla Khan a 'stately pleasure-dome' decreed:

> And from this chasm, with ceaseless turmoil seething,
> As if this earth in fast thick pants were breathing,
> A mighty fountain momently was forced . . .
>> Coleridge, *Kubla Khan*, lines 17–19

26. (p. 321) *Paradise . . . literally speaking, an island time out of mind*: 'And the Lord God planted a garden eastward in Eden . . . And a river went out of Eden to water the garden; and from thence it was parted, and became into four heads.' (*Genesis* ii, 8–10)

Manhattan, that one time 'Paradise', is some $12\frac{1}{2}$ miles long and $2\frac{1}{2}$ miles broad at its widest point. The island is bounded by the Hudson River on the west, New York Bay on the south, the East River on the east, and the 'narrow arm' of the Harlem River on the east and north.

27. (p. 321) *a portion of the Knickerbocker tribe of savages*: A term almost synonymous with 'Dutch'. Diedrich Knickerbocker, Washington Irving's pseudonym for his burlesque *History of New York* (1809), popularized the term. Some thirty-eight writers of the Knickerbocker Group and others represented by the *Knickerbocker Magazine* had been pilloried by Poe in 'The Literati of New York City' (*Godey's Lady's Book*, 1846).

28. (p. 321) *its first discovery by Recorder Riker, a knight of the Golden Fleece*: A 'Riker' who was certainly the first 'Amriccan' to strike it rich! Peter Minuit of the Dutch West India Company, so the legend goes, fleeced the Manhattan Indians, buying their island for 24 dollars' worth of trinkets (1624).

29. (p. 322) A MONUMENT TO THE MEMORY OF GEORGE WASHINGTON: The Washington Monument Association of New York in the 1840s attempted to finance the erection of a monument to the first President. The proposed location was to be Hamilton Square (at Third and Fifth Avenues, between 66th and 68th Streets). With appropriate fanfare a corner-stone was laid. But no design for the memorial had been agreed upon. The result was a fiasco – a prize example (for Poe) of democratic fickleness.

30. (p. 323) *'solitary and alone' . . . quoting the great Amriccan poet Benton!*: cf. the pedestal of Ozymandias, king of kings:

> Nothing beside remains. Round the decay
> Of that colossal wreck, boundless and bare
> The lone and level sands stretch far away.

But Poe is quoting not Shelley, but from Thomas Hart Benton's 'expunging' speech of 14 January 1837: 'And now, sir, I finish the task which, three years ago, I imposed on myself. Solitary and alone, and amidst the jeers and taunts of my opponents, I put this ball in motion.' The pompous pleonasm became a national byword.

The Missouri senator ('Old Bullion') was the devoted advocate of Jackson's hard money policy. Himself a victim of the panic of 1837, Poe had good reason to mock Benton's literary and financial and populist pretensions.

31. (p. 323) *one John, a smith, and one Zacchary, a tailor*; Zacchary Taylor ('Old Rough and Ready'), of course, was the twelfth President of the United States. Perhaps Pundita's inspection of the newspapers was so cursory that she confused Joseph Smith, founder of the Mormons (who had been murdered by an Illinois mob in 1844) with John Smith of Pocahontas fame (early investor in the Virginia Company and settler at Jamestown).

Select Bibliography

w. h. g. armytage, *Yesterday's Tomorrows: A Historical Survey of Future Societies* (London: Routledge & Kegan Paul, 1968)

burton r. pollin, 'Politics and History in Poe's "Mellonta Tauta": Two Allusions Explained', *Studies in Short Fiction* vol. 8 (1971), pp. 627–31

VON KEMPELEN AND HIS DISCOVERY

First Published

The Flag of Our Union (14 April 1849)

This imitation of a scientific report upon a supposed discovery of turning lead into gold was Poe's salute to the forty-niners in this year of the Gold Rush to California. Such synthetic manufacture or alchemy, he implied, had *political* implications for Californian immigrants. A technical advance in Bremen might yet undermine the Golden West.

At the same time he was courting two women and himself desperately seeking funds to start the *Stylus*. As he wrote to Annie L. Richmond:

. . . to be poor is to be a villain. I must get rich – rich. Then all will go well – but until then I must submit to be abused.

(21[?] January 1849)

Or to Frederick W. Thomas, editor of the *Louisville Chronicle*:

> I shall be a *littérateur*, at least, all my life; nor would I abandon the hopes which still lead me on for all the gold in California.

(14 February 1849)

Oddly enough he thought he had another 'Balloon-Hoax' on his hands. He really believed the public would be taken in. So he wrote to Evert A. Duyckinck,

> If you have looked over the Von Kempelen article you will have fully perceived its drift. I mean it as a kind of 'exercise', or experiment, in the plausible or verisimilar style. Of course, there is *not one* word of truth in it from beginning to end. I thought that such a style, applied to the gold-excitement, could not fail of effect. My sincere opinion is that nine persons out of ten (even among the best-informed) will *believe* the quiz (provided the design does not leak out before publication) and that thus, acting as a sudden, although of course a very temporary, *check* to the gold-fever, it will create a *stir* to some purpose.

But 'if you decline the quiz,' Shh! he gestures wildly in a postscript, 'please *do not let out the secret.*'

1. (p. 324) *the very minute and elaborate paper by Arago*: Dominique François Arago (1786–1853), Director of the Paris Observatory and Perpetual Secretary of the French Academy of Science.

2. (p. 324) *the summary in 'Silliman's Journal'*: Benjamin Silliman (1779–1864), professor of chemistry and natural history at Yale, founder-editor of the *American Journal of Science and Arts*.

3. (p. 324) *the detailed statement . . . by Lieutenant Maury*: Matthew Fontaine Maury (1806–73), head of the Depot of Charts and Instruments in Washington since 1842. Soon after his wind and current charts began to appear, culminating in *Wind and Current Chart of the North Atlantic* (1847). As early as June 1836 Poe had reviewed Maury's *A New Theoretical and Practical Treatise on Navigation* for the *Southern Literary Messenger*. But the peculiar relevance of Maury's charts, at the time of the Gold Rush, was their spectacular success in cutting the sailing-time between New York and San Francisco, via Cape Horn, from 150 to 133 days.

4. (p. 324) *By reference to the 'Diary of Sir Humphry Davy' . . . pp. 53 and 82*: At the end of an article on 'Alchymy', Isaac D'Israeli recorded: 'Sir Humphry Davy told me that he did not consider this undiscovered art an impossible thing but which, should it ever be

discovered, would certainly be useless.' (*Curiosities of Literature*, 1823)

'Diary' seems to refer to the two-volume *Memoirs of the Life of Sir Humphry Davy, Bart* (1836) written by his brother, John Davy. It was on page 53 of the one-volume abridgement (in the nine-volume *Collected Works* of 1839–40), however, that Burton R. Pollin discovered the reference to 'nitrous oxide' on which the whole elaborately protracted private joke appears to hang.

5. (p. 324) *to be found at the Athenæum Library*: The Baltimore Athenaeum Library.

6. (p. 325) *for a Mr Kissam, of Brunswick, Maine*: It was from the Maine Medical School in Brunswick that a young medical student, George Eveleth, had addressed Poe in 1846. A warm correspondence ensued between the eminent author and humble admirer. But, as Burton R. Pollin ingeniously argued, this reference to Mr Kissam (or Mr Quizzem, is it?) conceals a surreptitious stab at the youngster for daring to rival the grandeur of *Eureka* with his own cosmological theories and then consulting – to add insult to injury – a rival, Professor Draper, in New York City.

7. (p. 325) *so eminent a chemist as Professor Draper*: John William Draper (1811–82), once supported by Poe against the scurrilous attacks of the *North American Review* (1845), soon to be denounced in a letter to Eveleth as:

The chief of the very sect of Hog-ites to whom I refer as 'the most intolerant and intolerable sect of bigots & tyrants that ever existed on the face of the earth.' . . . A merely perceptive man, with no intrinsic force – no power of generalization – in short, a pompous nobody. He is aware (for there have been plenty to tell him) that I intend *him* in '*Eureka*'.

(26 June 1849)

8. (p. 325) *At page 13 . . . his researches about the protoxide of azote*: Garbled – not from a fantasy 'Diary' – but p. 272 of volume 3 of Davy's *Collected Works*:

Having previously closed my nostrils and exhausted my lungs, I breathed four quarts of nitrous oxide from and into a silk bag. The first feelings were similar to those produced in the last experiment; but in less than half a minute, the respiration being continued, they diminished gradually and were succeeded by a sensation analogous to gentle pressure on all the muscles, attended by a highly pleasurable thrilling, particularly in the chest and the extremities.

Researches, Chemical and Philosophical, chiefly concerning Nitrous Oxide and its Respiration (1799)

'Azote' was Lavoisier's term for nitrogen. So the whole send-up of Sir Humphry's stylistic shortcomings in his description of the physical effects of nitrous oxide, it turns out, is itself fuelled and inflated on laughing gas.

9. (p. 326) *in the 'Home Journal' ... several misapprehensions*: The *Home Journal* had, from the start, proved friendly to Poe. Yet an appeal published towards the end of 1846, to aid him while his wife lay dying, had rankled. The *'Viele Leiden'* (much suffering) so 'misconceived' and misconstrued by that paper – pointless in connection with Von Kempelen – 'poignantly illustrates the obsessive force of the last grim days of Virginia's life ... It also serves to confirm more substantially the transmutation of Poe into the successful gold-maker, Von Kempelen.' (Burton R. Pollin, *Discoveries in Poe*, p. 187)

10. (p. 326) *a late number of the Presburg 'Schnellpost'*: Or 'Courier' – a name, adopted from Berlin, for a New York German-language bi-weekly, started in 1843: *Deutsche Schnellpost für Europäische Zustände, öffentliches und sociales Leben Deutschlands*. Copies regularly landed on Poe's desk as associate editor, later editor, of the *Broadway Journal*.

Bratislava, a medieval city of Slovakia, was formerly the capital of Hungary. Usually spelt 'Pressburg' in German, the city was once renowned for the study of occult sciences.

11. (p. 327) *'The Literary World' speaks ... confidently*: As had Poe in writing to the editor of the *Literary World*, Evert A. Duyckinck. Yet that offer of 'the article' for ten dollars, or less, was apparently turned down.

12. (p. 327) *The family is connected ... with Maelzel, of Automaton-chess-player memory*: Poe's hoax ('Von Kempelen and His Discovery') figures a notorious hoaxer (Baron Wolfgang Von Kempelen) whom Poe himself had exposed (in 'Maelzel's Chess-Player' of 1836), though that too, in its way, was a bit of a hoax (being derived largely from Sir David Brewster's *Letters on Natural Magic*, 1832).

Clearly Poe saw something of himself in this Baron who 'had no scruple in declaring' his automaton 'to be a "very ordinary piece of mechanism – a *bagatelle* whose effects appeared so marvellous only from the boldness of the conception, and the fortunate choice of the methods adopted for promoting the illusion"' (*Southern Literary Messenger*, April 1836). But more hopefully, in this context, he must have identified with Johann Nepomuk Maelzel, the showman with a

Midas touch, who brought the chess-player, as well as metronome and Panharmonicum, to the United States.

13. (p. 327) *We were fellow-sojourners ... at Earl's Hotel, in Providence, Rhode Island*: Which is perhaps the key to the whole devious wish-fulfilment of Von Kempelen's 'Discovery'. For it was here that Poe stayed in 1848 while courting a prosperous widow of Providence, Mrs Helen Whitman. How he longed to be a prosperous suitor, able to match her cash with cash: 'were I wealthy,' he wrote, 'or could I offer you worldly honors ...' (1 October 1848). Yet even after Mrs Whitman had dispossessed herself of her property, at her family's instigation, Poe bungled the suit. For it was at Earl's Hotel too, on 20 December 1848, that Poe gave a public reading of 'The Poetic Principle', which dissolved in fiasco. A drunken bout at the bar finally put an end to the affair.

In 'Eldorado', published the following week in *The Flag of Our Union* (21 April 1849), the 'gallant' reappears not as an alchemist this time but a quixotic 'knight' with rueful countenance:

> And o'er his heart a shadow
> Fell as he found
> No spot of ground
> That looked like Eldorado.

14. (p. 328) *the house of Gutsmuth & Co ... in Gasperitch Lane*: Transmuting the names of two well-known authors of geography text-books – whom Poe had listed in a review four years earlier – the Germans Johann Cristoph F. Gutsmuths and Adam Christian Gaspari.

15. (p. 328) *the flash-name of the 'Dondergat'*: Poe's English coinage linked to his Old Norse and German producing an appropriately sham, or stage, effect of thunder and lightning.

Select Bibliography

W. K. WIMSATT, JR, 'Poe and the Chess Automaton', *American Literature* vol. 11 (1939), pp. 138–51

BURTON R. POLLIN, 'Poe's "Von Kempelen and His Discovery": Sources and Significance', *Études Anglaises* vol. 20 (1967), pp. 12–23; reprinted as *Discoveries in Poe* (Notre Dame: University of Notre Dame Press, 1970), ch. 10

THOMAS HALL, 'Poe's Use of a Source: Davy's Chemical Researches and "Von Kempelen and His Discovery"', *Poe Newsletter* vol. 1 (1968), p. 28.

Appendix

1745–6 Invention of the Leyden bottle

1747 Benjamin Franklin's work on electric forces

1749 Euler's *Analysis Infinitorum*

1750 Wright's *Theory of the Universe* (supported later by Herschel's discoveries)

1755 Kant's nebular theory

1758 Dollond's achromatic telescope

1760 Lightning-rods put up by Franklin in Philadelphia

1766 Cavendish isolates 'inflammable air' (called 'hydrogen' by Lavoisier)

1769 Watt patents his steam engine with separate condenser

1772 Bode publicizes Titius' Law of Distances (of the planets)

1773 Montgolfier brothers' attempts at flight with fire balloons

1774 Maskeleyne's test on the Earth's weight at Mt Schiehallion. Priestley isolates 'dephlogisticated air' (called 'oxygen' by Lavoisier)

1775 Volta's 'electrophorus'

1781 Herschel's discovery of Uranus

1783 Herschel's first list of double stars. First manned air flight in a hydrogen balloon

1785 J. P. Blanchard and Dr John Jeffries cross the English Channel by air

1786 Herschel's list of 1,000 nebulae. Galvani's observation of 'animal electricity'

1796 Laplace's *Système du Monde*

1799 First part of Laplace's *Méchanique Céleste* printed

1800 Invention of the 'Voltaic Pile'. Nicholson's and Carlisle's discovery of chemical effects of electric current. Herschel's discovery of infra-red rays

1801 Young's wave-theory of light. Piazzi's discovery of Ceres (orbit calculated by Gauss). Richard Trevithick's high-pressure engine – progenitor of all steam locomotives

1802 Wollaston's observation of seven dark lines in sun-spectrum. Herschel's third list of nebulae

1803 Herschel's theory of binaries

1805 Grotthuss' theory of electrolysis

1806 Herschel's theory of motion of the solar system in the direction of Hercules. Davy's work on electrolysis

1808 Dalton's *A New System of Chemical Philosophy* (2 vols., 1808–27)

1809 Gauss' *Theoria Motus Corporum Celestium* (1809–16). Sir George Cayley's theory of flight and fixed-wing flying model aircraft

1811 Herschel's theory of development of stars from nebulae. Poisson's mathematical theory of heat

1815 Prout's hypothesis (on atomic weights)

1819 Oersted's discovery of magnetic effects of current

1822 Lamarck's *Histoire naturelle des animaux sans vertèbres* completed. Ampère's *Obsérvations électro-dynamiques*

1823 Fraunhofer's observation of spectra of fixed stars. Faraday liquifies gases

1824 Arago's discovery of magnetic effect of turning copper plate

1826 Lobachevsky's geometry. Ohm's law

1827 First camera pictures made by Niepce. Ohm's *Galvanische Kette mathematisch bearbeitet*

1829 Faraday and Henry make observation on electromagnetic induction

1830 Lyell's *Principles of Geology*

1831 Faraday's electromagnetic rotation theory – foundation of the dynamo, motor and electrical industry

1832 John Herschel's observation on orbits of double stars

1833 Herschel's list of northern stars completed

1834 Faraday's laws

1836 John Ericsson's marine screw propeller

1837 Faraday's observation on electrostatic induction. Whewell's *History of the Inductive Sciences*. Wheatstone's and Cooke's electric telegraph

1838 Parallax of star (61 Cygni) measured by Bessel

1839 Gauss' general discussion of inverse-square forces. Parallax of *α*-Centauri measured by Henderson. Daguerre's process (camera-pictures)

1840 Draper takes camera pictures of the Moon. Whewell's *Philosophy of the Inductive Sciences*

1842 Discovery of Doppler effect. Weight of the Earth measured by Baily, using Cavendish's method of 1798

1844 Morse's telegraph transmits messages from Washington to Baltimore

1845 Discovery of Spiral Nebulae with Parsonstown telescope. J. C. Adams's computation of a new planet

1846 Discovery of Neptune from the work of Leverrier and Adams. Heating effect of the Moon measured by Melloni. Operations done under ether

1847 Sir John Herschel's *Results of Observations at the Cape of Good Hope*

[June 1848 *Eureka* published]

1849 Velocity of light measured by Fizeau

1850 Velocity of light measured by Foucault. Clausius' second law of thermodynamics

1851 Foucault's pendulum test on the Earth's motion

1864–7 Clausius' *Die mechanische Wärmetheorie*

1873 Clerk Maxwell's *A Treatise on Electricity and Magnetism*: laws of electromagnetic radiation, the foundation of radio, radar, television

1876 Clerk Maxwell's *Matter and Motion*